BATTLE
FOR
ROME

IAN ROSS has been researching and
writing about the later Roman world
and its army for over a decade. He
spent a year in Italy teaching English,
and now lives in Bath. Visit his
website: www.ianjamesross.com,
or find him on Twitter:
@IanRossAuthor.

TWILIGHT OF EMPIRE

War at the Edge of the World
Swords Around the Throne

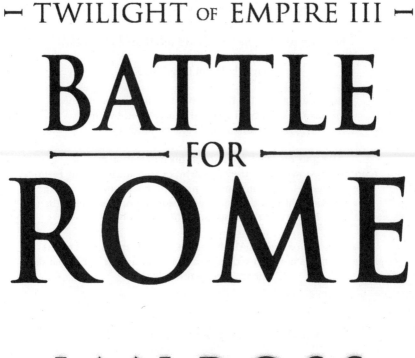

⊢ TWILIGHT of EMPIRE III ⊣

BATTLE
⊢ FOR ⊣
ROME

IAN ROSS

HEAD
of ZEUS

First published in the UK in 2015 by Head of Zeus Ltd.

9 7 5 3 1 2 4 6 8

A CIP catalogue record for this book is available
from the British Library.

ISBN (HB) 9781784081201
ISBN (XTPB) 9781784081218
ISBN (E) 9781784081195

Typeset by Ben Cracknell Studios, Norwich.

Printed and bound in Germany
by GGP Media GmbH, Pössneck

Head of Zeus Ltd
Clerkenwell House
45–47 Clerkenwell Green
London EC1R 0HT

WWW.HEADOFZEUS.COM

ἄπλωτα μὲν τὰ κατὰ θάλατταν ἦν οὐδ' ἐξῆν ποθεν
καταπλεύσαντας μὴ οὐχὶ πάσαις αἰκίαις ὑπάγεσθαι
στρεβλουμένους καὶ τὰς πλευρὰς καταξαινομένους
βασάνοις τε παντοίαις μὴ ἄρα παρὰ τῶν δι' ἐναντίας
ἐχθρῶν ἥκοιεν ἀνακρινομένους καὶ τέλος σταυροῖς ἢ τῇ
διὰ πυρὸς ὑπαγομένους κολάσει ἀσπίδων ἐπὶ τούτοις καὶ
θωρήκων παρασκευαὶ βελῶν τε καὶ δοράτων καὶ τῆς ἄλλης
πολεμικῆς παρατάξεως ἑτοιμασίαι τριήρων τε καὶ τῶν
κατὰ ναυμαχίαν ὅπλων κατὰ πάντα συνεκροτοῦντο τόπον
οὐδ'ἦν ἄλλο τι παντί τῳ προσδοκᾶν ἢ πολέμων κατὰ πᾶσαν
ἔφοδον ἡμέραν.

For the sea could not be travelled, nor could men sail
from any port without being exposed to all kinds of
outrages; being stretched on the rack and lacerated
in their sides, that it might be ascertained through
various tortures, whether they came from the enemy;
and finally being subjected to punishment by the cross
or by fire.

And besides these things shields and body armour
were being prepared, and darts and spears and other
instruments of battle made ready, and galleys and
naval armaments were collecting in every place.

And no one expected anything but to be attacked by
enemies at any moment.

Eusebius, Ecclesiastical History

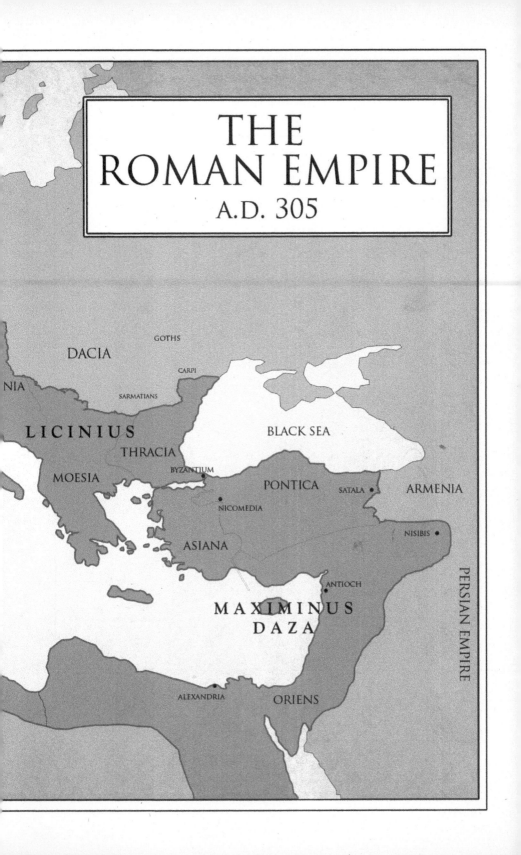

THE ROMAN EMPIRE
A.D. 305

GOTHS

DACIA

CARPI

NIA

SARMATIANS

LICINIUS

THRACIA

BLACK SEA

MOESIA

BYZANTIUM

PONTICA

SATALA

ARMENIA

NICOMEDIA

ASIANA

NISIBIS

ANTIOCH

**MAXIMINUS
DAZA**

PERSIAN EMPIRE

ALEXANDRIA

ORIENS

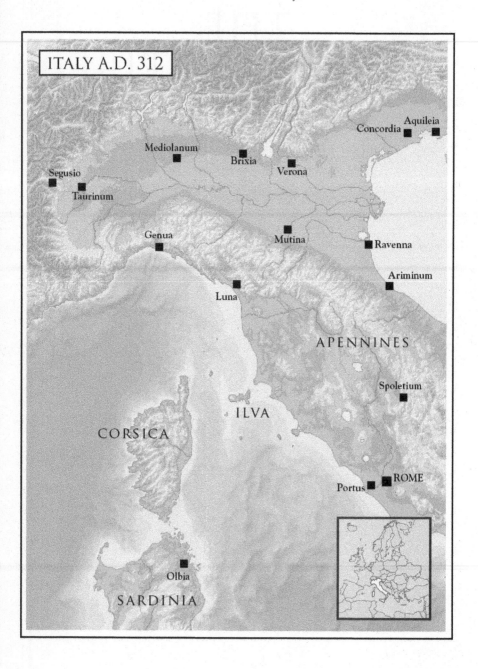

ITALY A.D. 312

Concordia Aquileia

Mediolanum
Brixia
Verona

Segusio

Taurinum

Genua
Mutina
Ravenna

Luna
Ariminum

APENNINES

Spoletium

ILVA

CORSICA

ROME
Portus

Olbia

SARDINIA

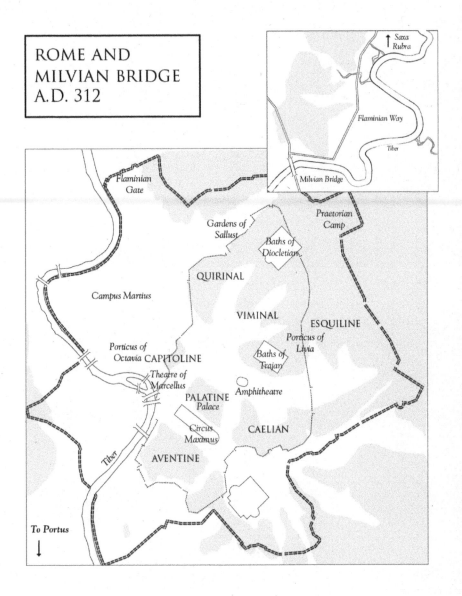

ROME AND
MILVIAN BRIDGE
A.D. 312

Saxa
Rubra

Flaminian Way

Tiber

Milvian Bridge

Flaminian
Gate

Gardens of
Sallust

Baths of
Diocletian

Praetorian
Camp

QUIRINAL

Campus Martius

VIMINAL

ESQUILINE

Porticus of
Livia

Porticus of
Octavia CAPITOLINE

Baths of
Trajan

Theatre of
Marcellus

Amphitheatre

PALATINE
Palace

Circus
Maximus

CAELIAN

Tiber

AVENTINE

To Portus

HISTORICAL NOTE

In AD 311 the Roman Empire stands on the brink of civil war. The unity established by the emperor Diocletian decades before has collapsed, and now four rivals contend for supreme power.

In the west, Constantine controls Gaul, Spain, Britain and the Rhine frontier. Licinius commands the central Danubian provinces, Greece and the Balkans, while Maximinus Daza rules the east and Egypt. Between them the usurper Maxentius, son of the former emperor Maximian, possesses the city of Rome itself, with Italy and North Africa.

The rival emperors prepare their troops and negotiate their alliances. All know that the coming war will decide the future of the Roman world.

PROLOGUE

Agri Decumates, Germania, December AD 311

The nine men were riding hard, bursting the silence of the winter forest. All trace of the road was gone, and they navigated only by the pale gleam of the sun through the weave of black branches overhead. Five hours the chase had lasted, and still they did not know who was pursuing them.

Up the slope between the trees, the riders crossed the bare summit of the ridge and plunged down the far side, into a narrower valley thick with dark pines. They had only ridden a short distance when the two remaining guides hauled on their reins and drew to a halt. One of them, the taller man with the red-dyed hair, raised himself in the saddle to peer between the trees, then called back. His breath plumed white in the frigid air.

'They are ahead of us.'

'How is that possible?' the tribune, Ulpianus, said. He had been wounded in the morning attack, speared in the gut with a javelin, and his face was grey from loss of blood.

'The valley goes like this,' the guide told him, sketching a wide arc with his right arm. 'They went around, I think.'

Ulpianus hissed between clenched teeth: 'Find out who they are.'

The two tribesmen slipped from their saddles and began to edge down the hillside. The cries of the pursuit had fallen away now, and the slow silence of the forest was ominous. Pines groaned in the icy breeze.

'Castus,' the tribune said, wincing back over his shoulder. 'To me.'

The rider behind him nudged his mount forward. He was a big man, with a thick neck and the ugly broken profile of a boxer. Like the others, he wore Germanic costume, and he had let his hair and beard grow out in a scrub of yellowish bristles. But the broadsword belted at his side and the gold torque at his collar marked him as a Roman soldier.

'They have us surrounded,' the tribune said. He sat hunched in the saddle, and the linen that bound his stomach was soaked through with blood. His strength was ebbing fast. 'If we have to fight, take the package in my saddlebag and break through. Alone if necessary.'

Aurelius Castus twisted the reins between his fists, exhaled slowly. 'I think we can make it if we stay together,' he said. 'I'm not leaving you, dominus.'

Ulpianus glanced at him. 'As a Protector of the Sacred Bodyguard, you're sworn to obey your commanding officer's every order!' He drew his lips back in a pained smile. 'However, I expected you might say that... We all have our duty.'

'*We will do what we are ordered...*' Castus replied, his throat tightening as he spoke the first words of the traditional soldier's oath.

Turning in the saddle, leather creaking beneath him, he looked back at the surviving members of the group. The attackers had hit their camp in the hour before dawn, howling out of the darkness in a swift raid that had left three men dead and two more wounded. Castus knew that they could all have been slaughtered, half of them in their sleep, but the raiders had only wanted to determine their strength, their

4

identity and their purpose. One of the guides had vanished too, captured or fled.

Two of those that remained – his friend Brinno and another man – were fellow members of the Corps of Protectores. Two more were mounted archers of the Equites Sagittarii: good soldiers, but close to exhaustion, and still shaken after the loss of their comrades. There was the single surviving slave, the tribune, and then the two guides up ahead. All them uncertain and confused.

Castus's hands were numb as they gripped the reins, and his face felt flayed and raw from the cold. A web of aches ran from his thighs up his spine and across his shoulders. The wind breathed ice across the back of his neck, and he tried not to shudder.

Six days had passed since they had left the imperial court at Treveris. Their mission was simple enough: they were to carry a sealed package to the court of the emperor Licinius, who ruled on the Danube. Only the tribune knew what the package contained, but whatever it was must be valuable to warrant sending such a strong despatch party through barbarian country in the dead of winter. In times of peace, they could have travelled south, around the headwaters of the Rhine and up through the province of Raetia. But the governor of upper Raetia had declared his allegiance to the usurper Maxentius, controller of Italy; now Maxentian patrols ranged freely through that territory. Whatever the dangers of the barbarians, the risk of the package falling into the hands of the usurper's men was far greater.

Castus eased back in his saddle, flexing his spine and his shoulders. He gazed at the forested hillsides around him. This wilderness between the Rhine and the Danube had once been part of the Roman Empire: the Agri Decumates, it was called.

Fifty years ago there had been farms in these valleys, roads and towns, settled villas. For the last three days Castus and his party had been following the line of the old fortifications, the overgrown ditch and collapsing palisades that had once marked the edge of civilisation, now just a dead-straight scar across a wild landscape.

This was Alamannic country, but the Alamanni were bound by treaties with Rome. Either their attackers that morning had decided to ignore the treaties, Castus thought, or they too were intruders in this land, and had no treaties to break.

He looked down the slope and saw the two guides clambering back up between the trees, returning from their brief reconnaissance.

'They wait for us, down in the valley,' the red-haired one said. 'They want to talk, looks like.'

'Who are they?' the tribune demanded.

'Burgundii,' said the other guide, and spat.

The guides were each from a different Alamannic tribe; the idea was, Castus supposed, that they distrusted each other more than they disliked Romans. With any luck, he thought, they hated the Burgundii even more.

'Castus,' Ulpianus said quietly. 'You and Brinno go down there with the guides. Find out everything you can.'

And make sure the guides don't betray us, Castus thought as he shook his reins.

They moved through the trees, leaning back in their saddles as the horses picked their way downhill into the valley. Castus was not a good horseman at the best of times; his mount was big, powerful, but it was also ill tempered and had a heavy gait. Ahead of him, Castus could see the two guides talking. They too seemed in a bad mood.

6

'What are they saying?' he asked Brinno, who rode just behind him. Brinno was a younger man than Castus, lean and sinewy; he was Frankish himself, a chieftain's son born in the barbarian lands near the mouth of the Rhine, but had lived in Treveris these last twelve years. The language of the Franks and the Alamanni was similar enough.

'The dark one wants to sell us to the Burgundii, I think,' Brinno said.

'And our red-haired friend?'

Brinno grinned, showing the gaps in his broken teeth. 'He wants to wait. Maybe we meet somebody who will pay better!'

Castus felt a knot of tension slip in his chest. Brinno was a good man to have at his side. They had trained together, and stood side by side in battle before. He trusted the young Frank as much as he had ever trusted another man. As much as he had ever trusted anybody.

The slope levelled, and they rode slowly out from the cover of the trees onto the open valley floor. A shallow stream flowed wide over a shingle bed, the water glinting with ice between the rocks. The air was so cold down here it hurt to breathe. Almost too cold for fear; Castus just wanted this to be over, and soon. He could see the moon, a perfect white half-circle low above the treetops; only an hour or two of daylight remained.

On the level ground at the far side of the stream the Burgundii were waiting. Four of them, sitting with careful idleness on their shaggy little horses. Castus glanced quickly right and left. As many again on either side, just within the trees. Beyond them the valley narrowed, with high spurs of rock showing between the pines. A bottleneck. He realised that their pursuers had been herding them to this exact spot. Reaching beneath his cloak, he tugged at his sword hilt, freeing the blade from the cold lock of the scabbard mouth.

Leaning forward over his saddle horns, Castus surveyed the enemy riders. They wore capes of animal pelts, and each man had a wolf's tail hanging from his shield. One had a red tunic, and his hair hung in neat braids – the chief, Castus guessed – but the others looked rough-edged and thick-bearded after many days of hard living. Their weapons were clean enough though, spears and broadswords, and the men had the look of fighters.

The two guides were talking, the Burgundii answering them in curt dismissive phrases. Castus heard Brinno sniff in disgust.

'How many do you count?' he said quietly, barely moving his lips.

'Four right there, four more up the slopes on each side,' Brinno replied.

Castus nodded. 'Twelve, and nine of us. Not bad odds.'

'You include the guides?'

'All right, seven of us.'

'One a wounded man who can hardly sit on a horse?'

'Six, then.'

'One a slave?'

'So, *five*... What are you saying?'

Brinno gave a slow shrug and widened his eyes. 'Nothing, brother. Only... if we go at them we have to go *hard*.'

Then he grinned again, and Castus found himself smiling back.

The conference was over, the two guides turning their horses and cantering back across the stream. Their expressions gave nothing away, but Castus already knew what they had to report. As they climbed slowly up the slope he told himself not to look back.

'They say we can pass, but we have to surrender our weapons

and horses,' he informed Ulpianus and the others waiting below the ridge. 'And the gold or *valuables* we're carrying too.'

'Valuables?' said the other Protector.

'The guide they captured this morning must have told them that,' the tribune said. 'Probably hoping to save his skin.' He drew himself up in the saddle, his face tightening with the strain. 'Listen,' he told them. 'We ride down there slowly, keeping close together, guides on the flanks. We get to within fifty paces of them, then at my signal we charge... every man for himself, cut your way through them and keep riding until we're past. Understood?'

Nods all round. No words were necessary. Castus caught the tribune's glance, and his eye went to the saddlebag.

Wind whipped at the treetops as they made their last preparations. Each man dismounted, checking his horse tack and equipment. Those who had wine or water drank and passed the canteens. Then they swung back into their saddles, loosening swords, the archers flexing their bows. Castus raised his arms above his head, warming his muscles, and felt the burn of blood flowing to his numbed hands. He retied the leather grip of his hunting spear, jabbed the weapon right and left, then propped it across his saddle bow and pulled the cloak back around him. Then they began the descent into the valley.

The Burgundii were still waiting on the far side of the stream, but their brothers had closed in from either side, watching as the Roman column moved out from the pines and forded the shallow icy water. Castus was riding in the lead, with Brinno to his right and Ulpianus just behind to his left. They were out of the water now, the horses shivering and blowing steam as they climbed the bank onto the level ground. Sixty paces. The Burgundii were shifting, spreading out ahead of them.

Fifty paces. No word from Ulpianus.

Forty. The Burgundii were lifting their spears, backing their horses. They had to attack now, Castus thought. Either that or halt.

He risked a glance back at Ulpianus. The tribune was swaying in his saddle, eyes closed, one arm clasped to his belly.

Gods below. Castus swept the spear free of his cloak and kicked his heels. 'Go!' he yelled, and the word rang in the frozen air.

His horse heaved, then surged forward into a headlong charge that almost threw him from the saddle. Behind him he could hear Brinno's scream of rage, then the noise of the wind erased all sound and for three heartbeats he felt airborne, flung forward with the spear whirling out and the bright blade flashing in the sunlight.

Two men ahead of him urged their horses together to trap him. Castus was almost on them when he hauled the reins sharply; his big horse jinked, forelegs off the ground, then slammed into the rider to the left. Castus swung forward with the impact, punching down with the spear as his horse kicked out at the other animal. The spear went wide; he pulled back his arm to strike again but the rider was already falling from the saddle, tumbling beneath the hooves.

A sword lashed in from his right, and Castus swayed backwards as the blade cut the air before his chest. He turned his spear clumsily and got the shaft of it up with both hands to block the next attack. The other rider was close, the two horses shoving together; the sword came down and chopped into the spearshaft, and when the Burgundian dragged his blade free the shaft broke. Castus hurled the stump of the broken spear at the man's head, then reached beneath his cloak for his sword.

His hand found only bunched wool; his belts had twisted

and the weapon was out of reach. The Burgundian's face was alight with triumph as he raised his sword for the killing blow. A jolt went through him; Castus's horse had lashed its head round and bitten the other animal on the neck. Castus leaned quickly from the saddle, ramming his arm across the Burgundian's shoulder and grappling his neck. Before the man could regain control of his panicking horse Castus had dragged him half out of the saddle. He punched his fist into the side of the man's head, once, twice, very fast; then the other horse bolted clear. Castus heard the crunch of the Burgundian's neck as he let him drop.

Sun was in his eyes, everything dazzling, and the air seemed too thin to breathe. Twisting, he looked back and saw Ulpianus slouched in the saddle as his horse circled and pawed the ground. Three enemy riders were closing in from the valley slope, whooping as they came; an arrow struck one of them and he flung up his legs and tumbled back over the haunches of his mount.

Cursing, Castus wrestled his own horse around and then seized the tribune's reins. Groping through the folds of his cloak he found the hilt of his sword and with a sharp tug he drew the weapon free. To his right, Brinno was in combat with another rider, the two of them circling as they traded grimly precise blows. The Burgundian chief, the man with the braids, had got behind Brinno and was raising his spear to strike. Castus urged his horse into a swift canter that closed the distance between them fast; the Burgundian chief was still watching Brinno as Castus yelled and slashed his sword down. The blade sheared off the back of the man's skull. Blood sprayed pink in the clean air, and Castus felt the heat of it spattering his face and chest. A moment later Brinno's adversary was down too.

'Go!' Brinno was shouting. 'We're clear – go!'

A rapid glance back to check that Ulpianus was still gripping tight to his saddle, then Castus was spurring on after Brinno, the tribune's reins burning as they dug into his fist. There were two more Burgundians up ahead, cantering down from the trees. One look at the bloodied, screaming riders galloping towards them and they turned and retreated.

Wind roared, hooves battered at stones and frozen turf, then the muffled darkness of the wooded valley rose on either side, and Castus knew, through the haze of violent energy, that they had survived.

They reached the dead town as dusk deepened into night. They had been following an old road that ran straight through the wilderness, and saw nothing at first but the trees and the undergrowth around them. Then the broken walls appeared from the gathering darkness, and the riders saw the pillars among the clumps of frosted ivy, the shattered hulks of buildings lost in tangled scrub.

'We should be safe here, for a time,' said the red-haired guide. His comrade had not made it through the fight; whether dead, fled or surrendered, nobody knew or cared. 'Burgundii don't come to these old places. Like tombs, they say. Too many ghosts.'

'What sort of ghosts?' asked the young slave from the rear of their little column. Besides Castus and Brinno, and the wounded tribune, only he and one of the archers remained of the despatch party.

'Ghosts of Romans!' the guide declared with a note of wry pride. 'Killed by my ancestors, maybe, hmm?'

They rode in silence, the town taking form around them even as the dark increased. The wide expanse of weeds and tangled scrub ahead would have been the forum once, Castus guessed. On the far side stood a large building, an old basilica perhaps, with a stepped entrance and part of the roof still remaining.

'In there,' he said.

Dismounting, they led the horses through the wide portal and tethered them at the back of the hall, amidst a wrack of fallen roof timbers and rubble overgrown with ferns and long grass. They lifted Ulpianus down from his horse; the tribune was feverish and mumbling, and they wrapped him in his fur-lined cloak and laid him in the far corner on a bed of ferns with the slave to watch over him. The shell of the old building protected them from the breeze at least, but outside it the night stood around them like a black wall of ice.

Castus took the first watch, with the guide. He pulled a fur hat down over his ears and crouched beside the open doorway, trying to suppress the shivers that ran through his body. As he stared into the darkness he began to make out the shapes of the ruins in the faint moonlight. Ghosts out there, he thought. The unquiet dead. He remembered something he had been told once, far away in the north of Britain. *One day all our works will be like this. Nothing more than hummocks in the turf, for savages to wonder over...* He remembered that the man who said those words was long dead too.

'River is south of here,' the guide said, mumbling through the fur edging his cloak. 'Two hours' good riding. Bridge is there somewhere. Far side – Roman territory.'

'Whose?' Castus asked. 'Licinius's or Maxentius's?'

He saw the man shrug, the slightest shift of the bunched furs, as if the affairs of Romans were of little interest to him. 'Licinius? But maybe best to ask first, hmm?'

Castus nodded. 'And the Burgundii? Will they come after us tomorrow?'

'Yes,' the guide said. 'They out there now.' His chin jutted towards the dark edge of the ruined town. 'They waiting.'

The hours passed, silent and fiercely cold, then Brinno came to relieve him and Castus crept back to the roll of blankets his friend had left still warm. He stretched out, his sword laid ready beside him, and pulled the blankets over his ears, but sleep did not come. For a long while he felt himself lying suspended in darkness, the cold pressing on him from all sides. Castus thought of his wife, Valeria Domitia Sabina; for six days, since leaving Treveris, he had tried to avoid thinking about her. Tried, and failed of course. Her image came to him now, keen and clear, warming his senses. He felt the blood stir in his body. He thought of Sabina, and of their son, only four months old when this mission had summoned him away from them. Every night they had filled his mind, and every morning he had banished them. It was too painful to imagine he might never see either of them again.

Memory eased him from wakefulness, and in moments he had plunged down into sleep.

'Dominus? Dominus!' The slave was shaking his shoulder. Castus woke quickly, one hand grabbing for the sword beside him. The cold flared against his skin as he pulled the blankets from his head. Still dark, deep night; the tribune was calling for him, the slave said.

Castus crossed the hall, groping in the blackness between the heaps of rubble, timbers and brambles. Ulpianus still lay where they had left him, but he was awake now, his eyes catching the faintest hint of moonlight through the broken roof. As Castus eased himself down beside him, the tribune reached out and seized his arm in a strong grip.

'Can't feel the pain now,' he said, and his voice was thin and strained but clear. 'Too cold... a mercy, at least. You must

14

take the package. Do it tonight, before dawn. I am consigning it to you. Take it and complete the mission. Deliver it to the emperor Licinius.'

'I understand, dominus,' Castus said. 'I'll do it.' There was no point in denying it now. Both of them knew that the tribune would not be leaving that place alive.

The horses stirred in the darkness. Castus went to move away but Ulpianus still held him, using the last of his strength. 'Don't you want to know what the package contains?' the tribune said. His voice was hardly more than a whisper.

'No,' Castus said. He glanced up, and noticed that the slave had crept back into the deeper shadows, out of hearing.

'You don't want to know what your life's worth?'

He could hear the smile in the tribune's words. *No*, he thought, *I do not*. Then he thought of Sabina, of his son. Of all that he could lose.

'Tell me.'

The grip on his arm slackened, as if the tribune was discharging something that had weighed him down for a long time. 'The package contains a letter,' he said. 'A formal offer of alliance between our emperor Constantine and his brother emperor Licinius… against the usurper Maxentius.'

Castus said nothing. He could have guessed as much.

'Also,' Ulpianus went on, halting, 'the letter requests that in the coming spring Licinius deploy his forces south towards the Alps… as if he intends to invade Italy from the north-east. This will cause the usurper to move his own troops towards Aquileia… to guard the eastern approaches. His western flank will be left open…'

'And Constantine will invade from the west,' Castus breathed. He sensed the tribune's nod.

'So you see,' Ulpianus said, 'the success of our armies is in your hands now. If the package is intercepted by Maxentius's agents... the plan will fail utterly.'

'It won't,' Castus said. But he was already feeling the weight of the burden.

'There's something else,' the tribune went on. 'An offer of marriage... with Constantine's sister. The package contains a portrait of her, an enamelled miniature. I've seen it – it hardly looks like her at all. She's... not glamorous. But Licinius... has no taste for women anyway...'

The words seemed to pain him now, and Castus could hear the gasp and lock of his breathing. Even in the cold air he could smell death.

'Castus,' the tribune cried, grabbing him again.

'What, dominus?' He hunched over the prone figure, leaning closer.

'Don't...' the tribune said, and his voice wavered and cracked. 'Don't let the dogs eat my flesh. Pile stones on me – promise...'

Castus gripped the man's shoulder, a reassuring pressure. He could feel the feverish heat of Ulpianus's body even through his thick clothing. 'And be careful,' the tribune said. 'Be careful in Treveris... you must... It's dangerous, brother. Your wife...'

'Yes...?' Castus said. Cold dread pushed suddenly at his heart.

He could hear the dying man struggling to breathe, struggling to form words. Something wet choked in his throat. The hand clasping his arm tightened, and then fell slack. Castus reached for the man's face in the darkness, holding his palm over the open mouth. He felt nothing, no slight warm stir of breath.

'Why did you say that?' he asked the dead man. Doubt clawed at his back, and he shuddered. Then he pulled the fur cape over the tribune's body.

* * *

They left the dead town in the first pale seep of dawn. The hooves of the horses were bound with rags, the men's weapons muffled, and they moved on foot, leading the animals behind them. It seemed even colder, the air itself frozen, and the world was almost eclipsed by white fog. Frost lay so thick on the trees and the overgrown ruins that the town seemed carved from brittle ice, and the ground creaked beneath their feet as they walked.

The guide had vanished in the night, and none of them were surprised by that. Now Brinno took the lead, with Castus and the slave following and the sole remaining archer bringing up the rear. Inside his tunic, Castus carried the package he had taken from the tribune's saddlebag. It was hardly larger than a man's hand, and sewn tightly into waxed linen. Such a small thing, he thought, to risk so many lives for.

Once they reached what looked like the town boundary they mounted up and began to ride, slowly at first. The fog swirled around them, and the sound of the padded hooves was a dull thudding on the old mossy paving of the road. The world around them seemed utterly deserted, devoid of life. But they had travelled only a mile from the town when the fog began to lift and they realised they were not alone.

'Left flank,' Brinno said under his breath. 'Three, maybe four.'

'Same on the right,' Castus said. 'They're shadowing us.' He kicked his heels and his mount broke into a fast trot. From the fog to either side came the sound of voices, calling and responding.

Cresting a rise, the riders saw the hills dropping away before them onto a wide flat plain, billowing with low mist. On the far horizon was a grey smudge, like a line drawn with a man's thumb on frosted metal. The Danube.

'Last ride!' Brinno said, grinning. The four of them had slowed, grouping together. Without another word they leaned from their saddles and clasped hands, the differences between them forgotten. From either side they could hear the wild cries as the Burgundian horsemen closed in around them. Then, as one, they whipped their reins and began to gallop.

Castus was in the lead now, hunched low over the saddle with the cold breeze rushing around his head and tugging at his cloak. The motion of the horse sent shocks up his spine; he tried to lift himself in the saddle but he was weary and his limbs were heavy. The world raced by in a blur of dirty whiteness.

A scream from behind him; Castus glanced back and saw the archer tumble from his saddle, the slim black shaft of a javelin jutting from his side. He knew he could not urge his horse to any greater speed: there were still miles to go before the river, and the animal was tiring fast. The young slave went galloping past him, flogging his lighter pony into a headlong charge. Another figure loomed from the mist; Castus thought it was Brinno, but then he saw the raised spear. He tried to shout but the wind punched the breath from his mouth. The spear flew, striking the slave between the shoulders and knocking him from the pony.

Brinno had a javelin stuck through the folds of his cloak. As Castus turned to look back at him, his friend plucked the weapon free and hurled it. One of the barbarians went down. There was another of them ahead, urging his horse up onto the road; Castus swept out his sword, levelling the long blade like a lance. The Burgundian barely had time to rein in his mount before Castus was onto him, driving the sword at his face. The man reeled, toppling from the saddle, and Castus rode on.

For a few long moments he was conscious of nothing but

speed and the cutting rush of the frozen air. The sun had risen, and lit the fog with an unearthly grey-white radiance, and Castus had the strange conviction that he passed from the world of the living into some cold hazy afterlife.

He realised that he was alone on the road. Only the noise of his own horse's hooves battering at the hard ground, his own heaving breath. Hauling at the reins, he looked back and saw Brinno some distance behind him, his horse lamed and limping. Around him dark shapes were moving through the grey murk. Without thinking, Castus wrenched at the reins and turned his horse towards his friend.

'Get up behind me!' Castus called to him. He was already shunting forward on the saddle. He saw Brinno shake his head.

'No time,' the younger man called. He raised his sword in salute, and grinned. 'Go!' he shouted. 'I'll hold them – go! Make this worthwhile, brother!'

The first of the Burgundians was already galloping towards him.

With a hiss of anguish Castus watched as the enemy riders closed in around his friend. He knew there was nothing he could do – except die at Brinno's side. And then all of their deaths would have been in vain.

We all have our duty... He dragged at the reins again; his horse reared, then spun on its rear legs and dropped into a heavy gallop towards the river. Castus closed his eyes, closed his throat against the wrenching cry trapped in his chest.

Ten heartbeats, and he risked a glance back. Brinno was still there, still fighting against the whirl of men that surrounded him. Then, at that very moment, Castus saw the spear darting in to strike his friend in the side. He saw Brinno crumple and fall from the saddle. Then he turned away, howling through clenched teeth into the steady snarl of the wind.

The road curved ahead of him; with a rush of choking horror Castus saw more of the riders appearing, coming from the flat misty plain to the right to cut him off. He sawed at the reins, swaying in the saddle as the horse crashed off the road and through the tangle of bushes onto the frost-crusted meadowland to the left. The river was there, clearer now, achingly close. It looked very wide, and there was no sign of a bridge. The horse was labouring over the broken ground, blowing hard, its neck and quarters steaming, and Castus could barely keep himself in the saddle.

As he neared the river he saw the ice, a pale grey sheet of it stretching from the bank to the ribbon of open black water in midstream. There was an island about fifty paces out, low and thickly grown with scrub, and the ice had filled the channel between it and the nearer bank.

Shouts from the right: the pursuers had left the road and ridden across country to meet the riverbank. More of them were coming up behind, their ululating cries carrying strangely in the mist. Castus let his horse slow as it neared the riverbank. He urged it on the last distance, through the crackling reeds and scrub to the edge of the frozen water. Birds burst up from the undergrowth and flapped wildly away across the ice.

The riders sounded exultant now, seeing him trapped against the river. Castus reached beneath his cloak and checked that the package was still safely secured inside his tunic. Then he slipped from the saddle, feeling pain burst through the muscles of his thighs and back. He looked again at the ice. It might carry the weight of a man, but not a horse. If he could get across to the island, would his pursuers dare to follow? He drew his sword, took a last glance back at the approaching riders, then slapped the horse across the haunches with the flat of his blade.

The animal flinched, then staggered up from the back, too exhausted to run. Castus was already scrambling down onto the ice, wrapping his cloak tight around his body, his sword held clear. He had thought to use it to probe ahead of him, but as soon as his boots were on the ice he was skating, flinging his arms out for balance. He could hear the approaching riders; from the corner of his eye he saw a flung javelin dart black against the sky.

Ice groaned beneath his weight, but he forced himself onward, legs spread wide for grip and balance. Too slow – he pitched forward onto his hands, feeling the cold striking into his arms; then he began dragging himself. Deep cracking noises came from beneath him. He could feel the water moving below the ice. For the first time he realised that he was about to die. He would lose his life in a frozen barbarian wasteland, and nobody would know. A gasp of laughter burst from his pit of his chest; then all he felt was a furious rage. He was scrambling on all fours, hands and knees sliding on the ice.

Get up, he thought. *Get up and run.* Another spear hit the ice to his left. He was shuddering, feverish, grinding his teeth as he tried to stand. With a heave he got his feet under him, hobnailed boots gritting into the ice. Three staggering strides and he felt the surface of the river beginning to break into a web of fractures. The island was only ten paces away now – he could make it.

With a noise like a heavy beam breaking, the ice beneath him gave and Castus felt himself pitching sideways. One snatched gulp of air, then the water burst around him and he was in the river, the weight of his heavy cloak and boots dragging him down. For a moment he was aware only of darkness; then the cold seized him like an iron fist closing around his chest, and he blew out air in a foaming torrent. Blood hammered in his skull; he could not tell where the surface was. He felt himself drowning, fighting, dying.

Then one hand struck the ice; he grabbed and gripped, hauling his head up above the surface. Cold burned him, and he was screaming as he tried to suck air. The ice broke up even as he tried to pull himself onto it. He was facing back towards the riverbank. Two horses, riderless, cantering in the distance. As he stared, everything looked very clear and bright. Something split the air above his head and he heard a cry. A man fell from a third horse.

Rolling, Castus managed to get one arm up onto the chunk of ice and look behind him. Heat flared in his chest, and he shouted incoherently. Out in the open stream of the river, moving from behind the island, was a slim twenty-oared patrol galley trailing a Roman pennant. Oval shields along the rail, and a pair of ballistae mounted fore and aft. As Castus stared he saw the catapult arms jerk, sending another bolt skimming across the frozen water at the Burgundians on the bank. A smaller boat was nosing through the shattered ice into the island channel, oarsmen pulling hard.

He tried to shout again, but the cold locked his throat, then a wave of violent shudders ripped through him and he lost his grip on the ice. Water closed over his head, and he knew only blackness.

Moments might have passed; maybe hours. He was aware of being dragged from the water, the sodden weight of his clothing hauling at his limbs. When he opened his eyes he was hunched on the narrow deck boards of the galley, and all around him were raised shields and levelled spears. A soldier's face, reddened by the cold, shouting at him.

'Who are you? Speak Latin? Identify yourself!'

He tried to speak, but he was shivering uncontrollably and gasping for breath. Pulling his shoulders up, he forced himself to meet the soldier's stare.

'Aurelius Castus...' he said, grinding out the words. 'Protector of the Sacred Bodyguard... of the Emperor Constantine...' He gritted his teeth, held his head up.

The soldier turned to somebody behind him. His red face twisted into a smile, and when he leaned forward again there was a leather mug in his hand.

'We're with the Fifth Cohort Valeria Phrygum,' he said. 'Loyal to Licinius.'

Castus took the mug in both hands, breathing in the scent of warmed wine.

'Drink deep, brother,' the soldier said.

PART ONE

CHAPTER I

January AD 312

In a sealed windowless chamber, deep in the bowels of the palace, two men sat facing each other across a low table. One of them was thin, middle-aged, with a bland colourless face beneath greying bowl-cut hair. His clothes were plain and undistinguished, but he wore the belt and brooch of an imperial official. The other man was wrapped in a robe and tight headcloth of white linen, and his face was concealed by a white lacquered mask in the shape of a dog's snout.

Neither man spoke. The lamp on the table between them guttered in a faint draught, and their shadows twined and twisted around the stone walls. Finally the thin man cleared his throat. 'Do you know who I am?' he asked.

The white dog mask moved side to side.

Julius Nigrinus concealed his satisfaction. As a tribune of the Corps of Notaries he was a highly placed figure in the imperial bureaucracy, but he did not care to be recognised. Sometimes anonymity can be a more potent weapon than fame. Besides, the masked man could be in little doubt of his authority; anyone able to have a man snatched from his bed in the middle of the night and conducted to this subterranean part of the emperor's palace by armed guards clearly wielded a certain power.

'But I know who you are,' the notary went on. He steepled

his fingers beneath his chin. 'You are Astrampsychus of Cunaxa, correct?'

'Merely a name I use for the public, dominus...' the other man said. His voice sounded muffled from inside the mask, but Nigrinus could tell he had a slight foreign accent. 'In reality—'

Nigrinus raised his hand abruptly, then shook his head. 'I am not interested in your real name. Or your appearance. That's why I had you wear your impressive mask. It's better if we each conduct ourselves solely in our... public persona, yes?'

The dog snout nodded. Nigrinus could hear the faint hiss and thud of the man's breath inside the mask. He could smell his sweat, and something else: the rank tang of urine. He suspected that Astrampsychus of Cunaxa was not a man of courage.

'Over two years ago,' he said, 'you were paid by the domina Fausta, wife of our emperor, to place a magical death curse upon the domina Minervina, her husband's concubine. Shortly afterwards, Minervina fell sick and was close to death. Thankfully, she survived, apparently owing to the prayers of some Christian priests.'

'Dominus...' the masked man breathed. 'I beg you – I did not know the identity of either woman! The ritual was com-missioned by a eunuch... I did not recognise the names...'

'And yet you created this curse anyway? Knowing that the use of magic in this way is a capital crime?'

'Dominus... I didn't know. When I discovered, I left the city. Only yesterday I returned for the first time...'

There was nothing very much the man could say in his defence. Nigrinus waited, letting the sorcerer sweat a little more in his constricting outfit.

'But that isn't why I had you brought here,' he said finally, with a light wave. He watched the man's shoulders sag forward. In the black holes of the mask his eyes were shining.

'It's not? Then why...?'

'I want you to tell me the future,' Nigrinus said. 'That's what you do, isn't it? You contact spirits and they tell you the secrets of the future?'

'Yes, but... what do you want to know?'

Nigrinus tightened his lips, as if he was considering. Then he smiled.

'Soon,' he said, 'in the coming months, there will be a war. Our emperor Constantine will cross the Alps and invade the territory of his rival Maxentius. All I want is the answer to a simple question. *Who will win?*'

He heard the intake of breath. Enquiring about the fate of emperors was as much a capital crime as issuing death curses.

'Have no fear,' he said, as reassuringly as he was able, and tried to contort his mouth into a smile. 'I already know of your past crimes, don't I? Assist me now, and I can see that those crimes are forgotten.'

The sorcerer hesitated, considering. Nigrinus held the blank stare of the mask's eyeholes. If the man had learned to control himself better, he thought, the outfit would look rather formidable. Nigrinus himself needed nothing like it, of course. His face was his mask.

'Upon your oath, I won't be harmed?'

'I won't lay a finger on you, I swear. In fact, I can see that you're rewarded. I too have certain *powers*, you might say... I can see that you want for nothing.'

A sigh, which sounded almost animalistic from inside the mask, and then the sorcerer lowered his head in agreement.

'The sack over there contains some... magical items,' Nigrinus said, 'which my men found in your lodging house. That should be sufficient?'

With obvious relief, the sorcerer turned and knelt in the corner of the room, taking objects from the sack and holding them up to the lamplight. Nigrinus watched with a sense of dull curiosity. Could people really believe that this quivering charlatan was in touch with the world of the spirits? Were hidden truths really accessed with such poor clutter, those feathers and scraps of cloth, those bundles of sticks? It was rather pathetic.

Julius Nigrinus did not particularly believe in the world of the spirits. Neither did he believe in the gods – or not the way most men did. If the gods existed, they obviously cared nothing about the affairs of mortals. However, he was not dogmatic in his disbelief. He wanted to see what this man would do, and what his exaggerated rituals might conjure up. After all, one never knew. Perhaps indeed there were dark powers beyond death; perhaps they really could whisper clues about the future. Sometimes it paid to be curious. Nigrinus himself had made a career out of it.

Besides, he thought as he watched the sorcerer assemble his arcane equipment, he needed all the clues he could get. The world was finely balanced, and his own place within it felt more precarious still. Just over two years before, Nigrinus had played a vital role in defeating an attempt to usurp the throne by the emperor's father-in-law. While his operation had not gone quite as he might have wished, he had still managed to expose the treasonous schemes of his own chief, the *primicerius* of the Corps of Notaries. By rights he should have got the man's job. That should have been his reward – it had been promised. But that reward had been snatched from him, at the instigation of men who felt his methods were unsound, unsavoury, perhaps even barbaric. Such men, Nigrinus thought, seldom needed to get their own hands dirty.

Instead, an ageing non-entity named Flavius Ummidius had been promoted to Chief of Notaries in his place, a man with little intelligence but many influential friends.

Nigrinus found that he was grinding his back teeth. Yes, he had been robbed, and the years had only stoked the flame of that injustice. But Julius Nigrinus was accustomed to being overlooked, accustomed to the scorn and even the hatred of other men. His father had been born a slave, and Nigrinus had worked his way up from nothing. Not surprising that he was distrusted. *They hate me*, he thought, *because they fear me*. That was good. And there would be time to make them sorry for their errors.

War was coming, he thought, that was true enough. And whatever was said publically in Treveris, the outcome was uncertain. Constantine was undefeated in the field, but so was Maxentius: the ruler of Rome had already seen off two imperial expeditions sent against him, without having to fight a battle. His armies were massive – Nigrinus had seen reports of up to two hundred thousand fighting men in Italy – and, if his troops were largely raw conscripts, Maxentius also had many thousands of experienced veterans from the Danube armies too.

But whatever happened, whoever was victor, Nigrinus was determined to make the most of it. This time he would do something that could not be denied, something brilliant and terrible. He would lay his enemies low. He would blast open every door that stood in his way. But he needed information; he needed to know which way to move. And at this point, he thought to himself, he would consider any option...

Down in his gloomy huddle, the sorcerer had constructed a rough tripod from woven sticks, only about two feet high, and piled greasy rags and feathers beneath it. Now, as Nigrinus watched, he lit a taper from the lamp and kindled his little pyre.

He crouched, tipping his mask up to blow on the twisting flame, and Nigrinus saw the silvery bristles on his exposed chin. The reek of burning filled the chamber, singed feathers and dirty smoke; a cough kicked at the back of Nigrinus's throat, and he stifled it.

Some time ago, this man Astrampsychus had made quite a name for himself, putting on his clandestine magical perform-ances all across Gaul, and even here in Treveris. Doubtless that was how Fausta, the emperor's wife, had got to hear of him. Nigrinus twisted a smile. Such things tended to impress weaker minds: slaves, eunuchs, women. Even a few of the imperial staff had been taken in. It was convenient that the sorcerer had made his reappearance now, and that Nigrinus's informers had picked up his trail before he came to public attention. The business of the death curse on the domina Minervina had not been common knowledge, and it was best that it stayed that way. The emperor's wife, after all, was supposed to be above suspicion.

'*CHAORA CHTHORA CHARABARAX!*' the sorcerer hissed, kneeling upright above his fuming little altar with his arms raised to the low ceiling. '*IAO CHANUMBRA!* O Chthonic gods! O Dis Pater! O Mother Hecate! Gods and Daemons of the Underworld! I adjure you to aid this divination. Rouse yourselves! Bring yourselves...!'

Smoke and stink were filling the room, and Nigrinus was struggling not to choke. His eyes were beginning to water. But he was fascinated, his gaze locked on the sorcerer's strange ritual. The man in the white robes appeared transfixed, swaying as he knelt, his hands fluttering in the smoke from the spitting blaze beneath the tripod.

'*ABRAXAS ABRAHATAS AOI AMARHA AMAAROTH!* Wake, demons, wake spirits! Bring me truths, I adjure you...'

Had the chamber got colder suddenly? Nigrinus realised that he was hunched forward in his seat, holding his breath. It seemed darker now too – but no, it was just the thick fumes in the air guttering the lamp flames. The blaze beneath the tripod seemed only to light the figure of the sorcerer, the smoke wreathing around him, until he seemed suspended in a shifting fog. His voice as he cried out his incantations was no longer the frightened breathy mumble of before; it was stronger, metallic-sounding, and seemed to come from somewhere deep beneath the stone floor of the chamber. Impressive, Nigrinus thought as he struggled to draw breath. Very impressive. But he was fighting the urge to run from the room.

The incantation had shifted now to a strange groaning mumble, the sorcerer fanning the smoke upwards towards his mask. The sweat ran down Nigrinus's brow and he felt slightly sick. Suddenly the flames beneath the tripod leaped – something thrown upon the fire no doubt – and then snuffed out. Reeling smoky darkness filled the room. The sound of the sorcerer's rasping breath came from down near the floor.

Nigrinus leaned forward and jogged the lamp on the low table, stirring the flame back to life. Now the smoke was clearing a little he could see the sorcerer slumped in the corner and the tripod fallen sideways over a heap of blackened ashes.

He coughed into his fist. 'Well?' he said.

'The spirits have given an answer to your question,' the man replied, his voice weak and hoarse from behind the mask.

'What did they say?'

'The spirits have told me... *Once battle is joined, the enemy of Rome shall perish...*'

Nigrinus waited a moment, hoping for more. He wiped his brow. 'That's all?'

The dog mask nodded.

'Well, they're certainly very diplomatic, your spirits.'

He stood up, his head spinning for a moment. He settled his cloak around his shoulders, then took a pace towards the door.

'Wait here,' he told the slumped figure in the corner. 'My assistant will come shortly to reward you and see you out.'

He crossed the chamber, and gripped the iron ring of the door handle. The thought of fresh clear air was delicious.

'One last thing,' he said, turning once more as if the thought had just struck him. 'When you placed the curse upon the domina Minervina... how was it done?'

The sorcerer had sat up, dragging his robes around him. The mask seemed to hang from his skull. His voice came slowly, wearily, from within. 'A figurine is made,' he said. 'A homunculus. Formed with clay from a dug grave mixed with the blood of a black cockerel. Items from the victim are placed within it – hair, or nail clippings – and certain words pronounced over it. Then iron nails are driven through the figurine in particular places. Head, heart, loins, stomach.'

'And then?' Nigrinus said. The words came out as an eager gasp.

The mask rose, the vacant eyeholes staring back at him. 'Then the figurine can be placed in a tomb,' the sorcerer said in a tone emptied of all feeling, 'or hidden somewhere close to the victim. In their bedchamber, for example. Beneath their bed, or where their food is prepared.'

'Interesting! And this is... effective?'

'Almost always, dominus.' The mask sagged again.

Nigrinus left the man sitting there and went out into the dark stone corridor, drinking the cold air down into his lungs. He coughed again as he pulled the door closed. His assistant was leaning against the far wall. Nigrinus nodded to him, then paced quickly along the corridor to the bottom of the stairs.

Night air breathed down from above, and Nigrinus stood for a while with his eyes closed and his head tipped back, inhaling deeply. He felt the dull fog of superstitious dread rising from him and dissipating. When he was fully calm and in possession of himself once more, he thought back over what the sorcerer had said. Behind him he heard a door slam, and the shuffle of feet on stone.

The enemy of Rome shall perish. Like a riddle. But so equivocal as to be useless. And yet, he thought, perhaps it meant something after all. If only he could find the right application for it... Maxentius was the master of Rome, Constantine his enemy. Yet Maxentius was a usurper – *the tyrant*, as those in Constantine's camp were learning to call him. Could he somehow be thought of as Rome's enemy?

With the vague intuition that he could make something of this yet, Nigrinus turned and paced quickly back down the corridor. His assistant was just leaving the chamber, a bundled sack under his arm. He was a dull sort of man, but at least he lacked the imagination to be treacherous. Nigrinus had experienced problems with his subordinates before.

'What should I do with this lot?' the man said, jogging the sack.

'Burn whatever's left,' Nigrinus told him. 'Throw the remains in the river.'

The assistant nodded curtly and moved towards the stairs. Nigrinus waited a moment for him to disappear, then eased open the door and stepped back into the chamber.

The lamp was still burning on the table, and the air was heavily charged with oily smoke. Only a few bent twigs and a blackened mark on the floor remained of the sorcerer's strange ritual. Of the sorcerer himself, nothing. Nigrinus nodded in appreciation.

He was just about to leave when something caught his eye – down in the corner, trapping a curve of shadow; Nigrinus bent and picked it up. The white dog-snout mask, still trailing the cord that had secured it to the man's head. It seemed tawdry now, a flimsy theatrical prop. Nigrinus studied the features of the mask. He had not broken his oath; he had not lied at all. Astrampsychus had been given his reward, and had been shown out. Nigrinus had not laid a finger upon him. And the dead want for nothing.

Turning the mask, he peered inside it. The dark hollow was spattered with fresh blood. Nigrinus flinched, squeamish, and tossed the thing away from him into the corner again. Then he snuffed out the lamp.

CHAPTER II

The imperial city of Treveris had rarely looked less impressive. Grey slush lay heaped along the sides of the streets and formed mounds under the dripping eaves of the porticos, threaded with the black runnels from the thawing drains. The light was fading, and the evening air smelled of damp smoke and latrines.

This did not feel like a homecoming. Castus had walked the three blocks from the palace, trailed by an unnecessary group of slaves carrying the meagre baggage he had brought back with him from his journey. After making his report that morning, he had taken the opportunity to bathe, change his clothes and have his hair cut. After going two months unshorn, his newly short-cropped scalp felt exposed in the chill breeze. He rubbed a palm over his shaved jaw, relishing the sensation of looking like a Roman soldier again instead of a barbarian.

But no amount of bathing and cleansing could unburden him of the weight of loss. Brinno's death still pressed upon his heart. Fourteen men had left Treveris two months before, and only Castus had returned.

Throwing his cloak back from his shoulders, he approached the house. The door opened before him, the porter and two other slaves stepping out to greet him. In the gloomy vestibule they took his baggage, and ushered Castus to a stool where he could sit while a boy removed his boots and placed soft-soled house shoes on his feet. Another slave brought a basin of warm water for him to wash his face and hands, while another held a linen towel for him to dry himself. All of it performed in sober silence. Castus unpinned his cloak and passed it to the door porter, then moved on into the heart of the house.

It was not a grand residence, by the standards of Treveris; in this area of the city there were scores like it, rented out to military officers, palace officials and their families. A suite of rooms on two storeys, around a brick-pillared central courtyard, the mosaic paving and painted walls just enough to give it an air of prestige. But it was several times the size of the quarters Castus had occupied as a centurion, let alone the spartan cell he had occupied in the precinct of the Protectores. And then there were the slaves.

They were waiting for him, gathered in the covered walks surrounding the courtyard. Castus scanned them quickly, barely taking in the faces. A dozen people, most of whom he did not recognise. How many of them did he own? He stepped into the alcove near the entrance door, where a shrine of Juno and the household gods stood with a clay lamp already burning before it. With his back to the throng of slaves he dipped his head, eyes closed for a moment in a prayer of thanks for his safe return. Then he took a pinch of incense and scattered it over the flame. The smoke curled around him, and he tried to stifle his cough. When he turned, the gathered slaves raised their arms in salute, greeting him with one voice.

A small man with a tight nervous smile stepped up to Castus, a scroll case and a heavy bunch of keys in his hands. Metro-dorus, Castus remembered, the freedman he had employed as procurator to oversee his household while he was away. He had never liked the man, but he had a reputation for honesty; Castus placed his hand briefly over the keys and the documents, nodded in acknowledgement, then walked on around the courtyard, the assembled slaves dropping their eyes as he passed.

Was it only in his blunted perceptions that they seemed to shrink back from him, to regard him with a sort of cringing distaste? He was the stranger here, the intruder; even after his bath, he felt he carried the scents of a different world, the sweat of long travel and hard living, the salt of blood and combat. As if he carried on his broad shoulders the burden of that other life, of which those gathered here know nothing: the life of warfare, which had made him, and raised him to this uncomfortable privilege.

Castus had never been particularly concerned about owning slaves himself; the few that were provided by the army had always sufficed. But decent households needed them, so his wife had explained. Twenty at least, in her opinion. Her father, she told him, had kept two hundred in his Rome townhouse alone. Castus fought down the sense of annoyance that was already rising through his fatigue. He had left instructions for Metrodorus to grant Sabina any necessary expenses – by law, he was not allowed to give her money directly, and after her father's execution for treason and the seizure of her property she had little wealth of her own. But he had also asked her not to use his money to fill the house with extra bodies.

He took a deep breath as he approached the doors of the reception chamber at the far side of the courtyard. He composed himself, tried to smile.

Valeria Domitia Sabina was seated on a folding stool in the middle of the chamber, a maid flanking her on either side. As he stepped up to the threshold, Castus felt a catch in his breath. For a moment he could only gaze at her, his mouth dry and his heart stilled. There was something austere, something almost aggressive in her beauty. He had forgotten how dangerously glamorous she could appear – when she wanted to. The words of a dying man in a ruined town came back to him: he had not forgotten Ulpianus's strange warning.

'Husband,' she said, standing up with a rustle of silk. Earrings of gold and pearls framed her face, a heavy gold necklace looped around her throat. Her hair was plaited into a mass of tight narrow braids, gathered in a golden net. Her face was a beautiful mask. She stepped up to him, kissed him lightly on the mouth, and he smelled that familiar perfume, musk and saffron, that had so intoxicated him when they had first met years before.

'Welcome home,' she said. Her hand lingered for a moment on his neck. But as she stepped back Castus noticed that she would not meet his eye.

Sabina led him to the back of the room, where couches and a low table were already set out for dinner. Castus settled himself warily, feeling not at all hungry. The evening had grown dark, and now the slaves closed the doors and the folding shutters against the cold damp breeze from the portico. Other slaves brought braziers to warm the room, oil lamps on tall iron stands, and amber wine in goblets of blue glass.

Castus reclined on the couch, sipping his wine, but his body was still locked into the rhythms of many days in the saddle, many weeks on the road. His hands as he gripped the glass felt clumsy and calloused, and he was aware of his chapped lips and wind-reddened face. Opposite him, his wife sat immaculate and reserved. How, he thought, had he come to be married to such a woman?

'We heard of your return this morning,' Sabina said. There was a slight catch in her voice, a ruffle in her silky poise. 'I'm sorry about your friend.'

Castus glanced quickly at her, a sound trapped in his throat. The black embers of grief flared briefly in his chest. His wife had never much cared for Brinno.

How much else did she know of what had happened, and what he had been doing? The mission to Licinius had been a strictly held secret. He had left Treveris back in early December under the cover of a routine escort duty to the Rhine and southern Gaul. But he had been away for two months, and it was not surprising that people had started to ask questions.

He had found Licinius at Sirmium in southern Pannonia, only ten days after his crossing of the frozen Danube. It had been a brief meeting: he had delivered the package as ordered, then waited only a day and a night before receiving the reply. Another sealed document, but Castus could guess that what it conveyed was positive. Licinius had sent twenty of his own mounted guard, plus a hundred *auxilia* of the Raetovarii, to escort him safely and swiftly back to the borders of Constantine's domain. Even now, Castus thought, that reply was doubtless being read and discussed in the chambers of the palace, plans made, strategies put into motion...

'You must tell me all about your travels – later,' Sabina said, with a strong note of suggestion in her voice. *When the slaves cannot overhear us*, she meant. Castus detected the hint of coldness in his wife's voice, the quiver of tension behind the façade of her courtesy. He stared at her across the table, trying to read her expression. He knew well her aristocratic disdain, although he had somehow managed to forget about it over the months of separation. This was something deeper, though. She was angry; angry at him, and only waiting for a moment when that anger could be safely kindled into rage and recrimination.

For so long Castus had dreamed of this homecoming, picturing it in his mind over and again: the joy of his return, the warmth of Sabina's welcome. How could he have been so mistaken?

'So,' he said, as mildly as he could manage. 'Tell me what you've been doing.'

The slaves were bringing food from the kitchens now: eggs in fish sauce, then steamed trout with asparagus, then peaches in syrup and cumin. Castus regarded the meal without enthusiasm; the cooks must have laboured at it all day, but he ate each delicately flavoured dish as if it were a bowl of beans.

As they ate, Sabina told him of her activities. She had spent much of her time at the palace, in the household of the emperor's wife, the *nobilissima femina* Fausta. Castus listened as she filled him in on the affairs of the court, the alliances and the rivalries, those who had risen in favour and those who had plunged into disgrace.

'Nepotilla's husband's become a Christian,' she told him. 'Or so they say. Apparently he's not a genuine believer, but he thinks it'll help his promotion. The rumour is that the emperor favours the sect more each day. Some say he's become a Christian himself!'

'Constantine?' Castus said, a mouthful of food catching in his throat. He swallowed heavily. 'Not likely.' He remembered well that strange moment over two years before, on the road north from Massilia, when the sun god had beamed his blessing upon Constantine from the sky. Now the emperor revered the solar deity above all others; his coins bore the proud image of Sol Invictus, the Unconquered Sun. So it should be, Castus thought. The idea of some bizarre and unsavoury foreign sect appealing to the master of the western world was a joke, a slaves' fable.

Sabina just shrugged, apparently uninterested. One of the maids approached her couch, leaning to whisper in her ear. 'The child is awake,' Sabina said. 'Would you like to see him now?'

Castus sat up quickly on the couch, not caring if he appeared too eager. Another slave came from the darkened passage outside the dining room, a blonde woman with a dimpled chin. Castus had not seen her before, but she carried a swaddled bundle in her arms. She bowed slightly as she approached, drawing the shawl away from the baby's face. Castus caught his breath. In the soft glow of the lamps his son gazed back at him, black-eyed, completely unfamiliar. These last two months had transformed the boy; he was half a year old now.

For a moment Castus felt only a strange baffled wonderment, his breath stilled, his body too tense to move. It was unwise, he knew, to develop feelings of attachment towards infants; so many of them died in their earliest years. But he could not help himself. They had named the boy Aurelius Sabinus, their names combined; Sabina had wanted to call him Honoratus, after her dead father. Perhaps, Castus wondered, she would have loved him more if they had.

He reached across to the swaddled bundle, and the baby stared back at him. Castus wondered if his own father had ever gazed at him in this way. Had that terrible old man ever felt this sense of tender awe? Sirmium was only a day's ride from the town on the banks of the Danube where Castus had been born. He could have gone there and found his father, stood before him and told him that he was a grandfather now, and his son a Protector of the Sacred Bodyguard. He had considered it, but he had not. Castus had not seen his father since the day he had attempted to kill the man with an ironbound bucket, then fled to join the legions. Most likely, he thought, his father was dead by now. If not, he could not bear the thought of meeting him.

No, this child was his own, and he was not his father. Everything would be different now. He smiled, and felt his chapped lips crack.

The baby's eyes widened, pools of black in the lamplight, then he smiled too. Castus felt the warmth rising through him, the joy of recognition. The moment lasted a heartbeat, maybe two, then the child's face creased, his mouth opened and he let out a wail of pure anguish.

Castus sat back quickly. *Gods, am I really so terrifying?*

'You are unfamiliar, that is all,' the nurse said, wrapping the child in her shawl again, soothing him. Her accent was Germanic, Castus noticed; a memory stirred in his mind and then sank. The nurse was carrying the baby away now, the other slaves bringing more wine, and Castus snatched up his goblet and drank quickly.

Sabina had barely glanced at the child. It was demeaning, of course, for any freeborn woman to nurse her own offspring, but Castus knew that his wife's lack of interest in their son went deeper than that. The pregnancy had been hard; it had almost killed her.

How different things had been when they were first married. The six months after the wedding had been filled with a passion that Castus had never before known. To have found himself married to a daughter of the Roman aristocracy had been strange enough, but that such a woman would be genuinely drawn to him, aroused by him, had been stranger still. His wife's moods, her maddening attitudes, were not surprising, Castus told himself – she had lived all her life in mansions and palaces. If she was sometimes arrogant and self-absorbed, it was only a legacy of her upbringing. He knew that there was more to her than that. He knew she was courageous – she had proved that in Massilia. He admired her intelligence, her effortless beauty and her curious subtle wit; she confused him, and he found her utterly enthralling. When he was away from her, he was clumsy and stupefied with desire. Brinno had laughed at him for it: how unmanly, he had said, for anyone to be so enraptured by his own wife...

Their happiness had not lasted long. By the autumn of that year Sabina was already growing impatient with him, caustic and frustrated by the limitations of her new life. He would listen to her describing the lost splendours of Rome, the stolen wealth of her family – the houses on the Aventine and the Caelian, the African estates at Thagaste and Thabraca, the villas in Lucania and Illyricum, all seized by Maxentius after the execution of her father and her first husband – and he knew that he could offer her little in consolation. Pregnancy had seemed at first like a release, but she had treated it as a further imprisonment. By the following summer Castus had been spending much of his time away from Treveris, or on duty at the palace. Their lives had resumed their separate courses. It pained him to have known such love – to know it still, despite everything – and to be daily reminded of the unbridgeable gulf between them.

The meal was done, the dishes with their half-eaten food cleared away. Sabina sat up, lifted her glass, still half full of wine, and drained it in one long draught.

'I shall retire to the bedchamber,' she said as she stood and wrapped herself in her silk shawl. 'You should speak to Metrodorus about the accounts, I suppose...'

Castus frowned as he watched her leave the room, strongly tempted to forget household convention and follow her, but the smirking freedman was already approaching with his scrolls and tablets. It was only some time later that Castus could finally dismiss the slaves and pace down the draughty darkened corridor to the bedchamber at the back of the house.

Sabina was in the inner room, seated close to the brazier in her sleeping tunic. Her loosened hair was like a spill of ink in the lamplight, and a handmaid stood behind her, running a comb through it and humming under her breath. Castus motioned to the woman, who bowed, placed the comb on the side table and left the room. Now, at last, they were alone.

But Sabina remained silent. Charcoal crackled in the brazier. Castus felt the silence pressing on his ears.

'Who was the *nutrix* with the baby?' he asked. 'I don't know her.'

'Elpidia? She's new. The old one had no milk, so I asked Metrodorus to buy another.'

He paced up behind her, placing his hands on her shoulders, the smoothness of her neck. He felt the cold links of her necklace, the warm silk of her hair.

'So you went to Pannonia,' she said. 'To Licinius.'

'How did you know that?' He had tightened his grip with intending it.

'Everyone knows,' she snapped, and reached up to seize his wrist. 'Everyone in the palace. You know how these things get passed around. You went through barbarian country and they killed everyone but you... You could have died! You could have died and I would have been a widow and not even known!'

She stood up quickly, throwing off his hands, and stalked over to face the wall. Castus heard her sniff; she was trying not to cry.

'What would you have had me do?' he said. 'Refuse? I'm a soldier. It's my duty. You know this...'

'Duty!' she cried, fierce with anger. 'Always *duty*... What about me? What about your son? You should have told me...'

'I could tell nobody,' Castus growled. He scrubbed at his chin, then ran a palm over his cropped scalp. His body felt racked with frustration, and he paced to the far wall and back.

'What do you think it's like for me,' she said, 'left alone in this draughty little house by myself, not knowing whether you're alive or dead, or where in the world you might be? Can you imagine? Are you even capable of imagining that?'

She spun around to face him. The distance closed between them suddenly, and she was standing before him, blazing with cold, contained fury. For a few moments Castus found he could not speak.

'Oh, but what do you know except *duty*?' she snarled. 'Never duty to me, your wife! Never duty to your family!'

'Consider for a moment,' Castus said, slow and heavy, 'that not everything in this world is about you.'

'What do you know of me! Nothing!' She raised her hand and punched his shoulder, then tried to shove at him. He grabbed her wrist, his fingers closing around the thin bones of her forearm. Wide-eyed, she stared back at him. 'How could you ever know me?' she spat. 'You're just a soldier, an uneducated peasant! How could you understand anything of what I feel?'

She swung at him again with her free hand, and he drew his arm back in a reflexive gesture.

'Oh, have I insulted you now?' she said. 'Have I insulted your precious honour? Hit me if you dare – isn't that what husbands do?'

He released her, shoving her away, and her choked cry of anguish echoed around the painted walls of the chamber. She swiped at her dressing table and the contents fell clattering onto the floor. Castus sat on the bed. He thought of the things he could tell her, but would not. The days of riding in the wilderness of Germania, the battles in the frozen forest, and the dead town in the white mist of dawn. Brinno's death, and his own plunge through the river ice. Would she even care to know of these things? Would they mean anything to her?

He got up and crossed the room, taking her by the shoulder as gently as he could. 'Sabina,' he said, the name forming deep in his throat.

She turned and flung her arms around his neck, her embrace sudden and fierce. 'Don't leave me like that again,' she breathed. Her kiss was hungry, desperate. 'Promise me you won't go off and get yourself killed without telling me first.'

The lamps had burned down, and only the last ebb of the brazier lit the room as they lay together in the ruck of blankets. Sabina eased herself up from his shoulder.

'So,' she said, 'do you have any interesting new scars to show me?'

Castus shook his head, watching her as she sat and scooped the hair away from her nape to unclip her necklace. Her veering moods no longer confused him as once they had. A slow wash of contentment ran through him, and he closed his eyes. Then he opened them again.

'Those earrings,' he said, lifting his hand to lightly touch the dangling pearls. 'Have I seen them before?'

'These? Oh, I don't know...' Sabina looked away, letting the hair fall to cover her face. Castus frowned. His wife's display of anger had been genuine, but she was hiding something else, something deeper.

'What's wrong?' he said, dropping his hand. She paused, glanced quickly at him, then looked away again.

'Nothing! I merely... I wanted to dress well – to welcome you home, I suppose...' She was already fiddling with the earrings, taking them off.

Castus tried not to let his disquiet show. The memory of the dying tribune's words came back to him, insistent and probing. *Be careful in Treveris...* But he could not help detecting something else, an evasive guilt that she was trying hard to conceal. What had she done?

Put it out of your mind, he told himself. *This is your wife, the mother of your child. Forget it – because if you knew, you would have to act.*

He let out a long sigh and forced a smile, then drew her down beside him again.

'What was he like then, Licinius?' Sabina asked, settling herself against the heavy muscle of his shoulder. Her voice still held a flicker of unease, and she was trying to cover it.

'Fat,' he told her. 'Very small eyes. Blue chin. I think his breath was bad.'

'I shan't envy the emperor's sister, then, having to marry him.' He had told her of that too – there seemed little point concealing things now.

'They told me at Sirmium that Diocletian's died,' he said.

'The old emperor? I thought he was dead years ago.'

Castus shook his head. He did not want to say more: that he had revered Diocletian as long as he could remember. The old man had rebuilt the empire, and held it together with iron strength. For years since his abdication he had lived in well-earned luxury at his fortified villa on the Dalmatian coast. Now that he was gone, there was nothing left to keep the rivals that had succeeded him from open war. Worse, some at Licinius's court had whispered that the old emperor had taken his own life, in despair at the ruin of his imperial dreams.

'If Diocletian's really gone,' Sabina said, her breathy whisper warm against his skin, 'there's nothing to stop Constantine from marching south in the spring, is there? Against Maxentius?'

'No,' he said. He sensed the shadows of unease cloud his mind. War had been Castus's life for so long, it seemed perverse that he should dread the prospect of this one so greatly. But he would be fighting against other Romans, men of the legions who had once been his brothers. He cast the thought aside. He had killed Romans before now, at Massilia, and it had not been hard. He could do it again, he told himself. It was his duty; it was what he was good at.

'Gods, let it be soon!' Sabina said. She raised herself on her elbow and ran her fingers over the roughness of his cheek. 'I can't stand another winter here! Another month, even... I hate this place...'

'But I thought you wanted me to stay here with you always?' he said, smiling.

'You don't understand,' she said, with a playful lilt in her words. 'If you're marching to Rome then you can go with my blessing. That's exactly what I *want* you to do!' She leaned closer, breathing into his ear. 'Go to Rome, my love. Revenge my family! *Kill Maxentius for me...*'

Castus frowned, but he was still smiling as he rolled her over onto the bed beneath him.

Later still, the brazier had died and cold stood over the bed. Castus woke suddenly, stifling a shout. In his mind he still saw the spears of river ice knitting above him, felt the water dragging him down. Brinno was reaching up from the black depths, grinning through broken teeth... Drawing quick breaths, Castus waited for his heartbeat to slow, then pushed the covers away from his body. Sabina lay sleeping, an arm draped across his chest. He slid from her embrace, and she mumbled something but did not wake. Cold tightened his muscles as he crossed to the far corner and drank deeply from the water jug. The bed was too soft for him; he had never got used to plump mattresses. Grimacing, he pulled on his tunic.

A thin cry came from along the passageway, a baby's waking wail. Castus left the bedchamber, stepping quietly over the slave sleeping at the threshold. Barefoot on the chilled tiles, he paced across the antechamber and into the passage. There was a flare of light from the courtyard portico, and then a figure appeared at the far end of the passageway: a slave holding a lamp. It was the new wet-nurse, Castus realised, the blonde woman, hurrying towards the child's room. 'Elpidia', Sabina had called her: a slave name. She paused as she saw him, glaring at him for a moment, then moved on.

Castus passed through the darkened dining room and along the shorter corridor at the far side to a small chamber, lightless and almost bare. A simple wooden bed stood against the far wall; he found it by touch, pulling the rough woollen blankets from the thin mattress and spreading them on the floor. Easing himself down, he stretched out on the hard tiles and pulled the blankets around him.

Sleep crept over him, comfortable and dreamless. Then, just at the edge of consciousness, he snapped back awake. He remembered where he had seen that blonde slave, the baby's nutrix, before. Years ago, in a forest in Germania. A valley of burning villages, troops paused beside the path as a file of prisoners went by. She had looked back at him; he remembered the moment with perfect clarity. The expression of proud defiance on her face. The undiluted hatred in her eyes.

CHAPTER III

Ten days later, on the open ground outside the walled city of Divodurum, a thousand men stood in serried ranks beneath a pearl-coloured sky. Low light gleamed off polished iron and burnished bronze. A thousand speartips glittered. A thousand oval shields shone in the greyness, each one freshly painted with the emblem of a red sun-wheel on golden yellow.

Castus rode slowly along the line of the front rank. Raindrops beaded his gilded helmet, and the breeze pushed at the tall plume of black feathers. When he reached the centre of the line he turned and rode up to the tribunal, slipping from the saddle and climbing onto the turf platform. Gathered behind him were the other senior officers, and the man holding the golden eagle standard of the legion; to either side of the tribunal were trumpeters and heralds. A groom led his horse away as Castus removed his helmet and clasped it beneath his left arm. He saluted the laurel-decked image of the emperor mounted on the standard pole, then turned to face the assembled men of his new command. Feet braced wide, one thumb hooked over his broad leather belt, Castus surveyed the ranks of soldiers. Blankly they stared back at him.

He coughed quietly to clear his throat, then drew a deep breath and threw back his head.

'Brothers!' he cried, his voice powering out to the far margins of the field. 'Men of the Second Britannica... Many of you know me. I served beside you in Britain, and on the Rhine. Many others do not. My name is Aurelius Castus, and by the sacred order of our emperor I have been appointed tribune, to take command of this legion and prepare it for war.'

Castus paused. He drew from his belt the slim gold-capped ivory scroll tube that contained his codicil of appointment from the emperor, the mandate that gave him command of the legion, and held it up for all to see. So many times he had stood through these sorts of addresses, from tribunals all over the empire; but always he had been in the ranks, silently dutiful. Standing up there before so many men, alone in the position of command, was a new and unnerving experience.

A herald stepped up beside him, taking the ivory tube and unrolling the document. In a flat and sonorous monotone, he began to recite the text of the codicil.

'*By the sacred pleasure of our lord and emperor Flavius Valerius Aurelius Constantinus Augustus, Invictus, the most distinguished Aurelius Castus, Ducenarius and Protector, is in honour of his virtues and services advanced to the rank of tribune...*'

As he listened, Castus remembered the ceremony, only five days before, in the huge audience hall of the imperial palace in Treveris. The slow steps he had taken across the polished marble floor, the smoke of incense from the altar where he had made sacrifice, the emperor seated high on his dais, blazing in purple and gold like one of the gods. The promotion was a reward, a recognition for carrying the despatch to Licinius. Only now was Castus beginning to digest its importance.

'*The said Aurelius Castus is hereby directed to take upon himself the command of the Second Legion Britannica, now at Divodurum, and with the favour of the gods and the sacred majesty of the emperor observe and execute the regulations of his command in obedience to imperial orders, and in all ways exercise and discipline the troops under his charge to attend the warlike demands of the state, in accordance with the glory and dignity of Roman arms. And for so doing this shall be his mandate.'*

The herald's voice died away into the damp February air. Castus took the scroll tube from him, then stepped forward to address the soldiers once more.

'War is coming,' he said in a lower voice. 'All of you know this. I cannot say whether we will march north, against our enemies beyond the Rhine... or against another foe. But we will be ready for anything that is required of us by our emperor.'

A ripple went through the ranks, and the speartips wavered like a field of long grass in a breeze. Every man there knew who that other foe would be. How many of them, Castus wondered, shared his misgivings about what lay ahead?

'You have been trained well over the winter,' he went on. 'Your *campidoctor*, Julius Macer, has lived up to his reputation.' He gestured to the man who stood just behind him on the tribunal, the legion's chief drill instructor. Macer was a veteran in his mid-fifties, solid and iron-stiff, with white hair and a face the colour of boiled bacon.

'You have done well so far,' Castus called to the assembled men. 'Over the coming months you will need to do even better. I will not ask you to do anything that I will not do myself. But by the time we are ordered to march, I want this legion to be the very best in the field army of Gaul. I believe you are the men to make it so.'

He stepped back smartly, nodding to Macer. The drill instructor took his position at the front of the tribunal, crying

54

out in a rasping yell. 'Salute to our new tribune, Aurelius Castus!'

Three times the men threw up their arms, shouting out the salute. Castus stood and gazed into the air above them. He felt dazed.

Macer the drillmaster stepped down from the tribunal, then turned to face Castus. He gave a smart military salute. 'Dominus!' he cried. 'Permission to commence drill!'

'Proceed,' Castus told him.

As the white-haired veteran strode away from him, already barking out orders to the centurions, and the brassy yell of the trumpets and horns sounded across the field, Castus watched the men carefully. This was an important moment, he told himself – he should be attentive, remember what he saw. This was the material of his command.

Legion II Britannica had only been formed the previous autumn, and had been billeted in Divodurum over the winter. Their first tribune had fallen sick soon afterwards, and Macer had been in effective command ever since. They were not a full legion, officially speaking; II Britannica only had the strength of two traditional cohorts, but there were several new units like this in the field army now. If required, their numbers could be bolstered by new drafts, but the smaller scale made them more flexible and gave them better cohesion than the old temporary detachments.

At the core of Castus's command were the men of the two British legions that had crossed the sea to Gaul for the Rhine campaign more than three years before; Castus himself had served with one of them, Legion VI Victrix from Eboracum, and had seen much of the other, II Augusta. As he watched them manoeuvre into their drill formations, he recognised many of the faces in the ranks. All of them had volunteered to remain in Gaul, rather than return to their old garrisons and their old legions. They were veterans, blooded in combat, men he could trust.

But the rest of Legion II Britannica were new recruits, some of them volunteers and others conscripted. They were an unknown mass; had Macer's winter of training moulded them into soldiers yet? Most of their centurions had been promoted from other legions of the Gallic army. Solid men, he assumed, but he had known many bad centurions in his time.

Now he watched them carefully, alert for faults, anxious for failings. He realised that he was holding his breath, the cuirass pressing tight against his chest. He forced himself to exhale, breathe, pay attention.

Castus had never looked for promotion or high honours, or expected them. In his twenty years in the army he had tried only to do his duty, support his emperor and his comrades, be the best he could and not disgrace his legion or his rank. And yet he had risen all the same. It felt precarious, daunting. Would he have the courage, the clarity of mind to live up to what was expected of him now?

As the troops reassembled in the ranks, and the trumpets rang out, Castus raised his eyes to the dull silvery gleam showing through the clouds. *Unconquered Sun, Light against Darkness... Let me lead these men well. Support me. Do not let me fail them.*

'They tell me you were with Galerius on the Persian campaign, dominus,' Macer said.

Castus nodded. They were in the main chamber of his quarters, a suite of rooms on the upper floor of an old bath-house, and his orderly slave, Eumolpius, was prising at the catch that fastened the breastplate of his gilded cuirass. Castus had bought the armour cheaply in Treveris just before he left, and it constricted his torso and rubbed at his neck uncomfortably. The catch came free, and the slave lifted the plates from his body. Castus inhaled gratefully, filling his chest, then swung his arms.

'I was in Persia myself, quite a few years before you,' the drillmaster went on, propping himself in the alcove of the window. 'I joined the legions in the days of the deified Aurelian. The Tenth Gemina – best legion there is, or it used to be...' He shook his head, narrowing his eyes. He had a thin mouth, almost lipless, and a voice like grinding gravel. 'Then I was on the Danube under Probus, and went east into Persia with Carus. After that I fought at the Margus in Diocletian's army, when he made himself emperor of the world. I came west with Maximian for the Mauretanian campaign, and here I've been ever since.'

Castus nodded again, then took a cup of wine from the table. Forty years, he thought – the drillmaster had served forty years, and never risen above a senior centurion's rank. Macer, he knew only too well, regarded the legion as his own. No doubt he resented a man twenty years his junior being installed above him. Castus knew that he needed to be careful – Macer could be an ally or an adversary, but he could not allow the older man to claim authority here.

'It's good to have an officer of such experience,' he said, his tone stiff and abrasive. 'I can see the men have responded well. Much of what I saw on the drill field was commendable.' He placed the cup down and spread his hands on the table.

'*Much*?' Macer said, shoving the word through the narrow slot of his mouth.

Castus sniffed. 'Your centurions are too keen to use the stick,' he said. 'Too often they push their men from the rear, watching out for stragglers. They should be in front, setting an example.'

Macer drew a long breath. His ruddy face coloured even more deeply, glowing up into the roots of his white hair. 'Soldiers need discipline,' he said.

'You herd goats with a stick. You don't lead men with one.'

It was an old saying, but it struck home. Castus could almost feel the heat of the drill instructor's anger radiating across the room. He noticed his orderly, Eumolpius, staring intently at the corner of the ceiling, and for a moment wondered if he had gone too far. From the portico below the window came the slow tread of a passing sentry, and a trumpet called the change of the watch.

'*However*,' Castus said, with deliberate emphasis, 'aside from that, I trust you to exercise the men as you see fit.' He leaned forward, his fists braced on the table, and stared at Macer. They had to work together, after all. A moment of stubborn silence, then the older man twitched his shoulder and glanced out of the window again.

'Tell me about the legion,' Castus said, easing himself down onto one of the stools. He picked up his cup and swirled the wine inside it.

Macer gave another curt half-shrug. 'Many of the men are fit and able,' he said. 'The troops from the old British legions, I mean. Most have served ten years at least. There's some rivalry between them – the Augusta men and the Sixth – but I find that it adds a sense of competition. Some of the centurions are good too: Attalus, Blaesus, Rogatianus...'

Castus knew Rogatianus well; the dark wiry African had joined the Sixth Legion back in Britain, and had fought against the Picts and on the Rhine. His optio, Modestus, was a familiar face too. Castus had known him from his very first days in

Eboracum, and had promoted him to his current position. There were others as well, men he knew and recognised. It was a reassurance to have them with him.

'What about the rest?' he asked.

'The rest are new recruits and conscripts,' Macer told him. 'They're a mixed lot – some are shaping up well. Couple hundred of the recruits are barbarians, sons of Germanic settlers. Can barely speak Latin, some of them. We've got a few *Christians* as well. I don't know what you make of that sort – personally I reckon old Diocletian took the right way with them. But so long as they don't mind fighting and don't try to peddle their funny beliefs to the others, I turn a blind eye. There's a Christ-temple near the south gate they go to.'

'The soldiers mix with the civilians, then?'

Macer curled his mouth sourly. 'Can't stop them,' he said. 'They're billeted all over the city. Not like the old days, when all the legions had their own fortresses...' He paused for a moment, with a look of intense nostalgia. 'Soldiers were soldiers back then. Not like now – hanging around the public baths, mixing with women and the scum of the streets... That reminds me,' he said, 'there's half a dozen men in the lock-up. I believe you've got the authority to try them, under military justice.'

Castus suppressed a groan, nodded, and gestured that the drillmaster was dismissed. Macer saluted, then strode across the room, his hobnails cracking on the tiled floor. He paused at the doorway.

'Mind if I suggest something... dominus?' he said.

'Go on.'

'The men know you're a soldier. Come up from the ranks. They can respect that. But if you go soft on them because of it, they'll despise you.'

'I'll bear that in mind.'

Macer left, slamming the door behind him.

From the wooden balcony outside the main chamber of his quarters, Castus gazed down into the courtyard below. Rogatianus was training a half-century of his men in *armatura* weapons drill, and the air was filled with the smack and crack of wooden swords on wicker shields, the cries of attack and injury, the centurion's encouraging bark. From the portico Castus could make out the rattle and click of knucklebone dice. He could smell woodsmoke from the bakery, and the yeasty stink from the brewhouse. All of it was familiar to him; he had known these sounds and scents for years, in legion fortresses and camps all across the empire. It was good to be back, surrounded by the life of the army once more after his long spell in the world of the palace.

But the duties of a tribune, he had quickly discovered, involved a lot more than the regular army life he had known as a legionary and centurion. More than just parading around in gilded armour too. With a heavy sigh he shoved himself away from the balcony and went back into the chamber. The large central table was spread with tablets and furled scrolls, shards of pottery scratched with rows of figures, all the great backlog of paperwork and administration that Macer had ignored for months but Castus could not. There were letters from the Primicerius of the Praetorian Prefect, from the Commander of the Field Army of Gaul, from the super-intendents of four different imperial arsenals, plus strength reports and inventories of arms and equipment that needed checking. Half the men needed new boots and tunics, and several hundred lacked armour.

'What's next?' Castus asked, pacing to the table and frowning at the impenetrable mess of paperwork.

'A report from the superintendent of the supply depot at Andematunnum,' Diogenes said, peering at a waxed tablet. 'Stating that the consignment of body armour sent by the *fabrica* at Augustodunum was returned as *faulty*...'

Musius Diogenes was another of the former soldiers of the Sixth Legion. Castus had known him since Eboracum: he had been a schoolteacher before joining the army, and with his slight build and fuzz of thinning hair he was the least military-looking man Castus had ever encountered. But Diogenes was tougher than he appeared, and had proved himself in battle; he was also a very skilled administrator, and Castus had appointed him *adiutor*, to serve as his personal secretary. It was a role that suited him well.

'Apparently,' he said in a dry tone, glancing up from the tablet, 'the prefect at Augustodunum sent the consignment twice, and both times it was returned...'

Castus rubbed his scalp. 'Faulty?' he said. 'What does that mean?'

'I suspect,' Diogenes replied, tossing the tablet aside, 'that the superintendent and the prefect have a ruse going on. They send a non-existent consignment of armour back and forth between them until it effectively vanishes, and split the payment.'

Castus hissed between his teeth. The knot of frustration that had been gathering in his neck gave another twist. 'So this pair of jokers are filling their purses while my men are expected to go into battle without proper body armour? Without even helmets?'

Diogenes shrugged. 'These abuses do happen, sadly, dominus.'

'Right. Take down a message to the prefect of the fabrica,' Castus demanded, snapping his fingers. He was pacing back and forth across the room. 'Tell him that I need two hundred and sixty mail or scale hauberks, plus one hundred and seventy helmets, delivered here by the ides of next month. If I don't get them, I'll write to the Praetorian Prefect himself and inform him of the, uh… the *treasonous and criminal actions* of him and his friend at Andematunnum!'

'I should mention that we don't have any proof, dominus…'

'Exactly! We don't have any armour either! Tell him also that if I don't get what I need I'll go over to his fucking fabrica and break a few of his ribs – that should teach him the advantages of body armour in a hostile situation!'

'Ah ha, yes,' Diogenes said, raising an eyebrow as he wrote.

Castus clasped his hands behind his back and peered out of the open door to the balcony. He could still hear the sounds of the exercise yard, the crack and shout, the laughter; he needed exercise himself, some hard physical activity to burn off the aggressive tension he felt building up in his body. He had always thought that tribunes and other officers had it easy.

'What's next?' he said.

'There's a… letter from your wife, dominus.'

'Sabina?' Castus turned quickly, surprised. He had heard nothing from her since leaving Treveris ten days before. 'What does she say?'

'Nothing of any great importance,' Diogenes said. 'Perhaps you'd care to look at it yourself?'

'No, no…' Castus told him, turning back to the window. 'Just give me the sense of it.'

Years before, Diogenes had taught Castus the basics of literacy. After spending most of his youth in the army, Castus had never learned to read and write, but with his promotion it had become necessary. It had been a hard task, and even now he could only make the slowest progress. The words seemed to dance before his eyes, letters scrambling and unscrambling, and he found it hard to concentrate on the meaning. Sometimes he wondered if his old army nickname – *Knucklehead* – was entirely justified after all.

'The domina Valeria Domitia Sabina greets you and hopes that you are well,' Diogenes read in a flat voice, clearly uncomfortable, 'as she is well, and so is your son. She asks whether you might be returning to Treveris for the birthday celebrations of the Augustus... some formulaic words of farewell... that's all.'

Sabina, they had agreed, would remain in Treveris rather than accompanying Castus to his new command. It was a wise choice; as she put it herself, she had no wish to live in an army camp, 'surrounded by farting soldiers'. He would return when he could, to visit her and their son, but both of them knew that Castus's duties would allow him few opportunities to do so. They had parted warmly, affectionately, but as he had ridden the fifty miles south to Divodurum Castus had been all too aware that his wife was probably glad to be alone again. The whole household had seemed relieved; he had been an awkward presence amongst them. No, he thought, Sabina would be much happier in Treveris, with the endless round of festivals and dinner parties, and the glamorous intrigues of the court. It was the world she knew best, just as he was far more comfortable here with his legion. But still doubt gnawed at his mind – and at his heart. He remembered all too well his sense that she was hiding something from him. And the words of the dying officer in Germania.

'Write back to her, would you?' he told Diogenes. 'Just tell her I'm well. But I won't be back in Treveris until at least the kalends of March.'

Diogenes nodded and picked up a fresh writing tablet. Castus was glad of the man's discretion. He knew he should keep his distance from his wife as long as possible, try and put her out of his mind as much as he could and concentrate on his duties. He would throw himself into the task of training his men, building their discipline, forming them into a legion to be proud of. Yes, that would be best – but the thought of her dragged at him constantly, pulling him back into unmilitary reveries.

Before leaving Treveris he had questioned Metrodorus about the baby's nurse. The Germanic slave was ideal for the job, the procurator had assured him; she was obedient, respectful, not at all dangerous. The child appeared to love her. Castus frowned at the thought. How could it be that a barbarian captured in war, a woman who must surely hate Romans, could be so trustworthy now? He shrugged the thought from his mind; slaves were different from free people. Their condition robbed them of genuine feelings. Or so he had been taught to believe.

He paced back across the room again, then went and peered over the secretary's shoulder.

'How can you write so fast?' he said, squinting down at the tablet.

'Shorthand,' Diogenes told him. 'I can teach you, dominus, if you like.'

'No, no...' Castus said. He took a step away, then paused. 'But, listen,' he went on in a lower voice. 'I need to practise. Reading and writing, I mean.' He cleared his throat. 'I haven't had much chance, and it's hard... Can you get me something simple to read? Something easy to follow...?'

Diogenes glanced up quizzically for a moment. 'I understand, yes,' he said. 'I'll see what I can find.'

Castus gave a curt nod. 'And not a word to anyone!' he growled.

Leaving the secretary to his work, he paced back to the open door of the balcony. How many months did he have? Two, perhaps, or maybe three. And then the order would come from the imperial staff, and Castus would lead his men on the road to war. He felt a tightness in his belly at the thought, a dry flutter of anxiety. Could he give them all the training they needed in that short time? From the courtyard below the balcony he heard Rogatianus's voice once more; yes, he thought, there would be time enough to prepare the men, he had only to trust his officers for that.

But as for trusting himself, he was less certain.

CHAPTER IV

The rain was easing as the legion marched into the town of Vidubia, but the road was churned clay and every man was muddied to the knees. They marched four abreast, dressed alike in hooded rain capes, with leather-covered shields and cloth-bound spears slung over their shoulders. Castus stood at the verge of the road and watched them as they passed him in the lowering light. He had marched beside them, on foot, setting the pace with his own mile-eating stride, and now he checked each unit, calling out to the centurions by name, judging the condition of the men. Eight days on the road, and they still looked strong. Only four soldiers so far had dropped out of the line, sprained or footsore, to ride in the baggage carts at the rear of the column.

Vidubia was barely a town, more a straggle of timber buildings bunched along the road, with an imperial posting station and an inn. The *mensores* had ridden ahead of the marching column, and already chalked their marks on the doorframes, allocating billets for the men. The luckier centuries were quartered in the stables of the inn yard, or in warehouses and dwelling huts; the others were left to put up their damp leather tents in the walled enclosure behind the posting station.

Castus had been given a pair of rooms on the upper floor of the station, large chambers with crude colourful paintings on the walls, probably the best accommodation in town. From the wooden balcony outside he gazed down at the lines of tents, the soldiers gathering around their smoking cook fires. He hear the curses and the corse laughter, breathed in the scents of smoke, damp wool and leather. He stretched his arms above his head, feeling the pleasant flex of weary muscles, the satisfying fatigue of a long day's march. As he walked back inside he stripped off his sweat-stained tunic and threw it over a chair. His orderly, Eumolpius, was busy scraping the mud from his boots.

A rap at the door, and before Eumolpius could get to his feet it opened and Macer walked in. The drillmaster raised his stick in a brief salute.

'Dominus. All the men are settled. They're too tired to cause trouble tonight, I reckon.'

Castus nodded, pouring himself a cup of watered vinegar-wine and gulping it back. 'They did well,' he said. 'If we keep up this pace we can break a day at Lugdunum. Then they can enjoy themselves.'

Macer gave a curt shrug. He had a new briskness to him since the legion had marched from Divodurum, although he seemed no more good-natured. The prospect of battle had clearly fired his spirits. Like Castus himself, Macer wore the gold torque around his neck, the reward of valour. He was a fighting man, but until a few months before all he had had to look forward to was a fat discharge bonus and retirement with the honorary rank of Protector. Now things were different. But he surely knew, Castus thought, that this campaign would be his last.

'There's still those four shirkers on the baggage carts,' Macer said. 'Can I suggest we sent Attalus and Blaesus to rouse a bit of life into them before tomorrow?'

67

'No,' Castus said. 'Force them to march now and they'll cripple themselves and be good for nothing.'

Macer's ruddy face flushed even deeper as he inhaled. 'If you say so... dominus. Sets a bad example, though, in my opinion. One of them's a *Christian*, it turns out,' he said, drawing his thin lips back tight against his teeth. 'You know what I reckon to that sort. Just saying what I think. Dominus.'

Or not, Castus thought. He gave a nod of dismissal, and Macer saluted tightly and stamped out of the room. Eumolpius raised his eyebrow. 'Back to work,' Castus told him, then leaned back against the table, sighing deeply.

The last three months had been hard. Macer had his own following among a few of the centurions, men like Blaesus and Attalus, who admired his methods and sought to emulate them. Castus knew that these men would never fully trust him. The rigours of training at Divodurum, the route marches and weapons drills, all those days of hard physical exercise, had welded the legion together. But they could not heal the rifts among the officers of Castus's command. He only hoped that the experience of battle would pull them together, and not drive them further apart.

There was another knock at the chamber door, and this time Eumolpius was quick enough to answer it. Diogenes came in, bearing his armful of tablets and scrolls, nodding a casual greeting.

'Reports are all in, dominus,' he said, spreading his documents on the table. 'A despatch too, by the courier from Arelate. All centurions report their men fit and well. Aside from the four you already know about.'

'Good,' Castus said, shoving himself upright. 'What does the despatch say?'

Diogenes glanced up briefly. Castus signalled his permission, and the secretary broke the seal on the tablet.

'*Orders from the office of Aurelius Evander,* comes rei militaris, *Commander of the Field Army of southern Gaul,*' Diogenes read. '*All units proceeding to Cularo are to leave their heavy carts and wagons at Lugdunum or Arausio and transfer their loads to mules or other baggage animals.*'

'Other baggage animals?'

'That's what it says, dominus.' Diogenes shrugged. 'Can they mean oxen, do you think?'

'Not without carts, surely. What do you make of it?'

'Presumably,' Diogenes said, setting the tablet aside, 'they believe that wheeled transport would be unsuitable for the mountain crossing, and they don't want a huge wagon park assembling at Cularo.'

Castus grunted. 'Makes sense.' He was still perplexed about the *other baggage animals* though. The army always used mules and ox carts.

'Elephants, maybe?' said Eumolpius, glancing up from his cleaning. For such a young man, he had a very deep and mournful voice. 'Did Hannibal not cross the Alps with elephants?'

'To strike fear into the Romans, I should think,' Diogenes said in a dry tone. 'Not to carry his baggage.'

'I have always dearly wished to see an elephant,' Eumolpius said wistfully.

Castus frowned at the orderly, who dropped his head and got on with his work.

'There is, of course, the account by Livius of Hannibal's crossing,' Diogenes went on, rubbing his chin thoughtfully. 'Perhaps it would be instructive to read it again? I might find a copy at Lugdunum, perhaps...'

Castus slopped more wine into his cup. He had crossed

mountains before. He had marched vast distances, seen and fought barbarians on three frontiers. But he had never been to Italy, never seen that great city at the heart of the empire, or expected he ever would. At least now there was no doubt about the final destination of their march.

'How far is it?' he asked. 'To Rome?'

'About a thousand miles.' Diogenes was smiling to himself as he gathered up his reports. 'I've always wanted to see the place for myself,' he said. 'Rome is the greatest city on earth. The eternal city, mistress of nations... Over a thousand years since the foundation, and there are one million inhabitants, so they say...'

Castus whistled through his teeth. The huge numbers loomed in his mind. A thousand miles, a thousand years. One million people... and how many of them had Maxentius conscripted into his new legions?

'Funnily enough,' Diogenes said, pausing by the door, 'there's a man in Rogatianus's century who claims to come from Rome. His name is Valerius Felix.'

'The one they call "Slops"?'

'Yes. Although I don't know if there's any truth in it. He seems a rather low sort of Roman, if he really is one...'

Once Diogenes and Eumolpius had left him, Castus sat alone at the broad central table, cleaning and polishing his weapons, armour and equipment in the light of a single lamp. Certain tasks he made a habit of doing himself. There was a solitude in command that he had never experienced before, and it made him uneasy. Once again, he found himself thinking of Brinno, and of his old friend Valens who had died in Germania. Even of Sallustius, who had turned out to be a traitor. All those men he had called brothers; all of them dead now. He missed Sabina too, and thought often of his son.

Stifling a yawn, he set aside his kit and wearily unrolled the scroll that Diogenes had given him to read back in Divodurum. He had been working his way through it for months, but had made little progress, and squinting at the letters made his eyes smart. *Caesars*, it was called, by somebody called Marius Maximus, a collection of biographies of past emperors of Rome. Diogenes had called it 'essentially frivolous', whatever that meant, but Castus was finding it dense enough. Originally the secretary had presented him with a children's book about talking farm animals, and Castus had stared at him until he removed it and fetched this one instead. So far he had battled his way halfway through the life of the emperor Commodus. Bizarre stuff, it seemed, and it felt somehow perverted, somehow treasonous, to be reading it – but Castus suspected that like most books it was almost entirely invented anyway. And he was getting faster at reading, more confident of picking up meaning from the squiggle of ink.

Outside his chamber the night had grown dark, and the noise from the encampment behind the posting station had stilled. Now there was only the distant cry of a sentry, the last hushed voices from the gate to the road. Castus sat back in his chair and rubbed at his brow. He pushed aside the scroll, letting it curl itself closed. No, he thought, the army was the life he had always known, the one he knew best. He picked up his sword, the long *spatha* he had been given by the emperor when he had been promoted to tribune. Drawing it from the scabbard, he admired the sheen of the lamplight on the patterned steel. The blade had twin fullers, and the gilded hilt was formed in the shape of an eagle's head. Always before he had trusted to the standard weapons of the legion armoury; he had never owned such a magnificent weapon as this. The symbol of his command. Up near the hilt, set into

71

the metal, were two facing figures in gold, each the size of a thumbprint.

Mars and Victory, Castus thought as he wiped and oiled the blade. He would need the aid of them both soon enough.

'Other baggage animals!' Diogenes said, with a bemused smile.

The line of beasts came swaying up the road towards the encampment, the heavy pads of their feet beating the dust, their curving necks shaggy with encrusted dirt. Once of them let out a roaring belch as they passed.

'Camels?' Castus said. 'We're crossing the mountains with *camels*?'

'Our emperor intends to outdo the great Hannibal in taking exotic creatures across the Alps,' Vitalis said. 'Although, as you can see, they are exceptionally good at carrying heavy loads. Three or four times the burden of a mule.'

Aelius Vitalis was a pale-skinned man with a neat beard and the lean muscles of an athlete. He had been in the Protectores with Castus; now he was a *tribunus vacans*, a supernumerary officer attached to the army staff. Castus had been glad to meet him so soon after arriving in Cularo.

'I have never seen one before,' Diogenes said, watching with great interest. 'They look quite ungainly. Are they capable of climbing mountains?'

'These are,' Vitalis told him. 'They've been specially bred for it. They terrify horses too – we have to keep them away from the cavalry.'

They turned to watch the line of animals trekking on up the road. Castus was no stranger to camels – he had seen them in the east. These had clearly been brought across from

Mauretania and up through Spain; the men leading them had the dark skin, short tunics and thickly braided hair of the Mauri.

Castus and his men had arrived at Cularo after eighteen days on the road from Divodurum, to find the army encamped in a broad green pasture set in a bowl of the mountains. The peaks were vivid in the sun, and all across the fields beyond the town were tents and palisades, troops and horses, a vast array glittering in the clear light.

The camel-handlers were not the only strangers in the camp. The field army contained men of all nations, or so it seemed. There were barbarian contingents from Germania, and auxiliaries from Spain and all across Gaul. New troops had come from Britain, and all the legions and cavalry squadrons of the Rhine army had sent their detachments. Even Legion VI Gemina, who had fought against Constantine at Massilia, had sent a pair of cohorts from Spain to join the force, many of the soldiers dressed in antique-looking segmented armour. More than twenty thousand men were encamped across the plain between the surrounding walls of the mountains.

'Remember Hrocus, the Alamannic king?' Vitalis asked, the trimmed beard giving his smile a leering quality.

'The one who hung around the court in Treveris, getting drunk?'

'That's him. His son, Hrodomarus, is camped just over the river with eight thousand of his Bucinobantes.'

They walked together away from the road, to their tethered horses. Castus had acquired a strongly built grey mare, a reassuringly placid animal that went by the very unmilitary name of Dapple. Never before had he felt so secure in the saddle, but he still preferred to walk if he could. Mounting up, he sent Diogenes back to the Second Legion camp, then followed Vitalis down towards the river. They were due to attend a meeting of the army staff and officers.

'They won't tell us much. The emperor's still up on the Rhine, in theory at least,' Vitalis said as they rode. 'Although we all know he'll be arriving here any day. Just a ruse to fool the enemy spies, like leaving it so late in the year before starting the invasion. By now Maxentius'll have decided that Constantine's campaigning on the Rhine this summer, and he'll move his forces east to Aquileia, against the feint from Licinius. But that would be thanks to you, heh!'

Castus smiled tightly. He did not like to be reminded of that nightmarish winter journey through the Agri Decumates and across the Danube. Maybe it had aided the emperor's strategies, but as far as he could see the expedition had not been worth the sacrifice of so many good men.

They rode down to the river and waded across. Just upstream, a party of soldiers were bathing in the shallows, laughing and splashing the cold water into glittering fountains.

'I saw the emperor, up in Treveris at the beginning of the month,' Vitalis said. Castus caught the uneasy shift in his voice.

'What happened?' he asked.

'Nothing really,' Vitalis said quickly. 'It's just...' He dropped his voice. 'They say he spends too much time with the Christian priests these days. There are so many of them at court, they fill the corridors like flocks of geese... It was Floralia when I was there, and I heard a rumour that the emperor refused to sacrifice to the goddess during the festival. I can't be sure – I saw nothing unusual myself. But people are worried, brother.'

Castus nodded, frowning. He had been so willing to deny the rumours when he had first heard them from Sabina. Perhaps, he thought, there was some other explanation?

'We'll see soon enough,' he said. 'There'll have to be a sacrifice before we march, to purify the army and ask the blessing of the gods. That and the divination by the haruspices. The emperor couldn't refuse that...'

Briefly he thought of the stories he had heard, stories told in military camps around smoking cook fires, of generals cursed by the heavens, signs of divine displeasure ignored, defeat and death preordained. Anyone refusing the gods their due came to a bad end, it was clear.

'I saw your wife at Treveris too,' Vitalis said, 'during the festival.'

Castus noticed that the ominous tone had not left his friend's voice.

'She was with the emperor's wife and her retinue, I suppose?'

'No,' Vitalis said, peering away towards the distant mountains. 'Actually she was with a man – a friend, I assume. I didn't recognise him, but he looked like one of officials of the palace—'

'Describe this man,' Castus cut in. It was absurd, he knew, but his heart felt clenched in his chest. Vitalis gazed across at him warily.

'A little younger than us, well dressed,' he said. 'They got into his litter together after the games. All his slaves were wearing the same light blue livery, I noticed. A wealthy man, I'd say.'

Castus turned his head, fighting to keep the look of consternation from his face. His mouth was dry, and there was sweat on his palms as he gripped the reins. He knew that Sabina had her own life in Treveris, of course he knew that – but his friend's words hinted at more. They hinted at a suspicion that Vitalis dared not express.

* * *

Two more days passed, and the force assembled at Cularo grew larger still. The men trained at arms, swam in the river, quarrelled and gambled away their donative money, while clouds gathered to wreath the mountains and the temperature dropped. Then, at dawn on the third day, the word passed rapidly though the camp: the emperor had arrived.

Constantine had ridden in under cover of darkness, having travelled by horse relays from the Rhine. All that day the soldiers waited, as if they would get the signal to march at any moment, but the emperor was secreted with his senior officers and army commanders. Another night went by, the talk around the fires in the encampment alternately loud and bragging, then subdued by anxious thoughts. Finally, on a damp grey dawn with a feel of thunder in the air, the trumpets sounded the assembly.

Castus led his men out in their finest array, fully armoured in gleaming metal, best parade tunics and uncovered shields. Marching in regular step, the legion followed the road across the plain towards the assembly field with their standards proudly displayed before them. The eagle was carried by a massive young man called Antoninus, one of the tallest and broadest soldiers in the army. Walking beside him, Castus felt almost puny by comparison.

All across the plain he could see the dispersed units of the field army converging. It was a bold sight, enough to stir the blood. Twenty-five thousand of the best fighting men in the world, primed for a campaign that would rival anything from history; or so the soldiers had been telling each other. Troops of cavalry cantered along the road, passing the marching infantrymen. Castus identified the Equites Dalmatae and Mauri, the Scutarii and Sagittarii, plus other units he had not seen before. The barbarian contingents were roaring out their warrior ballads, waving their spears as they sang. Some of them already appeared to be drunk.

At the far side of the field, in front of the imperial encampment, a high tribunal had been raised, built of stacked turf in the traditional way. Behind it the mountains were a towering rampart of gloomy stone, their peaks lost in the low cloud. Castus marched his men into position, then left Macer in command as he strode forward to the base of the tribunal to stand with the other officers. Turning, he looked back at the formations of troops that seemed to fill the plain between the rivers and the mountains.

Trumpets rang out, incense swirled in the damp heavy air, and a ripple went through the massed ranks as the emperor ascended the tribunal. Castus snatched a glance back over his shoulder. The platform above him was ringed with standards, the golden eagles of the legions and the banners of the cavalry mingled with the dracos and flags of the other contingents. In front of the standards stood the chiefs of the civilian staff and the senior army officers. All the military men were dressed in burnished gold cuirasses and white cloaks, the civilians in heavily embroidered capes and tunics. But his eye was drawn to the figure standing alone at the front of the tribunal, dressed in a simple purple cloak. Constantine looked gaunt, his face raw and his eyes rimmed with red. He stood stiffly, glaring out over the ranks of his army. Then he raised his hand.

'Fellow soldiers!' the emperor cried, and his voice was hard and abrasive in the morning haze. 'Fellow soldiers... I see before me an invincible army! I see before me an army that has conquered the wild tribes of Germania and Britain, which has crushed rebellion here in Gaul, which has restored security to our frontiers and peace to our provinces!'

His shout echoed slightly as he paused, a faint boom from the mountains.

'I see men conscious of so many glories, so many victories, and yet eager for more. I tell you now, the hour has come for you to surpass yourselves!'

A stir went through the ranks, like the low sigh of wind between the high peaks.

'Brothers, Italy is oppressed by a cruel tyranny! Rome herself, the mistress of nations, mother of our empire and centre of our world, is held captive by a monster who calls himself *emperor*! This man, this weak and impious man, has tried to blacken the name of Rome with his crimes. He has tried to extinguish the light of the world!

'Just as his father rose up in treacherous revolt against me, so has this man – whose name is too shameful to mention – committed treason against us all with his villainous reign... My friends, I cannot allow these crimes to go unpunished! Today, by the divine will and the sacred command of heaven, we begin a just war, a war of righteous liberation!'

Cheers burst from the assembled troops, the drumming rattle of spears against shields, the rising chant of *Constantine, Constantine*... Castus felt his heart swell in his chest, but already the centurions were calling for silence. The emperor had thrown back his cape to reveal the armour beneath, and raised his hand once more.

'Let no man say,' he shouted, his voice sounding ragged now, the words cracking, 'that I wished for this fight, or sought it! Instead, as the heavens are my witness, I have tried for months and for years to reason with this man, to persuade him from his evil course. But one cannot reason with insanity. So, enough false promises! Enough worthless pacts! No longer can I regard with indifference the mutilation of Italy. The honour of Rome imposes this war upon us... Our frontiers are secured behind us, the Rhine strongly guarded by your fellow troops. The enemy has a great army, but his soldiers are raw conscripts, weak and demoralised. Let the mountains ahead of us be the gateway to victory! Follow me, and the thunderbolt of your valour shall strike the foe and scatter him, and the road to Rome shall be open to our glory!'

'*Constantine! Constantine! Constantine...!*'

This time the cries of acclamation were universal: the whole army setting up the chant, the clashing of weapons almost overwhelming. Through it, Castus could make out the chilling war cries of the barbarians, and even the roaring of the camels. Trumpets brayed, horns blared and cymbals clashed, and in a reeking cloud of incense the priests began to lead the sacrificial animals in the ritual procession around the perimeter of the assembly.

As the priests made their way along the far side of the field, Castus let his eye wander over the groups of officers and officials gathered at the base of the tribunal. He gave a brief nod of greeting to those he recognised, but there were a great many he did not. Then he saw one face in particular, and a flush of anger rose through him. The ugly bowl-cut hair and thin, colourless features would ordinarily be forgettable, but Castus knew them only too well; Julius Nigrinus, tribune of the Schola Notariorum, had crossed his path too many times. Clamping his jaw tight, Castus forced himself to look away. With any luck, he thought, the man had not noticed him, and would not be accompanying the army into Italy. As far as Castus was concerned, he was quite welcome to go and work at his sordid intrigues elsewhere.

The procession of priests had circled the assembly, and they were leading their animals up the ramp onto the tribunal, where an altar was already smoking in readiness for the sacrifice. There were three animals, as tradition decreed: a pig, a sheep and a bull. The bull plodded along placidly enough, tossing the flower garlands that decked its horns. The pig too appeared unmoved by the noise and activity, but the sheep was terrified and stubborn, and the priests had to haul it along by force. Already a bad omen, Castus thought, then hastily tried to reverse the observation. Even thinking about bad omens was a bad omen – these things were sent by the gods. He struggled to clear his mind.

Up on the tribunal the emperor stood ready, freshly dressed in his ceremonial robe. The priests gathered around him in the smoke from the altar, and one by one the animals were herded forward. From where he was standing Castus could not make out what was happening, but he heard the thud of the axe and smelled the rich iron scent of the fresh blood. As each victim died a grunting sigh came from the assembled troops.

Now the haruspices moved in, their white robes stirring around them. They would be removing the internal organs of the animals for inspection, Castus knew. He had seen it done many times before. Next they would pronounce the message they had read in the bloodied chunks of flesh. Castus felt no worry there – he had never known them say anything negative. It was impious, but he had always assumed they were paid not to. The only true omens came from the sky, Castus had always believed.

There was a lengthy pause. Smoke eddied across the raised tribunal, and Castus could hear the troops beginning to shift and mutter. Here and there a centurion hissed for silence.

'What's happening?' Castus asked from the side of his

mouth. He dared not turn and look, not now. Whispers were passing between the men gathered beside him.

'The omens are bad!' Vitalis said under his breath. His face looked bone white. 'The diviners say the army must not cross the mountains!'

This time Castus did look back, craning his neck to see the emperor stalking down the ramp from the tribunal, a streak of blood on his white robe. Behind him, the priests were still gathered in the smoke from the altar around the carcasses of the sacrificial animals, several of them bloodied to the elbows. The mutterings from the troops were gathering to a low roar of suppressed sound.

'Look at them!' Vitalis said in a harsh whisper, his mouth twisting. Castus followed his glance, and saw a group of civilians gathered at the far side of the field. They looked like priests, most them with grey beards.

'*Christians*,' Vitalis hissed. 'They must be behind this – them or agents of the enemy...'

But now there was motion up on the tribunal. Aurelius Evander, Commander of the Field Army of Gaul, strode to the front and raised his arms for silence. Down in the ranks the centurions were yelling, the tumult of voices dying away, every man eager to know what would happen now.

'Soldiers of Rome!' Evander cried in a high and carrying voice. 'In the name of our lord and emperor, Flavius Valerius Aurelius Constantinus, Unconquered Augustus, I declare these omens to be void! Officers – prepare your men. The army will march, and we shall be victorious! Our mandate is granted by the Divine Will, and the command of heaven!'

The blood from the sacrificial victims was flowing across the tribunal now, running down the ramp in a red torrent as Evander turned and stretched his arms out to the skies, to the faint morning glow from the west. But the sun was hidden by cloud, and just for a moment it appeared that the commander was raising his arms in supplication towards Italy, towards the enemy.

Thunder rolled among the peaks, and it started to rain.

CHAPTER V

The stone road scaled the side of the mountain, rising in steep inclines and dogleg bends around the rocky outcrops and the stands of high pine. On one side were sheer cliff walls and slopes of dry scree; on the other the ground fell away into a huge gulf of empty air.

Reining in his horse, Castus stood at the edge of the road while the troops climbed past him. Normally he was terrified of heights, but the view before him was so vast it appeared unreal. The air was clear and bright up here, and he felt almost as if he could reach out across the valley and touch the far peaks, run his fingers over the bristle of dark pines and the weathered grey crags of the mountains.

Looking down, he saw the column of soldiers, mules and horses climbing the road below him, a long brown snake coiling up out of the valley. There was a sharp wind in the mountains, but here in the lee of the cliff the sun was hot on his face. The men climbing up the track were sweating hard; Castus knew how they felt – the ache of legs and the burn of lungs. He had walked with them most of the way, but had ridden up to the head of the column to check the camp ground at Druantium, just below the summit of the pass.

This was the tenth day in the mountains, and the going was good. They had marched out of Cularo under heavy cloud and flurries of rain, following a river valley that threaded its way between massive walls of looming rock. They had abandoned the last of the wheeled transport there, and also the mass of camp followers – traders, gamblers, prostitutes and beggars – that trailed any army like weed on the hull of a seagoing ship. They were a fighting force now.

The troops had been sullen at first, demoralised after the poor omens given by the haruspices. But no god had swept them from the high passes, or barred their way with landslides or unseasonal snowdrifts, and a few days later they had crossed the first high pass and dropped down to the fortress of Brigantio, and the spirits of the army had been restored. There was nothing like solid regular marching, Castus thought, to sweat the darkness from a man's soul.

From the next bend below him he heard the gargling roar of a camel, and a moment later spotted four of the beasts climbing ponderously up the road towards him, each led by a tough, barefoot Moorish handler. The camels had quickly proved their worth; for all their bizarre appearance, they were hardy and apparently indomitable, plodding steadily up the stony slopes. Each soldier carried seventeen days' rations in a sack slung around his body, but their waterskins could never hold enough for them to drink. The camels carried heavy panniers of water, and the soldiers had soon come to rely on them.

Castus felt his horse tremble as the camels approached; the grey mare blew and tossed her mane, trying to back up further onto the precarious verge. Castus leaned forward and rubbed at her neck. 'Don't worry, Dapple,' he muttered. 'They're ugly, but they won't hurt you.'

The camels climbed past, loping steadily upwards with the panniers flapping and slopping at their sides. Behind them came a column of infantry, red-faced and squinting in the bright sun. Castus glanced down again, looking for the position of his own legion on the road below. Coming round the bend directly beneath him he saw a party of officials, half of them on foot, all of them perspiring freely. He smiled – good to see the civilians working up a sweat – but just as he was about to look away he picked out the figure riding a pony at the back of the group. He grimaced, cleared his throat and spat from the saddle. It seemed the notary Nigrinus was accompanying the army after all.

He tugged on the reins and set Dapple's head downhill, letting the horse pick her way down the narrow verge clear of the marching column.

'Are you aware, dominus,' Diogenes said, 'that the road we've been following was originally built by the demigod Hercules?'

'Eh?' Castus replied. His secretary was sitting cross-legged in the scant light of a cooking fire, bent over the tablet in his lap to shield it from the wind. 'Did you read that in a book?'

'Oh, no, it's a well-known story. Apparently he came this way after stealing the cattle of Geryon, down in Iberia.'

Castus raised his eyebrows, then finished the last of his salt pork and hardtack and set his dish down on the springy turf. They were sitting outside his tent, a more capacious structure than Castus had used as a centurion. All around them, the night was filled with the glimmer of fires.

The army was camped on the broad mountain pastures just below the summit of the pass; there was a cold hard wind blowing from the west, and the fires trailed sparks out into the darkness. High above them to the east, the peak of Mons Matrona showed black against the night sky. A few last traces of snow on the summit glowed like cold blue scars.

'You should sleep,' Castus told Diogenes. Most of the other men had already crawled into their tents, exhausted after the long day's climb. He gulped vinegar wine from his canteen, swilling the last scraps of food from his teeth. 'What are you doing anyway? Writing letters?'

Castus had made no more progress with Marius Maximus and his *Caesars*. Too many other things to do to think about books. But the sight of the secretary's rapid, able scratching was fascinating all the same. Behind him, the wind heaved at the tent and the guy-ropes groaned.

'Well,' Diogenes said, with a slight cough of embarrassment, 'I'm actually making a few notes for a treatise I intend to write.'

'Really?' Castus said, doubtful. Diogenes had an endless ability to perplex him.

'Yes. I'm considering a scheme for the ideal form of government... A plan for reordering the state, to maximise the happiness of the multitude and end all war.'

Castus snorted a laugh. 'I wouldn't say that kind of thing too loud around here!'

'Why?' Diogenes said, dropping into a whisper. He glanced up at the night sky, then gave a rueful smile. 'Might the gods overhear me?'

'No, *soldiers* might overhear you. If you find a way to end all war, we'll be out of a job!'

'Ah, yes,' the secretary muttered. 'I should remember the fate of Probus...'

Castus shook his head, bemused, then stood up from the fire. His thigh muscles still ached from his long ride that day, and he needed exercise before sleeping. Eumolpius climbed wearily to his feet, but Castus gestured for the orderly to stay where he was. 'Get some rest,' he told the young slave as he threw his cloak around him. 'I'm taking a walk...'

Pacing away from the fire, he made his way between the tent lines of his legion. Here and there he greeted one of the centurions, or one of the small parties still gathered around the fires, talking in hushed, weary voices. Once he had checked that all was well, he carried on walking. Out past the horse lines, the mule corral and the enclosure where the camels were tethered, he moved into the deeper night. A sentry called a challenge, and he gave the response.

It was cold, and away from the glow of the fires the sky appeared huge and very black, the stars brilliant and numerous between the scudding clouds. Castus tipped back his head and filled his lungs with the clean thin air. Truly he felt as if he were standing on the roof of the world.

Still he felt a clawing doubt in his mind. Once again he remembered Vitalis's comment about Sabina. Jealousy was an entirely new experience for Castus; it left him unsettled, pained, disgusted with himself. But the thought of his wife in Treveris, enjoying herself with her well-dressed friend, was a constant goad... It was the way she had been raised, he supposed, the manners of the aristocracy; Sabina had been a married woman when Castus had first met her, after all. No, there was nothing he could do about it, he knew that. Not yet.

Shrugging, he pulled his cloak tighter around his body and turned back towards the spark-trails flung by the scattered fires. As he neared his own tent lines, he saw a figure running from the darkness. His heard his own name called.

'What is it?'

'Tribune Castus?' the messenger said. 'Dominus, you're requested to report to the quarters of comes rei militaris Aurelius Evander...'

'Lead the way,' Castus told him.

Moving fast, they strode through the smoky gloom of the troop encampments to the imperial enclosure on the level ground at the head of the valley. In contrast to the nocturnal quiet of the rest of the camp, the enclosure was still busy, the tents brightly lit from within. The messenger led Castus through the lines of mounted guards and Protectores, past the great white pavilion that housed the emperor, then threw aside the flap of one of the large tents beyond.

Castus stepped into lamplit warmth and the smell of leather and straw matting. There was a folding table at the rear of the space, with secretaries and slaves working. Other men, orderlies and supernumerary officers, came and went. The wind shoved at the tent walls, making the leather boom and the lamp flames waver.

'Tribune,' said a voice from the shadows. 'Come in and sit down.' Aurelius Evander, Commander of the Field Army of Gaul, was seated on a stool beside the brazier, a cup in his hand. Castus saluted, then lowered himself onto the other stool. He had known Evander back in Treveris, although with the difference in rank he had never felt close to the man.

'Have some wine,' the commander said, taking a cup from the side table. 'Better than the stuff your soldiers drink, I'm sure. I had it lugged up the mountain by camel, if you can believe it!'

Castus thanked him, and sipped politely. He knew he had not been brought here to drink wine. Evander was in his late forties, with tightly curled iron-grey hair and a look of vain self-approval. He was brisk, confident, keen on his own importance, but not a bad commander from what Castus had heard.

'Tomorrow,' Evander said, with no further preamble, 'we commence our advance down the passes into Italy. The enemy will certainly have fortified posts along the way, with signal beacons to send warning of attackers. They may have blocked the narrower passages, or set ambushes. I intend, therefore, to send a small, lightly equipped force ahead of the main army to clear and secure the road.'

Castus nodded. Sensible – he would have done the same himself.

'Obviously it's vital that the enemy positions are taken quickly. If any of the signal fires are lit, our advantage of surprise will be lost. Tribune, I want your Second Britannica to form the core of the advance guard, with you in overall command.'

'Thank you, dominus,' Castus said. He had not been expecting this.

'You'll have *exploratores* going ahead of you, of course, to scout the route. Your men will march unarmoured and lightly armed, but they should carry picks and axes in case there are barricades or fortified places in the way. I saw them on the march up here. They looked strong – you have a formidable drillmaster, I believe.'

'Julius Macer, dominus. He... has quite a bit of vinegar in his blood.'

Evander nodded, pursing his lips. 'Be careful he doesn't tax them too hard. You drive goats with a stick, not men.'

Castus felt a prickle of annoyance up his spine, remembering that he had used that old phrase himself. 'Yes, dominus, I'll make sure of that.'

'At least it seems that the business of the omens at Cularo has been forgotten,' Evander said. 'We must put our trust in the protecting gods, eh?'

Castus nodded dutifully and put down the cup, ready to be dismissed. As he did so, he noticed the strange stillness that had come over everyone in the tent. Evander stood up, then dropped to one knee. The secretaries and orderlies were doing the same. Castus glanced around, lowering his eyes quickly. All he saw was a pair of fine red leather shoes with jewelled straps, then he was kneeling as well.

'On your feet,' the emperor said, addressing the gathering. 'We're not at court now.' He had slipped into the tent without announcement, dressed in a simple soldier's cloak and hood.

Evander stood up and saluted, and the rest followed his lead. Constantine acknowledged the salutes with a raised hand. Then he looked around, and his gaze came to rest on Castus.

'I know you, do I not?' he said. 'Aurelius Castus, I think.'

Castus managed a curt nod. The emperor smiled and slapped a hand onto his shoulder. 'Evander here tells me your men will be forging our path down the mountains tomorrow.' His grip tightened. 'Clear out their strongholds, tribune,' he said gravely. 'Don't let our enemies know we're coming.'

'I will, dominus.' Castus felt a swell of pride filling his body. Not for himself, but for his men. His legion.

'Well, then. Are you ready for war?'

'*Ready*,' Castus said, and could not help grinning.

The valley was in shadow, but the peaks of the mountains were still blazing in the evening sun. Crouching in the cover of the trees, Castus stared down at the patchy grey-green fields and the stony stream bed crossing the valley floor below him.

'You see it, dominus?' the exarch said. 'Up to the right, on the slope above the bridge.'

Castus nodded. 'I see it now.'

The road descended a steep wooded ravine onto the flatter ground beside the stream, crossing the low stone bridge before angling to the left to follow the valley. High rocky slopes on all sides. Set above the angle of the road was a small fortification, little more than a high stone curtain wall enclosing some huts. As Castus watched, a heavy door in the wall swung open and a man stepped out. Military boots and leggings, a round fur cap: a soldier, but he wore no armour and gave no impression of vigilance. With a spear over his shoulder he strolled down to the stream and vanished behind some scrubby bushes.

'Now look up further, on top of the rocky outcrop there, above the trees.'

The exarch and his small unit of exploratores had scouted this position already, but they had kept carefully out of sight of the men at the guard-post. Castus knew that they had captured a few stray watchmen further up the valley – it was best not ask what had happened to them – but this was the first inhabited place the exarch and his men had encountered since descending the pass that morning.

Castus lifted his gaze from the fortification, up the thickly wooded slope to the crest of the outcrop overlooking the road. This time he saw it at once: a stone and timber watchtower, jutting up above the treetops. He could even make out the shape of the sentry standing on the platform at the top. No doubt they had a well-laid signal beacon up there too, ready to be fired.

'How many men?' Castus asked.

'My scouts reckon six up in the watchtower, dominus. Probably twice as many in the *burgus* down below.'

Castus grunted. He had brought two centuries of his legionaries down the ravine with him, and there were as many again of the Brisigavi, plus a score of exploratores. This little garrison of *burgarii* stood no chance against them, but all the enemy needed to do was fire their signal beacon and the fight was lost. Shoving his way backwards over the pelt of pine needles, Castus crawled between the trees and rejoined his men.

'There's no way to slip around behind them in any force,' he said. 'So we have to take them head on. First we need to deal with that signal tower and make sure they can't send a message down the valley. Then we have to seal the road beyond their post, so their runners can't get through. Once that's done, we can move.'

Nods from his men, quiet and confident. Rogatianus was leading one of the centuries, with Attalus, one of Macer's protégés, in charge of the other.

'Attalus,' Castus said, 'take half your men and work along the far side of the valley. Keep inside the tree cover and make sure you're not seen. When you're past the burgus, drop down and cross the river. Hold a position there and stop anyone trying to escape that way. Got it?'

The centurion casually shrugged one shoulder. He was a strongly built man with short-cropped black stubble dug into his hollow cheeks. Castus did not like him, but he led his men effectively.

'Get moving, then.'

Attalus and his group of men filed away down the slope towards the road. A short distance away, a group of Germanic auxilia, Alamannic warriors of the Brisigavi, squatted in the bushes. They reminded Castus of the guides that had led his party through the wilderness that last winter, and then deserted them. He hissed at their leader, and he raised his spear in greeting.

'I need you to take your warriors up through the trees above the burgus,' Castus said when the leader joined him. 'Don't break cover. You need to surround the signal tower, then close in and take it without causing any disturbance. Make sure nobody up there warns the others below. When the tower's yours, wave a branch from the rampart.'

'I understand, my friend,' the Alamannic leader said, and showed his crooked teeth in a wide grin. 'It's like you say: *We do what is told, and for the commands we are ready.*'

Castus straightened up, watching as the hooded warriors slipped silently across the hillside between the pines.

'Now we wait,' he said quietly, sinking down to squat on his haunches with his back against a tree. Rogatianus sent two of his men up the slope as lookouts, and the remaining soldiers wrapped their cloaks around their shoulders and sat clasping their spears.

Time passed slowly, the pines creaking and groaning as the wind gusting down the ravine caught their upper branches. Castus tried to keep his body relaxed, his mind idle, as he watched the slopes on both sides of the valley for the flash of movement. Now and again he saw one of Attalus's men clambering through the trees in the distance, but they would be invisible to the enemy down in their blockhouse. Of the Brisigavi he saw nothing. Two birds wheeled and spun in the air above the valley. Hawks, Castus guessed. He watched them for a moment, then looked back at the trees.

'Dominus,' Rogatianus said. The African centurion's face looked more than usually taut. 'It's been nearly an hour. Attalus and his men must be in position by now – can we wait any longer?'

'You're right,' Castus said, pulling himself to his feet. 'Form the men up on the road. Marching column, but have them keep their shields and weapons in their hands. At my signal, we change to battle formation. Silence, though...'

Rogatianus saluted and gave the word. With no undue noise or confusion the men scrambled down the slope to the road and into a tight column. Castus took his place at the front, and gave the signal to advance. The area of open ground before the bridge was too wide to cover at a run – the men would be exhausted by the time they reached the enemy. Their only hope, Castus thought, was to march over to the bridge, giving no signs of hostile intent. With luck, the men on watch in the burgus would not realise they were under attack until it was too late for them to do anything but defend their position.

Boots crunching on the gritty stone of the road, the legionaries marched down the incline and out into the open ground between the trees and the river. Castus had a sudden recollection of the meeting with the Burgundii, back in the Agri Decumates the previous winter. A troubling thought, and he tried to wipe it from his mind.

'Keep watching that tower,' he said over his shoulder to Rogatianus. There was still no sign of the Brisigavi up there. *What were they doing?*

Up ahead he could see two men running across the bridge and up to the door of the stone-walled burgus. A moment later the door opened and a file of men emerged, spilling across the road, some of them pulling on helmets. From behind him Castus heard Rogatianus calling to his men to keep steady, close ranks. He flicked a glance up the slope; from down here in the valley the watchtower was clearly visible against the sky. Nothing was waving from the top of it.

The noise of the marching men seemed unnaturally loud, the regular crunch of boot-studs on stone filling the valley. Castus was on the bridge now, his men close behind him. He could see the line of men on the road ahead beginning to edge closer together, raising their shields. A couple shuffled back towards the door of their fortification. One of them, the leader, stepped forward and yelled out a challenge. No chance of continuing the deception now.

'In the name of the emperor Constantine Augustus,' Castus shouted back in his parade-ground voice, 'I demand that you lay down your arms and surrender!' He was still marching as he shouted.

'Balls!' somebody called back. Another of the men threw a spear, but his aim was poor.

'Dominus! The tower – I can see a man waving...'

'That's it – *after me*!'

Castus dropped into a run, getting his shield up and drawing his sword from behind it. The burgarii were retreating back to their fortification now, but Castus could hear the thunder of his own men right behind him. A javelin arced over his head, then two more; the first missed, but two of the enemy were cropped down before they could reach cover. By now the legionaries were up off the bridge and onto the stretch of cobbles below the wall of the burgus; Castus felt his hobnails grate and slip on the worn stone, and staggered as he ran. An arrow zipped past his face, and he heard a cry of pain from behind him. When he looked up, he saw archers on the wall above.

'Shields up!' he yelled, his throat hoarse. More arrows snicked off the stones of the road, or thudded into the raised shield boards.

Then they were beneath the cover of the wall, the charging men slamming together into a tight testudo formation, raising shields to protect them from the defenders' missiles. Rogatianus was calling for axes and picks: the door was closed and heavily barred from inside.

Castus took three steps back from the wall. His heart was punching in his chest, his lungs heaving. The men with the tools were gathered at the door now, hacking at the solid oak planks with their axes.

'You!' he cried, seizing one of the soldiers by the arm. He was a young man named Salvianus, one of the Christians that Macer disliked so much. 'Hold your shield level against the wall...'

For a moment the soldier appeared baffled, his mouth opening and closing. He was terrified, Castus realised. Modestus stepped up behind him and clouted the back of his helmet. 'You heard the tribune! Shield against the wall!'

The archers inside the burgus were gathered to one side, shooting down at the party hacking at the door. Here the crest of the wall was clear. The young soldier was still paralysed, but two other men shoved him aside and crouched against the stones with their shields held level above them. Castus ran, crying out for Modestus to follow him; a moment of stark fear as he realised the danger of his action, then he leaped, got one foot on a shield and threw himself upwards at the wall's crest.

He had expected some kind of parapet or platform on the far side, but as he rolled across the crest of the wall he saw a sloping roof of worn tiles beneath him. No time to think: he swung his legs over and crashed down onto the tiles, sword in hand. The roof creaked beneath him, but the beams held and he was sliding downwards, kicking tiles loose, and then dropping from the eaves into the confined courtyard in a cascade of shattered clay.

Armed men all around him. Bodies turning in surprise from the barred door. Already he could hear others coming across the wall after him, Modestus's whooping yell. Castus scrambled to his feet, screaming wordless rage, and rammed the blade of his sword at the nearest man's face.

The defenders fell away from him, panicked. Castus held his ground, his features locked in fury behind the nasal bar of his helmet; only one man stepped forward, the leader, punching at him with a spear. Castus slashed the weapon aside, took one long stride inside the man's reach, and killed him with a raking backhand slash across his neck.

Modestus was with him now, two more soldiers dropping down from the roof and more still up on the wall crest.

Castus drew himself up straight, snarling, then flicked the spatter of blood from his sword. But the fight had gone out of the remaining defenders; they were throwing down their weapons, backing away into the far corner of the yard.

With the door unbarred the troops outside quickly occupied the burgus, securing the prisoners. Castus shoved his way through them. Up in the trees above the road he could see the Brisigavi warriors descending the slope from the watchtower. One of them was holding a pair of severed heads in his fist, gripping them by their hair.

'Good hunting!' their leader called. 'Killing Romans, heh!'

Before Castus could react, he heard the shouts and saw men pointing from the doorway. In the distance was a single fugitive, sprinting away along the road down the valley. He must have slipped over the wall somehow, Castus realised.

'Don't worry about him,' he said. 'Attalus's men will catch him.'

'Tribune!' Attalus called out.

Castus jerked his head around. The black-stubbled centurion was climbing up the slope out of the stream bed; his men forded the water behind him. For a moment Castus could only look from the centurion to the fugitive and back... then his teeth seized and his neck swelled.

'You in trouble here?' Attalus said.

'No, you are,' Castus said, holding back his rage. He flung out his arm, pointing at the running man. 'I ordered you to seal the road!'

Attalus braced himself against his knee, gulping breath. His expression flickered between shame and defiant denial. He could only shake his head and look away.

Castus stared at the dwindling figure of the runner, feeling the plummeting sensation of failure. He noticed Rogatianus gesturing to one of his men.

'Slops,' Rogatianus said.

The soldier who stepped forward was small and dark, with deep-set eyes and a long jaw. His arms were sinewy, and his hands were enormous. With no appearance of haste he scanned the road at his feet, then snatched up a single round pebble. He took a leather sling from his belt, loaded it with the pebble, then raised his head and peered at the distant running figure.

The soldier was named Valerius Felix, Castus remembered. The one who claimed to come from Rome. But the man seemed not to be doing anything, just staring along the road, his head raised. Around him was silence, everyone waiting.

Felix drew a long breath, leaned back, and whipped the sling up in an arc. Two sharp whirls, then he flung out his arm and snapped the stone free. The tiny missile sped upwards, dwindling into the sky until it was lost from view.

Castus was conscious that he was holding his breath. Everybody else seemed to be doing the same. Only Felix appeared indifferent. Castus looked down and saw the figure of the man still running. Then the fugitive seemed to stagger slightly, pitching forward. His legs folded beneath him and he dropped motionless onto the road.

A hoarse cheer rose from the gathered soldiers. Felix shrugged, spat, then walked back to join his comrades.

Stooping, Castus wiped his sword on the tunic of a fallen man, then slid it back into his scabbard. Over by the wall, he saw the young recruit, Salvianus, doubled over and vomiting.

One of the defenders lay dying nearby, a javelin stuck through his gut.

Castus blinked, and saw, as if for the first time, the corpses sprawled on the cobbles and around the scarred door of the burgus. He drew a deep breath and felt it catch in his throat. Only then did he notice that his hands were shaking.

CHAPTER VI

Seen from above, the town of Segusio was shaped like a clenched fist, with the knuckles facing the road that dropped down from the mountain passes.

The rear walls stood on the bluffs above the rushing river that Constantine's army had been following down the ravine for the last three days. To the south-west, at the angle of the walls, there was a citadel of solid masonry built onto bedrock; the road from the ravine dropped down a last steep incline to pass directly beneath its buttresses, before angling to the left under a weathered triumphal arch and descending to the western gate. All around, the mountains climbed from the narrow valley into the bright morning sun.

Castus surveyed the town from his vantage point on the craggy heights that rose steeply to the west. The walls were massive, taller than any he had known, with round towers every hundred paces. There were two gates that he could see, and probably another near the river to the east. Each one was a huge archway flanked by drum towers, fortified with triple-storey galleries above. The rows of arched windows suggested a serious array of defensive artillery in each gatehouse.

Squinting into the low sun, Castus ran his gaze along the tops of the walls, estimating the number of the defenders.

'That's one tough walnut,' Vitalis said.

Castus sucked his cheek and said nothing.

'You don't think so?'

On the western flank, where the walls ran down from the citadel to the river, there were fewer towers. There looked to be a jumble of ruins outside the walls down there, on the narrow strip of level ground before the crags. Castus knew that the town had been fortified back in Diocletian's day; he guessed that the builders had demolished any houses that remained outside the perimeter. There was some kind of necropolis down there too, and the remains of a temple, although it was hard to make out.

'It looks strong,' Castus said quietly. 'I don't think they've got too many men on those big walls, though.'

They were standing at the margin of a gathering of officers. Evander and the other senior commanders were peering at the fortifications, discussing the approaches in hushed and confidential tones. Beyond them, the imperial draco standard streamed its purple and gold tail away to the east in the wind from the mountains. The emperor himself stood alone at the summit of the crag, hands clasped behind his back. He appeared dangerously exposed, as if deliberately presenting himself to the defenders of the town below. But at that elevation he was well out of range of bow or ballista, and to the sentries on the walls he would appear only a tiny figure standing in the sunlight.

'Distinguished men!' Evander said, turning to Castus and the other tribunes. 'Below us you see Segusio,' the commander went on, gesturing. 'Strong walls, and a strategic position. We have no siege engines, no artillery at all, and blockading the place would give the enemy time to bring more troops from the east of Italy to oppose us on the plains. They have already refused our demand to surrender.'

He paused for a moment, scanning their faces. 'Our intention is to assault directly from the east, where the walls are lowest. The emperor, however,' Evander said, glancing with a respectful nod towards the figure standing a few paces away at the cliff edge, 'would hear the views of all his officers.'

Another pause, weightier this time. Castus had the impression that Evander's own views on the matter were quite clear. Constantine continued to gaze down at the walls.

'Dominus,' said Florius Baudio, stepping forward and saluting. 'The eastern walls look weaker, but there's a deep concealed ditch in front of them; I sent two men to scout around the perimeter earlier today.'

Baudio was one of Protectores assigned to the army staff, an older man with a very square head who had served ten years as centurion of Legion II Italica Divitensium. He had a grown son serving as optio in the same legion. Castus nodded to himself; Baudio knew his business.

'We could storm the east gate,' one of the other tribunes said. 'Use a ram, or incendiaries. It's not as heavily fortified as the others, by the look of it.'

Some of the other officers were grunting their agreement. Castus sucked his teeth and glanced away.

'Aurelius Castus,' Evander said. 'You don't agree?'

Castus took a moment to reply. He cleared his throat.

'Dominus, if we attack through the eastern defences we'll have to fight our way uphill through the whole town, with the citadel in front of us.'

'Good point,' Vitalis mumbled.

'And can you suggest an alternative course?'

'Dominus,' Castus said, and drew a long breath. 'You could send a party of men with ladders down into those ruins below the western wall, under cover of darkness. Then make a feint attack against the citadel or the gate, and send in the ladder parties while the defenders are distracted. They get over the wall, and take the gate and the citadel from the rear.'

Evander stared at Castus, narrow-eyed. Then he looked back at the town. 'We'd need some very high ladders,' he said quietly, as if to himself. 'Could it be done?'

Castus remained silent.

'It *will* be done,' another voice said.

Everyone turned, then dropped their gazes in deference. The emperor had paced back from the edge of the cliff. For a moment he stood and regarded the gathering of officers, his heavy-boned face without expression. Then he nodded once, decisively, and walked away. The cordon of his guards parted before him.

'Can't say I've ever seen a scaling ladder this big,' Macer said. Stripped to the waist in the hot sun, he was overseeing the construction work in the sloping field outside the legion encampment. His men had already felled several tall pines; now they were working with adze and saw to cut and shape the timber into lengths.

'We're having to make them in sections,' Macer went on. 'We'll need to carry them down and assemble them when we're near the walls.'

'Will they hold?' Castus asked him.

The drillmaster narrowed his mouth to a slot. 'Should do,' he said.

Castus nodded. The grass was muddied with bootprints and scattered with bright yellow wood shavings. Smells of fresh-cut pine filled the early-evening air, and the noise of the adzes echoed off the mountain slopes. The men looked stronger and fitter than ever before after their hike over the mountains, and they were throwing themselves into the work with fierce energy.

Motioning to the drillmaster, Castus led him over to a stack of felled logs, out of hearing of the men labouring on the ladders.

'You got something you want to say to me, tribune?' Macer asked. He stood with fists on hips, his tanned torso corded with muscle, grey hair bristling on his chest. Already he looked affronted, defiant. He knew what Castus was about to say.

'Salvianus. The recruit in Attalus's century.'

'What about him?' Macer's eyes were coldly hostile.

'You've ordered him to join one of the assault parties on the ladders tomorrow morning. Why?'

Macer screwed his mouth shut, his neck muscles tensing. 'You know as well as I do, tribune,' he said, after a moment. 'I heard what happened during that skirmish up the valley. He froze; he didn't follow orders. He was a coward. Men like that have to prove themselves.'

'You think he will?' Castus was speaking quietly, but the two men had edged closer. Macer's face was dark red with contained fury.

'I think he needs to be a *soldier*,' the drillmaster said, with savage emphasis. 'You know how it is, dominus. You stand in the line and you support your brothers, and if you fill your boots with piss and your breeches with shit, you know you've done your duty. That's the only way to break through fear. Otherwise it spreads, and your whole legion's rotted through with it.' He was spitting flecks of saliva as he spoke.

Castus leaned forward, his teeth clenched tight. 'Pull him back out of the assault party,' he said slowly. 'If he freezes halfway up a ladder, or decides he wants to run, then he's putting all the other men at risk. I can't allow that. You'll get another chance to weigh his balls for him, don't you worry.'

The two men stood glaring at each other. A fly buzzed between them, and Castus swatted it away. Then Macer inhaled, nostrils flaring, and stepped back.

'Call the centurions together,' Castus told him.

The drillmaster strode away, and Castus walked to the edge of the field and turned to stare down at the city. He heard the trumpet behind him, summoning the centurions. His shoulder and neck muscles felt tight and hard as boiled leather, and he breathed deeply and tried to relax.

In the last of the sun the towers of Segusio were glowing a pale golden grey. Castus looked at the walls, the height to the crenellated summit. All his life he had been afraid of heights; it was the only fear he could never truly conquer. He thought now of climbing those ladders, the effort of forcing himself upwards, the drop below him getting greater and greater...

Castus knew all about fear. He had seen it working in men all his life, and he knew how destructive it could be. The old Greeks, he had heard, believed that dread and panic were the sons of Mars, god of the battlefield. Phobus was one of the brothers' names, Castus remembered. But he knew that Macer was right: once fear gripped a man it could pass in the breath, in the motion of the air. It was contagious, and it broke soldiers, cancelled their will and their spirit and turned them into helpless slaves.

He raised his hand and touched the gold torque he wore at his neck. It was awarded for courage, for valour. The opposite of fear, supposedly. But, no, Castus thought: courage was what lay beyond fear. Why did some men possess it – Macer, Brinno, himself – and others did not? Salvianus was a Christian, he remembered. But Castus did not think that his religion made a difference. Their priests were with the emperor; the god of the Christians must surely approve of this campaign. Perhaps, he thought, some men were just not made for war.

Castus flexed his shoulders again, and grunted as the knot of muscle at the top of his spine loosened a little. Turning, he marched back up the field to the camp gate, where Macer and the centurions were waiting for him. All saluted as he approached.

Briefly, he told them what he needed them to do. It would not be easy: the advance around the walls in darkness, passing close to the citadel, then assembling the ladders and getting them ready. And that was before they started the actual assault.

'At first light,' he told them, loud enough for all to hear, 'half the army will make a feint towards the eastern walls. That should draw some of the defenders down there. At sunrise, men of the Twenty-Second and First Flavia Legions will begin an attack on the western gate, using incendiaries. Once the fires are started, the Second Britannica go in with the ladders.'

He paused, and checked each man, making sure they were following him.

'We'll be taking the right half of the wall,' he said, 'nearest the gate. We'll have archers with us to pick the defenders off the walls, and the Bucinobantes to support us once we get a toehold. The Divitenses will be attacking the wall to our left.'

Smiles went round the group, and a few good-natured groans. Legion II Italica Divitensium was another of the newer formations, and shared a numeral with Castus's command. There was a strong rivalry between them.

'We begin the assault on my order,' Castus went on. 'Six ladders: Blaesus, Rogatianus and Attalus go in first and the other three follow. Pick your leading men carefully.'

Attalus was standing at the back of the group with his arms folded across his chest. Castus had already reprimanded him for his failure during the skirmish in the valley. He could have taken the man's rank from him, but this was not the time for it. Macer had stood up for him: Attalus was a good soldier, and a good leader, the drillmaster had said; his men trusted him. Castus caught the implication. *And they don't trust you.*

After the centurions had been dismissed, Macer remained behind.

'Is it true,' he asked in a low voice, 'that you suggested this plan to the emperor yourself?'

Castus frowned and shook his head. 'You don't think the men can do it?' he asked.

'Oh, yes. They'll do it,' Macer told him. 'But for many of them, it'll be the last thing they ever do.' He sucked air through his teeth, and said, almost beneath his breath, 'A good soldier knows when to keep his mouth shut...'

The night was windy, the sky full of scudding clouds. The wind roared down from the mountain ravines, tugging at the bodies of the soldiers as they scrambled in the darkness with their ladder poles, shields and equipment. But the noise of the wind covered the sound of their movements, and as they crept up over the ridge beneath the citadel there were no cries of warning, no flight of wind-whipped arrows from the ramparts above them.

Crouched in the dry scrub behind a lump of broken brick wall, Castus sensed the darkness around him beginning to fade. There was no moon, but he could make out the grey shapes of the cloaked men beside him in the deeper grey of the bushes and ruined walls. Behind him, the craggy mass of rocks and trees that rose to the west of the town was taking form out of the night. Castus wore a infantryman's hauberk of bronze scale; it was heavier than his gilded cuirass, and stank badly of old sweat soaked into the lining, but did not constrict his chest so much. He took off his helmet and placed it on the wall, listening carefully.

'I believe,' whispered Diogenes from the shadows beside him, 'that the white object over there is the *heroon* of Cottius.'

'The what?'

'The *heroon*. A kind of monument, a cenotaph. Cottius was king of these mountains, and Segusio was his capital. That old arch there below the citadel wall was built by the deified Augustus in his honour. Three hundred years ago, or maybe more...'

Castus sniffed, and rubbed his knee. He had grazed it on a chunk of masonry on the way here. Probably a bit of some other *heroon*, he thought.

'I found a book in Lugdunum, in fact,' Diogenes said. 'Pacatius's *Guide to the Cottian Alps*...'

'Quiet!' Castus hissed, then raised his head above the mossy crest of the broken wall. He could hear it clearly now: the shouts of men, away to the east. The feint attack on the far side of the town had begun. Trumpets echoed off the mountains, startling flocks of birds into flight along the river valley.

Still they waited. When Castus looked up he saw the eastern sky lit by the colours of dawn, the battlements showing stark black against it. From this angle, from below, the wall looked all the more impressive. Once again Castus wondered whether the ladders would be long enough to reach the top. At Massilia, he remembered, the attackers had badly underestimated the height of the walls... He had been inside the city then, watching the failed assault, but the memory of that scene was vivid in his mind now: the ladders smashed by rocks from above, the men lying broken and twisted in the ditch below the wall.

His body was running with cold sweat, and he suppressed a shudder. *Phobus*, he thought. Panic dread, killer of courage.

The thought came to him that if he died today his son would never know him. His mouth tasted sour and his breath was short. He drew his sword part way from the scabbard and slammed it back again.

Beneath the wall the ground was still in predawn shadow. Castus could see nobody moving up on the ramparts. Just as well, he thought – very soon any sentries up there would have a clear view of the men gathering in the ruins below them. Dawn sun was illuminating the great bluffs that rose directly to the west; perhaps they had a little more time yet. When he glanced to his left Castus saw the men in the dry scrub around the ruins assembling the ladders, wedging the lengths of timber together, tapping in the rungs and lashing them tightly.

'Tribune!' somebody called in a harsh whisper, and Castus turned to his right. For a moment it looked like a section of the hillside had detached itself and was rolling down the slope towards the gatehouse; he blinked, craned his neck, and saw the mass of men running, carrying huge bundles of sticks and dry brushwood over their heads. The first cries came from the gatehouse now, but there were archers moving towards the gates too, and a volley of arrows rattled off the stones around the high windows.

Crouching, Castus raised his hand and made a fanning gesture, trying to keep his men silent, keep them concealed while they still had time. He could see defenders moving along the top of the wall, helmeted heads appearing between the crenellations, but they were running along the parapets towards the gate.

Shouts from the gatehouse: a block of soldiers was advancing down the road, shields locked and held above them in one huge testudo formation. The noise of their boots stamping on the cobbles was amplified by the covering of shields; it sounds like a vast rattling torrent coming down the hill. As the horns wailed from the ranks of Constantine's army, a sharp snap came from the gatehouse, then another; the formation buckled as the twin ballista bolts slammed into it. But the advancing men held, doubling their pace. Inside their fortress of shields they carried bales of pitch-soaked straw, and more of the heavy combustible fascines.

Arrows spat down from the gate towers, but the archers on the ground were far greater in number and returned six shots to every one from the defenders. The tramping block of soldiers divided as it reached the gates, the fascines passed forward hand to hand and then flung to join the head-high mass heaped against the gates. Then the shields rose again and rattled back into formation, the testudo retreating up the slope. A stone from a catapult crashed into it, raising screams from inside.

Castus watched it all, trying to breathe slowly, trying to calm his racing pulse. Any moment now, he thought. Any moment... He heard somebody moving behind him: Eumolpius was there, handing him a leather flask of watered wine. Castus drank deeply, then passed the flask to Diogenes. He pulled his helmet on and tied the laces securely beneath his chin.

Burning torches appeared in the morning grey, the flames rushing in the hands of running men. Two more men carried a fire-pot between them, grey smoke streaming in the wind. The men in the towers were yelling now, archers leaning from the embrasures to try and pick off the runners before they could ignite the heaped tinder against the gate.

One man fell, then another. But the torches were still coming, arcing through the greyness as the men flung them. The fire-pot went swinging after them, smashing against the stone of the gate arch and spewing burning embers onto the packed dry brushwood of the fascines.

Grey smoke boiled up from the arch, and a moment later Castus saw the first bright tongues of fire licking against the scarred old wood of the gate itself. Within three heartbeats the whole heaped mass of wood, pitch and straw had ignited and fire was seething from the archway.

'Go!' he said, and slapped the shoulder of the man in front of him. The messenger jogged forward, his back bent, and Castus heard him pass the word to the first of the ladder parties. All along the strip of ground to his left he saw men rise and begin to advance, hefting the heavy ladders between them. Archers were moving up too, arrows nocked, ready to shoot at any figures appearing along the rampart. Beyond them, the men of the Divitenses were already approaching the wall, racing their rivals of the Britannica.

Fanned by the wind from the mountains, the fire at the gate was burning more fiercely, the smoke rising to shroud the arcades above the arch. Trails of grey and black enveloped the towers, darkening the dawn sky. Castus felt the coiled tension in his body; he wanted to run forward, to charge onto the open ground beneath the walls where, even now, his men were wrestling their ladders upwards. But he needed to stay back, watch what was happening and order in the reserves when they were needed.

Beside him an archer stood up, took aim, and released. When he looked up, Castus saw the shapes of men along the parapets. *Where did they come from?*

The wind sent the smoke from the burning gate eddying along the line of the wall, and snatched streams of sparks from the fire. Up the slope, the soldiers of the other legions had formed into a shield wall, archers and slingers positioned just behind them. But the artillery in the gate towers made no response, the men up there too busy trying to douse the flames beneath them. Water splashed down from the embrasures, but it turned to steam almost immediately.

Now the first of the ladders was swinging upwards against the wall. Men below heaved on long poles, guiding the ladder head up against the masonry; Castus heard the crack as it fell into position. He exhaled: the length was right. Already the knot of men on the ground were scrambling onto the rungs, hauling themselves upwards with bent heads, shields strapped to their backs. It was all about speed now: they needed to reach the crest of the wall before the defenders could muster to drive them back. The more men on the ladder, the heavier it became and the harder it was to dislodge.

Two ladders were up, then three. Yellow and red shields rose in streams, like bright-coloured beetles scaling the shadowed cliff of the wall. To the left, the men of the Divitenses were already climbing towards the bright glow of the parapet. More archers were loosing shots, running forward from cover to aim up at the crenellations.

A gasping cry, and Castus shifted his gaze just in time to see a heavy stone plummet down from the top of the wall. It hit one of the ladders, caught a climbing man of Blaesus's century and knocked him down, but his comrades kept on pushing upwards. The next three assault parties were already running forwards.

Castus was on his feet now – no point in remaining concealed – the blood pumping hot and fierce in his head as he yelled to his centurions. Blaesus's men were almost at the top of the wall when there was a loud crack, then a scream: the damaged ladder snapped beneath the weight of their armoured bodies, and the climbers fell with a sickening crash of breaking timber.

Further along the wall, another ladder went down. Now Castus could see the ballistae mounted in the wall towers, angled down to shoot along the line of the wall. A heavy bolt spat from the tower nearest to him, narrowly missing Rogatianus and his men. There were too many defenders, suddenly. *They knew we were coming...*

The fire in the gate had spread, driven upwards by the wind, and now the gatehouse itself was burning, flames curling from the embrasures and dancing away on the breeze over the town. Castus could see four of his ladders in place against the wall, but as he watched, one of them toppled sideways, pushed by the men on the parapet above. The climbers leaped clear as the ladder fell, but the screams of injured men lying in the murky shadow at the base of the wall were getting louder.

'Forward, *everyone forward*,' Castus shouted. They needed numbers now, or the assault would be driven back. Rogatianus was almost at the top of his ladder, a column of men packing the rungs below him, but the defenders above were pelting spears and stones down, and Rogatianus could only cling on with his shield held over his head. The billowing smoke from the gatehouse was fogging the air, and everything stank of burning.

Castus was on his feet and running forward into the gulf of blue shadow at the base of the wall. Over to his left he could see the men of the Divitenses lit up by the sun as they battled their way across the ramparts. Unless Castus's men could also gain a foothold on the wall, their comrades from the other legion would be cut off. A thrown javelin darted towards him, and Castus dodged it; a spent arrow rebounded off the wall and flickered against his helmet. As he ran, he swung his shield around to carry it on his back.

'*Britannica!*' he roared. '*Britannica – with me!*'

He leaped over a fallen body, and then he was in among the confused mass of men at the base of the wall. A figure reeled towards him – it was Macer. The drillmaster was bleeding from a head wound, one eye masked with blood.

'Tribune! There are too many of the bastards up there – we've got to pull back!'

'No!' Castus yelled. He grabbed Macer by the arm and shoved him towards the wall. He would not turn back now; he would not admit defeat.

Snatching up a fallen ladder he started wrestling it back upright; others sprang to help him, lifting the heavy timbers between them and swinging the ladder up and across to fall, jarring, against the wall. Castus felt the rage powering him. He knew he was endangering the lives of his men, risking everything to prove himself as their leader, but there was no time for thought now. Sweat greased his palms as he grabbed the rungs and began to haul himself up. The wall towered black above him, threaded with smoke, and he felt the weight of his body pressing down on every rung. The ladder felt so flimsy, and there were other men behind him. Violent tremors ran through the wood as the men scrambled upwards, and Castus could hear the top of the ladder rattling against the stone of the wall.

Up, then further up. He concentrated only on the rungs in front of him, only on lifting his arms to grip and pull, his legs to push. The ladder was creaking beneath him, bending the further he climbed. Something struck his helmet and he felt the impact ringing in his skull. Another missile fell; he ducked his head towards the rungs and the stone crashed against the shield on his back. When he paused for a moment he felt the man beneath him grasping for his ankle.

Head down, hunched beneath the rim of his shield, he pulled on upwards. The stones of the wall were almost within reach now. Castus glanced down quickly, and the drop beneath him veered away. His head reeled and he could not breathe. The strength was leaking from his arms, his legs would give and he would fall...

Motion from the corner of his eye; he turned his head and saw something dark shunted onto the crest of the wall above the next ladder. A black iron pail: it tipped, and a torrent of burning charcoal, cinders and steaming ash cascaded down onto Rogatianus and his men. Screams, and the stink of burning flesh, then the sound of men falling, dying. Castus blinked as the plume of hot ash washed past him. When he looked again, Rogatianus was still clinging to the top of the ladder but most of his men were gone.

'Tribune!' a voice cried from beneath him. Castus looked down: it was Felix, the slinger, just below him on the ladder. The man raised one enormous hand, pressed his palm against the heel of Castus's boot and pushed his foot up onto the next rung. Castus tried to gasp his thanks but his throat was hot and dry, and felt packed with cinders.

There were men above him now, men on the wall, grasping for the top of the ladder and trying to shove it away. Fury propelled Castus upwards, and he stamped at the rungs and hauled himself hand over hand. As he neared the top the sunlight almost blinded him. A speartip came from the light and jarred against the back of his shield.

Castus flung his right hand downwards.

'Spear!' he managed to shout.

Felix stretched from below him, and the shaft of a spear slid into Castus's palm.

His body pressed almost flat against the rungs, Castus struck overarm with the spear into the glaring haze of smoke and sun. He was striking blindly, but he felt the jarring impact as the blade bit. A few more rungs: he heaved himself up, trying to swing the shield off his back and get the grip into his left hand. For a moment he was wavering, balanced almost upright on the narrow rungs at the head of the ladder and feeling the world tilting around him. Then he wrestled the shield around his body and lashed with the spear, jabbing at the men packing the gap between the merlons.

Felix was right behind him, clambering up into the space below his raised shield. Others below him too, armoured bodies pressed tight at the head of the ladder. Castus jabbed again with his spear, roaring, and then flung himself forward at the edge of the wall.

His shin struck the stone, his shield banged against the merlons and the spear was wrenched from his grip, but then he was in over the battlements and onto the narrow walkway beyond. Hunched into the hollow of the shield, he got his legs beneath him and pressed his back against one of the merlons, warding off blows until he could free the sword from the scabbard. Felix was climbing over after him, empty-handed: he threw himself onto one of the defenders and they fell grappling to the stone walkway.

Castus shoved forward, driving two attackers back with his shield boss. A spearhead jarred off his armoured shoulder. Then the sword was free, the oiled steel blade and eagle hilt gleaming for a moment in the bright sun before a billow of black smoke blew down across the top of the wall. He slashed, the blade whining in the air, then stamped forward and swung the blade up backhanded, feeling it hack through a spearshaft and slice across the face of a shield.

The fight was boiling across the narrow walkway now, more men piling in over the wall behind Castus. Felix was on his knees, face set hard and grim, striking a fallen enemy with his fists. Castus saw an enemy soldier aiming a javelin; he lashed out, and his sword took the man's hand off at the wrist. Everything seemed easy now; everything was happening very quickly. Bodies pressed in around him, and he barely had room to swing his blade. But the feel of solid stone beneath his feet was joyful: for a moment Castus felt the battle was already won.

When the wind parted the smoke, he saw flames rising from the buildings inside the wall. Over to his left, a party of the Bucinobantes had swarmed into one of the wall towers; they had already butchered the defenders, and were furiously hacking the ballista on the roof to pieces with axes. From the other direction, a knot of men were charging down the walkway towards Castus, helmeted soldiers with red shields. The Divitenses, he thought... but then one of them flung a javelin that passed so close he heard it whistle.

'*Shields up!*' he shouted, and his voice snarled and cracked. A man died beside him: friend or foe, he could not tell. The smoke eddied again as the shields rose around him and butted together, rim against rim, blocking the walkway.

Bright streamers of flame were coiling up from the burning town. The enemy troops had halted, spears levelled at Castus's men advancing along the walkway towards them. Then the knot of red shields broke apart, the enemy turning to flee for the sanctuary of the nearest tower. With a bellow of triumph, the men of the Second Britannica charged after them. They kicked aside the bodies of fallen men, scrambling over the debris of stones, broken spears and discarded shields that clogged the walkway. Castus saw one soldier crouched back against the rampart wall, hands raised in surrender. He noticed the smuts on his tunic from the fire-bucket, and rammed his blade through the man's neck.

Further along the wall he could see another band of his men scrambling across the rampart. The centurion leading them – it was Attalus – lifted his spear briefly in salute, then began forming up his men on the walkway. Everywhere the defenders were in retreat, piling back into the towers or rattling down the wooden stairways on the inner side of the wall into the swirl of smoke.

'*Constantine!*' Castus yelled, sword raised. '*Victory to Constantine!*'

The men around him took up his cry at once, their cheers ringing along the wall. The slate and thatch roofs of the town were spread before them, the narrow streets and alleys boiling with smoke that rose black against the sun. Shreds of straw and wood whirled on the wind, sparking into flame as they flew, and when the smoke eddied and cleared it looked as though the whole town was burning.

PART TWO

CHAPTER VII

Arelate, Southern Gaul, June AD *312*

Heat lightning split the sky to the south, flickering over the delta of the Rhodanus. Sabina stood at the open window and watched the flashes of illumination as the warm night breeze flowed over her skin and stirred the long drapes. Anxiety twisted in her stomach. The breeze carried the scent of the distant sea, and for a moment she imagined an escape: a fast ship from Massilia that would carry her to North Africa or to Spain. She had some coin, a little jewellery she could sell. Perhaps she could make a new life for herself, and avoid the mess she had made of this one. But no – there was no escape. She would have to confront the mistakes she had made. She would have to endure their consequences.

Already she could hear the voices from the courtyard downstairs, the tread of the men climbing to the upper portico. But she did not want to turn from the window yet; did not want to acknowledge what would surely happen next. Leaning slightly across the sill, she could see the rooftops of Arelate spreading beneath her, a tiled terrain greyish in the moonlight. She had arrived here only two days ago from Treveris, with the rest of Fausta's household and attendants; in Arelate they were closer to the Alpine passes, and the messengers that would bring news of the war in Italy.

More than two years had passed since Sabina had last been

in this city. She had become engaged to Aurelius Castus in a chamber of the imperial residence, only a few blocks away from the house she occupied now. The memory deepened her sense of shame; she had been happy then, the marriage had been all she wanted. A new life; the chance to become a new woman. A virtuous woman. She had been unfaithful to her first husband many times, but with Castus things would be different. For all his uncouth ways, his ugly Pannonian accent, his lack of social graces, she loved him. And he had loved her back, in his rough and awkward way. It had all seemed so perfect, at the time.

Gods, what have I done? How have I allowed this to happen?

It had been the pregnancy, and the difficult childbirth; in her pride she had pushed her husband away, just when she needed him most, and he, in his ignorance, had believed she wanted solitude rather than attention. She tried to tell herself this was the reason, but she feared it was more than that. It was in her blood somehow, in her heritage. She was born to duplicity.

And how easy it had been, how predictable. First the exchange of glances, the flirtatious words. Then came the gifts, the jewellery and the perfumes, so well suited to her tastes – she realised later that he had bribed her slaves to tell him what she liked. The man was handsome, cultured, educated and witty; everything her husband was not. A rising official in the imperial ministries. He was also from Rome, her birthplace, the city for which she hungered. She had fallen fast, and hard. She had desired him; she had even come to believe that she loved him. But then, back in the spring, she had suddenly found the affair too much to endure. Something in his attitude had changed, and she became suspicious of him. The trip south with Fausta and her retinue had been a merciful relief.

And now he was back, making demands upon her. The note he had sent was no lover's plea either. It was a threat, naked and plain.

Footsteps from the hallway outside, and the sound of muffled voices. Sabina stepped away from the window. The room was dim, lit only by a pair of lamps on tall stands. The flames barely moved in the still, close air. She crossed quickly to one of the pair of couches and sat down, trying to keep her manner neutral. At the last moment she realised that the bracelet she wore on her forearm had been one of his gifts – one of his bribes. With a gasp of revulsion she dragged it off over her wrist and thrust it beneath one of the couch cushions.

A glass wine cup stood on the low table beside her. She raised it, drained the wine in one long swallow and set it down again. The alcohol bloomed in her head, and she took a deep breath. Then the men appeared at the doorway.

Metrodorus was first, smiling and smug as he introduced the visitor. The procurator had been bribed early, and lavishly. He stepped aside, with an obsequious bow, and the man entered the room.

'Leave us,' Sabina said over her shoulder to the two slaves waiting beside the couch. The women bobbed and departed, following Metrodorus out. Then she was alone with him.

He paced towards her, with that smooth prowling step she had once admired. She could tell that he had just come from the baths; he still carried the scent of perfumed oil. Smiling, he seated himself on the other couch and faced her.

'You should not have come here,' she said, the words catching in her throat. Her breath was tight, and she could feel the sweat gathering at her hairline.

'How could I keep away?' he replied with a casual gesture of his hand. 'I was travelling to join the army in Italy, and it was only natural that I should pause here to pay my respects to the nobilissima femina Fausta. And to see you, of course...'

Being so close to this man was harder than Sabina had anticipated. She wanted to move along the couch, away from him, keep her distance. But at the same time the memory of what they had shared was shamefully vivid in her mind. Did she really still want him? The sense of danger that he carried with him repulsed and excited her at the same time.

'Don't lie to me,' she said. 'You've used me, all along. Whatever you're doing, I want no part of it.'

'Oh, but you seemed so eager to be used...'

She raised her hand, wanting to slap him, but his quick smile told her that he expected it, perhaps wanted it. She let her hand drop.

'And, yes,' he went on, 'you have been quite convenient. Wife of a noted military commander, close to the emperor's wife. Very useful. But you see, you're already a part of what I'm doing. Those messages you sent for me, to our friends in Rome – who would have suspected you of passing treasonable correspondence? And the information about Fausta, and the things your husband told you...'

Sabina's heart was beating wildly now, and for a few moments she could not speak. But she had known – known and not wanted to admit it to herself. In those first days of their affair she had told this man so much. How stupid she had been, how guileless. And how easily he had snared her. She had even told him of Castus's mission to the court of Licinius – the realisation of her mistake burned in her mind.

'But there's no reason that I alone should benefit,' he went on, still in that artful sardonic drawl. 'We can do great things together, you and I. Everything you desire, I can give you.'

'You think I'd do anything to aid Maxentius?' she said, choking. 'I wish only destruction upon him! He murdered my father and my first husband—'

'They were *traitors*,' he broke in. 'They were plotting against him. Of course he had to kill them – any emperor would do the same. Constantine, certainly, would not hesitate.'

She caught the suggestion in his words. It was true – already she was implicated in this man's treachery. A cold flush passed through her. If she informed on him, she would be denouncing herself too. She would be questioned, tortured – nobody would believe that she had acted in ignorance. The thought of pain, of indignity, filled her with a sick terror.

'Do you really think,' he said, settling himself a little further forward on the couch, 'that Constantine can take Rome? Already two imperial expeditions have failed. You know the power of the eternal city, the strength of the walls. Maxentius has an army of one hundred thousand men, many of them veterans from the Danube legions. If Constantine fails – as he surely will – then you will be left with precisely *nothing*. I offer you an alternative.'

He was twisting the heavy gold ring on his middle finger as he spoke. Twin leopards, clasping a pearl. 'Assist me, and I can see that all your family wealth and property is restored to you. To you, *and to your son*. I know you, Valeria Domitia Sabina – I know what you are. You are more than just some soldier's wife. You are a daughter of the Roman aristocracy. Let me return your birthright to you...'

He was edging closer now, dropping his voice to a purr.

'My husband would kill you,' she said.

'He would kill *you too*. Or try to, if he found out. We must hope that no word of this reaches him, eh? But perhaps, if we're lucky, he will not be around for much longer...'

'What's happened?' she said, suddenly afraid. 'What's happened to him?'

'Nothing – yet... But the war will be fierce, and the fighting hard. And who knows what accidents may befall a soldier so noted for his reckless courage?'

Sabina glanced at his hands, those well-manicured fingers. She remembered Castus's hands, how different they were, rough and calloused. A warrior's hands. She felt a sudden need for her husband. A desire for him to return with all his justified rage. But what if that meant her own death? He had offered her security, and she had betrayed him. She had betrayed everything, poured it out like water onto the ground, and now only this other man, this sly and deceptive creature, offered her any chance of avoiding her fate.

He shifted once more, smooth and subtle, and came to sit beside her on the couch. Sabina did not move. She kept her back straight and tried not to flinch as he raised his hand and caressed the nape of her neck. For a moment she imagined herself seizing the glass cup from the table and smashing it into his face, slashing that smile to bloody shreds. The image shocked her with its intensity.

'If this thing happens as it must,' he said, breathing the words, 'then those who have acted well will be rewarded. Think about that. Think about what you desire, and how to get it.'

The grip of his hand tightened, pulling her towards him, and he leaned and kissed the bare skin of her shoulder. Panic beat in Sabina's chest; she felt entirely powerless, as if she lay in the coils of a snake that might strike her at any moment. Be calm, she told herself. Be calm and endure, for now. And pray that some chance of freedom comes.

But even as she thought this, she felt the echo of his words deep within her, his suggestion finding an answer from her hidden core, that dark part of herself she had tried to deny.

'What do you want from me?' she said quietly.

CHAPTER VIII

'Feathers?' Castus asked, shoving himself back from the table. The folding stool creaked beneath him.

'That's what it says, dominus,' Diogenes replied. He was reading out the latest field orders from the army commanders. 'All soldiers of the Gallic army are to fix a plume of feathers at the front of their helmet, to aid identification.'

'Hmm. Makes sense, I suppose.' With the troops on both sides armed and equipped the same, and so many of the shield designs similar, it was proving difficult to tell friend from foe. During the storming of Segusio, some men of the Divitenses had been killed by Prince Hrodomarus's Bucinobantes, who mistook them for the enemy. Whether a plume of feathers would make a difference in the heat of battle Castus could not say, but perhaps it would make the troops feel more secure.

'What sort of feathers?'

'The order doesn't specify, dominus. I should think goose feathers would serve... or the tail feathers of a cockerel?'

'First camels, now cockerels...' muttered Modestus from the tent door. 'The barnyards of Italy must be quaking already.'

Castus turned to address his orderly. 'Eumolpius, rip the feathers out of my crest and fix a couple to the front of my helmet. Better set an example... Right – next,' he said to Diogenes, 'how are the new men shaping up?'

'Well enough, dominus. They're Roman soldiers, after all. They've made their sacred vow...'

Legion II Britannica had taken losses in the assault: eighteen dead and over thirty disabled by wounds. Castus had listened as Diogenes read out the names of the fallen: some of them were men he had known for years, since the old days in Eboracum; others were completely unknown to him. He tried not to consider that he might be responsible for their deaths, but every name had jarred in his mind.

Now the gaps in the ranks were filled by volunteers from among the prisoners taken when the town had fallen, scattered between the different centuries. They were conscripts from Carthage and Sicily for the most part, with a few Dalmatians, and even a Syrian. The growing diversity of his command did not bother Castus: as Diogenes said, the new men had sworn an oath to the standards. Swapping one emperor for another could not be that difficult. But he was struck by the odd fate that had brought these men to the legion, to serve alongside other men who had been trying to kill them not long before. At the time, as he had scaled the ladder and stormed in over the parapet, Castus had thought nothing of the men he was fighting. They had been the enemy, that was all. But they had been Romans too, and the memory of that fight troubled him. He remembered the soldier he had slain on the parapet as he had tried to surrender. It was war, he told himself. He had done his duty to his emperor and his men, and that was all that mattered now.

Castus was glad to be away from Segusio anyway: the town stank of burnt thatch, and for days after the capture dead bodies were still turning up in the blackened ruins around the east gate. The fire had not been Constantine's intention: the strong wind and a wooden storage shed for animal feed just

129

inside the western gate had seen to that. It was the emperor who had saved the town from the flames. Before the surrender had been formally agreed, he had ordered his troops into the streets to help fight the blaze. Men who moments before had been locked in bloody combat now joined forces, heaving up water from the river and pulling down buildings to make fire-breaks. It would not, Castus supposed, have looked good if the first town liberated in Italy had been destroyed in the process.

Now evening was coming on, and the shadows outside the open flap of the tent were growing longer. The army had marched eighteen miles east from Segusio, down the valley of the Duria River towards the open plains before Taurinum. Morale was good. The men of the legion were proud that they had been at the forefront of the assault – an honour disputed with their rivals the Divitenses, of course – and Castus felt his command of them to be more secure than ever. But he could not allow himself to get complacent.

He had seen little of Macer since the attack. The drillmaster had been wounded; he had lost an eye, and spent several days in the camp hospital. Did the man still think Castus had been wrong to press the assault? If he did, he said nothing about it. Perhaps, Castus thought, the drillmaster's weakness at the foot of the wall had shamed him into silence now.

'Send in the first of the men,' he called to Modestus.

The optio shouted, and a soldier marched into the tent with four long strides and stamped to a halt before Castus. He was a short man, but there was still barely enough headroom in the tent for him to stand upright.

'Valerius Felix,' Castus said. 'In recognition of your bravery during the storming of Segusio, I am recommending to your centurion Rogatianus that you be advanced to the grade of *immunis*, with a raise in pay and provisions, and exempted from fatigue labour.'

The man's expression did not alter; he stared straight ahead at the rear wall of the tent. Did he remember Castus's moment of fear and indecision at the top of the ladder? If he did, nothing in his manner showed it. 'Thank you, dominus,' he said, tight-lipped.

There had been a rumour, back in Divodurum, that this man Felix was an escaped slave. It had caused the usual bad feeling: slaves were forbidden to serve, under penalty of death, and even the suggested taint of servitude disgusted soldiers. Castus had ordered the man to swear before the gods that he was freeborn, and the issue had seemed resolved. But his comrades still called him 'Slops'. He was certainly odd-looking, with his bony face and long jutting jaw, his huge dangling hands. Although, Castus reminded himself, he was hardly in a position to judge on appearance...

'My adiutor tells me you were born in Rome,' he said.

'That's right, dominus.'

'So how did you end up enlisting in Gaul?'

Felix sniffed, clearly uncomfortable.

'I took a walk one day. Gaul was where I ended up. Dominus.'

Castus lowered his brows, alert for the hint of insolence. But, no, the man was speaking truthfully. Perhaps he had been a slave after all? In which case, the less Castus knew of it the better.

'Dismissed,' he said. Felix turned and marched out, and Modestus sent in the next man.

'Sentius Salvianus,' Castus said. 'Your centurion Attalus reports that you are a Christian. Is this true?'

'Yes, dominus,' the young man said. He was no older than eighteen, and appeared very nervous. But his voice had an educated tone. 'I believe it is no longer forbidden, dominus.'

'Quite so,' Castus growled. 'Very soon, we will face the enemy in open battle. I ask you now: is there any reason why you should not stand in the ranks with your comrades?'

'No, dominus!' Salvianus was sweating, but he looked sincere.

'Your... *religious feelings* will not stop you fighting, killing?'

'Not at all.'

'Good. As you know, cowardice and dereliction of duty carry the death penalty. If you flinch or fail, everyone around you is endangered by it.'

The young man nodded quickly. Castus studied him: he had seen men like this in the army before, but very few of them. And not many serving as common soldiers.

'You're a volunteer, I think,' he said. 'Why did you enlist?'

'I... wanted a different life, dominus.'

Castus gave a tight smile, nodding. Something in the young man's voice, in his face, told him all he needed to know. Castus had wanted a different life himself when he had run away from home and joined the legions. He doubted that young Salvianus had tried to murder his own father in the process, but maybe it was much the same. Even wealthy men, he guessed, could be tyrants.

'Honour your oath, soldier,' he said. 'Do that, and nobody will fault you for it. Dismissed!'

Outside the tent, Castus stood up straight, stretching his back. The evening light was soft over the camp, turning the smoke of the cooking fires to a glowing haze. Across the tent lines, he could see a line of naked men queuing at the big bathing pavilion, shoving and joking. He would like a bath himself, but he had another duty to attend to first.

Eumolpius stooped out of the tent, passed Castus his cloak and helmet – a pair of long black feathers now fixed securely above the nasal – and then dropped into step behind him. As they marched down the avenues between the tent lines, Castus heard the sounds of female laughter: the army had already begun to pick up its trail of camp followers. The troops had baggage carts again too now, some of them mounted with the ballistae taken from the walls of Segusio.

Above the camp to the south-west loomed a last summit, rising like a dog's tooth, but to the east, for the first time in nearly a month, the horizon was flat. The advancing army was leaving the mountains behind it now, and the expanse of open sky, unconstrained by jutting peaks, was a liberating sight.

A convoy of camels was coming up the road towards the camp perimeter, bringing up supplies from the surrounding countryside. The sentries at the camp ditches raised their hands in mock salute. '*Beuuuurk!*' a soldier yelled, and the rest laughed as one of the beasts returned his call with a throaty roar of its own. Behind the camels, at a discreet distance, was a single figure on foot. Castus paid the man no attention at first, assuming he was one of the camp slaves.

'Tribune,' the man said, pausing.

Castus squinted, focusing on his face, but already he had recognised the dry, rasping voice. He should have known that he would encounter Julius Nigrinus sooner or later. His expression tightened to a sneer of displeasure.

'I have yet to congratulate you on your promotion!' the notary said.

Castus just grunted; he had no desire for this man's congratulations.

'I hear your men were at the fore during the taking of Segusio too,' Nigrinus went on, his tone angled and sardonic. 'I hope the casualties were not too heavy? It appears that the defenders of Segusio were forewarned of our attack plans!'

'You think so?' Castus said, frowning. He had thought as much himself, but had voiced his suspicions to few people.

'Certainly. Their garrison had clearly been reinforced, and recently, if the prisoners I've questioned are telling the truth. Granted, they did not expect the burning of the gate, or the near-incineration of the entire town... The people of Segusio have only the humanity and celerity of our emperor to thank that they are not currently the citizens of a mound of ashes!'

'No doubt somebody's writing a panegyric about it even now.'

Nigrinus gave a feigned chuckle, nodding. His words had raised fresh suspicions in Castus's mind; no doubt that was their purpose. The thought of treachery within the camp, perhaps within the emperor's own command, felt poisonous. Was Nigrinus spreading these ideas widely? Did he hope that he would be granted further powers of investigation and subterfuge? Castus shrugged off the thought: anything like that just weakened morale. Better to face the enemy square on, rather than worrying about hidden foes.

'But you must be on your way to the commander's conference,' Nigrinus said. 'I shall not detain you further – no doubt our paths will cross again soon!'

Not if I can help it, Castus thought as he watched the man pacing away towards the camp gates. The sentries at the gates barely noticed him passing; the notary was so unobtrusive as to be almost invisible. A grey-brown shade, insubstantial in daylight.

* * *

Aurelius Evander had set up his headquarters in an abandoned farmhouse next to the road station. Ad Fines, the place was called. The sun was gone by the time Castus arrived, and he joined the group of other officers, tribunes and prefects, waiting in the courtyard. There was a big olive press at the rear, and Evander climbed onto the stone platform to address them.

'Soldiers,' he said, then coughed and cleared his throat. Thirty officers gazed back at him. 'As most of you are aware, our cavalrymen have been skirmishing with the enemy scouts since this morning. It seems that the enemy are preparing to make a stand in the hills to the east of us, and contest our advance to Taurinum.'

All across the courtyard, men straightened slightly, squaring their shoulders. They had been expecting battle for so long – now it was almost upon them.

'Their numbers match our own,' Evander said, 'but they also have a large force of *clibanarii* with them. We lack the strength of horse to attack them effectively from the flank, so our Augustus has devised a strategy to confront them from the centre using our main infantry force, and to destroy them.'

Castus felt his brow contract in a frown. Few of the men around him had ever encountered the heavily armoured lancers called clibanarii, but he had faced their Persian equivalent many years before, at Oxsa in Armenia. As Evander described what was to be done, Castus could hear the slight intakes of breath around him, the shuffle of feet. This was the emperor's own plan, so the commander had said – could any man speak out against it?

'Are there any questions?' Evander called. Even he sounded unconvinced by what he had just told them.

'It seems risky, dominus,' said Leontius, Prefect of Legion VIII Augusta, raising his flaring sandy eyebrows.

'Opening the line like that...' another officer added, from the side of Evander's improvised podium. 'Has it been done before?'

'It has!' Evander proclaimed. 'Scipio Africanus did something very similar, as did the deified Aurelian. We must trust that the military genius of our Sacred Augustus is quite equal to the situation!'

But his words did little to ease the minds of his officers. They filed out of the courtyard in silence, exchanging troubled glances. In the gathering dusk, they rejoined their orderlies and separated quickly. Castus was just about to follow them when he heard somebody call his name.

Two men of the Protectores were standing beside a gate in the courtyard wall. He recognised them from his time in the Corps, but did not know them by name.

'Wait for me here,' he told Eumolpius, then followed the two men through the gate and into the olive orchard behind the house.

The trees smelled dusty in the darkness, and the ground was dry underfoot. Lights showed through the trees from the encampment in the open ground beyond. The emperor's own quarters, Castus realised as he saw the mounted guards and the purple draco standard. He surrendered his sword to one of the Protectores, then the other pulled back the flap of the largest tent and ushered him inside.

Castus had expected an open space within, but instead there was only a panelled antechamber, dark and reeking slightly of incense. More figures stood in the shadows, not armed men this time but slaves or eunuchs, and there were thick mats covering the ground. An inner curtain of gold-embroidered purple hung partly open, and as he stood in the antechamber, the sweat prickling beneath his tunic, Castus could make out a scene in lamplight beyond.

The emperor was seated, a small round table at his side holding a goblet of wine, a glass jug and a dish. Opposite him sat another man, old and white-haired but vigorous-looking, with dark features stretched with intent. They were speaking together, too quietly to be overheard. As Castus watched, inclining his head slightly to peer through the gap in the curtain, he saw the older man lean forward and touch the emperor on the arm, then on the forehead.

'Who's that?' he whispered to the Protector, who had followed him into the tent.

'That? One of the Christian priests,' the man replied. 'A bishop from somewhere in Spain. Corduba, I think?'

Someone made a hushing sound from the shadows, and Castus straightened up. Shortly afterwards, a man in a damask robe drew the curtain back and gestured. Castus recognised him: Festus, the emperor's eunuch, the Superintendent of the Sacred Bedchamber. He had seen him often enough in Treveris.

'Tribune Aurelius Castus,' the eunuch said in soft and breathy tones. Castus stepped through the parting in the curtain and dropped to kneel upon the matting.

'You may rise,' said another voice from the far side of the chamber.

Castus stood, feet braced, careful not to look directly at the figure beside the table. The older man, the Christian priest, appeared to have left by another exit, but Castus was aware of others in the darkness around him: slaves and attendants. The emperor was never truly alone. From the corner of his eye, Castus could make out the figure slumped in the chair. The lean profile and heavy jaw were almost in silhouette against the light of the lamp.

'You were at Oxsa, tribune?' Constantine said. His voice was rough with fatigue, and his Danubian accent seemed more pronounced.

'Yes, dominus.' Castus was aware of the quietness around him, no stir of voices or activity, as if the layered walls of the imperial pavilion were made of some padded substance that deadened sound.

'I remember you, I think. Or perhaps I met you later... it doesn't matter. You faced the Persian cataphracts then. Do you think my troops are strong enough to hold off these clibanarii tomorrow?'

'Yes, dominus!' Castus answered at once. 'If the gods are with us...'

He had spoken without thinking, and was aware of the tense pause that followed his words. Under his breath, he cursed. The figure in the chair shifted, reaching for the cup of wine.

'They're slightly different, these clibanarii, from the Persian armoured cavalry,' Constantine said, fingering his cup. There was a faint slur to his voice, Castus noticed. Not only fatigue. 'They're trained to charge against infantry lines directly, rather than waiting for horse archers to create gaps they can exploit... It's a...' He paused again, taking a sip of wine. 'It's... They use *fear* as a weapon, do you understand?'

'I think so, dominus.'

'They terrorise their opponents, break them. Our lines held at Oxsa; they must do the same tomorrow. They must hold, and then *destroy* the enemy.' He clenched his right hand into a fist, punching it into his palm. 'Do the other tribunes, the other officers, understand what must be done? They know the formations and the manoeuvres?'

'They do, dominus.'

As he spoke, Castus realised that the emperor was not tired, not drunk at all. Constantine was nervous; he was gripped by anxiety. Perhaps – it seemed impious to even consider it – the emperor was afraid. Phobos. Even the thought of that unstoppable armoured cavalry crashing into the ranks of the foot soldiers brought dread and panic. Castus knew now why he had been summoned here.

'All of us are confident, dominus,' he said in as firm a voice as he could muster. 'The men too. They're as strong as any troops I've known, and if you ordered them to smash through a wall of stone, they'd do it.'

Constantine rubbed his brow with his thumb, nodding. 'Yes,' he said quietly, 'I expect they would.'

Castus exhaled slowly, and wished he could believe it himself.

CHAPTER IX

The sun had climbed from the horizon and burned off the thin scrim of cloud, and now the day was getting hot. On the exposed plain the troops stood and sweated in their formations. Just over a quarter-mile away, across open fields of scorched stubble and parched grass, the ground rose to a long low ridge. Up on the ridge, in plain sight, the enemy cavalry sat in a compact mass with the sunlight gleaming from their armour. To the men on the plains below, they appeared like a fortress of glittering metal.

'There's not too many of them,' Antoninus said. The massive young standard-bearer stood just behind Castus, at the right of the legion formation. He was bare-headed, and held the eagle standard planted proudly in the ground before him.

'That's just the tip of their wedge,' Castus told him. 'The rest of the army'll be deployed on the reverse side of the ridge, where we can't see them.' *Or determine their numbers*, he thought. Glancing to the left and right, he scanned the horizon. There was a lot of dust rising from the far side of the ridge. How far did the enemy flanks extend? The Constantinian line was bunched heavily towards the centre to repel the cavalry, the legion detachments in two close formation lines, each eight men deep; if the enemy had strong forces out on their wings, they could swing forward across the ridge and envelop the flanks...

Castus told himself not to think about that – to concentrate only on the ground before him, the narrow stretch of baked earth and burnt stubble that would be his battlefield.

Horseback messengers were galloping back and forth along the lines. Castus spotted Vitalis, and raised his spear in salute. The other tribune waved back, then cantered closer.

'General advance, one hundred paces!' Vitalis cried, then rode on. A moment later, the trumpets sounded.

The men of the Second Britannica hefted their shields, lifted spears, and began the slow steady march forward over the dry ground. Dust rose; Castus felt it in his nostrils. All morning he had been remembering that battle at Oxsa many years before; he had been as young then as many of the men in the ranks behind him. But he had been in the reserves that day; he had not had to witness the charge of the Persian cataphracts directly.

Gazing up at the mass of cavalry sitting immobile on the ridge, he tried to estimate the distance, and guess how long it would take them to reach the infantry front line. Less than the time it would take him to count sixty heartbeats, if they rode at the gallop. They would come slower, though, at least at first, keeping their formation. A horse would not charge directly against formed infantry: that was the maxim that every foot soldier held dear. But could any infantry line hold firm in the face of that terrible advance? These clibanarii wore such heavy armour, horse and rider encased in metal, that even at a walk, even a standstill, they could face the bristling spears and locked shields and force their way through by weight and invulnerable strength alone...

Don't think, he told himself. Already he could feel the tension in his chest, the kick of his heart. Beneath his hauberk of bronze scales his body was flowing with sweat, and his scalp itched under his helmet. He gripped the shaft of his spear more tightly, and felt the moisture of his palms.

The trumpets sounded again, and the marching men came to a halt. In the eddying dust the centurions moved along the ranks, straightening the lines. Castus looked to his left, along the front rank of his assembled men. One hundred and twenty shields, each with the bold red sun-wheel on golden yellow. Every man wore a pair of grey feathers above the brow of his helmet. Beyond them were the auxilia troops of the Batavi, and on the far side the red shields of the Divitenses stretching away into the haze. To Castus's right, across the narrow lane between the units, were the warriors of the Bucinobantes, and beyond them the legionaries of I Minervia, their shields a solid-looking wall of black. Every unit had their standards at the front, the eagles glinting, the long tails of the draco banners streaming in the dusty breeze.

Already the men of the Germanic auxilia were raising their war cries, the weird reverberating shouts booming across the plain towards the distant enemy. Between the waves of noise Castus could make out other sounds: the dry tapping of a man's teeth; somebody else muttering under his breath, either prayers or curses. Then, from along the lines to the left, a burst of cheering.

Every man strained forward, peering between the ranks of their comrades as the emperor came galloping along the front line. Constantine rode hard, not turning his head but only raising his hand to acknowledge the acclamation of his troops. Behind him came his staff officers and orderlies, and the rider carrying the long purple imperial standard.

'*Constantine! Constantine!*' the men cried, a massed roar of voices barrelling from the ranks of the infantry. A tumult followed, thousands of spears drumming against shields, the surge of noise rolling down the battle line and echoing away across the plain.

But the emperor did not pause to address his men; there would be no rousing speech from Constantine. Already Castus could see him riding to the fore of his right-flank cavalry, the standards dipping as he approached.

Calm settled back over the army, breathless and tense. The ground ahead was misty with airborne dust now, shot through with sun. The riders up on the ridge had still not moved: impossible to make out their numbers, or even distinguish them clearly. The legionaries were passing waterskins along their lines, each men tipping his head to drink. Castus swilled water, swallowed a little and then spat the rest in a dark starburst at his feet. He could smell sweat through the dust, hot metal and leather, the rank scent of fresh urine.

Plumes of brown dust were rising in the distance now, and as Castus turned his head he could hear the shouts, the dry rattle of spears. His blood quickened as he realised that the flanks of the army had already moved forward, up on the ridge to attack the enemy wings. The battle had begun.

Breathing slowly, one eye on the massed cavalry waiting on the ridge, he paced down along the front rank of his men. Soldiers called out to him as he passed – *dominus… dominus…* – the centurions raising their spears in salute. He saw Rogatianus among them, his face and arms pitted with dark burn-scars from the flaming embers thrown down on him from the walls of Segusio. He greeted all of his officers by name. All looked fierce, steady.

Castus reached the extreme left-hand end of the line, where Macer stood. The drillmaster nodded to him as he drew closer. His mouth was set firm, and the bandage over his eye showed beneath his helmet rim.

'Ready?' Castus said quietly, and the old man nodded again. 'Remember, we're closing from the right,' he went on. 'Keep your men locked here, don't let the lines drift.'

'You don't need to tell me my business, lad,' Macer said.

Castus felt his shoulders tighten under the heavy hug of his scale armour. But he caught the glint in Macer's single eye: the old man had meant no disrespect. He twitched a smile, jutting his jaw, then turned and paced back along the lines.

He saw the faces of the men. Some of them expressionless, blankly determined. Others, in the second and third lines especially, looked pale and drawn. Many would not meet his eye. Fear was stalking through them. Castus kept his own face set hard. *The mask of command.*

At the centre of the line he paused and took two steps outwards. It was an effort to turn his back on the enemy, to lose sight of that forbidding mass of horsemen even for a moment, but he faced his men and raised his spear above his head. The ranks rippled, every man straightening, the low hiss of whispered words falling into silence.

Castus felt the sun pressing down on him. Sweat broke beneath his helmet rim and itched at his eyes.

'Fellow soldiers!' he yelled, the words catching at the dust in his throat. 'Very soon, that bunch of shiny bastards up there are going to come down on you with everything they've got!'

He swung his spear to point up at the ridge behind him. A stir of drawn breaths, feet shuffling in dust, clink of metal.

'They're going to swing a punch at you and try to make you flinch!' His voice snarled, hoarse. 'When they charge, they'll make the ground shake!'

Castus clenched his jaw for a moment, trying to moisten his mouth.

'Don't worry about feeling afraid,' he cried. 'Everyone feels it – you're *supposed* to feel afraid! But remember this... *you are stronger than them!* Stand your ground. Keep your shields up and your spears level, and don't flinch. Trust to your brothers, the men beside you and behind you... Hold your positions, listen for the trumpets and only move when you hear the order.'

He paused, watching the lines shift and blur before him. He blinked the sweat from his eyes.

'When they come down at you' – his voice rose again – 'remember this: those riders have never faced an enemy in battle! All they've done is trot around the drill field at Mediolanum. They're more scared of you than you are of them! They think they can break us... but we're going to show them different!'

He could see the smiles now, the nervous grins. From somewhere in the rear ranks came the sound of a spear tapping against a shield rim.

'Here's to victory!' Castus roared, punching his spear above his head. 'Here's to Constantine! *Britannica! Britannica!*'

And the shout came echoing back, the drumming of spears gathering to a rhythmic crash. Through it, another chant: '*Knucklehead! Knucklehead! Knucklehead!*'

Castus stared at Rogatianus, and saw the centurion grinning back at him. For a moment he felt a hot flush of anger – how had his old army nickname followed him yet again? – then he threw back his head and laughed.

Then a roar swept along the front line, a clattering of shields, and the cry went up from the right wing: '*They're coming!*'

Castus jogged back to his position next to the standard-bearer. When he turned, his breath caught: the whole gleaming mass of cavalry had begun rolling down the ridge towards them, dust boiling up from beneath the hooves of the horses. Horns wailed from both sides, the rival signals blending to a high brassy scream. Staring through the haze, Castus saw the numbers of the clibanarii double, and then treble, more of the horsemen crossing the ridge and falling into one massive blunt-headed wedge.

'*Gods*,' somebody gasped from behind him. 'Gods, there are thousands of them...'

Already the ranks of the legion were shuddering, men backing up a step, then two steps, pressing towards the men behind them. Castus could hear the centurions yelling, trying to straighten the lines.

The noise of the oncoming cavalry reached them now, the rolling thunder of hooves on dry baked earth, the ringing of metal. The blunt head of the wedge was already down the ridge and onto the flat ground, coming on at a fast trot. Their formation was tight, every horseman appeared knee-to-knee with the rider beside him, and their long lances wavered in the haze above them.

Castus ground his boots into the dirt, as if he could take a firmer grip on the ground. Behind him he could hear Antoninus spitting words through his teeth, '*Come on, you bastards. Come on, you fuckers...*'

A gust of wind swept the field, parting the dust, and suddenly the huge wedge of cavalry appeared very close, their armour clear and bright, every rider distinct. Castus felt his throat tighten. The sight was fearsome, awe-inspiring. The riders looked huge, and godlike in their casing of gleaming mail and scale. Every man wore a polished mask of gilded metal, moulded into the form of a perfect and expressionless face: they appeared inhuman, like automatons. Even their armoured horses were masked, blinkered in filigree bronze. They looked utterly unstoppable.

Castus heard groans of anguish from behind him, and high gasps of terror. The centurions were yelling, but more of the men were shuffling backwards, trying to put another few feet between them and the oncoming cavalry. Castus felt his own chest filling with a dark pressure; his heart was tight against his sternum, and his legs felt weak. Deathly fear was stealing his resolve. *Hold! Hold...!* Now the ground was shaking, the dust jumping.

One hundred paces, then fifty. Still the armoured wedge ploughed closer, some of the leading riders beginning to break formation as they urged their horses into a faster gallop.

'Javelins!' Castus cried, raising his spear. The word seemed to ignite something in his body, in his muscles. Suddenly he felt alive, and everything was happening very fast.

The lines rippled, every man in the rear four ranks taking a step forward and hurling his javelin over the heads of the men in front, and for a moment the air was dark with flying metal. Arrows were whipping from the archers at the rear.

'Shield wall! Repel cavalry!' Castus shouted, and heard his words echoed by the centurions along the front line. The rolling dust cloud was almost on top of them as the men of the front rank dropped to one knee, shields grounded and spears angled upwards. The second-rankers stepped up close behind them, raising their own shields to lock with the ones beneath. The noise was enormous, deafening: shield rims slamming together; men yelling as they formed the wall. In a heartbeat, the wavering front line was a solid bulwark bristling with spears.

Dust reeled, and when he looked forward again Castus saw the first riders break from the haze and swerve at the sight of the obstacle before them. Some had already been felled by the missile storm: horses rolled and kicked in the dirt, their trapped riders crushed beneath them. But as the momentum of the charge died so more horsemen filled the gaps in the enemy line: they were milling now, some riders forcing their mounts on towards the shield wall, others turning, readying their long-reaching lances.

Now, Castus thought. *Now, or we won't hold them...*

With a sharp stab of panic he realised that he could no longer hear the signal trumpets. All he could distinguish through the cheek guards of his helmet was the screaming of men all around him, the neighing of panicked horses and the clatter of javelins, and Antoninus yelling crazed defiance at the back of his head. Had the signal to change formation already been given?

From the rear ranks men were still hurling javelins forward, arcing them over the shield wall into the packed mass of cavalry. Castus saw one javelin strike a rider full in the chest; the man just shuddered slightly in the saddle, and the javelin bounced away from him, harmless. *Our weapons cannot touch them...*

There were more of the horsemen now, and they were pushing their mounts forward at a walk, angling their lances down in a two-handed overhead grip. Darts and javelins flickered around the scale-armoured flanks of the horses, but Castus could already see the lines of shields beginning to bow inwards, the forest of spears swaying and separating as men bunched together to oppose the advancing riders.

'Hold your positions!' Castus was yelling, but he could not hear his own voice. The noise around him had merged into a steady rushing scream. There was nothing within striking range of his spear, and he kept his shield up and stared over the rim.

Then sudden motion from his right. For a moment Castus felt the panic rising in his throat: the solid block of Bucinobantes warriors holding his right flank were breaking apart, throwing down their shields and retreating. He felt a heavy grip on his shoulder, a hand hauling him backwards.

'The signal!' Antoninus screamed in his ear. Castus remembered that the standard-bearer was not wearing a helmet, and could hear better. He shoved himself backwards against the shield behind him. The fleeing Bucinobantes were streaming in through the gaps in the legion formations to either side of them now, leaving open lanes between each block of legionaries and the next. As they pushed their way though the ranks, the men at the front lines drew in closer, every man taking a shuffling step to his right. Shields meshed tighter, armoured bodies pressed together.

Castus kept shoving back, forcing himself through the gap between two shields. Men shouldered against him from both sides, and he could feel the shaft of the standard jabbing against his right arm. 'Back!' he shouted. 'Further back – move!'

But already the enemy cavalry had taken the bait: horses swerved and reared as their riders hauled at the reins, and a solid knot of clibanarii came powering out of the dust cloud, aiming directly for the open lane between the legion's shields. For a few heartbeats Castus could only stare, convinced that the charging horses would ram straight into him... then they were streaming past him into the gap, scaled bardings flapping, hooves kicking aside the litter of fallen shields. A hot wave of dust engulfed the legionary lines, rank with the stink of horse sweat and metal.

The riders were surging past so close to him that Castus could almost have touched the flanks of their horses. One turned aside at the corner of the formation, his horse shying back from the spears; he raised his lance overhead and then plunged it down, driving the long steel point through two overlapping shields. Castus roared, lunging forward with his own spear. He felt the tip strike the rider on the thigh, then glance off the iron bands that encased his leg. The horse reared, striking out with its hooves, and the dense mass of legionaries shrank back from it. Tightly pressed together, they could only hold their shields before them as the horse kicked. A sling whirred close to Castus's ear, and he saw the rider knocked sideways as the lead shot struck his head. He toppled, sliding back off the saddle, and a bellowing cheer went up from the legionaries as the horse spun away from them.

More of the clibanarii were forcing their way through the gap between the lines, so many that their charge had stalled, men and mounts crushed together. *Now*, Castus thought, *now they see their mistake...*

All along the front line, the shield wall had opened broad lanes between the units. But the men of the reserve legions held steady in their formations, and the armoured horsemen sweeping into the gaps found themselves facing a second line of troops, drawn up in a solid wall and blocking their path. As the leading horses faltered, turning aside, the riders that followed collided with them. In moments the formidable armoured assault had collapsed in a milling crush of men and animals, with the flanks of the legionary blocks pressing in on either side like huge barbed teeth, grinding and crushing the trapped horsemen.

But the clibanarii were more dangerous at close quarters, and now the packed horsemen were lashing out at the infantry to either side. Castus saw one rider lean from the saddle and stab downwards with his lance, reaching over the shields to impale a man deep inside the formation. His horse shuddered – somebody had sliced its exposed leg – and with a whinnying scream collapsed sideways. Horse and rider slammed down onto the shields, crushing the men beneath them. Another horse bucked suddenly, almost throwing its rider from the saddle; the rear hooves kicked out, blasting one man's shield to splinters, bursting the helmet of another.

'Bludgeons!' Castus shouted over his shoulder. 'Bludgeons to the front *now*!'

Already he could see the centurions shoving their men forward, funnelling them though the close-packed ranks. Some pushed between the shields, others dropped to crawl between the legs of their comrades. All of the men had thrown down their own shields and spears, and armed themselves with blunt weapons: long-handled cavalry maces, or simple wooden clubs encrusted with iron hobnails. A few carried pickaxes and entrenching mattocks.

While their comrades held the milling cavalry at bay, the clubmen scrambled in between the horses. Castus saw two men with maces strike an armoured rider; the iron mace-heads rang off the man's cuirass, but the *clibanarius* dropped his lance and slumped from the saddle. A soldier grabbed at a horseman's arm and dragged him downwards, another man aiming two swinging blows of a studded club at the rider's head.

The lane between the legion flanks was a violent chaos now, the dust choking. More of the clubmen were streaming in from either side, battering at horses and men alike. One of the horses went down, staggering under a blow to the legs, then another toppled beside it. A kicking hoof caught a clubman in the head and killed him instantly. The flank of shields bowed suddenly inwards as a third horse fell, the armoured rider spilling from the saddle to sprawl on his back in the dust. Immobilised by the weight of his armour, he had no defence: for a moment Castus stared at him in dazed fascination. Then a foot soldier swung a mattock over his head and brought it smashing down onto the fallen man's head. The brilliant golden mask crunched inward under the blow, and blood sprayed from the eyes and mouth.

A breeze swept the line, churning the dust to a red-brown fog, and for a few heartbeats Castus could see nothing. When it cleared, he saw a horse charging straight at him from the packed mass of enemy cavalry; it had managed to turn in the confined space, and was bolting back for open ground, but the hedge of spears had panicked it. Castus threw himself back against the men behind him, lifting his shield. He saw the rider lurching in the saddle, trying to angle his long lance to strike. Then the horse lunged forward, jaws wide; the animal's head passed over Castus's shoulder, and he heard the ghastly crunch of bone as it bit at Antoninus's face. Blood spattered against his shoulder, but at once a mesh of blades had struck the animal, jarring in through the gaps in its armour. It stumbled and fell, and the rider tumbled from the saddle.

Castus stepped forward, raising his spear to strike down at the fallen man. Too late he saw the long cavalry lance angled upwards; then pain exploded through his head. He staggered, but the bodies of men all around him held him upright. His mouth filled with blood; he coughed, and it ran down his chest. More blood, filling his throat. He was choking on it. The lance had slipped in behind the cheek guard of his helmet and stabbed him through the side of the jaw – for a moment, he had felt the sharp point of it in his mouth. He spat broken teeth.

Pain was ringing through him, and his whole face felt split wide open. His leg went from beneath him and he was kneeling, vomiting blood, propped on his shield. Around him the noise of the battle became a vague rushing roar, and all he could feel was the ripped wound in his head and the taste of cold iron.

'*Britannica! Britannica!*' somebody was shouting. When he opened his eyes he could see a dying horse only a few paces away, legs thrashing as it blew bloody froth. Antoninus was sprawled beside him, the front of his skull crushed to pulp. Castus felt his strength ebbing, his consciousness beginning to blur. *Get up*, he thought. But he could not. *Don't fall on your back; you'll drown in your own blood.*

He tried to speak, but the motion of his jaw sent a bolt of agony through him, and he plunged down into blackness.

CHAPTER X

They rigged the forks at noon, on the old drill field outside the walls of Mediolanum. The troops of four legions were drawn up in parade formation, four sides of a hollow square facing inwards towards the punishment ground.

The condemned men wore only loose unbelted tunics, the stripes and patches that marked them as soldiers cut away. All three were bruised, unwashed and stumbling. One of them had to be dragged across the parched grass to the forked punishment poles, and then the three of them were bound in place, their arms raised, and their tunics ripped from their backs.

From his position at the head of his legion, Castus watched with sober disgust. The day was very hot, his head was aching, and one side of his mouth was packed with a poultice of mashed herbs in sour medicinal gum. Twelve days had passed since the battle on the road to Taurinum, and the wound on his jaw was still healing; the jagged hook-shaped scar was coated in sticky brown paste, but itched furiously. Castus felt like tiny flames were flickering up the side of his face. At least the surgeons had removed the thick linen bandage that had swathed his head for so many days, but his tongue kept probing at the mauled left side of his mouth, rubbing at the stitches, and at the jagged gap where he had lost two teeth: the jolts of pain were becomingly maddeningly familiar.

It could have been much worse – only the tip of the lance had jabbed through his flesh. If it had been driven with any force it would have broken his jaw, or speared him through the back of the head. The wound had been clean, and there was no infection. But Castus could not rid his tongue of the taste of iron, the vile sensation of the lance-head penetrating his mouth.

Watching three men being flogged and then beheaded was doing nothing to improve his mood. Squinting slightly, he tried to ignore the flickering itch and the throb in his jaw, and the constant desire to spit. Behind him, his men were drawn up in silence, all of them perspiring in the midday sun with their full kit and shields. The only sounds were the regular swish and crack of the rods on the backs of the condemned men, the howls and gasps of pain. The rods were bloody in the hands of the torturers now, spattering gore with every blow.

Two of the prisoners had been soldiers of Legion I Martia; the third was from the *numerus* of Batavi. All three had been stripped of their rank and status, dishonourably discharged and sentenced to an ignominious public death. Their crime, sup-posedly, had been treason: they had been discovered while trying to set light to a storehouse of army grain and oil. Apparently two of them had confessed to being paid by agents of the tyrant to disrupt the emperor's advance. It was widely implied that they had also been responsible for informing the enemy of the plan for the assault on Segusio.

So the official story went, anyway. Castus found that he did not believe it. Most likely the men had been drunk when they were caught, and trying to steal supplies rather than destroy them. Their confessions meant nothing; a weak man under torture would tell his masters whatever they wanted to hear. Whether the rest of the army believed it or not seemed unimportant. The executions would be an example, and a deterrent. Castus had wondered whether Nigrinus might have been behind the arrests. But, no, this was too crude to be the notary's work.

At the far side of the hollow square, beyond the ranks of the Divitenses, Castus made out the figure of Aurelius Evander, commander of the field army, watching the proceedings from horseback. Had he ordered this? Did he believe the men were guilty? No doubt, Castus thought, their deaths answered some important official requirement. Perhaps they were intended to silence the rumours about treachery... *Gods*, his head hurt... *Let this be over soon.*

The prisoners were limp as the guards cut them down from the forks. Two of them looked dead already. Castus glanced away as the *speculatores* moved in with their drawn swords. In his current state, the sight of beheadings was too much to endure. He heard it, though: the chop of the blade quite distinct, three times. From his left he heard a man choke and vomit. Strange, he thought, that soldiers can watch men die in battle or in the arena and be completely unmoved, but to see their own former comrades beaten and executed was painful, sickening. He felt the pain of it himself. Perhaps these three had been traitors. Perhaps they had betrayed their oath, given aid to the enemy. Still, they could have been killed cleanly.

Finally it was done. The three corpses were dragged away by the heels, their severed heads gathered up by the torturers, and the horns wailed. A collective sigh rose from the assembled troops, a ripple of release, as if they were shaking off the weight of what they had just witnessed. One by one, the legion detachments turned and marched back towards the city, every man eager for the delights of the baths, the wine shops and the races. Out on the plain, only the forked poles remained, and the puddles of blood drying slowly into the dust.

* * *

'I've got to say,' Vitalis said, peering at the side of his face, 'I think it's an improvement...'

Castus lowered his brow.

'I mean it!' Vitalis declared, eyes wide. 'The scar, I think, distracts the eye from your oft-broken nose, your bull-like neck, your perpetual frown...'

'Get to Hades,' Castus muttered from the side of his mouth, then leaned and spat between the seats.

'Did he say something...? Ah, but I'm joking. You look fearsome! You look like a gladiator!'

Castus smiled, and felt his face aching. The ugly welt of scar tissue on his left jaw seemed to have frozen the muscles on that side; the surgeons had told him he would have a crooked smile for the rest of his life. It was still hard to speak, almost as hard to eat and drink.

It was the penultimate day of the Games of Apollo, and the great circus of Mediolanum was packed. Down on the sand, chariots and horses careered around the track in the hot sunlight. A sudden roar went up from the crowd, and from his position high on the southern curve of seats, beneath the awnings, Castus glanced down to see what had happened. For a moment the light dazzled him.

'Red team's crashed onto the barrier,' Vitalis said, jumping to his feet. He smacked his hands together. 'Nasty!'

Castus had never understood the fanatical obsession of so many men for chariot racing. It seemed immaterial to him who won or lost the race, and he suspected most people just watched it for the accidents. He had never known any women who got at all excited about it, not even Sabina, with all her passion for the delights of city life. Then again, he thought, rising in his seat to gaze over the heads of the crowd as two of the Blue and Green teams came racing round the bend in a smooth neck-to-neck arc, it was quite dramatic...

'Beat him!' Vitalis was shouting. 'Whip him! Fuck him! Come *on*, you chicken-hearted bastard!'

All around him the crowd were yelling, cheering their favourites and screaming abuse at their opponents. Volleys of noise went up from the stands, as gangs of rival supporters raised chants or rhythmic handclaps. The racing teams of Mediolanum had recently suffered a reversal in popularities: Maxentius was known to favour the Blues, and Constantine was widely rumoured to be a supporter of the Greens. Now the Blue teams were getting little support, and a lot of heckling.

Today, the rivalries of the racing factions seemed like the only feud in town. All around him Castus could see off-duty soldiers, many of them from his own legion, mingling with the civilians. They had reason enough to celebrate: it was high summer, and their emperor was everywhere victorious. Like Taurinum before it, the city of Mediolanum had thrown open its gates to the conquering new emperor. The greatest city in northern Italy, the Queen of the Plains, one of the capitals of the empire, had fallen without a single blow, and the citizens had lined the streets and clambered onto the rooftops to cheer and throw rose-petals on the imperial retinue as Constantine made his ceremonial entrance. Castus had gained only the vaguest impression of it all; the imperial *adventus* was a clash of bright colour, noise and thronging crowds, seen though a mist of fevered pain. Now the men of his legion were billeted in the city, and Castus himself had been allocated another smart townhouse as his quarters; it was the former property of a Maxentian supporter who had fled for Rome.

It was almost as if, Castus thought, the war was already won.

Despite himself, he felt the mood of the crowd lifting his spirits. His wound had depressed him; close brushes with death often had that effect. Was it only chance that he had lived? In the past he had found it easier to shrug these things off, but life now seemed both fuller and more precarious. He had so much more to lose.

But for all the enthusiasm of the city's population, the rapturous panegyrics hailing the godlike conqueror as a bringer of a new golden age, Castus knew there were plenty here who had no love for Constantine. Even less love for his army: to the cultured citizens of Mediolanum, the soldiers billeted among them must have seemed barbarians, uncouth foreigners from the edge of the world. Their streets were packed with legionaries from the far frontiers of Gaul and Britain, with swaggering warriors from the forests of Germania, drunk on their wine, filling the air with guttural barracks Latin and vomiting on the marble steps of their temples and theatres.

Castus sensed the tensions in the crowd around him, the knots of gathering threat. The city was like dry tinder, waiting for a spark. But this was the festival of Apollo, the sun god, Constantine's own protecting deity. An aspect of the great god Sol Invictus. It was only right, he told himself, to celebrate. And over in the enclosure of the imperial gallery, Constantine himself sat watching the races, a tiny figure between the white and gold pillars.

'I hear the nobilissima femina and her retinue will be arriving here soon,' Vitalis said, leaning to speak over the noise of the crowd.

'Fausta?' Castus mumbled. He had heard nothing of it.

'Fitting that the wife of the Augustus should join her noble husband, no? Besides, she spent many years in the palace here, when her father was alive.'

Mediolanum's imperial palace lay only a short distance away, flanking the circus: both had been constructed by Maximian, father of both Fausta and the tyrant, when he was senior Augustus. But every time Castus thought of Maximian, he remembered the old man's face swollen in death, the body turning slowly as it hung from the rafters of the residency in Arelate. He suppressed a quick shudder. His wound was flaring badly, and he fought the desire to scratch at it.

If Fausta was coming to Mediolanum, would Sabina be coming with her? Hard to imagine that she would remain behind in Treveris. The prospect of seeing his wife so soon, so unexpectedly, quickened Castus's heart. But he felt uneasy: why had she not written to tell him? Was she intending her arrival to be a surprise?

Unlikely. All that he knew of his wife suggested that she did not enjoy surprises. Her life had contained too much chaos, he supposed, too many reversals; now she relished routine, careful planning, order and clarity. He wondered how she would react to his appearance. Would the scar repulse her?

Leaning forward on the stone seat, he spread his knees and flexed his shoulders. The race was approaching its climax now, the remaining teams galloping up towards the curve once more before swinging round into the closing straight. All around him men were getting to their feet, waving, screaming. Vitalis had climbed up onto his seat and was stropping the air wildly, shouting to one driver or another. Unmoved by the frenzy of the crowd, Castus squeezed the wad of leaves between his back teeth, then dipped his head and spat again.

The noise crested as the winning team crossed the line, the whole stadium roaring. Then, gradually, the cheering and the shouts of victory died away, the spectators dropping back into their seats. Some looked smug, triumphant, others desolate. The Greens had won, it seemed.

'You did well?' Castus said.

'Not I,' Vitalis replied, shaking his head. 'I had money on the Whites. Their lead driver was supposed to be a wild beast. Not today, though...'

'It's all fixed anyway. Isn't it?'

Vitalis shoved at his shoulder, grinning. 'Let it never be said that you're too clever for your own good!'

They got up, joining the columns of people queuing for the exits. The imperial gallery was already deserted: the emperor must barely have stayed to see the finish of the race.

'Of course,' Vitalis said in an undertone, 'the real money's on what happens tomorrow morning. The ceremony.'

'What about it?' Castus asked. He knew what his friend meant: at dawn the following day, the last day of the games, the emperor with his chief ministers and the priests of the city would make public sacrifice to Apollo. An ox with gilded horns, two goats and a heifer. It was tradition. It was required. The smoke of sacrifice was the divine nourishment of the gods, or so he had always been told.

'There's a rumour,' said Vitalis in a conspiratorial whisper, 'that our Sacred Augustus won't attend...'

'He has to,' Castus hissed back. 'It would be sacrilege otherwise.'

'Maybe. Or maybe he just wants to avoid any more bad omens... Or maybe those Christian priests have talked him out of it. They're very opposed to *carnal sacrifice*, apparently...'

Castus remembered the scene he had witnessed in the emperor's pavilion, the night before the battle. The white-haired Christian priest leaning forward to touch the emperor: a sign perhaps, or a blessing? It could not be true: no commander who shunned the gods, who failed to give respect to the deities of Rome, could ever hope to win victory. Divine favour would desert him. More importantly, his troops would desert him.

The crush in the stalls was very great now, people shuffling along in herds towards the arches of the upper exit gates. The sun was hot, and Castus heard raised voices, tremors of violence. Without the race to focus the attention, the aggression of the crowd was turning inwards. Down in the lower stalls a few brawls had already broken out. Neither Castus nor Vitalis carried swords, just a dagger and a staff each. Both were plainly dressed, with no insignia of rank; they could have been off-duty centurions. Castus still wore the gold torque around his neck, a decoration for valour, but few seemed to notice. The circus had always bred a democratic spirit. Perhaps that was why there were so many riots at the games?

Vitalis took his arm, and Castus paused. 'You remember I said that I'd seen your wife with a man in Treveris?' Vitalis said in a low and confidential tone. Castus gave a quick nod, feeling his senses sharpening at once.

'He's here. At least, I'm fairly sure that's him...'

Castus gazed down into the milling people filling the lower stalls; at first in the light and confusion he could not make out any single figure. Then a flash of colour caught his eye. The scene leaped into sudden focus. Four slaves in sky-blue tunics flanked another man, clearing a path through the throng for their master.

'That man down there?' he said, quiet and urgent, and Vitalis nodded.

The man was moving through the meshes of the crowd with unhurried assurance. He was in his mid-thirties, perhaps, and despite the heat he was wearing a dark cape across one shoulder, richly embroidered in gold. Hawkish profile, a high forehead, receding black hair slicked with oil. Castus watched him for a moment, noting the shape of him, the way he moved. Not a fighter, but his slaves would fight for him. He captured the man's image in his mind, flicked a glance towards the exit gate, then stepped up onto the back of the curve of seats and began clambering through the crowd.

He heard Vitalis calling after him. 'Careful, brother – do nothing rash. Least, not in public!'

Men turned, shoving at him, some of them snarling abuse as he climbed between them. Dropping down onto the next row, Castus moved steadily towards the archway, glancing down every few steps to track the progress of the man in the dark cape. It would have been impossible to climb all the way down to cut him off before he reached the lower exit; Castus knew he would have to try and intercept him as he left the stadium. He had no real idea what he intended: the man was a stranger to him, and he had no evidence against him. Only the shadow of a suggestion. An intuition. What would he do if he managed to confront him? Castus was not sure. He just wanted to look the man in the eye, watch for a flicker of recognition. Then he would know.

At the arched exit gate the crowd was thick. Castus forced his way into it, using his bulk to forge a way through. Several men pushed back against him, or turned with angry stares, but one look at his expression and the raw, glowering scar twisted into his lower jaw and they moved aside. A woman with dangling earrings and a heavily powdered face screeched as he shoved past her; he heard her spit, and mumbled an apology over his shoulder. Then he was through the arch and into the dense echoing gloom beneath the stalls.

After the bright sunlight, it took a few moments for his eyes to adjust, but Castus kept moving. He shouldered his way past a knot of men – one swung a punch at him and he swatted it aside – and reached the broad stone steps. Down the flights, he doubled the corner and paced quickly across the entrance hall of the stadium. There was no flash of blue between the bodies, no sign of the man in the dark cape. Castus cursed under his breath as he moved towards the big arches that led outside: the man must have passed through the entrance hall much quicker than he had anticipated.

Squinting across the sunlit plaza on the far side of the arches, he saw the waiting litter at once. Black wood, sky-blue drapes pulled closed all around. More slaves in livery surrounded it on all sides, keeping back the crowds that spilled from the exit gates of the circus.

Castus hesitated for a moment, drawing back against the warm stones of the wall. He was scanning the crowd for his quarry, but there was no sign of him. Probably he had already left the circus, and was inside the litter now. Surely the same litter, Castus realised, that Vitalis had seen Sabina getting into, back in Treveris...

He walked fast across the plaza, steering between the thronging people. One of the liveried slaves, a big man with a shaved head, folded his arms across his chest as he noticed Castus approaching. He drew himself up, squaring his shoulders.

'I want to talk to your master,' Castus said, stepping in close to the big slave.

'Got an appointment?' the slave replied. Castus was not sure if he was joking.

'I don't need one.' He spat from the corner of his mouth, then raised his staff, pointing to the gold torque he wore at his neck. The slave's expression did not waver. Castus's intention had been only to look at the man he was following, to find out his identity; he had been determined, but still calm and detached.

Now, suddenly, he was angry. The scar on his jaw flared hot, and he felt the quickening of his blood. Other slaves were joining the shaven-headed man now, drawn by the confrontation. One blow in the face with the head of his staff, Castus thought, and the big man would go down; the slave on the right, the one with the stye in his eye, was no threat, the other he could manage, and then... He pictured himself ripping aside the drapes of the litter...

'Tribune Aurelius Castus!' a voice cried. Castus saw the big slave's eyes flick to the left, then drop in deference as he stepped back. He turned, and the man in the dark cape was directly behind him.

He was not alone. At his shoulder walked Aurelius Evander, commander of the field army, with a dozen dismounted troopers of the Schola Scutariorum surrounding them both. It was Evander who had greeted him.

'Excellency,' Castus said, touching his brow. The two men had been talking as they approached, and did not appear to have overheard his exchange with the big slave.

'I didn't know you were a man for the races, tribune,' Evander said. 'A fine victory for the Greens!'

Castus could only reply with a tight nod. The man beside Evander looked familiar now; Castus was sure he had seen him before. His brooch was set with jewels, and the heavy gold ring on his finger was shaped like a pair of leopards clutching a pearl. Not a man to fear the crowd, clearly.

'Castus here is one of the heroes of Segusio, and the battle on the road to Taurinum,' Evander was explaining to the man with an easy smile. 'It's good to see him recovered from his wound!'

The man in the dark cape did not speak, but he peered at Castus with a cool appraising glance, the most subtle of smiles. *I know you*, the look said.

'And may I introduce,' Evander said to Castus, gesturing to the man, 'his excellency Claudianus Lepidus, just arrived from Treveris. Lepidus is to be our new Master of Dispositions...'

Yes, Castus thought, he had surely seen this man before. Back at Treveris, when he had served in the Protectores: this Lepidus would have been one of the horde of officials and minor ministers who had passed continually through the marble halls, begging attendance upon the emperor. Castus had always tended to ignore civilians, but he recalled the man's face now, that hawkish profile and glossy receding hair. Clearly the man had done well for himself. Lepidus was still looking at him – the glance had lasted only a couple of heartbeats, but it was eloquent in its disdain.

Castus breathed in slowly. He wanted to kill this man, and Lepidus knew it, and did not care.

'Well, we must go,' Evander declared, taking the man by the arm and motioning towards the litter. 'Tribune, will you join us for dinner later, perhaps? I have some particularly fine squid, sent up from Genua...'

'Another time, excellency,' Castus managed to say. But Evander was already walking away, the bodyguard forming around him and Lepidus. They crossed to the litter, and one of the slaves drew aside the sky-blue drapes for them to climb inside.

Castus watched them depart, motionless in the plaza with the crowd eddying around him. He was burning with an intense feeling of humiliation. The man had as good as challenged him. And there was nothing – nothing whatsoever – that Castus could do to respond.

'I still don't believe it,' Vitalis was saying, pacing across the mosaic floor of the reception chamber. 'I mean, I suspected it… but to have it happen, or *not* happen…' The single lamp on the table threw his shadow wheeling around the painted walls. Castus just shrugged.

'Hold still, please, dominus,' Eumolpius muttered in his usual doleful tone. 'This buckle is rather tight…' The slave hissed between his teeth, then gave a last tug at the leather strap and stood back.

Castus raised his right hand. He bent his elbow, and heard the faintest whisper of polished metal, a slight creak of leather. His arm gleamed in burnished bronze, articulated curves of metal armouring him from wrist to elbow. A *manica*, it was called; Castus had seen them often enough, but had never worn one himself. It was lighter than he had expected, and not at all cumbersome. Flexing his arm, he clenched his fist a few times, then strode to the table and drew his sword. Two slashes and a stab at the air: the armour did not hinder his movements.

'He was there,' Vitalis was saying, still pacing near the door. 'We all saw him – he stood before the altar of the god with his head covered, looking like he was praying or thinking… He made the supplication of wine and incense, but when the sacrificial victims were led in, he turned and walked out of the temple. Like he was offended by the sight of them. It was… *unseemly.*'

'Completely,' Castus said. He shared Vitalis's dismay. But the emperor's failure to sacrifice to Apollo that morning was only further darkening his already black mood. The memory of his encounter with Lepidus the day before had turned ceaselessly in his mind. Castus had murdered the man a hundred times, but the thought did nothing to ease the deep anguish of his humiliation. *He is my wife's lover.* But, no, he had no proof, no evidence at all… Only the knowledge in the man's eyes, the certainty of that challenge.

'Perhaps, dominus, you would like to try the new cuirass as well?' Eumolpius said. 'I'm not sure if the shoulder armour will work with it...'

Castus nodded. The muscled cuirass was plain polished bronze, but large enough to fit his frame. Like the manica, and a great deal more weapons and armour, it had come from the garrison arsenal of Mediolanum, seized when the city surrendered. Diogenes had got in there quickly, and had managed to requisition enough to outfit sixty of Castus's front-line troops with plate cuirasses. Several of the other units had done the same, but when Legion II Britannica next took the field, they would be arrayed like gods.

'The helmet too?' Eumolpius said, as he fitted the two halves of the cuirass around Castus's torso and buckled the straps. 'I managed to find an armourer in the city to repair the buckled cheek-piece, and a goldsmith to regild it, although it's not an exact match...'

'Bring it,' Castus said, holding out his hand. For an army slave, Eumolpius made a bizarrely efficient orderly. It was almost unnatural.

While the slave fetched his helmet, he swung his arms, inhaled and filled his chest. The cuirass, and the linen arming vest beneath it with fringes of straps at waist and shoulder, felt tight. But it weighed less than a scale hauberk, he could breathe freely, and the shoulder-piece of the manica moved easily when he lifted and turned his arm. Eumolpius handed him the helmet and Castus put it on carefully, wincing as the cheek-plate touched his scar. But he felt no stab of pain.

'You look like Mars descended to the earth,' Vitalis said, leaning against the doorframe. 'You should find a mirror and admire yourself, brother!'

Castus gave him a crooked smile, then gestured to the slave to help him off with the armour. Vitalis had asked him what had happened after they had left the circus the day before, but Castus had told him little. He lost the man in the crowd, he said. Even to speak of it was painful, and felt strangely demeaning.

And soon Sabina would be joining him. Fausta and her retinue had already crossed the mountains, and were at Taurinum; Sabina, surely, was travelling with them. At least, Castus thought, she would approve of the accommodation: this requisitioned townhouse was larger, if older, than the one he rented in Treveris. It had a large pillared central courtyard, several reception chambers and a smaller private garden to one side. There was little furniture – Castus slept on the floor on his bedroll – but that could be arranged.

The thought of seeing his wife again, of confronting her about her relations with Lepidus, was unnerving. Castus had considered questioning the procurator, Metrodorus, about it beforehand, but the idea felt dirty and underhand. Far better to speak to her directly. And then what? If she confessed to infidelity he would be obliged to act, it was the law: he must divorce her, denounce her, she must be punished. It would be a public disgrace; it would be shameful. The thought of losing Sabina, and the idea that he might be accusing her unjustly, ached in his bones. Castus had no proof of his wife's guilt, and part of him desperately wanted to disbelieve it.

Vitalis had left, and Castus was sitting alone when Diogenes tapped at the doorframe, cleared his throat and saluted.

'Macer's here, dominus. With Attalus and the three prisoners.'

Castus groaned wearily. His head was aching, the side of his face itched furiously, and mosquitoes were whining in his ears. Mediolanum might be the Queen of the Plains, but it was also the kingdom of the mosquito. He swatted at his neck, clapped at the air and then studied his palm. No trace of blood.

'Show them in,' he said.

There had been a handful of disciplinary cases since the legion had taken up billets in the city. Not surprising: off-duty soldiers, civilians and lots of alcohol were a poor mix. Castus had ordered fatigue duty and ration cuts: he had never been fond of harsh discipline, whatever Macer advised, and the memory of the three men flogged and executed on the drill field a few days before was still fresh in his mind.

He seated himself heavily on his folding stool, facing the door, as Macer and the other men marched in from the courtyard. The three accused were from Attalus's century, and their centurion was accompanying them. All wore their tunics unbelted, and had suitably woeful expressions.

'Dominus,' Macer declared, standing stiffly with his baton clasped in both hands. 'Three soldiers presented for judgment! Scutio, Trocundus and Gaetulicus, all from the century of Attalus.'

Castus gazed wearily at the three men. Trocundus he knew: a veteran. The other two were newer recruits. 'What are they accused of?'

'Dominus,' said Macer, gravel in his voice, 'the owner of their lodgings accuses them of raping his wife.'

'All three of them?'

Macer nodded.

Attalus stepped forward, looking surly. In a low voice, the centurion outlined the men's exemplary service, their clean record, their military excellence. Trocundus had fought in the front line at the battle on the road to Taurinum; Gaetulicus had scaled one of the assault ladders at Segusio.

Castus felt the pressure massing in his head. His neck ached, and he wanted a drink of water. 'What have you got to say for yourselves?' he asked the accused men.

'Dominus,' said the older one, Trocundus. Clearly the leader of the trio. 'It wasn't like the man says. It wasn't rape, I mean.'

'What was it?' Castus felt his knee jumping. He forced himself to breathe slowly.

'She wanted us to do it!' the second man said. Scutio. With a jolt of appalled disbelief, Castus noticed that the man was trying to hide a smirk.

'Explain yourself.' It was all he could do the force the words out. Macer was glaring at him; Castus saw the muscle bunching in the drillmaster's jaw, his knuckles tight as he gripped his baton.

'Well, dominus, you could tell... She was always showing herself off, wearing these thin gowns that let you see everything...'

The third man was smiling to himself now. Even Attalus looked vaguely amused. Only Trocundus maintained his sober grimace.

'You could tell she wasn't getting any from her husband,' Scutio said, with something like a wink. 'Only natural she goes looking for it elsewhere. You know how it is, dominus! You leave women alone and they go wandering...'

Castus drew a long breath. Then he stood up sharply, crossed the room in three long strides, grabbed Scutio by the throat and slammed him back against the wall. With one blow he broke the man's nose with the side of his hand. Blood spattered on the painted plaster.

Behind him he could hear Macer's hiss of surprise. The soldier named Gaetulicus let out a fearful whine. Castus rammed Scutio's head against the wall again.

'You don't talk like that to me,' he said quietly. Then he released the man, letting him slide to the floor.

Turning on his heel, Castus seized Trocundus by the neck of his tunic, then kicked his leg out from under him. Trocundus dropped and lay on his back, hands lifted before him, eyes wide.

'Tribune!' Attalus cried. 'This isn't right...'

Castus just glanced at him as he strode back to the table. He felt very calm, sure of himself, as he did in the heat of battle. He picked up his sword and drew the blade from the scabbard, then turned to face the accused men. He could smell urine; one of them had pissed in his breeches.

'Dominus,' said Macer in an urgent growl. 'Control yourself.'

'You three' – Castus pointed the sword at the three rapists – 'have *disgraced* the name of soldiers.' He realised he was shouting – his words echoed back from the far wall. 'You deserve the most severe penalty, all of you! You deserve to be discharged without honour, flogged and executed, like those poor bastards on the drill field the other day...'

Scutio, the man he had struck, was curled in a protective crouch at the base of the wall, choking back tears of pain. Gaetulicus was still standing, looking faint with fear, while Trocundus lay on the floor at his feet.

'Drillmaster,' Castus said. 'When the deified Aurelian was a tribune, how did he punish rapists?'

Macer replied in a low voice. 'I believe he tied them between two bent trees, dominus... then released the trees so they were torn limb from limb.'

Castus nodded coldly, then slapped the blade into the palm of his hand. Already he could feel his anger shifting to a strange distant loathing. Not just for the three cringing prisoners either. He knew that the rage he felt sprang from a deeper well; it was personal. And he had already crossed

172

a dangerous line. Suddenly he felt very tired, very heavy. He seated himself on the stool again and laid the sword across his knees.

He would gladly have sent these men to their deaths. It would be justice. He would have killed them himself. But he knew, all too clearly he knew, that his own shame and humiliation were propelling him. He thought of the victim, some woman he would never know. Would her ruined life be improved in any way by the deaths of these men? Castus was an officer; his authority came from the emperor, and through him from the gods. His justice must not seem arbitrary, or it would be nothing but tyranny. Besides, he did not know if the morale of the troops could take another round of floggings or executions. The symmetry of the three rapists and the three men that had died on the forks was unappealing.

Exhaling, he pressed his fingers into his brow, kneading the bunched flesh. 'We are at war,' he said, thick-voiced. 'Therefore, the traditional punishment for this crime will be suspended. But all three of the accused will lose their immunities of service and be reduced to the lowest grade.'

'Dominus!' Attalus said quickly. 'I must protest – Trocundus is a twelve-year veteran, he was about to make optio...'

'Silence!' Castus said. His glare swept the room. Macer was chewing his cheek; even Diogenes, by the door, had a look of startled apprehension. 'All three will be placed on double fatigue duty for the next four months, and their rations will be cut by half. Also, they will pay an indemnity to the victim to the value of two pieces of gold per man.'

'But the men aren't paid for another month!' Attalus cried. 'They don't have that amount of coin!'

'Then the money will be taken from the funeral fund of their century.'

Attalus tightened his jaw, affronted. Castus did not care; he had not forgotten the centurion's expression of amusement moments before.

He stood up, sheathing his sword. 'Get them out of my sight,' he said. 'Dismissed!'

Macer lingered by the door as the centurion escorted his men out through the courtyard.

'What is it, drillmaster?' Castus asked with his back turned. 'You don't approve?'

'I just think you might remember the fate of the deified Aurelian,' Macer said.

Castus glanced back at him, raising an eyebrow.

'He was murdered,' the drillmaster said. 'By his own officers.' He snapped a quick salute, then turned and followed Attalus.

Diogenes came back in, bringing a couple of slaves with a sponge and water to clean the blood off the wall and the urine from the tiled floor. 'I honestly thought you were about to kill those men,' the secretary said. He still had a look of bemused fright on his face, but it was not that far from his usual expression.

'I wanted to,' Castus said in a low growl. 'They deserved to die. I wanted to hack off their heads and boot them round the room... But I need living soldiers, not dead ones.' This too, he supposed, was part of command. Knowing the limits of power, and when to hold back. Even so, he felt a cold roiling anger at what had just happened.

Send us to the battlefield, he thought. *Gods, deliver us from the temptations of leisure...*

Barely an hour had passed when he heard voices from the courtyard and an orderly from headquarters came stamping into the room, flinging a salute. Castus listened to his message with numbed surprise.

'Eumolpius!' he cried, striding from the room into the court-yard. 'Eumolpius, gather my kit...'

Seldom, he thought, had his prayers been answered so quickly.

The army was to march against Verona at first light.

CHAPTER XI

The grey-green river rushed down from the mountains and flung a tight loop around the city, protecting it on three sides. On the fourth side, massively fortified walls closed the neck of the loop, studded with drum towers. And before those walls, the emperor Constantine's triumphant advance across the plains of northern Italy had faltered and stalled.

From the edge of a plundered orchard Castus gazed at the city shimmering in the late-afternoon sun. There were twenty thousand men inside those fortifications; the ramparts bristled with spears.

'There's the bastard,' Brocchus said.

'Are you sure?' Castus squinted at the figures on the top of the wall.

'See the white draco?' Brocchus replied. 'That's his personal standard.'

Brocchus was the new eagle-bearer of Legion II Britannica. A stocky veteran with a creased face, he had served nearly twenty years in the Augusta legion in Britain. He also had extremely sharp eyes, it seemed.

The amphitheatre of Verona had originally stood outside the fortifications, but newly built walls connected it to the main circuit. It was a citadel now, an outwork of the main defences. The double row of massive arches were sealed with masonry, and a rampart had been constructed around the top. It was from that rampart, Castus now saw, that the enemy commander stood to survey the siege works around his city.

'Decent shot from a ballista could pick him off,' Rogatianus said, shading his face with a level palm.

Castus had been thinking the very same thing. Pompeianus, the commander of Verona, was Maxentius's Praetorian Prefect and leading general. Without him, the resistance in the north would surely crumble. Castus knew that Constantine's agents had been in communication with him during their stay at Mediolanum, trying to induce him to change sides. Pompeianus had stuck to his allegiance. A loyal soldier, if nothing else. Castus could respect that, but he still wished the man dead.

The march from Mediolanum had taken six days, on dead-straight roads across the widest flattest country Castus had seen since leaving the Danube. Outside Brixia they had met a force of cavalry, but the enemy horsemen had fled after the first skirmish and the infantry had just watched and cheered from their battle lines. Pressing on eastwards, they had skirted the southern shore of Lake Benacus, the water stretching away ice blue to the snow-capped mountains on the horizon. And then they had reached Verona, and the advance had ground to a halt.

Already two direct assaults on the walls had failed. Men of the Primigenia and Flavia Gallicana legions had stormed the ramparts each time with ladders, and each time they been thrown back. Casualties had been high; there had been no further attempts since. From his vantage point at the edge of the orchard, Castus watched the troops toiling in the trenches that ran across the neck of the river, hacking at the dry ground with picks and mattocks. There were scorpion catapults along the walls, and the garrison had plenty of archers; now the attackers were throwing up breastworks of fascines and felled trees to cover their own artillery. The siege was solidifying, tightening its grip.

A hundred paces from where Castus was standing, a group of engineers was adjusting the torsion drum on a heavy stone-throwing catapult. There were other machines waiting nearby, taken from the arsenals of Mediolanum, Taurinum and Segusio. Soon they would begin to add their missiles to the hail of stones and bolts that had been battering the walls of the city for days.

Taking off his cap, Castus scratched at his scalp and the nape of his neck. The mosquitoes of Verona were, unbelievably, even more vicious than those of Mediolanum. His neck, legs and the backs of his hands were covered in swollen bites. *Sweet blood*, Diogenes had told him. It seemed unlikely, but nobody else seemed to suffer as much.

If the insects loved him, many of his troops did not. Rumours of his outburst against the three condemned men, and the punishments he had given them, had spread through the legion during the march east from Mediolanum. Had he really been so unjust? Castus thought not, but he knew that soldiers had a strange and often baffling code of justice. He had shared it himself, before he had been in command. Now his legion was more divided than ever, all the unity and purpose won at Segusio and the battle before Taurinum dissipated. Centurion Attalus openly glowered in his presence, and Macer seemed to be keeping his distance, wary of how the dice might fall.

If only they could break this siege. Castus had wanted battle, movement, momentum, but instead there was only stalemate. With the legion sitting around in siege lines in the growing stink of their own latrine trenches, or forced to labour in the hot sun under the sting of the enemy artillery, dissent bred fast.

At least, he thought, the expedition of the night ahead would change that.

The river at Verona flowed too deep, the current too strong, to be forded, and the only two bridges were inside the fortifications. To the north, beyond the loop of rushing water, a low spur of hills rose to a summit directly above the riverbank. Strongly walled, it was a bridgehead for the city, and the road led east from its gates along the far side of the river, towards the Maxentian garrisons at Aquileia and Concordia. As long as that road remained open, the city could always be supplied or reinforced, and the besiegers could never hope to blockade the place.

The expedition would leave after dark, moving upstream to find a river crossing that was not screened by the enemy cavalry. Then a reverse march along the far bank and over the spur of hills to circle around the bridgehead and descend on the other side of the city, cut the road and complete the blockade.

It sounded simple, but Castus knew that it was not.

Still, he had argued hard for his own legion to be included in the expeditionary force. Anything to get them moving, and work some shape back into them. His arguments, for once, had paid off.

'Let's go,' he told Rogatianus and the eagle-bearer, and they turned and made their way back through the ripped stumps of the orchard to the legion encampment, where the men were cleaning and checking their armour and kit, their shields and mail shirts laid out across the parched grass like an armourers' fair. All of them would need to rest as much as they could before the sun went down.

The night was humid, still warm with the day's heat, but the waters of the river were cold and bracing. By the time the men of the legion clambered down the slope of the bank and began fording the torrent, the auxilia and cavalry vanguard had already established a guarded perimeter on the far side, and rigged ropes across the water to guide the troops in the darkness.

Leading his horse, probing ahead of him with a spear, Castus waded out into the river. The current tugged at his legs, then pushed at his thighs, and after a few paces he was waist-deep and shivering with the water surging around him. The riverbed was gravel and loose stones, and with every plunging step forward he felt his boots slip and skid. A few men had already fallen; one, from another unit, had been swept away downstream. Nothing could be done for him now. The crossing was supposed to be silent, but the noise of five thousand splashing, tramping men would carry for a mile down the valley. If the enemy had scouts in the area, they would soon be alerted.

Up the far bank, sliding in the rutted greasy mud, Castus hauled himself onto dry ground again. His breeches were soaked and his boots slopping, but there was no time to dry out. Pulling himself up into the saddle, he sat and watched the last of his men crossing behind him. There was no moon, and in the blackness all he could see were toiling shapes in the black water.

With the last men of the column across, they formed up on the road that followed the far bank. Shuffling and muttering, they hefted their wet kit as the centurions hissed and prodded them into line; they knew they were in enemy territory now. Castus waited, patting his horse's neck as he felt the water drain down into his boots. A rider came along the column, making hand signals to the unit commanders. *Ready to march.* No trumpets, no orders called; the column just gave a lurch and spilled into motion, the troops shunting forward until the ranks opened out and they fell into the familiar marching step.

Twelve miles back down the riverbank and across the spur above the bridgehead; they would have to cover that distance and take up their positions on the road before first light. If the men were tired, they did not show it. Every man carried fifteen days' hard rations in his shoulder bag, full armour and equipment, shields, spears and javelins. Their waterlogged boots crunched the gravelled road, and their soaked clothing squelched and dripped as they marched. But there was a sense of discipline and purpose in them now. Castus could see that even in the darkness.

Night marches were always difficult, especially with no moon to show the path ahead. Individual units could become separated or lose the route, gaps could open in the column or close suddenly and create confusion. Riding beside his marching men, Castus felt a strong sense of unreality, as if he had slipped into a dream. He dismounted, hoping that having his feet on the ground would keep him focused. Instead, as he led his horse, he found himself thinking about Sabina. Would she be in Mediolanum now? Was the other man, Lepidus, there too? Castus wondered if his wife had brought their son with her; there was little hope of seeing either of them for months now, but the possibility was tantalising even so...

With a jolt he became aware that the column ahead of him had halted. They were surely approaching the last bend that would take them within sight of the city. A shout went up from somewhere along the road, then a cry, and a horseback messenger rode past at the gallop.

'Cavalry!' somebody yelled. 'Prepare to repel cavalry!'

At once the column stiffened. Shields rattled and banged together as the men slung them from their shoulders, readied their spears and fell into two rows, facing outwards. Cursing, Castus pushed his way between them, handed the reins of his horse to the man beside him, then jogged forward up the line.

Macer had the vanguard, with the standard-bearer Brocchus. As Castus reached them he saw the troops gazing forward into the gloom. The air was thick with the smell of sweat, damp clothing, muddy boots. Ahead he could make out the faint trace of the road, empty between trees. For a moment there was only stillness, then he saw the darkness thicken into the forms of running men. The soldiers around him swung their shields to face forward, clashing them into a solid wedge.

'They're charging us!' Macer shouted. 'Javelins – ready!'

'Wait,' Castus told him, raising his hand. There were four other units ahead of them in the line of march – had they been cut off? The column must stretch for a mile in front, another mile behind; if an enemy force had managed to infiltrate between them it could be a disaster...

'Tribune,' Macer yelled in his ear, his javelin raised, 'they'll be right on top of us unless—'

'I said *wait*!' Castus seized the drillmaster's arm, dragging it down. '*Liberator!*' he called at the top of his voice. The darkness swallowed the echo. 'LIBERATOR!' he cried again.

The rush of men seemed to part, slowing and scattering before the wedge of shields and spears. Around him Castus felt, rather than saw, the javelins drawn back to throw.

Then a heavily accented voice called back. '*Strong in victory!*'

A gasp of release went through the legionaries at the correct response to the watchword. But the shields stayed up. Now the scattered men on the road ahead were gathering on the verges under the trees, appearing to congeal out of the shadows. Castus made out their bare heads, their long hair, the glint of their spears. Germanic auxilia.

'*Where is your commander?*' he hissed loudly at the nearest group.

'Here!' a voice called back. 'Who are you?'

'Second Britannica!'

The shape of a man formed from the blackness, walking carefully back down the road towards the wedge of shields, raising an open palm.

'A false alarm, I think,' the Alamannic commander said. 'My men were falling back...'

'So I see,' Castus growled. He slapped Brocchus on the shoulder, and the man raised the eagle standard. Tension flowed out of the column, and a few men snorted quiet laughter, but Castus could sense the anger behind him as the legion formed up again to march.

'Get your men out of the road,' he said to the Alamannic leader. 'We're going through them. You can fall in behind when we're past.'

He caught the brief angry intake of breath, then the man was gone.

'Fucking barbarians,' Macer said.

An hour later the column swung off the road and traced a path up the hillside above the river. Now they were out of the wood the stars were clear overhead, and the long stream of marching men felt very exposed. Mounting his horse, Castus rode on up the line, trusting Dapple to pick her way forward on the snaking path between the climbing soldiers. As he neared the summit of the ridge he heard the men ahead of him talking, hushed voices calling back to their comrades behind them.

'What's happening?' he said, sliding from the saddle. A small group of officers was standing on the summit. Even in the darkness he could pick out the gleam of their armour and ornaments.

'Castus – is that you?' Valerius Leontius, Prefect of Legion VIII Augusta and commander of the expeditionary force, peered at him as he approached, then gripped his shoulder. 'Look down there,' he said, pointing down the slope beneath them. 'And listen.'

From the summit Castus could see the city at the base of the hills, the loop of riverbank and the grid of streets marked out by pinpricks of lamplight. At the far side of the grid was a bar of darkness: the city wall, and the no man's land beyond it. And then, spreading across the plain outside the walls, the camp fires of Constantine's besieging army. At his feet, seemingly only a few hundred paces away, was the fortification of the bridgehead, the hill inside its walls rising up to a black crest of tall pines. Castus could hear nothing at first but the steady creak and stamp of the men climbing over the ridge behind him. Then, trying to ignore the noise of the marching column, he heard the other sounds, distant shouts and thin high screams carried on the night air. The clash of arms.

'They've sallied from the walls,' he said. Some of the other men around him nodded and grunted their agreement. Even as he spoke he could see the flare of fires in the gap between the city fortifications and the siege camp. 'Looks like they're burning our artillery.'

'Trying,' Leontius said grimly. He shook his head. 'All the better for us – they won't be paying so much attention to what's happening behind them!'

The prefect snapped out an order, and the gathering of officers broke up. Castus remained on the summit, standing beside his horse while he waited for his own troops to come up the track and cross the ridge. Staring at the flicker of fires down on the plain had spoilt his night vision, but it was an entrancing sight. Men were dying down there, victory and defeat hanging in the balance, all of it so far away that it was like the combat of ants. *This,* he thought, *is how the gods must feel.*

They descended the ridge, straggling down an oblique valley that brought them to the riverbank a mile beyond the bridge-head. There they formed up, stumbling, tired men falling into rank and file behind their standards, but there was no enemy force guarding the road, and the few scouts had already been scattered by their approach. The battle on the western bank of the river was over, and smoke was rising from the siege works in the pale light of the coming day. The sally had been driven back.

As the first bright rays of dawn threw their shadows across the road ahead of them, the *cornicines* of the expeditionary force sounded their horns in unison, signalling that the blockade had been accomplished. And from the far bank of the river, they heard the answering trumpets, the cheers of the main army, as the soldiers raised their arms in salute to the sun. The city remained silent, brooding behind its walls.

CHAPTER XII

'It looks almost peaceful, don't you think?' Diogenes said, the tablets in his lap apparently forgotten as he gazed across the river.

'Hmm?' Castus replied. He had been pondering the lists of provisions the secretary had been compiling; after ten days in their new camp, supplies were running low, and the foraging parties were ranging ever wider over the surrounding countryside.

'The city over there,' Diogenes said. 'Absurd to think that we are a hostile army, intent on taking the place by force.' They were sitting on folding stools on the grassy meadow that ran down from the camp fortifications to the riverside. Much cooler there than in the stifling confines of the tent, and the slight breeze from the water seemed to keep the insects at bay. For a moment Castus considered reminding his secretary of the correct form of address in the army, but let it drop. There were only two sentries standing nearby, and they were not listening. Besides, he thought, it was true. It hardly felt as though they were at war.

He would not have had it that way himself. When he looked to his right, along the curve of the riverbank, he could see the walls of the bridgehead. Just above them, inside the perimeter, rose the arcaded façade of the city theatre, the ranks of seats dug into the hillside facing the water. It looked as if the defending troops were using it as an arms depot now. One swift strike, Castus thought, and they could capture the bridgehead, storm across the bridges and take the city from the rear. It could be done – with a few thousand more men it could be done with ease. He had suggested it to Prefect Leontius, with as much respect and deference as he could manage. Leontius had been firm: they would sit tight, maintain the blockade, wait for the city's surrender.

Castus stood up, idly smacking his fist into his palm. He had never been inclined to delay, to long strategic thinking. These long summer days of siege were becoming a frustrating ordeal.

Narrowing his eyes, he looked across the river. The buildings of the city came right to the water's edge in places, unconfined by walls. The curve of houses and quays was only a long bowshot away – during the first days after their encirclement of the defences, archers had lined the banks and conducted a lengthy, and mostly fruitless, duel of arrows. Now the defenders no longer bothered to shoot at them. Instead boys leaped off the stone embankments, laughing and shouting, to swim upriver against the strong current and climb the bridge piers. Sometimes groups of civilians came down as well, to stare across the loop of the river at their besiegers. They seemed curious rather than afraid.

A few citizens of Verona had even swum across the river, escaping the city by night to join their families in the surrounding countryside. Prefect Leontius had posted sentries all along the banks to apprehend them and bring them to him for questioning. Castus never knew whether he learned anything from them. Some of the more enterprising and athletic young women of the city had taken to swimming the river too, to prostitute themselves to the soldiers. Castus imagined them swimming back afterwards, coins clasped between their teeth.

It did seem absurd, he thought, despite his loyalty to the army and the emperor. A Roman army besieging a Roman city in the heartland of Italy. At least with both banks of the river under their control the army had managed to throw a bridge of boats across, downstream from the city and anchored with heavy cables. Now the men camped on the east bank had their tents and baggage, and even a few ballistae to lob shots at the bridgehead fortifications.

'Perhaps,' said Diogenes in a distant musing tone, 'I could use this as an illustration of certain points I shall make in my treatise? Surely such disharmony offends the gods, I mean – if humanity learned to work together towards a common end—'

'Time you got back to working towards a common end,' Castus said firmly. Diogenes blinked, raised his stylus in brief salute, then went back to his tablets.

'So… eighteen pigs, dominus, twelve cows and eight hundred *modii* of grain brought in by the foragers these last two days. We're down to the last reserves of oil; we have hardtack and bread for seven more days…'

Castus yawned heavily, feeling the muscles around his scar stretch tight. He had not shaved for several days, and his jaw felt coarse with stubble. He had hoped that a beard might hide his scar, but the hair did not grow around the torn flesh. He knew it was vanity, a strange and unfamiliar urge. Once again he thought of Sabina, of his son, both of them surely now living in the house in Mediolanum… Several times he had caught himself thinking about a life beyond the army. A domestic life, as a husband and a father. He could see his son grow, raise him properly, as he had never been raised himself. His rank as a former tribune and Protector would guarantee a secure upbringing for the boy at least… But, no, he thought. It was a fantasy: his wife consorted with another man, and his future held nothing but confrontation. A familiar anger massed at the back of his head, a black frustrated rage that had no outlet, no ease.

Movement to his right caught his eye, and Castus turned to see three men passing through the camp gates. All three wore dirt-spattered tunics, and each carried a yoke across his shoulders, a brimming pail of ordure slung on both ends. The leader – Trocundus – noticed Castus watching him and pulled himself up straight, sneering. The other two disgraced legionaries could not meet his eye, but Castus felt their hostility. He forced himself to continue watching them, tracking them as they passed along the camp perimeter and down towards the riverbank below the city, until they vanished into the distant haze.

The road east from the bridgehead ran along a low causeway, lined on either side with tall cypresses, not yet cut down for firewood or construction material. Four centuries of Castus's legion were stationed there on night watch, guarding the approaches to the city across the plain from the direction of Aquileia and Concordia. Castus made sure to inspect the troops at regular intervals: there was a screen of cavalry scouts further to the east, and in the warmth of the night it was too easy for the men to grow careless. Several times he had caught sentries half-asleep at their positions.

'Where's your centurion?' he asked one group of men as they clambered hastily to their feet. They glanced around, peering along the darkened road and between the trees. Attalus's century, Castus remembered. He had seen nothing of Attalus for days.

'He was here a moment ago, tribune,' one of the soldiers said.

Castus grunted and moved on, glancing back to check the men were still on their feet, looking attentive. Across the road he doubled back through the avenue of cypresses. A fire smoked in the darkness, and he saw the shapes of men gathered around it, their voices low and carrying in the heavy night air. Not for the first time, Castus wondered whether the men talked about him around their fires and in their tents. It would not be unusual if they did, and for a moment he considered creeping closer, trying to catch what this group were saying. He thought better of it – it was not his business what the soldiers thought or believed. His only concern was keeping up a proper watch on the road: somewhere out to the east there were strong enemy garrisons, but there had been no sign or word of an advance, no attempt to relieve the besieged city.

Moving away from the road, and the glow of the fires, Castus pushed his way through the dry scrub below the causeway and stared eastwards into the night. The plain stretched away, empty under the crescent moon. No movement on the flat horizon, only the black pillars of cypresses and the low mounds of wooded copses growing around isolated farms to break the horizontals of dark land and black sky. Nevertheless, as he stared he felt a tight sensation at the nape of his neck, the familiar intuition of danger. He glanced around – nothing. A pair of crickets away in the bushes to his right was rasping loudly, and the air was thick and still.

There was a pressure in his bladder, and he took a few more steps to a thicket of bushes, unlaced his breeches and pissed into the shadows. He grinned to himself; perhaps that was all that was causing his unease? But then, as he tied his breeches again and straightened his tunic, his senses flared. A shout of warning came from the darkness away to his left, and he turned.

A shape leaped from the bushes, swinging a blow, and Castus threw his head forward and felt the rush of air over his back. Crouched low, he spun on his heel, his hand already at the grip of his sword. There were three of them – no, four – closing fast around him.

Brambles caught at his feet and he stumbled, just in time to evade the second swinging blow. They had clubs, he realised, or axe handles. Confusion still gripped him; he was acting on instinct alone, ripping his sword free of its scabbard and whirling the blade at the second attacker. A clumsy strike, but it was enough to send the man dancing back to trip and sprawl in the bushes.

Castus grabbed breath, the stunned numbness in his head fading, cold clarity rushing in. He was surrounded and out-numbered. The fourth man was hanging back, and the fallen one had not yet scrambled to his feet.

Yelling, Castus wheeled his blade, the honed steel whining through the air. His attackers were dressed in short army capes, their faces covered by scarves. *Keep moving. Keep clear of them.* He was circling sideways, sword drawn back to stab at the next man who got within his reach, but the ground was treacherous underfoot, tangled scrub and tree roots, and in the darkness he was aware only of the cloaked shapes pressing forward at him again. He saw the cold glint of a javelin head, the shaft drawn back to throw. He stabbed, the point of his blade catching in the woollen folds of a cloak and ripping free. Then he felt the ground snatch at his feet again, and he tripped and fell to one knee.

The note of a horn cut through the heavy air, high and brassy. Then another, cracked and discordant. The alarm signal. Castus heard one of the attackers gasp something to the others. *I know that voice.* The fourth man had already gone, melting back into the darkened scrub; now the other three were backing away, throwing down their clubs and turning to run. Castus was back on his feet and he charged them, slashing wildly; one of the cloaks ripped free and he saw the back of a dun-coloured tunic as the man fled.

Again the horn sounded. Castus stumbled towards it, then saw another figure in the bushes ahead of him. The man who had shouted a warning.

'Who's there?' he shouted, the scar on his jaw rippling with pain.

'Tribune.' The figure advancing towards him had his hands up. 'Valerius Felix, tribune. I saw people moving down here...'

'Gods...' Castus dropped forward, bracing himself on his knees. Tremors were running through his body, fast and hard from his gut. For a moment he felt sick; then he straightened up, sucking in air.

But now he could hear men shouting on the road, the clatter of shields and weapons. From somewhere through the trees came the noise of horses riding fast.

'Back, quick,' he said. He held his sword high as he began to run, keeping the blade clear of the bushes. Ten staggering strides and he was free of the scrub and pounding up the slope of the causeway with Felix close behind him.

On the dark road between the trees, they met a confusion of panicking men.

'Form up!' Castus shouted. 'Centurions! Form your men...!'

Where was Attalus? He should have been in command here... And then Castus realised. *The fourth man.*

A horseman appeared out of the trees to the left, blasting through the soldiers on the road like a black wind. Now there were more of them coming, a torrent of them bearing down on the disarrayed infantry, the hooves of their horses suddenly very loud on the gravel.

'Hornblower!' Castus shouted. 'Sound *prepare to repel cavalry!*'

The man was standing right next to him, and blew a deafening brass yell into Castus's right ear. Already the riders were almost upon them, scale-armoured men with horsehair plumes, mounted on powerful horses, charging out of the night. Some of the soldiers had managed to form a rough knot of shields in the middle of the road, but the horsemen just rode around them. Castus saw one man step out, shield raised, in the path of a galloping horse; he raised his spear, but the animal was on top of him before he could throw. The hooves smashed him to the ground.

Castus raised his sword above his head, wrapping his cape around his left arm. Hot breath behind him, the batter of hooves, and then Felix threw his arms around his chest and dragged him off his feet. Castus fell hard, trapping the smaller man beneath him, and the cavalry horse stepped over them both and cantered on down the road.

As he raised his head, Castus saw the whipping tail of a white draco, the horseman that rode behind it glancing back at him for a moment. Then the torrent of horsemen was gone, leaving a wrack of dying men in their wake.

'Explain to me,' Leontius said, pacing ferociously, 'what in the name of Hades happened last night?'

The prefect's whole body appeared to be glowing with rage, his flushed face making his eyes seem unnaturally blue. Not just rage, Castus knew; the man was scared.

'I've already had a message from across the river,' the prefect said, flinging out a hand towards the wall of the tent. 'The Augustus is... very disappointed in us, shall we say. *Extremely* disappointed. He threw a cup of wine at Evander, and Evander threw a cup of wine at me, in a manner of speaking. And now I'm throwing a cup of wine at you, tribune! And *what are you going to do?*'

'Nothing, dominus,' Castus said. He was standing stiffly on the matting floor of the commander's tent. Bright sunlight from outside, the sound of voices, even birdsong. And in here, the unravelling of a disaster.

'Nothing?'

'No, dominus. The responsibility lies entirely with me. I failed to attend sufficiently to the readiness of my men. They share no blame in this.'

'So you're entirely responsible,' Leontius said slowly, with sober gravity, 'for the escape of the supreme commander of the enemy forces in Italy? For letting Pompeianus break out of the city, no doubt to ride east and join his reserves at Concordia? You were supposed to be guarding the road!'

'Against advances *from* the east, dominus,' Castus said, fighting to keep the anger from his voice. 'We were attacked from behind, by surprise.'

'Yes, well,' Leontius said, frowning until his eyebrows almost covered the blue glare of his eyes. 'That was an error of our scouts... Who would have guessed that Pompeianus would leave from the far side of the bridgehead and follow exactly the same path we'd used to outflank him...? Even so. This looks bad, brother.'

It was much worse than the prefect knew, of course. Castus had mentioned nothing about being attacked by his own men moments before the enemy had ridden through their lines. Nothing about one of his own centurions apparently supporting the attack; the same centurion that was supposed to be in charge of the piquets on the road. No, he would be passing no more blame on down the ladder. Attalus he would deal with in his own time. If, that was, he had any time left...

'They say there are forty thousand men camped at Concordia,' Leontius said, rubbing his face and then fretting at his fingernails with his teeth. So it seemed his nocturnal swimmers had told him something after all, Castus guessed. 'Apparently the tyrant's ordered that Verona must not be allowed to fall. He plans to trap us against the walls of the city, no doubt. So we can expect Pompeianus back here soon, leading a relief army. The gods only know what we're going to do then...'

Leaving the tent, Castus drank in the clean fresh air and the morning sunlight. He had not slept all night, and fatigue was dulling the violent whirl of his mind. He scrubbed at the grizzled thicket of his beard: he needed to shave, and find a bath. He wanted to lie down for a very long time in a cool, shaded room.

As he walked back towards the legion lines, Macer fell into step beside him. Castus was startled: he was so weary, he had not noticed the drillmaster's approach.

'What's the damage?' he said, before the other man had spoken.

'Only five dead,' Macer said through thin lips. 'Another eleven wounded, but none badly. We didn't pay much in blood. But our reputation took a beating, tribune. The other legions are already calling us craven. There've been fights.'

'I don't doubt that,' Castus said. He would have thought the same himself.

'There's been another fatality since,' Macer said, dropping his voice to a strained stiff whisper. 'Scutio. One of your rapists. Found in the river at sun-up with his wrists slashed to the bone.'

Castus remembered the name: Scutio was the man he had struck, back at Mediolanum. That left two of them, and Attalus.

'He killed himself?'

'They tried to make it look that way. Didn't do a good job of it. You could tell from the direction of the cuts. I'd guess he had a loose mouth.'

Castus inhaled sharply through his teeth. He stopped walking, and Macer paused beside him. 'You know about what happened, then?'

Macer nodded, the leather patch he wore over his injured eye twitching as he frowned. 'If you want to do something about Attalus,' he said, 'I'll support you. They may have had a grievance, but what they did went way over the line.'

'*Over the line*?' Castus said, biting down hard on each word. He drew himself up, closing on the drillmaster until only a hand span separated them. 'You consider that trying to murder an officer in the dark, by creeping up behind him while he's having a piss... is *over the line*? Which *line* are you talking about?'

'Are you surprised they hate you? You took away everything they had – everything they'd gained since they joined the legions. You took their *honour*.'

'I'm sure they were thinking of their honour when they raped that woman in Mediolanum. We all have to face the consequences of our actions, drillmaster.'

For a moment Macer held his gaze, the anger rising in his face. Then he breathed in, tightened his lips and glanced away.

'Listen to me,' Castus growled. 'Nobody says anything more about what happened last night. You hear the slightest word about it from anybody and you shut him up quick. I've just eaten shit in that tent back there to try and save the legion's name. Now you're going to help me pull the men together. That rider we let through last night's coming back here with an army behind him. We've got a tough fight ahead of us.'

The drillmaster nodded again, his expression unflinching.

'And another thing,' Castus added, as he turned to go. 'From now on, you back me in everything I do or say. *Everything.* You're not neutral any more. Understood?'

Macer's single eye blinked once. 'Understood,' he said.

CHAPTER XIII

Across the open plain stretched the far-flung battle line. Taking two steps forward from his position in the front rank, Castus could see the cavalry moving out on the left wing, towards the edge of the high ground almost a mile away. He looked to his right and saw another mile of troops, a wall of shields and proud standards vanishing into the distant haze. An impressive sight. But when he glanced to his rear, back through the sun-shot ranks of his own legionaries, he saw only open space; the second line had already been redeployed to widen the flanks. Now the whole army was arrayed in a single shallow formation. There were no reserves, no support. Castus thought of the membrane of skin over a healing scar: if the line ruptured at any point, the whole army would be torn in half.

Behind the troops the sun was already low, shadowing the ground in front of them. The sky to the east was still filled with light, a perfect blue fading to green near the horizon. And the horizon was filled with the enemy.

'Like a sea of gold,' said Brocchus, the standard-bearer, standing at Castus's shoulder. The vast array opposite them was lit by the evening sun; the helmets and mail of the enemy soldiers burned in the hot shimmer of light, their shields were bands of glowing colour and their speartips were a forest of dancing flames. The dust stirred up by their movements hung in a low golden penumbra above their lines, and the distant cries of their officers echoed across the darkening plain.

'Why don't they move?' somebody said. 'Why don't they attack now?'

'They're waiting till the sun's gone down,' Castus said calmly. 'They don't want to advance with it in their eyes.'

'So they want to fight this battle in the dark, eh?' Brocchus laughed nervously.

No reason why not, Castus thought. They had the numbers for it: all they needed to do was keep pushing forward. But he said nothing, worried that his words would betray his apprehension.

Six days had passed since Pompeianus had slipped through the siege lines at Verona, and for all that time, sweltering in the midsummer heat, Constantine's men had been in a state of nervous tension. The news that Maxentius's general was marching back against them at the head of an army came as a relief; now at last they could move, and bring the enemy to open battle. Twenty thousand men would counter-march against Pompeianus, to confront him in the field before he could raise the siege; half that number would remain behind in the lines to keep the city garrison penned up inside the walls.

They had been so eager, Castus thought, as they had marched out of the siege lines earlier that day. Aggressively enthusiastic, urging each other on. But they had not expected to fight until the next morning. Only ten miles from the city, they had been digging their camp trenches and lighting their cooking fires when a man on a lathered horse had ridden in with the news that the enemy vanguard was already in contact with the scouts and approaching fast. Confusion ensued, men falling back into march column, or battle formation, units split up, officers missing as the horns sounded the alarm and the signal trumpets blared out *enemy in sight* and *form battle array.*

Now at least the lines were steady, the formation set, although Castus had ended up with men from at least three other units mixed in with his own.

From the lines of the opposing army came the thunder of spears clashing against shields, the noise swelling and fading ominously across the plain; a moment later, Constantine's army raised their own tumult, and for a few heartbeats it seemed to Castus as if both sides were halves of the same army, answering each other. But then he heard the booming of the Germanic war cries from along his own front line; the enemy had no answer to that.

Flexing his right arm, he felt the leather straps of the manica pull against his shoulder and the banded bronze of the armour tighten over his biceps. His cuirass, with its thick linen padding, felt unnaturally heavy on his torso. He paced slowly along the front line of his assembled men, drawing his sword and holding it high, to catch the last rays of sun.

'Second Britannica!' he cried, the muscles of his cheek dragging against the scar. 'All of you know your positions – hold to them! Keep your lines steady. *Do not yield*, and do not allow the enemy to draw you into an advance. This ground,' he shouted, swinging his sword down parallel to the front ranks, 'is where we fight. We halt their advance here. All we need to do is hold them! If we hold them, *we win...*'

He kept on along the line, repeating his hollow words, hearing them echoed back by the centurions to the men behind them. Important that the men see him and hear him at least. But he found his eyes skating over their faces, avoiding their gazes. *How many*, he thought, *know of what happened six nights ago?* Even as he shouted, he felt the dark pressure building in his chest, the grim sensation of impending disaster. *Do not think that,* he told himself. *Do not even consider it.*

They were stretched too thinly; the troops were not ready. The enemy had forced them into a battle they could not win. *Do not allow these thoughts to take hold.*

Was it age counting against him? Never before had he felt this unnerved before a fight. He had known fear, mortal dread, but never this ebb of strength and focus, this sense of gathering panic. Phobos. When he gazed across at the enemy lines he thought of his wife, and of the man Lepidus back in Mediolanum. He thought of his son growing up fatherless. He remembered that moment in the last battle when the lance had punched through his face and his mouth had filled with blood.

Turning back to face his men, Castus breathed a curse through gritted teeth. He needed to get a grip on his nerves. He needed to set an example. He found that he was facing Attalus's century: the centurion would not meet his eye, but Castus saw Trocundus and his friend glaring back at him. He breathed in, smelling dust and sweat, narrowing his gaze until the men looked away.

Now a roaring noise came rolling up the lines from the left, a swell of voices raised in acclamation. *Thank the gods,* Castus thought as he saw the imperial party cantering along the lines, the emperor mounted on a champing grey with his purple cloak billowing and the last fire of sunset glowing all around him. Slamming his sword back into its sheath, Castus threw up his arms in salute.

Constantine was calling out to the troops as he rode, the feather plumes on his jewelled helmet swaying, but his voice was almost drowned out by the fierce chanting of the men in the ranks. Castus caught only scraps of the emperor's speech.

'... before you the army of the tyrant! Destroy it and the road to Rome is clear...'

'*CONSTANTINE! CONSTANTINE! CONSTANTINE!*'
'... when the Unconquered Sun rises once more before us...
The god's light will reveal the scale of our victory!'
'*CONSTANTINE! CONSTANTINE! CONSTANTINE!*'

At least, Castus thought, there could be no doubts about their emperor's religious beliefs today. Before leaving camp at Verona, Constantine had sacrificed, publicly and lavishly, to Mars, Jupiter and Sol Invictus. In the blood of beasts and the swirl of incense he had petitioned the gods to give strength and victory to his army, and the soldiers had cheered him to the echo. The Christian priests had not been in evidence: rumour suggested they had gone back to Mediolanum in disgust.

The emperor rode on; the sound of his voice and the waves of chanting died away into the hanging plume of dust, and now all could hear the signal horns wailing across from the enemy formation, sounding the general advance. Castus felt the ripple of movement run through the lines as every man braced himself, the front ranks kneeling behind their shields, everyone readying spears and javelins. The sun was gone, the ground between the opposing armies dark, but the evening sky was still luminous blue as the enemy troops began to roll forward over the plain in their attack columns.

They came on slowly, keeping their shields up and their formations solid. Castus felt the breath catch in his throat – there were far more of them than he had thought. As they drew closer he made out the designs on the shields in the grey light of dusk; many of them were plain, but others he recognised from his years in the Danubian army: to one side was the Neptune emblem of Legion XI Claudia, to another the lion of IV Flavia. Then, with a clench of his heart, he spotted the Hercules blazon of II Herculia. Castus had served over ten years with the Herculiani, and still thought of the legion as his home, his true family. *Great Lord Sol*, he prayed, *Unconquered Sun, do not allow me to kill my brothers...*

He was relieved to see that the unit directly opposite him carried a shield he did not recognise: blue with the symbol of a wolf suckling two infants. Romulus and Remus, he thought; no doubt it was one of the newly raised legions from Rome, but there could still be many veterans in their ranks.

Steadily the distance between the armies narrowed, the Maxentians closing in with a regular step, formidably disciplined. At thirty paces the enemy columns came to a halt, dust billowing up between them. All along the Constantinian line men were hurling darts and javelins; a moment later, the barrage of missiles was returned from the enemy lines. Castus kept his head down, watching from behind the rim of his shield.

A javelin arced down to his left, and he heard a cry of pain. From the corner of his eye he saw the stricken man fall, the others surrounding him carrying him back through the ranks and another soldier taking his place at once. Castus could see that the legion was taking casualties all along the line, but the enemy were suffering too. Now the men in the rear ranks were passing fresh missiles forward. The air was filled with hissing steel.

With a bellowing shout the enemy column to the left surged forward, shields up in a wedge formation; they closed the distance to the Constantinian line with frightening speed. Castus could not see whether it was his own men or the Divitenses to their left who took the brunt of the assault, but he heard the noise: like a storm wave breaking against a cliff. The ripple of concussion passed along the line, men bunching into the shelter of their neighbour's shield, turning to stare at the clash to their left.

'Eyes front!' Castus yelled. 'Watch the men ahead of you!' He could hear the centurions repeating his words all down the line, wielding their sticks to straighten the files. But already the formation opposite was lurching into motion, another massive assault wedge bearing down on Castus and his men.

'Steady!' Castus heard himself shouting. 'Keep formation…!' His words echoed back at him from the hollow of his shield, and a heartbeat later the ground in front of him was swallowed up by the rushing wall of armoured bodies.

Castus threw his shoulder behind his shield, and the next instant felt the shock of impact. All around him men staggered back, and the noise of the collision was like a single vast crash. Distance was gone; light was gone. Castus felt spears passing over his head. His shield rim took a blow, then another, and a blade skated down the armour of his right arm. Roaring, stamping his boots into the dust for grip, he pushed forward into the lock of combat.

All along the line the mesh of shields pounded and surged, men braced in the stance of wrestlers, stabbing at each other overarm. Some men staggered and fell, down among the milling boots and kicking legs, the churning dust. Castus had no thought but to keep pushing forward against the solid tide of attackers, shoving with his shield and striking out with his spear. He felt the tip clash against shield boards and grate over mail, and when he felt a gap open he thrust forward with all the strength of his arm. He could not tell what he was striking, or whom.

Beside him a man fell; his comrades dragged the body back by the legs, and another soldier clambered forward to take his place in the line. Castus felt something moving beneath him, an enemy crawling beneath his shield. He rammed down with the rim and felt it strike the man's back, then stamped down with his boot. A moment later a spear darted forward between his knees, and he heard the man beneath him choke and die.

Two shields butted against him, and he heaved them back and punched out with his spear. A jarring impact up his arm; the spearshaft was hacked through. He hurled the stump at the enemy, then reached down for his sword. The blade grated across his cuirass, and then it was free in his hand and he was striking wildly, thrusting and cutting over the rim of his shield. A helmeted head rose before him; he stabbed it between the cheek guards and it dropped again.

The only sounds now were the grunt and hiss of breath, the battering of shields and the high clink and rasp of steel. Every time Castus sucked breath his mouth filled with dust and the stink of blood and sweat. An enemy soldier lurched forward from the mass of attackers, slamming into the wall of shields; the man swayed, his head rolling on his shoulders, and with a clench of horror Castus realised that the man was dead, a corpse held upright by the solid press of the fighting.

He was swinging blows now, hammering at the press of attackers like a blacksmith beating hot iron. He felt his blade bite into flesh, pulled and heard the scream, but did not see the man fall. Behind him his own men were pushing forward, supporting the front line with their own weight.

The enemy line gave suddenly. Castus felt the pressure on his shield slacken; he staggered, and almost fell to his knees, but somebody behind him grabbed the neck of his cuirass and hauled him back to his feet.

Gasping breath, still hefting his shield, Castus gazed at the gulf of open space opening between the lines. Already he could hear the ragged cheer going up from his own troops: the enemy were retreating; the attack had been repelled. He was grinning, and tasted blood in his mouth.

To his left he could see the front-rank man taking a step back. He was about to shout at them to hold steady, but then saw the mound of bodies piled in front of their lines. Two and three deep in places, many of the fallen were still alive, writhing and crying out. Spears flicked out from the shield wall, silencing the enemy wounded.

Only fifty paces away, Castus could see the enemy line re-forming. With a jolt of surprise he noticed that the moon was clear in the sky now, a bright white disc beaming through the haze of hanging dust. The moonlight flooded the space between the lines, picking out the fallen bodies and the bristle of spent missiles and casting the ground between them into utter darkness. The slain men appeared to be floating in a lake of ink, their upturned faces grotesquely lit, like the masks worn by actors in the theatre. Castus shuddered at the sight.

A touch on his arm, and he turned. Eumolpius was beside him, with a skin of water. Castus took the skin and tipped it, letting the water wash over his face before gulping it down.

'Thanks,' he said, and cuffed the young orderly on the shoulder. He passed the waterskin to Brocchus, then caught at Eumolpius's sleeve. 'Now run over to Macer on the left wing,' he said. 'Find out how he's doing and report back to me. Go!'

Eumolpius vanished into the press of men behind him. Glancing around, Castus saw the glint of teeth in the moonlight. He heard men laughing, joking together at what they had endured. It was not over yet, Castus knew, but he was glad. Some of the men in the front ranks had begun to shout across to the enemy, challenges and abuse, cruel laughter.

'*Come on, cocksuckers! Come and have another go!*'

'*Hey, bastards! I'm pissing on your slain!*'

Almost immediately the cries came back from the enemy horde, ringing across the black field of fallen bodies.

'*Traitors!*'

'*Barbarian scum! Fuck off back to Germania!*'

Back and forth went the screams and shouts. Castus realised that he had lost all sense of time, and had no idea how long the battle had lasted. Squinting up at the moon, he was shocked to see that several hours must have passed. From somewhere to the north there was the sound of distant fighting; the battle was still raging on the wings.

'Tribune! Messenger at the rear!'

Castus turned, handed his shield to Brocchus and began shoving his way back through the ranks. He slapped men on the shoulder as he passed, growled words of encouragement and congratulation. Several saluted him, or gripped his arms, joyful in momentary victory. By the time he moved out through the rear of the formation Castus was elated. His legs were shaking beneath him and he was breathing hard, but he felt his spirits rising warm and strong; he felt invulnerable, suddenly. He knew he could win.

A man came limping along the rear ranks, and Castus recognised him in the spill of moonlight. 'Attalus!' he cried, and strode over to the centurion. A reckless humour gripped him. 'Want to try and kill me now?' He flung out his arms. 'Go ahead and try!' Laughing, he watched the centurion shrug and turn away. But then he saw the lines of bodies laid out behind the rear ranks, the wounded and dead of his legion, and the laughter died inside him. Many of the wounded men were writhing and groaning, the surgeons moving between them.

'Castus!' Vitalis said, sliding down from the saddle beside him. 'What's your situation here?'

'We held them,' Castus replied. He realised that he was shouting. Both of them were shouting, their voices hoarse. 'They're forming up again for another try though. What's happening on the wings?'

'Our cavalry on the left have pushed back the enemy flank,' Vitalis said, 'but they've been held by their infantry reserves. We're losing ground on the right, though – can you spare any men to reinforce them down there?'

'None,' Castus told him. 'I need every man I've got here.' As he spoke he was glancing back at the formation. It looked ragged, great gaps driven through the files where men had moved up to replace the fallen in the front ranks. 'I need reinforcement myself.'

Eumolpius came jogging out of the darkness, panting.

'Macer's firm,' he gasped. 'But he needs more men.'

'We all need more men,' Castus said grimly. He gripped Vitalis by the shoulder. 'Can any be spared from the left wing? We need to hold the centre – I reckon they'll throw everything against us next time.'

Vitalis bared his teeth, staring off up the line. 'There are four centuries of the Thirtieth pulled back into reserve. I could bring one of them up to reinforce you, maybe...'

'Do it,' Castus said.

Vitalis nodded, then swung himself back into the saddle and spurred his horse into a gallop. Dust funnelled up behind him, pale grey in the moonlight.

Forward again, pushing through the ranks, Castus reached the front line and took his shield from Brocchus, then lifted his head to check the formation of his legion. They resembled a mob now, all order frayed, penned in behind the defensive wall of shields. Already Castus could hear the enemy signals, and see the vast indistinct horde opposite stirring into motion once more. Rhythmic shouts were going up, a chant, but he could not make out the words.

Seizing a fallen spear, he clashed it against the rim of his shield. Two strikes, four, and then the men around him took up the rhythm.

'BRITANNICA!' Castus yelled. 'BRITANNICA!' He felt the force of battle flowing through him again, the fighting spirit powering his blood. All along the line, men joined the chant, the clash of spears and roar of voices filling the night.

Across the darkened enemy lines, the moon lit a fluttering banner. The white draco of Pompeianus. Castus fell silent, tightening his jaw. He dropped the spear and drew his sword. Then, a moment later, the enemy let out a single vast cheer and began their charge.

They moved from the centre, forming as they ran into a blunt-headed wedge aimed directly for Castus's legion. Castus heard himself shouting, crying out the familiar commands, but everyone around him knew what was happening now: bodies tensed, feet braced, they counted their heartbeats until the shock of impact.

The force drove Castus back, the whole line buckling around him, and then there were spears darting and jabbing around his head. Pushing back upright, he shoved himself forward, feeling dead men beneath his feet. He was clambering over corpses piled knee-high. A shield rim punched against him, ringing off the manica that cased his right arm; Castus flicked his blade out and heard a yelp of pain. The men behind him were pressing at his back, and he was shouting, incoherent, as the two masses of men ground together.

He swung a blow overarm and felt his blade cut into an enemy shield; he tugged, but the sword was stuck fast. Another wrenching tug, then the weapon came free, but when he drew back his arm Castus saw only a stub of broken metal above the gilded hilt. He dropped it, reaching down into the crush beneath him for another weapon. His hands skated over the backs of fallen men, a bloodied face. Then he was crouching, his shield raised above him as he groped blindly in darkness. A sharp edge beneath his fingers; he ran his hand along it and felt a hilt, a worn grip. Closing his fist around the sword Castus surged back to his feet, but he was disorientated now. The crush swirled around him, a wild melee, and for a few moments he could not tell friend from foe. He heard somebody shouting: 'HERCULIA! HERCULIA!'

Then he saw the feathered helmets of his own men, and struck out in the other direction.

A man came pushing through the ranks beside him. Castus saw only a helmet crested with horsehair, a shouting face. 'Form a wedge on me!' the man was yelling. 'Form wedge and advance!'

Castus gaped at him for a moment. '*Who are you?*' he screamed. 'Get back in line!'

But the man was already ploughing his shield into the mass of the enemy. There were more men behind him, shoving their way up through the ranks. But not enough of them, Castus thought. Not enough to make a difference.

'Hold your positions!' he bellowed into the clattering din. 'Hold steady!'

The man with the horsehair plume was still pushing forward, the line stretching in his wake as some of the front-rank men obeyed his command. With a stab of shock, Castus realised that he had recognised the man: the infantryman's helmet had confused him, but suddenly he was certain. '*Gods below!*' he said under his breath.

'Brocchus!' he cried, glancing around him. There was no sign of the eagle-bearer. 'Brocchus! Hold the men back – keep the formation steady!'

'Tribune.' A figure staggered up beside him, grasping his arm. Rogatianus's dark face was almost invisible behind the nasal bar of his helmet. 'Tribune... was that...?'

Castus nodded, teeth clenched. He could see the horsehair plume swaying over the enemy ranks, the armoured figure of the emperor hacking a path into the heart of the opposing formation. Ice filled his veins, and he remembered the battle in the forests of Germania years before, Constantine's mad horseback charge across the flooded valley at the barbarian fortifications... It was happening again. It was happening again, and there was nothing he could do to stop it...

'We have to get him back!' he shouted to Rogatianus, and the centurion nodded sharply. 'Form two files of your men behind me, quickly – shields to the front and we go!'

Already the enemy formation, thrown into turmoil by the sudden foray, was massing again, pressing forward to seal off the emperor and his band of followers. Castus felt the jostle of men at his back, the clash and rattle of locking shields. Then he swung his hand up, a dead man's sword lifted high, and yelled the order to advance.

At once the enemy closed around them, spears hedging them on all sides. Castus wielded his shield like a weapon, smashing aside bodies, punching the boss into the faces of men ahead of him. When he looked up he saw the horsehair plume still dancing in the moonlight. Beyond it, far beyond it over the massed gleaming helmets of the enemy, waved the white draco of the enemy commander.

The mad bastard, Castus thought. *He wants to fight his way through to Pompeianus...*

Fury surged through him, and a roar burst from his throat as he fought. All of this was about Constantine. The emperor's glory, the emperor's victory. The men whose corpses Castus stamped underfoot had died for that. The lines of dead and wounded sprawled behind the legion lines had fallen for that. Reeling on his feet, still battling forward, Castus felt a sensation of hatred flooding him. Who was this man, this emperor, to order such slaughter? For so many years Castus had followed the man, saluted and acclaimed him, bled for him, fought his battles, killed his opponents. He had risked everything, and laid a path for Constantine in the blood of other men. Only now, lost in the frenzied mesh of battle, did his heart recoil from that truth.

'*Constantine!*' he screamed, and he did not know if it was a battle cry or a curse.

There was no sign of the horsehair plume now, but when the mass of soldiers ahead of him fell back for a moment Castus saw the body sprawled across a mound of the slain. He yelled again, plunging forward; Rogatianus was right behind him, with a knot of other Britannica men, and the enemy were falling away from them.

'Shields around me!' Castus called over his shoulder. A last few strides, swinging his blade, and he stood over Constantine's body. The emperor was wounded, but was still moving, trying to stand.

'Rogatianus – two of yours to help carry him.'

A javelin smacked into his shield; another flicked over his shoulder. His men had formed a ring, surrounding the fallen emperor. When he looked down Castus saw Rogatianus on his knees, a javelin jutting from his neck. He cried out, but the centurion had already dropped at his feet.

Throwing down his shield, Castus seized Constantine under the arms and wrestled him upright. The emperor was soaked in blood: his own, or the blood of other men, Castus could not tell.

'Forward,' the emperor gasped, staggering on his feet. 'We must go forward.'

Castus seized him by the shoulders. 'No!' he shouted, spit spraying from his mouth. 'Listen to me, you insane idiot – you're killing my men! How many more do you want to die? Back to the lines – *now*!'

Dragging the emperor behind him with one hand, sword levelled in the other, he turned and began fighting his way back to safety. Rogatianus's few surviving men raised their shields around him, and together they beat a path through the enemy.

Chaos all around them, shouting men falling back, others pressing forward. Castus could feel hot blood coursing down his body inside the bind of his cuirass; he had a cut on his neck that he had not noticed. Behind him the emperor was still staggering, head down. The noise of battle had become a constant rumble and hiss, like the hoarse breathing of a giant. Blades clashed and flickered in the moonlight, but Castus felt numb, heedless of the danger all around him, intent only on forcing himself forward.

Then, ahead of him, the enemy ranks opened and he saw the wall of sun-wheel shields. He was shouting, the words ripping from his throat, men tumbling out of the line to surround him and draw him back between them.

Then the shields closed around him, and he was safe in the heart of the battle once more.

The field was rutted with the dead. The sun was still below the eastern horizon, but there was light enough in the sky to make out the corpses lying in mounds on the blackened grass. Castus walked slowly, stepping across the bodies, and with every step he felt his boots sink into the blood-soaked ground.

He had no idea how long the fighting had lasted, or truly when it had finished. The men in the battle lines had been too exhausted to cheer; they had just sunk to their knees among the bodies of their fallen comrades. Still the slaughter had continued, even after the messengers had ridden across the field with news of the victory. Hundreds, perhaps thousands more of the Maxentian soldiers had died, either trying to retreat or in desperate refusal to surrender. Pompeianus had been found dead on the field, Castus had heard, surrounded by the men of his bodyguard. He had seen nothing of Constantine after dragging him out of the battle.

Far across the field in the slow leak of daylight, Castus could see other parties moving among the bodies. Some were soldiers, searching for their fallen comrades, others were civilians who had appeared from the surrounding villages to loot the dead. A patrol of cavalry passed, their horse, stepping warily among the corpses. Castus raised his hand in tired salute; it had been the cavalry who had won the fight in the end, breaking the enemy's right wing and rolling up their flank.

Exhaling, Castus felt the ache in his body, the slow churn of nausea in his belly. He was still wearing armour, his dented helmet clasped beneath his arm, and a thick pad of bandages tied against his neck. How many men had he lost? He had known many battlefields, but none quite like this. None where most of the fallen were Roman soldiers.

'Dominus!' Eumolpius cried from away to his left, raising a fallen shield. Castus made out the sun-wheel emblem, distinct in the greyness. 'There are more here,' the orderly called. 'This was our position, I think...'

Castus nodded, then strode over to join him. He had not been sure where his legion had been placed, but now he saw it plainly. The dead were piled in front like a low uneven rampart, and spilled away behind.

'Stack up some shields here as a marker,' Castus said. 'Then run back to the lines and fetch the stretcher parties.'

Already he could see surgeons and army slaves moving around between the bodies, kneeling beside some with bandages and water flasks, shaking their heads over others. Pacing heavily, Castus followed the line that his legion had held.

It was getting lighter now, and he could make out the faces. He forced himself to look at them, to remember their names. Fifty paces on and he paused, staring down at the choked knot of bodies sprawled together at his feet.

Salvianus, he thought. The young Christian recruit lay on his back, his face blank and oddly peaceful, sightless eyes rolled upwards in death. Beside him, lying against the piled corpses of other men, was Trocundus. Castus could not tell which of the two had fallen first, but their outflung hands were almost touching, as if they had reached out and found some unlikely companionship in death.

Castus breathed deeply, feeling the pressure in his chest. He had seen so many dead men; it should hardly matter to him. But when he raised his blood-crusted hand to his face he felt tears well from his eyes. Tired, he thought. Exhausted. He forced himself to turn away from the bodies and continue along the line.

A flash of gold, down in the muck of dust and blood. Castus stooped, groaning with the effort, and picked up the hilt of his broken sword. He was surprised nobody else had taken it yet: the gilding alone was worth a good price. He stuck it through his belt, then turned to gaze out over the plain.

'Brother,' a voice called weakly. 'Brother – you got water?'

Castus paced forward, peering into the gloom. The fallen soldier lay a short distance away, propped on one elbow. Even as he approached, Castus could tell he was from the opposing army. He could also tell that the man was dying; one of his legs had been almost sheared off, and he was lying in a congealing pool of his own blood. It was amazing he was still conscious.

'Fucking parched,' the soldier managed to say. Castus knelt down beside him, feeling the blood soaking the knee of his breeches. He pulled a flask from his belt and held it to the soldier's lips.

'Wine!' the man said, after sucking down a mouthful. He grinned, let out a shuddering gasp, then drank again. 'Now that's decent of you, brother...'

Castus recognised his accent. Pannonian, like his own. He could not see the fallen man's shield, but he knew where he was from.

'Herculiani?' he said. The soldier nodded, then tipped his head back with a groaning sigh.

'I was ten years in the Second Herculia,' Castus told him, and his voice caught as he spoke. 'Primus's century, then Dexter's. Ever heard of them?'

The soldier blinked, and his eyes seemed to clear a little. 'Valerius Dexter I know,' he said. 'He's a tribune now, so they say. Haven't seen him in years.'

'How come you're here?'

The soldier stirred, then gasped in pain. Castus took him by the shoulder to support him. He could smell the blood all around him.

'Came down with Galerius,' the soldier said. 'Six years ago, was it? Whole detachment went over to Maxentius... He's the emperor in Rome, so we said he... must be the proper one to support. Right?'

Castus snorted a laugh, then lifted the flask for the man to drink again. It seemed the only help he could offer.

216

'So what about you? How'd you end up fighting for Constan-thingy?'

'Long story,' Castus said in a breath. He wondered if he might somehow save the soldier, carry him to a surgeon; he glanced around for a slave he could call to help him. But no – the man's life was ebbing fast. Even to move him would kill him.

'Go on, then,' the soldier said. 'I've got all the time in the world...' A shudder racked him, and he tensed. 'Ah!' he cried. 'No, I haven't... ha ha!' He was laughing through clenched teeth, still grinning.

Castus felt his own body shaking, tremors of cold running through his limbs, as if the man's pain were soaking into him. He could not speak.

'Oh, well,' the dying man said. 'They're all the same, eh? You follow yours, I follow mine, but they're all fucking bastards when all's done...' His face had turned grey, and his brow was beaded with sweat. 'Hey,' he said, the words seeming to leak from him. 'Is it true your one's turned Christian? That's what we heard...'

'I don't know about that,' Castus replied. He was holding the dying soldier to his chest now, feeling the slow creep of death.

'Ah,' the soldier said again. 'Well... reckon I'm done, brother. Can't feel a thing... Give my regards to the old Danube, if you get that far... How about another drop of that wine, eh?'

Castus lifted the flask to the man's mouth, his hand trembl-ing. The soldier's lips did not move. He gave a last twitch, and then the light faded from his eyes.

Easing the body down, Castus knelt for a few moments. A sudden shudder locked his shoulders, and his chest heaved against the breastplate of his cuirass. He drew another breath, then hauled himself to his feet. Away across the plain, the first rays of sun were lighting the sky.

* * *

Vitalis met him as he strode back into the legion camp. Castus could see men looking at him, muttering words to each other. He assumed it was because he was covered in blood.

'Did you lose your mind?' Vitalis hissed, grabbing him by the shoulder.

Castus stared at him, then shook himself free and walked on. Vitalis fell into step beside him.

'What were you thinking?' the other officer said in a low voice. 'I mean... the heat of battle's one thing... but that's no excuse!'

Ahead of him Castus could see the command tent already raised, horses and men gathered around it. Diogenes was there, with Brocchus and Modestus. They turned to stare at him as he approached, their faces blank.

'What's happening?' Castus said as they parted before him. Nobody spoke. He pushed past them and on into the tent.

'Aurelius Castus,' a voice said. A young man, a staff officer by the look of him, was leaning against the folding table. Macer stood beside him, with a couple of orderlies. The young man straightened up.

'By the sacred order of the emperor, Constantine Augustus,' he said, 'you are hereby relieved of the command of the Second Britannica Legion. Aelius Vitalis will take command in your place.'

Castus blinked, feeling the air rush from his body. He looked at Macer, and the old drillmaster shook his head sadly and turned away.

Taking the gilded sword hilt from his belt, Castus tossed it onto the floor. Then he turned and walked out of the tent, into the clean morning sunlight.

'I'm sorry, brother,' Vitalis said from behind him.

CHAPTER XIV

The oval of the old amphitheatre resembled a gaping mouth, filled with broken teeth. Amidst the heaps of fallen masonry and the scarred stonework, nearly ten thousand prisoners from the defeated army filled the bowl of seats and the open space of the former arena. Stripped of their weapons, armour and belts, they sat in huddles, dressed only in their loose tunics. Archers lined the parapets above them, but the prisoners seldom glanced upwards. They seemed more intent on keeping out of the direct glare of the sun.

Stepping from the dark archway high in the upper tiers, Castus heard the iron gate swing closed behind him and the key grate in the lock. Slowly, hands clasped at the base of his spine, he descended the steps between the tiers of seating. Two soldiers walked behind him, armed with spears, but none of the defeated men made any hostile move towards him. Some just stared as he passed; a few of them hissed abuse. On their faces Castus saw anger, humiliation, tired resentment.

He shared their feelings. Since his command had been taken from him he had felt all of those emotions. He was still an officer, but he had no fixed role in the army now; he was a tribunus vacans, a supernumerary, available for any duties that nobody else wanted.

This was such a duty. His task was not difficult, but neither was it honourable. Many of the prisoners were wounded, and flies swarmed around them. Cooking fires sent grey smoke swirling between the huddled bodies, and the air stank of stale sweat, urine and excrement.

Following the curve of seats around to the eastern gateway, Castus mounted the steps to the podium. He could see the mass of men shifting and stirring, many gathering on the open space below him, others keeping their distance. Most of them were from the garrison of the city, which had surrendered as soon as news had come of the battle, but some had been captured on the field and marched back here under heavy guard. Standing up before them, feet braced, he stuck his thumbs in his belt.

'Soldiers,' he called out in his best parade-ground voice. He saw with vague pleasure the flinch of pride that ran through them, the instinctive stiffening of posture, the vestiges of military discipline. Castus waited for them to settle, then addressed them.

'You are defeated men. You have lost your honour. But you are still Romans, still soldiers.' The words felt stiff and awkward in his mouth. Truly he hated this job. The mass of prisoners gazed up at him blankly.

'You have the opportunity to redeem yourselves,' he went on. 'All you have to do is walk through this gate below me.' He gestured downwards at the shadowed archway beside the podium, where a strong force of guards waited. 'Walk through there, and declare your willingness to serve in the army of Constantine Augustus. Your service under the tyrant Maxentius will be forgiven, and you will be able to take up arms once more and stand proudly under the standards of our legions.'

He paused, trying to make himself smile. The scar on his jaw gave him an unfriendly look, he knew.

'Get to Hades, you lying Pannonian fuck,' one of the prisoners called out. 'And take your *Constantine Augustus* with you!'

'Give us food!' another shouted, and a chorus of agreement
followed.

Castus glowered down at them, setting his teeth and drawing
up his heavy shoulders. The two soldiers behind him edged
forward nervously, but Castus knew there was no real threat.
The archers all around the parapets already had arrows nocked
on their bowstrings; any prisoners attempting an attack would
be shot down at once.

'You will get all the provisions you want if you agree to
serve,' he called out. 'Just take the oath of allegiance, and you
will be restored to the dignity of soldiers and receive full pay
and allowances.'

Already he could see knots of men sloping forward, many
looking ashamed of themselves, and vanishing into the archway
beneath him. There were scuffles breaking out, some men trying
to restrain their comrades from leaving.

'Think on it!' Castus cried. 'I'll be back here tomorrow to
repeat the offer!'

With a shudder of relief, he stepped down from the podium.
How much longer, Castus wondered, would the last hard core
be kept in this place? Several thousand had already gone over
to Constantine's side, but thousands remained. What would
be done with them? He had already had more than enough of
hectoring them like this; personally, he would rather die than
betray his oath. Encouraging other men to do so sickened him.

As he climbed back up towards the barred exit gate on the
upper tiers, Castus saw a group of prisoners blocking the steps
above him. Hard-looking men, most of them in bloodstained
tunics. They stared coldly at him as he approached.

'Clear the path,' one of the guards behind him growled,

raising the butt of his spear. One of the prisoners stood up, clearly the leader of this little group. He was thin and muscular, with a bald, sunburnt skull and a scrubby rust-coloured beard.

'Name and rank, soldier,' Castus said.

The red-bearded man stuck out his chest, his hand going to a sword hilt that was not there. 'Claudius Sergianus,' he said. 'Centurion, Ninth Praetorian Cohort.'

Castus sniffed, nodded. 'Got something to say to me?' At the periphery of his vision he could make out the shapes of archers silhouetted on the parapet above him.

Sergianus tipped his head back, giving Castus a lean and unblinking stare.

'Me and my boys won't turn traitor for you, or anybody,' he said. 'You can go and tell your emperor that.' He made a kissing sound with his teeth, then spat on the stone steps.

'Can't say I blame you,' Castus said. He climbed another two steps, until he was level with the centurion. 'Right. You've said your bit. Now get out of my way.'

The centurion flicked his gaze between Castus and the spears of the men behind him. Castus knew what he was thinking. He saw the challenge die in Sergianus's eyes, and the prisoner stepped back.

Climbing the steps to the gate, the sun hot on his neck, Castus tried to appear calm and unconcerned. Only when the iron gate had swung closed again and he was in the cool darkness of the tunnel beneath the stalls did he allow the angry tension to shudder through him.

'It's impossible, as I've told you before.'

'Dominus – did you even pass on the message?'

'Listen to me. *He will not receive you.* The Augustus isn't even here at the moment – he's gone to a villa on Lake Benacus. Leave it, Castus...'

Leontius was reclining on a couch in his quarters, eating grapes. He appeared grander these days, Castus noticed. His valiant command of the left infantry flank during the battle had gained him a promise of promotion; now, with Evander leading half the army eastwards to besiege Aquileia, Leontius had been left in effective command of the troops at Verona.

'Dominus,' Castus said, uncomfortable with pleading, 'if I could just be allowed to see the Augustus once... apologise to him...'

'Apologise?' Leontius said, incredulous. 'Brother – what apology could ever be acceptable? You're lucky you only lost your legion – you could have lost your head!'

'So what was I supposed to do?' Castus said angrily. He had refused the offer of a chair, and remained standing. 'Leave him to die in the middle of the battle?'

Leontius winced, scrubbing at his bristling eyebrows with a thumb. 'Not only,' he said, pained, 'did you lay hands upon the sacred person of the emperor. You also screamed abuse at him, and refused his order to advance!'

'The order of a madman, in the circumstances. I saved his life.'

'Brother, please. You do not accuse the Invincible Augustus of being a madman, or a... what was it? *Insane idiot!*'

Castus frowned. Had Constantine himself remembered that remark? It seemed incredible. Perhaps the emperor was just so unaccustomed to abuse it had stuck with him? His guts churned with acid heat.

'Give it time,' Leontius said, slumping back on the couch. 'The emperor is tired. We're all tired... This campaign's taking its toll. Nobody's even sure if we're going to march against Rome this autumn or remain here in the north until next spring. We lost nearly four thousand dead or maimed in the battle – the enemy lost four times as many, but even so. Now the men are going down with campaign fever... They're puking and shitting themselves to death.'

Castus grunted. He had heard the rumours. 'That bad, eh?' he said.

'Worse. There are stories going around that Maxentius has cursed the army. That the fever's caused by a magic wind sent from Rome! As if we needed that...' Leontius laughed grimly. 'A man like you,' he went on in a more placatory tone, 'will always be needed, sooner or later. Just keep your head down and wait until the time's right. Then I'll do what I can for you.'

Castus exhaled, letting his shoulders drop. 'Just don't send me back into that amphitheatre,' he said, glancing towards the bar of hot light at the tent door. 'Give me some other duty. Even supervising the latrines...'

'Ah, the amphitheatre...' Leontius shrugged. 'Yes, you've probably done as much as you can there. The gods know what we'll do with the rest of the prisoners. There's talk of forging their swords into manacles – I don't even know if that's possible...' He paused, popping another grape into his mouth and chewing thoughtfully. 'Why not go back to Mediolanum for a while?' he said. 'Your wife's there, isn't she? I can write you an order to, I don't know, check the arsenals or something.'

Sabina, thought Castus. And Lepidus too. But he nodded, mumbled his thanks.

'Take some of these grapes before you go. They'll be too ripe to eat soon. Everything's going rotten in this heat...'

* * *

Castus made the journey in two days, riding in a fast two-horse carriage of the imperial despatch service. He stayed a night in Brixia, and reached Mediolanum early the next evening. All the way he had tried not to think what would happen when he saw Sabina again, tried not to imagine what he would say, or what her reply might be. Let it happen, he thought. Let the dice fall.

He was already in a state of barely subdued anger as he arrived at the house. The evening light was warm, and the street stank of hot drains. He banged on the door, then announced himself to the startled porter. Slaves conducted him into the vestibule and fussed around him, bringing water to wash the dust of the road from his face and slippers for his feet. He was glowering as he marched through the doors into the pillared central courtyard.

'Dominus!' cried the procurator, Metrodorus, raising his hands. 'You grace us with an unexpected visit!'

'Don't worry,' Castus said, 'I won't be needing much, Just have some food prepared and the water heated – I need a proper wash.' He had seen the fear in the procurator's eyes at once; the man was almost trembling with nerves.

'At once, dominus, at once...'

Castus seated himself on the low wall between the courtyard pillars. He unpinned his cloak and tossed it aside. Metrodorus was still bobbing about nervously, with a look of unctuous concern on his face. His fingers were greasy and he had food on his tunic; clearly he had been disturbed over his evening meal. Castus did not care. He found that he disliked the man more than ever.

'Bring wine for the dominus!' Metrodorus snapped at the two slaves standing slack-jawed by the entranceway. 'And have the furnace and the oven lit! Summon the cook!'

Glancing around while the slaves dashed to their duties, Castus quickly judged that his wife was not at home. Through the open doors he could see furniture in some of the rooms; Sabina had clearly closed up the house in Treveris and moved everything down here. How much, Castus wondered vaguely, would that have cost? There was a gilded cage hanging in one corner of the courtyard, between the pillars. Inside, a silent and disconsolate-looking songbird. Had Sabina perhaps intended that as a hint?

'Come with me,' Castus told the procurator as he stood up. He strode towards the main reception chamber, with Metrodorus bobbing behind him. The sense of angry urgency that had propelled him all the way from Verona had shifted now; he felt unnaturally calm. He knew the mood was deceptive; it was similar to the intensely charged stillness he sometimes felt before a fight.

There was still a faint smudge of blood on the plastered wall of the reception chamber, where Castus had smashed the nose of the soldier accused of rape. He wondered whether Sabina had ever noticed it there. It looked brown now, unidentifiable. Walking to the recessed apse at the back of the room, Castus ordered Metrodorus to dismiss the slave attendants and close the doors. The light retreated at the creak of the hinges, and shadow filled the chamber.

'Where is my wife?' Castus said, turning to confront the procurator.

Metrodorus swallowed hard, but stood his ground. 'She left five days ago, or perhaps six,' he said. 'She disliked the heat in the city, and said she was going to a villa in the hills, or perhaps somewhere near Comum – she was not clear...'

'She went with the emperor's wife? Or was she alone?'

'Ah, no, dominus... that is, I believe...'

Castus closed the distance between them in three strides and seized the procurator by the front of his tunic, bunching the cloth into his fist and hauling the man up onto his toes. 'Tell me the truth,' he said through bared teeth. 'All of it.'

'With a man!' Metrodorus stammered. 'She went with a man, forgive me!' Sweat beaded his face, glimmering in the faint light.

'Which man? His *name?*'

'I do not know! He... sent his slaves here with a litter. I have never seen him... But he is a man of wealth, a powerful minister, I believe...'

'These slaves wore livery? Light blue tunics?'

Metrodorus nodded quickly. 'Dominus, I... I thought you *knew!*'

It took a moment for the man's suggestion to register. Then Castus roared, hurling the procurator away from him. Metrodorus staggered sideways, collided with the wall and slid to the floor, raising his hands before him.

'*How long?*'

'For many months...' Metrodorus said, struggling to speak. 'Since we were in Treveris, perhaps even since the winter...'

'Why didn't you *tell* me?'

Castus was advancing on the man with clenched fists. Metrodorus quailed back against the wall. From somewhere inside him he summoned a vestige of courage.

'With all respect, dominus... it was not my job! I am your procurator. I oversee the affairs of your household...' He winced at the unfortunate phrase. 'The financial matters, the... domestic economy. I am not here to report on your wife's behaviour!'

'Report now,' Castus said, grinding out the words. 'How would you describe my wife's *behaviour?*' He wanted to hear it all. The bitter truth, which he could no longer pretend to ignore.

'The domina Sabina...' Metrodorus got to his feet and straightened his tunic. There was a hard look in his eyes now, the pouched flesh of his cheeks tightening. 'She has disgraced you. She has abused your household and acted like a courtesan. It is my opinion that she is no better than a common whore.'

Castus stood in the centre of the room, clenching and relaxing his fists. He wanted to destroy something. The procurator's words hung in the air, and he knew he could kill the man without thinking. But pain was flashing through his mind, and he felt a black gulf opening inside him, a sinking sense of weakness and futility. Violence had been his answer to so much, but it would solve nothing now.

'Get out,' he told the procurator. ' I don't want to see you again.'

As he moved through the house Castus noticed everyone shrinking away from him. Slaves turned quickly as he approached, vanishing through doorways or just pressing themselves up against walls. Nobody wanted to look at him. They were afraid, he knew. Dull with anger and grief, he recalled stories of slave-owners flogging their entire households for some supposed failing.

In the dining room there was a simple meal laid out, and he ate standing, hardly conscious of what he was doing, tasting nothing. Fantasies of vengeance flickered through his mind as he dipped bread into olive oil: he could find this villa in the hills, or near Comum, or wherever it was. He could kill them, kill them both... But he knew it was hopeless. He had lost everything. His legion, his honour, and now his wife too.

A faint cry came from outside. *My son*, he thought suddenly, pausing as he raised a piece of bread. *How could I have forgotten my son?*

Cursing to himself, he threw down the bread and stalked quickly from the room. Of course Sabina would not have taken the child with her; he should have known that at once, but his mind had been fogged with other concerns. The courtyard outside was suffused with warm evening light, and Castus stood for a moment glancing around – he still felt like a stranger here – before he heard the cry again. It had come from the small garden court at the side of the house.

Stepping through the gateway into the coolness beneath the brick colonnade, he saw the figure of a woman in a plain green dress, walking slowly as she clasped a large bundle to her shoulder. The blonde woman, he realised, the barbarian nursemaid, carrying his son. She was whispering to the child, soothing him with words in her own language. As she turned the corner of the colonnade she noticed Castus and tensed, cupping the back of the child's head as if to protect it.

'Don't speak loudly,' she whispered, in her accented Latin.

Castus moved a little further into the garden court, feeling the sense of slow shadowed tranquillity easing his mind slightly. Leaning against one of the brick pillars, he waited for the woman to draw nearer.

'Sabbi was sleeping, but the noise woke him,' the slave said, sitting down carefully on a bench against the far wall, the baby cradled in her lap. The child was quiet now; he lifted a hand from inside the shawl that wrapped him, and Castus saw the woman put the tip of her finger into his mouth. *Sabinus*, he thought. The male form of his wife's name seemed all the more inappropriate for the boy now. He must be almost exactly a year old, Castus realised. Hardly a baby at all, although he still looked so small and fragile cradled in the woman's lap. Leaning forward, Castus saw the dark silky hair covering the child's head, the soft pink eyelids.

'You want to hold him?' the nurse asked.

'No!' Castus said quickly. He folded his arms. He felt calmer, strangely at ease now, but he knew the desolate rage was still inside him. He had the terrible sensation that he would injure his son somehow if he touched him.

'I remember you, I think,' he said. The woman raised her head, and her eyes appeared to gain focus. She was perhaps a year or two younger than Sabina, with blonde hair pinned up loosely, a broad forehead and a deeply dimpled chin. She did not smile, and there was a sharp clarity in her blue eyes that Castus found slightly unnerving. He had never been comfortable in female company. But this woman, at least, was not afraid to look at him.

'Perhaps I too remember you,' she said, then looked down at the child again.

'You're of the Bructeri? It was summer, four years ago, I think...'

'I remember,' the woman said again, her words clipped. She did not look up. 'You came to my country, you burned my village, you murdered my people, killed my husband and took me from my child. Yes, I remember.'

Castus had pushed himself away from the pillar and was standing upright, his muscles drawn taut. He stared at the woman, at his son cradled in her lap. He could feel the heavy pulse of blood in his neck, the urge to leap forward and take the child from her. With a deep breath, he forced himself to ease back.

'What's your name?' he said.

'Elpidia. My name is Elpidia.'

'That's a slave name. What's your real name?'

She looked up at him, slow and suspicious. 'Ganna,' she told him.

'How did you come to be here?' He knew he was speaking curtly, the way a master addressed a slave. He had a strong sense that he should keep his distance from this woman.

'When your army destroyed my home,' she said, 'I was taken to a market and sold, like an animal. A woman bought me. She was old, and not unkind. In her household I learned your language, and I was there two years.'

'And then?'

'The old woman was sick. She needed money to pay the doctors, so she sent me back to the market. My next master was a cruel man.'

'He mistreated you?'

'He beat me every day, and every other night he raped me.'

The woman's voice had not changed, still that same accented monotone, as if she was completely unconcerned. Such things happened often enough, Castus knew. Most men with female slaves used them for sex. He had heard people joke about it; the act did not even count as adultery. But he had never heard a slave speak of it. He eased himself down against the pillar to squat facing her.

'Then what?' he said, almost grunting the words.

'Later I was pregnant, and he left me alone. I waited eight months, then I took just enough poison to kill the unborn child.'

Castus started forward, the breath choking in his throat.

'It was better that way,' she said with sudden fervour, returning his stare. 'I would not give birth to a slave! I sent the life back to the gods, to be reborn in freedom.'

The child stirred in Ganna's lap and let out a sleepy cry, and she stroked his cheek and then put her finger in his mouth again. With the breath tight in his chest, Castus nodded for her to continue.

'That was last autumn,' Ganna said. 'My master never knew. It was an inconvenience for him to lose property, that was all. So he sold me, and I came here.'

Castus braced his arms against his knees.

'You must hate Romans,' he said quietly.

'Of course. All Romans are murderers.'

'My son is Roman,' he growled at her. 'If you ever—'

She let out a snort of laughter, cutting him off. 'If I harm him? Sabbi is a child. All children are innocent. Of course I will always protect him from harm. I would never hurt him.'

'And when he grows up?'

The flesh between her eyebrows puckered into a frown. 'When he grows up,' Ganna said, gently rocking the child in her arms, 'you will teach him to be an honourable Roman soldier, like you. A *killer.*'

Castus held her gaze for a moment, then glanced away. He could hardly blame the woman. He would have felt the same, in her position. But still it was a shock to hear a slave express their bitterness and pride so openly.

'Who was your old master?' he asked in a low growl. 'Did you ever see him again?'

'Of course. I saw him often. He is the man your wife goes with now.'

Castus drew a sharp breath, his stomach clenching. 'Lepidus?'

He saw the woman shudder quickly and nod.

'You know where he is now?'

'No,' Ganna replied. 'Just that she has gone with him. You people think slaves are like furniture. You forget we have ears. But he has some hold over her, I think.'

Despite all that he had heard, all that he knew, Castus still could not fully believe that Sabina had simply deserted him. He told himself he was being foolish, grasping for hope when there was none, but the woman's words spun in his mind. Braced against the pillar, he stared into the darkness.

'You learn some truths as a slave,' Ganna told him quietly. 'You learn that some things you cannot change. They are outside your power. These things you must endure.'

'What else?' Castus said.

'That you must be patient,' the woman said, dipping her head to attend to the child. 'Be patient, and guard your strength. So when the chance comes to act, you are ready.'

PART THREE

CHAPTER XV

Northern Italy, September AD *312*

The two men sat on folding stools in uncomfortable silence. There were no lamps, nobody around to bring lamps, and the large chamber was becoming increasingly dim. The men did not move; both of them wore the heavy embroidered robes and insignia of members of the Roman Senate. They were not accustomed to fetching and carrying things for themselves.

As the darkness increased so did their discomfort. Both tried to appear unconcerned, maintaining their dignified composure, but each flicked a glance towards the doorway when he thought the other was not looking. How long had they been sitting here now? An hour? Had they been forgotten? Where were the slaves? It was past time for dinner...

Eventually, when the far corners and the high ceiling had almost vanished into the gloom, the man concealed in the passageway outside cleared his throat and paced quietly into the chamber. The two men on the stools suppressed their jolts of surprise.

'At last!' one of them said.

'Who are you?' the other demanded.

The newcomer had an unprepossessing look, his clothes drab and very plain, his thin face and bowl-cut hair almost deliberately bland.

'Greetings, *clarissimi*,' the man said, with the touch of a smile. 'I am Julius Nigrinus, Tribune of Notaries. I'm most sorry for having kept you for so long...'

Nigrinus was not sorry at all; he had spent quite a while in the passageway, observing them from the shadows and enjoying their discomfort.

'But why are you sitting in the dark?' he said in a bemused tone; then he turned to the far doorway. 'Lights!' he called. At once a pair of slaves walked in carrying lamps on tall tripods, which they placed on either side of the seated men. A third slave brought a stool for Nigrinus, and he settled himself upon it, facing them. The two senators pulled themselves together, peering at him warily.

They were not, Nigrinus thought, very attractive specimens of the ancient Roman aristocracy: the 'conscript fathers', as senators liked to call themselves. Both were prestigious enough, one a former praetor and the other a former deputy consul, and their names advertised the length and weight of their lineage. Lucius Turranius Venustus Gratianus, one was called. The other was Quintus Aurelius Cornificius Gordianus. Nigrinus himself cared nothing for lineage, or prestige. His own father, after all, had been born a slave.

'We have been waiting here for a considerable amount of time!' announced Gratianus. He was a large man, fleshy and bulbous, with a small chin bobbing between pendulous jowls. The other senator, Gordianus, was long-limbed and stiff, with a head like a block of wood and a forbidding scowl.

'And we placed ourselves in considerable danger coming here too,' Gordianus said. 'May I remind you that we are senior members of the Roman Senate? I had expected that I would be given an audience with Constantine immediately!'

'Ah, yes,' Nigrinus said, with the slightest smirk of apology. 'The emperor, you understand, has many pressing engagements. The ongoing war against the tyrant of Rome occupies almost all of his time, and he is currently with his troops. But I assure you that he will be happy to meet with you as soon as he can.'

This was not actually true, Nigrinus reminded himself. The emperor Constantine was at that point little more than a hundred yards away, in another wing of the villa, enjoying a late supper with his military commanders and drinking a very great quantity of wine. But there was no need for these men to know that.

The two senators were among a dozen or so wealthy individuals, most of them with significant property in the north, who had so far slipped away from Rome and travelled to Verona or Mediolanum to present themselves to Constantine. Most, Nigrinus considered, were like them: convinced of their own importance, full of the perils of their journey, surprised that they were not received with rapturous praise by the emperor himself. Instead, all had been accommodated in isolation, and brought separately to this villa on the shores of Lake Benacus to be questioned. All of them, Nigrinus knew, had networks of family and dependants left in the capital, ready to vouch for them if the course of war swung the other way.

Gordianus and Gratianus had apparently crossed the Apennines to the Adriatic coast and paid a fisherman to take them up to Ravenna, then a donkey-driver to conduct them safely to Verona. They claimed that they had been threatened with death by Maxentius, their property seized, their wives imprisoned. Perhaps some of it was even true. Still, it amused Nigrinus to think of the flabby Gratianus and the inflexible Gordianus hunched in a stinking fishing boat, trying to maintain their dignity amid the nets and tackle.

'Anyway, since we have some time to wait,' he said, 'perhaps you could tell me something of the situation in Rome at the moment?'

Gratianus cleared his throat and pursed his lips a few times, clearly ill at ease speaking to someone of such inferior standing. Gordianus just maintained his wooden frown and waited for his colleague to say something.

'The tyrant redoubles his depredations daily,' Gratianus said, shrugging his round shoulders. 'So many of the best people have now been attacked, accused of false crimes and had their property seized that whole areas of the city resemble a desert, with nothing but boarded-up houses and armed guards on every corner!'

'Really?' Nigrinus said, finding the claim hard to believe. 'And yet so few of your fellow conscript fathers have chosen to flee the city and join the party of Constantine. Are they held in severe bondage, perhaps?'

Gordianus raised both eyebrows. 'A senator of Rome will only abandon the eternal city under the greatest duress!' he said. 'I and my esteemed colleague here travel as... spokesmen for our fellows. Ambassadors, you might say.'

'Indeed,' Nigrinus said, with a mollifying smile. He had long made it his business to train his eye in detecting signs of duplicity in the human expression. But even a child could have seen that the men before him were concealing their true motives. The ancient Senate of Rome had long been a political backwater; the senators still held their old ceremonial offices, but successive emperors had very sensibly robbed them of any executive power. It was, however, a backwater populated by extremely wealthy men. The richest men in the world, in fact. These two before him, Nigrinus knew, were probably worth their weight in gold, which in the case of Gratianus in particular was a considerable sum.

No, he thought, the elite of Rome did not really care which emperor claimed power over them. The Senate had been among the first to acclaim Maxentius as emperor when he had seized power with the help of the Praetorians six years before. If they despised him now, it was only because he had failed to live up to their expectations. What mattered to them was the maintenance of their wealth, the protection of their property and the respect paid to their dignity. Perhaps Maxentius really was making life difficult for them: he had certainly executed a few senators in recent years. But more likely these so-called conscript fathers were just keeping a foot in both camps, making sure they had men placed to take advantage of victory, whoever it looked like the victor might be.

And it's my job, Nigrinus thought, *to steer them in the direction of the right man.*

'How are the populace of Rome disposed towards the tyrant and his government, would you say?' he asked, careful to keep his questions respectful.

The two senators exchanged another quick glance. 'The mob are fickle as usual,' Gordianus said. 'A few years back there were riots in the streets. Domitius Alexander had seized power in Africa and cut off the grain supply, and famine was a real possibility. Now the tyrant's soldiers have defeated the rebellion, the grain flows and all is well—'

'In fact his granaries are full to overflowing!' Gratianus broke in. 'And yet still he extorts money from the aristocracy, to pay his troops and bribe the populace with games and shows!'

'How appalling,' Nigrinus said.

'He's a great one for festivals,' Gordianus continued. 'In fact, he's invented half a dozen new ones, in honour of Mars and the Dioscuri, even his dead son Romulus – imagine naming one's son after the founder of Rome – and then declaring him Consul at the age of five...!'

'He uses his purloined wealth to fill the city with new buildings,' Gratianus said. 'There are construction sites everywhere. In summer the dust and noise are intolerable... Apparently he wishes to be remembered as the founder of a new Roman era!'

'Yes, well,' Nigrinus broke in. 'This is all very interesting... but it sounds from what you're saying that Maxentius is making himself quite popular. Are there any – besides yourselves and your fellow senators – who oppose him? The Christians, perhaps?'

'Them?' said Gratianus. 'Oh no, they're quite fond of him. When they're not fighting among themselves, that is... He does still hold a lot of their property, seized by his father during the Persecutions. But they had so very much to begin with, you see...'

'The Roman people love those who love them back,' Gordianus said in a tone of great gravity. 'As I say, the plebs are easily swayed. The city *collegia*, the trade guilds that is, the circus factions, the burial societies: all can be bought, if the price is right.'

'But then, forgive my ignorance,' Nigrinus said, leaning forward slightly, 'if the members of the Senate wish to be rid of the tyrant, why do they not simply *pay* the people to overthrow him?'

Gratianus pursed his lips again: his expression of mild pique, Nigrinus supposed. 'It is beneath the dignity of the Senate to bribe the populace!' he declared. 'Besides, it would set a bad precedent.'

'Absolutely,' his colleague added. 'And how could we know if our expenditure would be worthwhile? Maxentius has a vast army camped in and around Rome. He has rebuilt the

Praetorian Guard to full strength using drafts from his Illyrian detachments, and enrolled six new legions from Italy and Africa. The walls of the city are powerful, and have already repelled two imperial field armies sent against them. If we back your man Constantine, and he loses, we would all suffer!'

'And even if he were successful,' said Gratianus, 'could we guarantee that he would uphold our honours? We could merely be swapping one oppressive ruler for another.'

So here it is, Nigrinus thought. A simple bargain – that was why these men had come here. *One hand washes another.*

'I really think, you know,' Gratianus went on, 'that these are matters we should discuss with Constantine himself, face to face. Rather than with... a subordinate.'

Nigrinus managed a pale smile, consoling himself by wondering how this fat senator would fare under torture. There was always the chance the man was a spy, after all: civil wars bred traitors like a corpse bred maggots. But that would hardly send the right message.

'Certainly you are correct,' he said, hiding his annoyance with an ingratiating gesture. 'And, I assure you, the Augustus will be happy to speak with you some time... very soon.'

He got up, excusing himself and pacing silently from the chamber. What the senators had told him only confirmed what he already suspected: that despite the glib words spoken in Constantine's camp, Maxentius still enjoyed widespread support. A few victories in the north would not be enough to shake the allegiance of the Roman people. And to judge from the prisoners taken after the recent battle, many of the tyrant's soldiers were still firm in their loyalties too. Half of the prisoners had agreed to change sides, but the rest had not. Only two days before, there had been a riot in the amphitheatre at Verona where they were being held, and in the confusion nearly a hundred had escaped; the fugitives had still not been rounded up.

No, Nigrinus thought to himself: Maxentius was in a strong position. The walls of Rome were formidable, and if defended by a large enough garrison Constantine would be powerless against them. Verona had halted him, and Aquileia was still holding out against Evander. If the tyrant chose simply to sit in his palace and wait out a siege, he could well win...

Was it worth it? Nigrinus often found himself considering this question. In private, even in secret, he saw little to commend Constantine over Maxentius. One of them had to win: their ambitions would not allow compromise. But it seemed immaterial which of them came out on top. All so wasteful, Nigrinus thought. So inefficient. If he were to conduct a war, the fighting would be over before it even began. His enemies would all be discreetly killed in their beds, before the first trumpet had sounded. But such things would not accord with Roman honour.

If only he had a reliable agent in Rome itself. Someone who could report accurately on what was happening there, who could intervene and shape events. Ideally somebody placed very close to the tyrant's court, or to the other powerful groups in the city. But there was nobody that Nigrinus could trust in that way. He was acting blindly, having to piece together what was happening through the biased and self-serving narratives of men like Gratianus and Gordianus... It was intolerable.

Loitering in the dark passage, he peered back through the doorway into the chamber behind him. The two senators were still seated, waiting for something to happen, somebody to conduct them to their lodgings, their dinners, the emperor himself. The lamps guttered: Nigrinus had purposely cut the wicks very short, and they were almost burnt out.

If you want something done, he told himself, best do it yourself. Or find somebody expendable, who asked no questions, and get them to do it for you... The method had worked for him the past. But already his mind was working, spinning schemes, composing the plausible-sounding story he could feed to his superiors. *Yes,* he thought, *yes, it just might work...*

In the room, first one lamp went out and then the other. Nigrinus edged back down the corridor, smiling as he heard to the voices of the two senators echoing through the darkness, their angry demands turning to nervous confusion, and then to panic.

CHAPTER XVI

The night was hot and close, and there was a cricket rasping in the garden outside his sleeping chamber. Noise, too, from a nearby house: flute music and voices, snatches of laughter. Castus lay awake, sweating under a single sheet, alert for the high whine of mosquitoes.

He wondered what the men he had left at Verona were doing now. Had Modestus been promoted to centurion in place of Rogatianus? How was Diogenes faring under a new tribune? And what about Macer – was he pleased that Castus had gone? Once again the familiar sense of loss flooded through him. Over these last six months, Castus had come to regard the Second Britannica as his home. The men of the legion, even those that clearly resented and despised him, were his family. He belonged with them. He belonged with the army. Thumping at the bolster beneath his head, he closed his eyes and tried to force himself into sleep.

No use. He sat up, throwing off the damp sheet. Pulling a loincloth around his hips, he paced out into the garden court, calling in a low voice for the slave who usually slept under the colonnade. There was no reply, only the cricket rasping from the darkened bushes; the court was deserted in the yellow moonlight. Barefoot on the warm tiles, Castus crossed to the low wall between the pillars, stepped across it and sat down facing the garden. The night air was soft on his skin, but his body felt stiff and ached with tense frustration.

A footstep behind him, and he turned quickly. The barbarian slave was standing in the shadowed gateway from the main courtyard.

'Where's the child?' Castus asked.

'He's sleeping. Dorcas is with him. The other nurse.'

The woman advanced into the court, her bare feet silent, and leaned against one of the pillars in a patch of moonlight. Her hair was loose, her expression solemn. 'It's too warm here,' she said. 'In my country it's never like this.'

Castus nodded, rubbing at his scalp and feeling the prickle of sweat. At least the flute music had stopped now.

'You cannot sleep?' the woman said. Her voice was softer, he noticed. Her accent less harsh.

'Too much on my mind.' It occurred to Castus that it was unusual to be talking like this with one of his slaves, a nurse-maid, a barbarian at that. He sensed the rest of the household sleeping around him, the quiet city empty under the moon. Only the insects were awake.

Quietly the woman paced over to stand behind him; he tensed, flinching as she laid her palms on his shoulders.

'You are wounded,' she said.

'This?' He lifted a hand and brushed the scar on his jaw. 'It's nothing.'

'Not that,' she said. Her fingers pressed into his flesh, squeezing at the hard muscle. She put her thumbs on either side of his spine and began massaging his shoulders and back. Castus was surprised at the strength in her hands. After a moment of resistance he let his head fall forward and relaxed. He felt the knots of his body begin to ease.

'You said you have a son?' he muttered.

'Yes. Back in my homeland.' Her hands were still working, kneading at his shoulders. 'If he lives, he will be six years now.'

'What will happen to him?' Castus felt his words slowing, thickening.

'He will grow to be a strong young man,' Ganna whispered. 'A great warrior.'

Castus smiled. A great warrior who would kill many Romans, no doubt... He thought of his own son, of Sabinus; over the last few days at Mediolanum he had seen more of the boy. At least the child seemed to recognise him now, and did not recoil from his attempts at fatherly attention.

As Ganna massaged his shoulders, he noticed something on her wrist: a simple blue glass bead on a leather thong.

'What's this?' he said, flicking lightly at the bead. It was scratched with faint symbols or words.

'An old woman I knew gave it to me, a cook in my first house,' she said. 'It's a charm. It protects me from evil.'

Has it worked? he thought. But he remembered what she had told him of her former master, and said nothing. Her palms tightened around the muscles of his neck, her thumbs still kneading at his spine. Castus could feel the weight of her body pressed against his back, her hair against his shoulder as she leaned closer over him.

'When will you go back to your war?' she asked.

'Whenever my war calls for me.'

She bent forward, her hair falling to shadow her face, and her breath was warm and soft on his skin of his neck. He felt strangely vulnerable, and a disturbing sensation of tenderness was running through him.

'You should take me with you, and your son,' she whispered. Her fingers lightly traced the scarred welt on his jaw. 'Then

Sabbi can see his father leading his warriors, and I can make sure you don't get injured again.'

Castus reached up, and his hand found the nape of her neck. Twisting, he drew her down to him and kissed her hard on the mouth.

For two heartbeats they were locked together, then he stood up abruptly and took her in his arms. Confusion and desire coiled through him. As he ran his palm down her back he felt the stipple of old whip-scars through the thin fabric of her tunic.

'I don't want to be like your old master,' he said.

'No, you're not. Slaves must do what their master commands. But in my heart I am a free woman, and I decide what I want.' She kissed him again, and he felt her smiling. What god, he thought, had allowed him this?

But then a child's cry drifted through from the far wing of the house, and the other nurse began calling Ganna's name. Her slave name: *El-pi-di-ahhh!*

She stepped away, neatly evading Castus's reaching hand, and without another glance she strode barefoot through the darkened gateway.

Castus woke to the sound of voices from the outer courtyard. It was daylight, and the slanted shadow on the wall of his sleeping chamber told him that the second hour of the morning had already passed. He cleared his throat, stretched, then threw himself to one side and stood up off the bed in one smooth motion. The flex of his limbs pleased him; he was still supple, after so many indolent days. Scrubbing at his head and his unshaven jaw, he paced out into the colonnade of the garden court.

'Tribune Aurelius Castus?' The figure at the gateway of the court wore the dusty cape and boots of a military despatch rider. Castus realised that he was still completely naked, but he could not retreat back into his room and fetch a tunic. He just nodded, with a curt grunt.

'Message for you, dominus,' the rider said, offering a slim folded tablet. The man had a disapproving look on his face, which Castus found quite understandable; what sort of military officer was still lounging around naked in bed at this hour?

'Thank you,' he said, taking the tablet. He called for one of the slaves to take the man to the reception room and give him food and drink, then retreated into his chamber. Dropping the tablet on the side table, he drank a cup of warm water and dressed himself quickly in tunic and slippers. Already his mind felt focused, his body tight with anticipation. He had noticed the wax seal that closed the tablet, the imprint of the imperial sigil.

Out in the garden court again, he sat down on the wall between the pillars, broke the seal and peered at the message inked on the wood. He was glad the despatch rider was not there to see him puzzling over the letters. But it was simple enough, and after he had read it out loud to himself, slowly, there could be no doubt.

He was to present himself at the Villa Decentiana, on Lake Benacus, at the earliest available moment. Castus knew the place; he had passed it on the march to Verona, and on the journey back west. He knew that the emperor was staying there.

'Philo!' he called, summoning the slave who currently acted as his orderly. 'Philo – hot water and a razor! Pack my clothes and bags, pack everything...!'

He was on his feet, pacing back and forth between the pillars and the door of his chamber. He wanted to run, or dance. He wanted to set off immediately. Instead he turned, and his wild lopsided grin slipped as he saw Ganna stepping through into the court, carrying his son at her shoulder. On her face, sober regret mingled with pride.

'You are going back to your war?' she said.

Castus nodded. 'If the gods will it,' he said.

She stepped forward, holding the child out in her arms. 'Take him,' she said.

Clumsily, Castus reached out and took his son from her. He still did not feel comfortable holding the child, the soft wrapped weight so delicate in his arms, but at least now the boy looked up at him with an expression of recognition, even of pleasure. Castus felt the side of his mouth twitch into a smile again.

Ganna slipped off the leather thong with its blue glass bead. As Castus stood holding the boy, she tied it around his right wrist.

'For protection,' she said. 'You need it more than I.'

Exactly two days later, Castus stood waiting in an antechamber of the Villa Decentiana, gazing out through an open window at the dark blue waters of Lake Benacus and the distant mountains glowing in the September sun. He was still dusty and saddle-sore from his journey, and since his arrival he had gained no idea of the reason for the summons, or who had issued it. The emperor was nowhere in evidence. Castus stood easily, chewing slightly at the ridge of scar tissue inside his cheek and trying to subdue the sense of trapped irritation fluttering in his chest.

The slave beside the far doorway cleared his throat, and Castus nodded, paced heavily across the chamber and stepped through into the next room.

'The distinguished Aurelius Castus, tribunus vacans,' the slave intoned, then closed the door firmly behind him.

There were five men seated on the couches at the far end of the room, with a stool set before them. Castus saluted, then crossed to the stool and sat down. One of the faces he recognised at once: the vigorous-looking white-haired Christian priest that Castus had seen speaking to the emperor in his tent. A moment later, with an unpleasant sense of premonition, he noticed that another of the men was the notary Julius Nigrinus.

'Greetings, tribune,' said the man seated at the centre of the group, with a papery smile. He was the oldest of them, plainly dressed but with an air of importance. For a moment the group appeared to be studying Castus, saying nothing.

'Well, he doesn't look like a spy!' the priest said.

'All the better,' commented the old man. 'Tell me, tribune,' he went on, 'have you ever been to Rome?'

'No, dominus.' Castus felt his scarred jaw itching. The sense of subterfuge and conspiracy in the room was almost palpable, and he liked it not one bit.

'Good, good,' the old man said. 'You do know, however, that many of the tyrant's soldiers come from the Danubian territories, just as you do? Rome at present is full of Pannonians and Moesians, it seems.'

Castus just nodded, frowning. The five men on the couches appeared to be conducting a silent conversation in slight shifts of expression alone.

'Domini,' he said, with heavy emphasis. 'I was summoned here for some purpose, I think?'

The old man gave his fragile smile again. 'Forgive us, yes,' he said. 'First, you should know who we are. My name is Flavius Ummidius, and I am First Secretary of the Corps of Notaries of the Sacred Augustus. My colleague Nigrinus I believe you already know.'

Nigrinus inclined his head in greeting. Castus felt his guts tense, and managed a tight nod in reply.

'Here on my left is his excellency Burrius Agrippinus, *princeps* of the *agentes in rebus*, and on my right the esteemed Bishop of Corduba, Hosius. With the bishop you see one of his young deacons, Stephanus.'

Christians at a meeting of imperial ministers? Castus hid his unease. The young man beside the bishop had a fervent stare, slightly bulbous eyes and a small, pursed mouth.

'As to our purpose in summoning you here,' Ummidius went on, 'we have a certain matter in which you may be able to assist us, and in so doing assist yourself!'

Did this man, Castus wondered, always speak like this? He forced himself to pay attention, and pick out the meaning from the circling politeness of the words.

'Some days ago, a young man arrived here from Rome. His name is Publius Pomponius Bassus Pudentianus, and he is the son of a senator recently proscribed by the tyrant. He left the capital with the stated intention of travelling to his family's estates in Sardinia, but instead sailed north and then travelled here to offer his services to the Sacred Augustus Constantine. It is our intention that Pudentianus travel back to Rome, with certain verbal messages and assurances to the members of the Senate that might aid in winning them to our cause.'

'Young men of the aristocracy,' said Agrippinus, the head of the agentes in rebus, 'never travel without a retinue. Slaves, bodyguards, attendants... So we have an opportunity to infiltrate a number of our own people into Rome, to gather intelligence and make contact with dissident factions in the city.'

'The most important task of the mission,' Ummidius said, 'would be to undermine the tyrant's bases of support, by any means available. He will be less inclined to try and wait out a siege if he thinks the city populace may turn against him. We can defeat him in open battle, but if he remains behind the walls of Rome, well...'

Castus grunted in affirmation; Verona and now Aquileia were demonstrating how difficult sieges could be. It seemed a good enough plan. But the idea that he had a part to play in it seemed ominous. He glanced at Nigrinus: this, he knew, was his doing.

'We thought, perhaps,' Ummidius went on, 'that you would be especially effective in liaising with the tyrant's soldiers, bearing in mind your common origin. Perhaps determining their dispositions, their morale and the strength of their loyalty. Even sowing the seeds of unrest among them...?'

It was the amphitheatre at Verona again, Castus thought. On a massive scale. Every muscle in his body felt tense, and he was struggling to keep his expression neutral. This was insane; it was a death sentence. More importantly, it was also extremely dishonourable. For a tribune of the Roman army, a man who held the rank of ducenarius of the Corps of Protectores, to conceal his true identity was bad enough; to do so in order to try to incite disloyalty and mutiny was even worse.

'You would be travelling with several others, of course,' Agrippinus said. 'Stephanus here will accompany the group. Once in the city he will endeavour to make contact with the Christian leaders of Rome and assure them of Constantine's regard for their faith. Also, Julius Nigrinus will be going, in the guise of the young man's secretary. He will carry letters of credit to raise funds in our interest, and coordinate negotiations with the Senate and with the city factions.'

Nigrinus was saying nothing, but Castus recognised all too easily the attitude of nervous excitement concealed by the man's blank expression. Several times already he had found himself trapped in the notary's schemes. Each time, men had died. Castus would rather have throttled Nigrinus with his bare hands than agree to go along with another of his intricately unpleasant projects.

'What role would I be expected to play, then?'

'We thought you would make a convincing bodyguard for Pudentianus,' said Ummidius. 'A former gladiator, perhaps, from the Carthage arena; that would explain your battle scars, of course. And as a freedman, you would be immune from conscription into the tyrant's army, which would be inconvenient!'

A couple of the men laughed. Castus did not.

'You don't have to agree now,' Agrippinus said. 'Although we'll need your answer by the end of the day. The mission is set to depart imminently; Julius Nigrinus would be able to brief you further, if you accept. I would add that a service of this nature would certainly commend you to our Augustus, and serve to wipe away any... lingering taint on your reputation.'

'If, on the other hand, you decline it,' Ummidius added, 'I'm afraid that the highly confidential nature of what we have told you would mean that you could not be further employed until the tyrant is defeated. In fact, you would be obliged to remain under house arrest, for security purposes.'

Castus sat up straight on the stool, but felt his body reeling with what he had been told. Two avenues of possibility lay before him: on the one hand, ignominy and virtual imprisonment; on the other, a desperate and dishonourable mission into the heart of the enemy camp, under the direction of a man he detested. Neither seemed appealing.

'Take a few hours to consider,' Agrippinus said. 'If you need them.'

* * *

Castus was sitting on the steps of the outer portico when Nigrinus found him, watching the last of the sun lighting the snow-capped mountains on the far shore of the lake. Fishermen were dragging their boats up the stony beach below the villa – at least, Castus assumed they were fishermen. In his current mood he could almost believe them to be undercover agentes in rebus.

'I can quite understand,' the plain-looking notary said as he leaned against a pillar of the portico, 'why you would be dubious about this proposal.'

'Was it your idea?' Castus said, glancing around at him.

Nigrinus was gazing out at the lake. 'I made a few suggestions,' he said. 'I would add that, although the more political aspects of the situation would be under my control, you would have total freedom of action. I would not be giving you orders, I mean.'

Castus was not sure if the comment was intended to be conciliatory. Surely Nigrinus knew of the bad blood between them. The very great quantity of blood spilled between them over the years.

'I sometimes wonder,' Nigrinus went on in a blandly musing tone, 'what a man might do if, say, he got close enough to the tyrant to strike a mortal blow...'

'Don't even think about it,' Castus said, shuddering as he understood the implication.

'I'm only imagining.' Nigrinus smiled. 'But it's intriguing, no? One man, one blow, and this whole war could end. All those lives saved! You saw the field that morning after the battle. Thousands of dead and injured. All of them Roman soldiers. How many more must die, do you think?'

Castus made no reply. His jaw was set tight, and the gap in his back teeth ached with the pressure.

'Ah, but you think such an act would be dishonourable, I suppose?' Nigrinus said quietly. 'Perhaps. Far more honourable for thousands to be slaughtered in battle than for a tyrant to be struck down in his own palace...'

'If this is what you're thinking, forget it. I won't be your executioner.'

Nigrinus spread his hands, still smiling. His voice had a sibilant quality; Castus thought of a snake's tongue, dryly flickering.

'That's a shame,' the notary said. 'I doubt the gods would be displeased. It could hardly be said that Maxentius is an honourable man, after all. He is... fond of luxury, they say. A rather sordid individual, a sensualist. And a debaucher, who has dishonoured many women. Your wife among them, in fact...'

'What did you say?' Castus turned sharply, rising to a crouch. He saw Nigrinus's expression of pleasure, heard the faint rasp of his laughter.

'Oh, yes – although I'm sure the domina Sabina has never told you of that particular episode!'

'When?' Castus demanded. '*How...?*' His mind reeled and dived; he knew the notary was entrapping him, probably even lying, but he was snared. Nigrinus clearly knew it too.

Castus stood up, stepping towards the man, but the notary did not flinch.

'It happened in Rome, years ago,' Nigrinus said. 'Soon after your wife's first marriage. She would have been seventeen, eighteen... Around the time of the Persecution edicts, I suppose. I don't know how willingly she went with him – but it must be hard to refuse the son of the senior Augustus of the west!'

'How do you know about this?' Castus was telling himself to draw back, relax, refuse the bait. But the notary's words had struck at his weakest spot.

'Oh, I have my sources. They say Maxentius made her perform some very humiliating acts. Sexually, I mean. Things you'd blush to ask of a whore, let alone a senator's daughter. Why, they say he even made her—'

'Enough!' Castus cried. He paced across to the inner wall of the portico, then back again. Nigrinus watched him, as a man watched a trapped animal. *I could do this now*, Castus thought. *Kill him, as I've wanted to do for so many years...* But that would truly be the end. He would never see his son again, never see his wife, or Ganna.

'If you happened to find yourself close to Maxentius,' Nigrinus said, 'you might ask about him and Sabina. Discover what really happened.'

'How would I ever get myself into that position?'

'I suppose that's what your wife said to him!'

Castus halted, fearful for just one moment that he would not be able to stop himself from seizing the notary and smashing his body to pulp against the tiled floor. He inhaled slowly, held the breath inside him, compelled himself to remain still.

'You didn't need to tell me all that,' he said as he exhaled.

'No? Your mind is already made up? Shame – I'm sure

the emperor would have been extremely grateful, had you agreed...'

Castus turned away from him and stared at the lake, the deep dark blue of the water and the fire on the distant mountains.

'I'll want to bring two of my own men with me,' he said. 'You can dress them as slaves and add them to the retinue. They'll be under my command alone. I won't take orders from you, and I won't sacrifice myself or my men for your schemes.'

'Entirely reasonable, tribune,' the notary said. He appeared to stifle a yawn, then stretched his back and shoved himself away from the pillar. 'I shall go and inform my colleagues of your very sensible decision.'

CHAPTER XVII

Hot sun, a bright sky, and the broad Tyrrhenian stretched blue to the far western horizon. To the east, Italy was a flat shore and a blur of distant mountains. Between sea and sky, the Ligurian coaster *Thetis* rode southwards across the swells, her upswept prow and stern alternately rising and sinking, her big mainsail sheeted hard against the pressure of the wind.

Leaning out over the rail, Castus squinted into the salt spray and looked back at the wake. Two sails on the far horizon, but they were moving towards the coast, and neither was the one he expected to see.

'Triangular, you say?' the shipmaster rasped, moving up to stand beside him at the rail.

Castus nodded. 'Like this,' he said, sketching three corners in the air. He had seen a ship with a triangular sail at Genua just before they had sailed the previous morning. He had seen it again in the evening, coming in shortly after the *Thetis* had anchored in the bay of Luna. And twice more today it had appeared, flickering across the horizon, dogging their wake.

'Plenty of boats have sails like that,' the shipmaster said. He was a short stocky Corsican, with no neck and a windblown grin, a man as blunt and weatherly as the vessel he commanded. 'We could too, if we was running across the wind; you just swing the yard round and bring the leeward arm down, then brail up the sail to the arm and you've got your three corners, so it looks. Ain't triangular really, though, truth be told.'

Castus squinted at him a moment. 'But we're running before the wind, not across it. And so are they, if they're following us.'

'Fair enough,' the shipmaster said, showing his yellow teeth. 'But you'd be better looking the other way, keeping an eye out for any of them cruisers up from Misenum. They're more to worry about!'

There had been no sign yet of warships patrolling the sea lanes. The only ones Castus had seen were the pair of liburnian galleys in the harbour at Genua, but they were crewed by Constantine's men; they had seized the port in the emperor's name only ten days before, but the citizens of Genua did not appear to mind the change of allegiance. The naval base at Ravenna on the Adriatic had also recently declared for Constantine, so Castus had heard, but with the territories of Licinius on the far shore that sea was still too dangerous to travel.

Pushing away from the rail, Castus made his way towards the stern, leaning into the pitch of the deck. He was dressed in a simple tunic of dark blue wool, with plain leather shoes. The gold ring that marked his citizenship, and the golden torque that signalled his rank and prestige, he had left behind in Verona. He felt almost naked without them, and without the military belt and boots he had worn since he had first joined the army nearly two decades before. He carried no weapon either; there was a shortsword concealed in his bedroll, but it did little to reassure him. Castus had the unnerving sensation that he was going into the heart of the enemy camp dangerously underequipped.

The *Thetis* was a small vessel, not much bigger than a fishing boat; her scarred and greasy timbers creaked and wailed with every shift of the wind, but she was seaworthy enough and would draw little attention. There were six crewmen, all of them slaves, and they went by nicknames: Fish-hook, Donkey, Gizzard... They roamed naked over the deck, joking in gnarled accents, leaping over the rail sometimes to swim beside the ship, or even dive beneath the hull and surface on the other side.

In contrast to the high-spirited crew, the members of Castus's little party appeared very subdued. Felix sat in the scuppers with his back to the rail, playing knucklebones with one of the young nobleman's slaves. Of all the party, Felix seemed to inhabit his assumed role with the greatest ease; Castus wondered if there was any truth in the stories about the man once being a slave. But Felix knew Rome, or so he claimed, and Castus had wanted a guide he could trust. The man had saved his life on the night that Pompeianus had broken out of Verona. Twice, in fact: he had warned him of the attackers in the bushes, and then dragged Castus out of the path of the charging horse. The man was tenacious, and quick-thinking, and those were attributes that Castus knew he could use.

Felix, however, hated the sea. Even now, after nearly two days' sailing, he kept his back to the waves and tried not to look at the water. He had been badly sick for the first few hours after leaving Genua. Castus himself was immune to seasickness; he had often thanked the gods for that.

In the lee of the little kennel-like deckhouse near the stern, Diogenes was still debating with the Christian priest. The former schoolteacher had not been Castus's first choice for the mission. He would have taken Modestus, perhaps, or Brocchus: a man with military bearing and muscle. But Diogenes had found out what was planned somehow, and petitioned Castus to join the party. It would be dangerous, Castus had explained; maybe they would not return. Diogenes had been unmoved; perhaps, Castus thought, the man would have his uses after all.

The slatted door of the deckhouse swung open, and Nigrinus clambered out into the daylight, blinking as he raised his head.

'How is he?' Castus asked.

'Still asleep,' the notary replied, with a sour grimace. 'Probably dreaming he's back in Genua, lying in a pile of prostitutes.'

The young senator's son, Publius Pomponius Bassus Pudentianus, was supposedly the leader of their party. Castus and Nigrinus were his freedmen; the others were his slaves. He was a necessary liability, but since the party had left Verona he had caused nothing but aggravation and delay, and his habit of treating them as if they were genuinely his slaves and dependants endeared him to nobody. Most recently, he had vanished for forty-eight hours in Genua, just as Nigrinus had finally managed to arrange passage on a ship for Sardinia. Castus and Felix had tracked the young man down to one of the city's most expensive brothels, and he had been so drunk by then that they'd had to carry him aboard the *Thetis* wrapped in a cloak.

Since leaving harbour, Pudentianus had done little but sleep and vomit. His two slaves tended to him most of the time, but Nigrinus made it his business to check on the young man as well: it was vital for the success of the mission that he remain alive and in reasonable health. It was almost worth enduring the irritations of Pudentianus's presence, Castus thought, to see the notary so obviously ill at ease.

Clambering past the helmsman and the tiller bars that connected the two big steering oars, Castus pulled himself up onto the little platform beneath the sweep of the stern. Gulls wheeled and darted in the wake of the ship; beyond them, the horizon was clear. No sign of a triangular sail, or any other vessels at all now. Castus wondered if he was becoming delusional. Perhaps, he thought, he simply could not believe how easily the journey was going so far? And it was a relief, he had to admit, to be moving again, covering distance with a firm destination in mind, with hundreds of miles separating him from Constantine and his army, from Ganna and from Sabina, from Lepidus. Out here on the open sea his spirits felt liberated, the sea air singing through him. No, he thought: he should enjoy it while he could, and not look for shadows where there were none.

The plan itself, as Nigrinus had explained it back at the villa on Lake Benacus, was simple in its essence. They would take ship from Genua down the western coast of Italy and across the narrows of the Tyrrhenian to Corsica, and then to the port of Olbia on Sardinia. From there they would hope to pick up one of the big cargo ships from Carthage that often called at Olbia before crossing to Portus, the harbour of Rome. With any luck, they could blend in with the other passengers travelling from Sardinia or Africa, and by the time they reached Rome there would be nothing to say that they had come from the north.

To aid the deception, each member of the party carried coins taken from the prisoners at Verona: copper and silver pieces, minted in Rome and stamped with the head of Maxentius. On the other side was the figure of the goddess Roma and the legend *PRESERVER OF HIS CITY*. Castus had peered at the portrait of the enemy emperor, surprised to notice that it looked so much like Constantine. But coin portraits were seldom accurate: the tyrant's father Maximian had appeared much the same.

The real danger during the journey lay in the sea crossing between the Italian coast and Sardinia; Maxentius's galleys from the naval base at Misenum were reported to be cruising in the straits around the island of Ilva. And then, Castus thought, they had Rome itself to tackle. The eternal city, the mistress of nations: the camp of their enemy. As the plan went, once they had done all they could in the city, they would slip out by different routes and make their way north to Spoletium on the Flaminian Way by the ides of October, hoping to meet the vanguard of Constantine's army there as it advanced across the Apennines.

It was vague – too vague – and Castus still had little notion of what challenges the city itself might hold. His only concern at the moment was getting the party to Rome without being discovered by the enemy. After that, he would take things as they came.

Dropping back down off the stern platform, he picked his way forward to the lee of the deckhouse once more. As he approached, he heard Diogenes still locked in passionate debate with the Christian priest Stephanus, their voices raised against the whine of the wind.

'But your cosmogony is opposed to all reason! As Aristotle said, nothing can come from nothing… so how can you claim that your god existed before everything else and somehow created the cosmos from a void?'

'What is impossible with men is possible with God!' the Christian declared. 'God is uncontainable and immutable, therefore nothing can exist outside God – a common craftsman can fashion inert and pre-existing matter; only God can create matter from nothing!'

'Nonsense! Is your god immune from the laws of nature, then? Or are you suggesting that he somehow *shat* the universe into existence?'

Castus grinned ruefully, then climbed around the far side of the deckhouse and forward to the mast. In the bows, one of the sailors stood poised with a three-pronged harpoon, catching fish for the evening meal. Off to the west, the sun was slipping down towards the horizon, and the waves were fired with gold. A stirring sight, Castus thought. So why did he still feel so wary? Again he glanced back to windward, and just for a moment the low sunlight seemed to flash off the white peak of a following sail.

The mission to Rome was a closely guarded secret, or so Castus had been told. But he already knew that the information had leaked to the imperial court; he'd had proof of that before he'd left the villa on Lake Benacus. A eunuch dressed in court robes of deep wine red had been waiting for him outside his room when he'd returned from dinner; he had provided no information but only requested that Castus follow him. Already Castus could guess the identity of the eunuch's mistress.

Years had passed since he had last spoken to Fausta, nobilissima femina, the wife of the emperor Constantine. He had seen her often enough, both at official functions and around the palace in Treveris, and with Sabina so often in her retinue he had heard a lot about Fausta as well. If she'd paid any special attention to him, she had been careful never to show it, and he'd acted likewise.

He found her in her private chambers, seated on a couch with several other ladies and eunuchs around her; she dismissed them all with a gesture, and in a flurry of silks and scents they were gone. Castus heard the eunuch who had brought him softly closing the door behind him.

'Be seated, please,' Fausta said, offering him a place on the facing couch. Castus crossed the room and sat down. He was very conscious that he was alone with the emperor's wife, although he knew that he would be observed, and anything he said overheard.

Fausta had been only seventeen when they had last met. She

was around twenty now, a grown woman; the change in her appearance and manner were remarkable. Castus had noticed before that she had shed the plumpness of adolescence, the soft roundness of face that had given her a childish look at times. Now he saw how poised she had become, how regal. He noticed the hard clarity in her deeply lidded eyes. The 'gilded piglet', the crueller courtiers had called her once, in Treveris. She was far from that now.

'You are being sent to Rome, I hear,' she said.

Castus did not attempt to deny it.

'Have they ordered you to murder my brother?'

'In a manner of speaking, domina,' he told her. 'I said no.'

'I'm glad.' Her expression barely altered, but Castus sensed her warming towards him. 'I did not think you were the sort of man for that.'

What sort of man, he wondered, *do you think I am?* Being in her presence again brought back charged memories. He had last spoken to her before the siege of Massilia, during her father's attempt to seize power from Constantine. Maximian had died by his own hand soon afterwards, and Castus had been the last man to see him alive.

'My brother,' she said, 'is not the monster that so many here like to believe. All this talk of sorcery – complete nonsense! He's entirely devoted to the traditional superstitions. Quite the champion of piety, in fact.' She paused, moving her lips slightly, as if deciding how much she ought to say. 'I was never very close to him,' she went on. 'He's more than a decade older than me, and by the time I was able to think of him as my brother he was sent off to join Galerius as a staff officer. But every man I've known has been ambitious for power, excepting slaves. I can't blame him for wanting what my father had, or what my husband also desires.'

Castus nodded slowly, still uncomfortable under the frank-
ness of her gaze. She had put her trust in him once, back at
Massilia; Sabina had been her gift to him, a reward for service.
But there had been more between them than that. Both of them,
in that warm, scented, dimly lit chamber, were aware of the
deeper connection they had once shared.

'You know he must die,' Castus said. 'If we win.'

Fausta just shrugged slightly, and her brief pout made her
appear once more the child she had once been. 'I know that,'
she said. 'All my life I've had to accept these things. I'd just
rather it was decided... fairly.'

Back at Massilia, Castus had realised that Fausta had made
a decision to support her husband over her father. That was
where she saw her best interest. But now, he realised, she was
undecided. What would she do if her brother was victorious,
and her husband was defeated? What future would there be
for her then? She still had no child by the emperor; rumour
was that Constantine continued to prefer the company of his
concubine Minervina to his wife. He could set Fausta aside at
any time. If she had chosen to leave matters to the will of the
gods, Castus could not blame her.

'I'm sorry I haven't had the chance to speak with you since my
father died,' Fausta said. Castus felt a brief flicker of surprise at
her cool candour. He reminded himself that this young woman
had never known love, or been loved herself. 'I understand
you played an important part in what happened at Massilia. I
should have thanked you for that.'

Castus inclined his head. 'There's no need, domina.'

She gave a quick laugh, and her smile had a capricious look.
She was lounging on the couch now, no longer so regal. 'No
doubt my husband will be grateful once more if you succeed
in your mission to Rome.'

'The Augustus...' Castus began, then paused, uncertain how to continue.

Fausta laughed at his discomfort. 'He's still very angry with you, yes. He thinks you're a very *insubordinate* soldier.' She widened her eyes a little. 'If only he knew,' she said.

Castus felt the heat rush to his face, but Fausta was still smiling. A private, knowing sort of smile. Since entering the room he had been trying not to think about that night in the garden house of the Villa Herculis, the darkened bedchamber where she had played the role of Sabina. But she surely knew he was thinking about it now. For a couple of heartbeats he allowed himself to meet her gaze. The distance between them felt suddenly very slight, but it was an unbridgeable chasm. Memory kindled desire; desire brought shame.

'Your wife is being foolish,' Fausta said, her voice barely more than a whisper. 'But perhaps don't judge her too harshly until you know the truth.'

'What is the truth?' Castus said, his voice thick.

'That's what you have to discover,' she told him, with another sly flicker of a smile. 'Maybe in Rome you'll find out?'

They camped on the beach that evening, in the shelter of a low headland that broke the straight ribbon of the shoreline. The sailors brought the *Thetis* in under oars, then ran her up onto the beach; as soon as the keel grated onto the sand Castus jumped over the side and waded through the surf. Clumsy on dry land after two days at sea, he stamped up the beach and through the fringe of coarse grass to the pines that covered the flat land inshore. No sign of habitation: this entire coast seemed deserted. No sign of a sail out on the horizon either: war had emptied the sea lanes. Content that their landing had been unobserved, and no concealed enemies lay in wait for them, Castus swung his arm, and the rest of the party came ashore.

The sailors secured the ship with anchors high on the beach, then gathered driftwood and cut branches from the myrtle bushes for a fire. The sun was low over the sea to the west, and evening was gathering beneath the pines. Insects flickered in the warm light as the sailors lashed oars together and covered them with sail canvas to make tents in a clearing between the trees. Pudentianus, the young nobleman, sat on a folding stool on the sand, drinking wine and admiring the last glow of the sun over the sea while his two slaves waited on him.

In the woods above the beach Castus cut two short straight sticks. He handed one to Felix, and they stripped off their tunics and went down onto the sand to practise their armatura drill. It was different fighting without a shield, and without the reach of a spatha, but Castus knew that any fighting they did over the coming month would be like this. When they closed to spar together, both men instinctively shifted into wrestling stances, sword-sticks drawn back to stab, their left hands stretched out to grab and grapple. Felix was much smaller than Castus, but fast and agile, and his unnaturally long arms gave him a killer's reach. Circling, kicking up sand, they fought until both were breathing hard.

'A good show!' Pudentianus cried, as Castus pulled Felix to his feet for the last time. He and his slaves had gathered in a circle with the sailors, as if they were watching a gladiators' bout. Castus spat in the sand and wiped a forearm across his brow. He had not intended to create a spectacle, but on an open beach there were few places to exercise discreetly. Besides, he thought, perhaps it was better to let the civilians know there were real fighters defending them.

Diogenes passed him a flask of watered vinegar wine, and Castus drank deeply. After so long aboard ship it was good to stretch his muscles and feel his blood flowing. Even the sting of sweat in his cuts was invigorating. Further down the beach the sailors were grilling fresh fish over the charcoal, and the smells of the smoke and the sea mingled with the scent of the pines. Castus breathed it all in, and felt his spirits rise. Just for a moment he allowed himself to imagine Ganna on that beach, with his son in her arms, both of them gazing out over the waves.

'They tell me you're a tribune,' Pudentianus said, appearing beside him. Castus blinked away the brief reverie. He nodded curtly.

'I've never really met any soldiers before,' the young man said, with the faintest note of apology, 'so I wasn't entirely sure.'

He was about eighteen or nineteen, Castus guessed, and his face still had an adolescent look, rather thick-lipped and pimply. Nigrinus had told him that the youth came from one of the most highly placed families in Rome, but Pudentianus had never spoken directly to him before, and seemed to find conversation with his social inferiors difficult. He was looking sideways at Castus now, as if dubious about his status.

'It's good to know that a warrior of your experience is accompanying us to Rome,' he said, with an awkward smile. 'Although I hope there won't be any occasion for fighting...!'

'I hope so too,' Castus said. If the youth was going to drop the formal address, so would he.

'Tell me something,' the youth said, pacing across the sand towards the trees, hands clasped behind his back. 'What do you make of our friend, the notary?'

Castus realised that he was expected to follow. He lingered a moment, pulled on his tunic, then tied his belt as he strode to catch up with Pudentianus. Nigrinus was still sitting on the sand near the fire, well out of hearing.

'I mean,' Pudentianus went on, 'do you trust him?'

'I wouldn't trust him beyond the reach of my arm,' Castus said in a low tone. 'But I think he's on our side, if that's what you mean.' Even as he spoke, it occurred to Castus that he was only assuming they were all on the same side.

'I suppose that's what I was asking, yes.' Pudentianus paused, scuffing the sand with his foot. He gazed over at Nigrinus and frowned. 'It's just... he seems such a crude sort of person. I wonder why the emperor would trust him with a mission of such delicacy?'

Castus snorted a laugh. 'He's *delicate* enough when he want to be.' *Like a surgeon*, he thought, and remembered the torture chamber Nigrinus had shown him in the cellars beneath the city of Arelate. No, he did not trust the notary at all: he had seen and experienced enough of his work over the years.

'When we reach Rome,' the youth went on, 'I'm concerned that the meetings with the aristocracy should be left in my hands. I mean, my father was Consul, and I'm personally acquainted with many of the best people. I... I was on the board of the Centumviral Court last year; I can expect entry into the Senate very soon... But I fear that the notary might wish to take control of things, and his... his more *abrasive* attitudes might cause offence...'

Castus tightened his lips against a sneer. It was all politics, he thought. This puking lad, who'd spent the last ten days either complaining, sleeping or sick, was making a bid for control, and wanted Castus to back him. Perhaps he had a point – no doubt Nigrinus lacked the charm for diplomacy – but the idea that this boy could do any better was almost laughable. Was that really how things worked in Rome?

'My only business at the moment is getting you both to the city alive,' Castus said, stepping closer and speaking quietly. He was a head taller than Pudentianus; the young man nodded quickly, swallowing. 'Once we're there,' Castus went on, 'you can thrash things out between yourselves.'

He did not rate the young man's chances if he pitted himself against Nigrinus. Then again, the city was Pudentianus's home territory. Shaking his head, Castus left him and strode back to the fire, where the sailors had finished preparing the evening meal.

The sun had still not set, but the sea to the west was glowing. Castus stood just above the surf, eating grilled fish and chewy flatbread and washing it down with watered wine. From behind him he could hear Diogenes and the Christian priest, still locked in their intractable debate.

'... but what about the bodies of those who've been cremated, or dismembered in battle? Will they be stuck back together, at this *resurrection* of yours?'

'After the Day of Judgement the righteous will take on heavenly bodies, yes – they will be resurrected in the incorrupt flesh, as they were in life, and those bodies will be immaculate...'

'So how was it that when your Jesus came back to life he still had wounds upon him? Didn't he tell his followers to stick their fingers in his scars? And he had to eat and drink too – doesn't it say that in your books? How come he needed earthly nourishment, if he had an immaculate heavenly body? No, this is clearly childish nonsense! Plato, on the other hand—'

'I'm afraid you are an extremely ignorant man...'

Finishing the last of his meal, Castus paced along the beach. Philosophical debates had always confused him; how could people spend so much time arguing about things they could not see or feel? When he looked out towards the horizon, he

273

saw the sun sinking towards the rim of the sea. That was god, surely. The light of the world. Beyond that light there was nothing. Castus kissed his fingers lightly, then raised his hand in salute to the sun. *Sol Invictus. Lord of Daybreak.*

The headland above the beach was lit by the evening glow, and Castus had a sudden desire to climb up to the heights and survey the surrounding country. He wished he had done it earlier, but if he hurried he knew he could get up and back before nightfall. Doubling back quickly to the camp, he took the shortsword from his bedroll and threw the baldric around his shoulder. Felix glanced up from his meal and then made to stand; Castus gestured for him to stay where he was.

Moving away from the fire and the voices, he crossed the sand and jogged up the rise through the grass. There was a track between the trees, he noticed, but still no other sign of human life. He started climbing, the slope growing steeper and more rocky as he pushed his way through the dry scrub. Then, before he had expected, he was at the summit of the low headland, clambering through a last screen of tangled bushes and out onto the stony ridge above the sea. The air smelled strongly of thyme, and now he was no longer moving Castus could hear the noise of the insects from the darkening land behind him.

Down on the beach, the camp fire was a glowing ember. Beyond it stretched the pale ribbon of empty sand and the ranked trees, following the shallow curve of the coastline as far as the distant hills. But when Castus glanced down to the other side of the headland, he caught his breath. On the beach about half a mile to the north, another vessel was pulled up on the sand. It was small, with oars piled across the thwarts and a lowered mast, but Castus felt almost sure that it was the same one he had seen in Genua, and in the bay of Luna. The ship with the triangular sail.

It must have crept in along the coast under oars, he realised, screened by the headland. Peering at the distant shape, he could make out one or two figures sitting on the sand beside the beached craft. There had surely been more, to work the oars, but there was no sign of them now. No fire either, or any encampment.

Castus had already reached for the hilt of his sword. He slid the blade free a short way, then tapped it back into the scabbard. Then, slow and smooth, he eased down into a crouch in the bushes; no watchers on the beach would see him silhouetted against the evening sky. Keeping low, he began to edge back through the scrub bushes. Almost at once he paused; now that he was listening more carefully he could clearly make out the sounds of men moving in the near distance. At least six of them, he estimated, and no more than a couple of hundred paces away. The dry bushes and scrub crackled and hissed as they crossed the ridge and descended into the pine woodlands behind the beach, and all the time Castus stayed still, tensed and hardly breathing.

When the last of the men seemed to have passed his position he eased himself back into motion, stepping carefully over the tangled bushes and picking his way down the steep stony track. The sun had long gone now; only a trace of light remained in the western sky, and the hillside was being consumed by the darkness. Insects rustled and rasped on all sides.

By the time Castus had scrambled down to the beach, he estimated that the group of men ahead of him would have almost circled around through the trees behind the camp. Lifting his sword clear of his waist, he started running along the hard wet sand at the edge of the surf. The camp seemed further away than he had anticipated. He could make out the fire, still burning down to embers on the sand, and the dim shapes of the makeshift tents just below the trees. He was running hard, yet

275

trying to conserve his strength: if he could get to the camp in time he could warn Felix and Diogenes, perhaps counter-attack before the newcomers could spring their ambush...

A shout reached him, then a scream from the camp. Castus doubled his stride, a curse bursting from his lips. Swerving up the beach and across the dry sand, he saw the figures running in the trees, one of them outlined briefly against the light of the embers. Smoke swirled, and Pudentianus's two slaves dashed from the closest tent. Castus could see a body on the ground, the dim shapes of struggling men.

Stooping as he ran, he snatched up the three-pronged fishing spear from beside the fire. The man on the ground was one of the sailors; the combat between the trees was indistinct, frenzied. Castus yelled out a battle roar; his sword was in one hand, the trident in the other. There were pale faces in the darkness, a haze of kicked-up dust, incoherent shouts. Then suddenly the attackers seemed to melt back into the darkness; Castus saw one man turn and flee, his cloak whipping behind him. He canted back the fishing spear, aimed at the fleeing man's legs, and threw.

The man screamed as the blow knocked him down. 'Get him!' Castus shouted. 'Get him alive!' He was closing fast, sword in hand; but one of the sailors was faster. Standing over the fallen attacker he raised a club in his fist.

'They killed Fish-hook!' the sailor yelled, then smashed the club down on the head of the wounded man with a meaty chopping sound.

Light rushed between the trees, flinging shadows. Diogenes had a flaming torch in each hand, and passed one of them to Pudentianus.

'Who were they?' the young nobleman was saying, clearly shaken as he stared into the reeling shadows between the pines.

The sailor stepped back from the body of the fallen man, flinging down his bloodied club as Castus approached. The attacker was quite obviously dead: the harpoon had struck him in the thigh, but the club had crushed the side of his skull.

'Bring the torch closer,' Castus said, still heaving breath after his run along the beach. He considered going after the other attackers; but, no, that would be disastrous.

Diogenes stepped up with his torch, and Castus shoved the dead man over onto his back. What was left of his skull was shaved bald. Castus leaned closer, studying the ruined features in the flickering light of the flames. Then he stepped back.

'Can you tell who he was?' Pudentianus said, wincing.

Castus just shook his head. But he had a good idea all the same. He was sure that he had seen this man before, back at Mediolanum, and he had been dressed in a sky-blue tunic.

CHAPTER XVIII

'I believe we're in luck, dominus,' Diogenes said, emerging from the stairway.

'Don't call me that,' Castus told him.

'Sorry!' Diogenes said. Sardinia had declared for Maxentius, and the port of Olbia was enemy territory; they all knew it was important to keep to their assumed roles here. Floorboards creaked as he crossed the room to join Castus by the window. From this vantage point on the upper storey of the harbourside inn, they could see the high curving gooseneck stern of the big ship moored at the far end of the quay.

'She's the *Fortuna Redux*,' Diogenes said. 'Left Carthage two days ago. She sails tomorrow for Portus and Rome, and there's room aboard for passengers.'

Castus nodded in satisfaction. The gods were smiling on them once more, it seemed. They had only arrived at Olbia a day ago, and here already was the means for their onward journey... There was no sign of the ship that had followed them from Genua either; Castus had scoured the stone quays and the wooden jetties, and peered out over the long reach of the harbour, but had seen nothing of that distinctive triangular sail or low hull.

The master of the *Thetis* had assumed that the men who attacked them on the beach were common pirates, taking advantage of the chaos of war to prey on travellers. A reasonable explanation, although Nigrinus had clearly not been convinced. Castus had said nothing about recognising the dead man. He did not trust the notary enough to share his suspicions, and if Lepidus was behind the attack, Castus would keep the information to himself for now. Surely, he thought, he could not have been the target himself; there had been plenty of opportunity for Lepidus to strike against him in Mediolanum. Which left only the possibility that his rival was intending to destroy the mission, for reasons of his own. Was Lepidus an agent of the enemy, then? Castus remembered Fausta's parting words. *Maybe in Rome you'll find out...*

After the attack, the *Thetis* had put to sea at first light, leaving only two rough graves beneath the pines to show that anything unusual had happened there. All the way along the coast of the island of Ilva they had been prepared for another attack, the sailors armed and ready, but there had been no further sightings of the supposed pirates. Instead, off the southern cape of the island, the *Thetis* had been intercepted by a warship coming out from the land. Castus and the rest of the party had concealed themselves in the deckhouse, while the shipmaster had answered the galley's summons in his thickest Corsican accent. It had been enough to dissuade them from any further investigation: the *Thetis* was too small, and too obviously a local coasting vessel, for the Maxentian marines to bother boarding her.

Since then there had been no more trouble, and after their voyage down the Corsican coast and across to Sardinia the *Thetis* had landed the party at Olbia and sailed away again, the master and crew clearly glad to be rid of their dangerous passengers.

Staring down from the inn window into the dazzle of sunlight, Castus saw the familiar greyish figure of Nigrinus walking along the quay towards the moored ship, with Felix trailing behind him. He suppressed a quick smile: he was one step ahead of the notary in finding onward passage, it seemed. Pudentianus and the rest of the party were lodged in a different inn a short way up the street. Since their arrival in Sardinia the young nobleman had kept himself away from the brothels and wine shops. This was home territory for him, Castus supposed. He only hoped that Pudentianus did not go too far in playing the local magnate's son. They were supposed to be keeping a low profile here, after all.

'How are you getting on with that Christian?' Castus asked Diogenes. 'Has he managed to convert you yet?'

'Far from it,' Diogenes said, with a wry smile. 'In fact, I've been steadily undermining his beliefs one by one, and exposing them for the childish and illogical fantasies they surely are! I do believe I might be close to convincing him...'

'Careful with that,' Castus said. 'We don't want him too undermined; he's got to persuade the Christians in Rome that we're on their side yet.'

'Ah, yes, I suppose so...'

Down at the end of the quay, Nigrinus was talking to a pair of men in sailor's clothing. Castus saw him gesture at the ship. Seagulls were whirling and hacking around the quays, and the masts swayed in the sunlight. Behind the notary, Felix stood waiting. What had Nigrinus told him? Seeing them together like that made Castus uneasy; no doubt the notary was angling to recruit Felix to his schemes.

Dropping his gaze, Castus scanned the figures moving along the broad paved expanse of the nearer quayside. Nobody down there seemed to be paying special attention to Nigrinus and Felix. In the bright sun, the scene appeared quite peaceful; hard to imagine that a desperate war was being fought over on the mainland. Then a party of soldiers went striding past, off-duty marines from one of the warships moored on the far side of the harbour. Castus heard them singing and laughing, boisterously heedless of the civilian life around them. Frowning, he turned from the window. The less time they spent in Olbia, he thought, the better for them all.

The *Fortuna Redux* sailed late the following afternoon, gliding out of the sheltered harbour on the land breeze. As she cleared the headland, her hull began to roll with the motion of the deep-sea swells. Rigging wailed as the big main yard swung to the wind, and by early evening the craggy coastline of Sardinia had sunk below the eastern horizon, and the ship was sailing out of sight of land.

There were a score of passengers aboard, most of them from Carthage. A plump lady named Magnilla was travelling with her small entourage of slaves and eunuchs; then there was a troupe of pantomime actors from Hippo Regius, and three or four merchants with their own slaves. As they felt the currents of the deep sea take them, all filed up to the shrine beneath the raised gooseneck stern and made their sacrifices for a safe voyage. The *Fortuna Redux* was a stout and broad-hulled bulk freighter, her hold packed with amphorae of wine, fish sauce and olive oil. There was a big deckhouse aft, with cabins for the owner, shipping agent and sailing master, and a few of the wealthier passengers: Pudentianus had secured accommodation in there for himself, Stephanus and Nigrinus. Everyone else had to berth on the open deck, or down in the stinking recesses of the hold above the slopping bilge waters.

Clouds covered the sky, and the wind was whipping spume off the wave crests. As the light faded Castus stood on deck and watched a party of sailors rigging ropes and tackle near the stern. Others ran along the decks, hauling on the lifts and braces to draw the big mainsail up close to the yard. One of them paused for a moment and bent over the water butt beside the mainmast, drinking deeply.

'What are they doing?' Castus called to him, gesturing to the party at the stern.

The sailor straightened up and wiped his mouth. 'Fixing relieving tackle to the steering oars,' he said in a slurring African accent. He nodded to windward. 'Greasy sky, see. Feel those big swells from the south-east? Comin' on to *blow*. Be a dirty night, I'd say.' He grinned. 'Best get yourself below and hang onto something!'

Castus grimaced. He could already feel the deck heaving and pitching beneath him, the breeze coming in hard from the north. The sailor loped away again, but Castus remained where he was; he did not fancy spending the night down in the bilges, in the stinking rat-scurrying darkness with a pack of wailing, frightened slaves.

Further towards the bows, Castus made out the figure of Valerius Felix crouched against the rail, clinging onto one of the main-yard lifts. Moving with long swaying strides, reaching out for support, Castus made his way forward up the pitching deck until he stood beside the man. Felix had a blanched and queasy look as he stared out over the darkening waves; clearly he had still not shaken off his seasickness. He just nodded a greeting as Castus approached. For a while they stood in silence, gazing at the rise and fall of the grey horizon.

'How long since you were last in Rome?' Castus called above the noise of wind and water, the wail of rigging and the groan of the ship's heavy timbers. Felix took his time answering.

'Twenty years, more or less,' he said at last.

Castus nodded. He realised that he had little idea how old Felix was. About his own age, he guessed, which would make him barely more than a boy when he had left the city.

'You still know any people there?'

Felix shook his head. 'Not people,' he said, with a tight grimace. 'Places.'

He seemed unwilling to say more. Ironic, Castus thought, that he had chosen a man even more taciturn than himself to accompany him on this mission. Once again, he wondered if the stories he had heard about Felix were true. Had the man really been a slave? And what had driven him from Rome at such a young age? Clearly there were things about his past that Felix did not want to discuss. Castus could understand that. As the soldier's commanding officer, he had the right to demand answers, but in this unusual situation he was content to let the matter drop, for now. There were other things he wanted to discuss.

'The notary was talking to you, back at Olbia.'

Felix pursed his lips sourly, then his face split into a quick grin. Gone almost at once. 'Oh, yes,' he said. 'He talked.'

'And said what?'

Felix looked at him, a knowing glint in his eye. 'He was sounding me out,' he said. 'I wasn't interested. I know his sort.'

'Good,' Castus told him, and could not resist smiling too. Somehow he still felt he could trust this man, although the gods knew he had enough reason not to.

'Tell me something,' he said. 'Back at Verona, that night the enemy commander broke through our lines. You saw those men coming after me?'

Felix swallowed heavily. He nodded again. 'I knew what they were about,' he said. 'Heard them talking, back in the tent lines.'

'You could have reported it.'

The man's expression closed, his eyes growing dark. 'I never been much of an informer,' he said. 'Nor liked the sort that were. Reckoned I'd just follow and see what I could do.'

Castus grunted, low in his throat, and gazed back at the sea again. This too he could respect, in a way. Felix had certainly saved his life back there, although he might have wished the man had not left things so much to chance. But he was decisive, at least, and capable of taking action.

The noise of the wind had increased, and the *Fortuna Redux* was pitching heavily now, her bows bursting the water and scattering spray back along the decks. There was still a bit of light in the sky to the east, greenish and shredded by cloud, but the ship was moving into the night and the weather out there was dirty, just as the sailor had predicted.

'You should go below,' Castus said, but Felix just frowned and shook his head.

'Better up here,' he said in a choked voice.

Castus could only agree. They said nothing more, huddled against the rail in the blast of the wind as the spray soaked them and the ship rolled and dived. Darkness all around them now, shot with flashes of moonlight, and when Castus peered out over the far rail he could make out the wave crests rolling past higher than the ship's side, boiling white with foam. The mainsail had been furled, and the ship laboured along with only the headsail to give her steerage way. In the brief gleam of light between the clouds Castus could see the figure of the helmsman, standing rigid on the roof of the deckhouse with the big tillers of the steering oars clasped tight, the wind whipping at his grey hair.

Every time the ship dived, a chorus of screams rose from the slaves and other passengers down in the hold. Castus did not envy them: for all the cold and wet out here on deck, at least he could see the sky and sense the motion of the waves around him. Down below, he knew, there would be nothing but lurching darkness and fear. After a few hours, the sounds of terror decreased, the people below decks stunned into silence, praying fitfully. Only the occasional despairing wail or nauseated groan rose from the hatches.

Castus had eaten nothing since leaving port, or taken anything to drink. Now that the motion of the ship had grown more regular he felt hunger pinching at his belly. He could ignore that, but thirst was more pressing. He clapped Felix on the shoulder, gestured, then began crawling back along the scuppers towards the water butt beside the mast. When he reached it, he found the liquid slopping inside to be undrinkable, so much salt spray had got into it. Cursing, he crawled further towards the deckhouse: he had a flask of vinegar wine and some food stowed in his baggage in the narrow shelter beneath the overhanging roof.

As he passed the deck hatchway, Castus heard a rattle and a thud from the ladder, and a figure came groping up from the darkness below. Pausing for a moment, startled, Castus watched as the man crawled out of the hatch and crouched on the deck. It was one of the actors from Hippo Regius, from what he could see; the man turned, and Castus caught the glint of his smile and the exaggerated gasp as he breathed in the fresh night air.

Pulling himself onward along the ship's rail, Castus reached the overhang of the deckhouse and found his bundle of belongings. He dragged out his cape, damp now from the sea spray but still dry on the inside, then found the flask of wine and drank deeply. He was just shoving the flask back inside the bundle when he heard the scream from inside the deckhouse.

A woman, it sounded like. But immediately afterwards there was a man's cry. 'Murder! Help – murder!'

Castus's hand grasped the hilt of the shortsword concealed in his baggage and drew it free, and immediately he was moving. He pulled his way back along the wooden wall of the deckhouse, braced against the steeply tilting deck, until he reached the corner and swung himself around to the doorway.

The door was latched shut from the inside, but Castus hurled himself against it and the thin slats burst apart. Dragging the door open, he lurched through the opening with the sword held low at his side.

Two steps down to the deckhouse floor; partition doors hanging open in the wheeling light of an uncovered lantern. Castus took in the scene in a heartbeat: the plump lady, Magnilla, poised at an open door, her mouth gaping in a silent scream; Pudentianus peering from behind her shoulder. Opposite, a blanket-covered body with three bloodstained knife-holes. There were others gathered in the shadows, figures waking from huddled sleep to panic and horror.

He did not see the man crouched in the shadow at the foot of the steps until it was almost too late.

The attacker seemed to curl upwards from the floor, the knife flowing into a stabbing strike. Crying out, Castus slammed himself sideways against the doorframe. He felt the blade cut through the cloth of his tunic and rip free, then he grabbed at the man as he tried to push past him and through the door. The deck plunged suddenly, and they were thrown together as the lamp in the deckhouse snuffed out.

Screams in the darkness as Castus tried to grapple the man, and get his sword around to strike. Stumbling on the steps, he half fell and the man writhed free of his grip and bolted out onto the open deck. Castus was at his heels, the sword in his hand.

Wind flung spray over the rail, and ahead of him Castus saw the man running with a lurching stride towards the mast. He was thin, dressed only in a short tunic, and he still held the short stabbing knife.

Felix was moving down the deck from the bows, a heavy maul clasped in his fist. As he reached the mast, the fugitive saw that he was trapped and turned at bay. In the moonlight Castus could see the man's face twist into a desperate snarl. He threw a glance at Felix, then looked back at Castus. Advancing steadily, Castus kept his blade low and level; if the man tried to jump him again, he would be ready. There were others behind him too now, sailors clambering up from the deck hatch.

The killer took one more desperate look up and down the deck, then flung himself wildly towards the rail and vaulted across it. The dark surge of water took him at once, and he was gone.

Dawn came up fiery red in the east, and the morning sun shone clear across a placid empty sea. The storm had blown itself out in the night, and now the sky was a clean-washed blue, only a trail of little white clouds along the horizon. A fine sight, but the mood aboard the *Fortuna Redux* did not reflect it.

Passengers and crew gathered on deck, all of them grey-faced and weary after the disturbed night, as the sailors sewed up the body of the murdered man in a blanket and tied a ballast rock at its feet. One of the Carthage merchants claimed to be a Christian of sorts, and muttered a short half-remembered prayer over the body before the sailors heaved it up and carried it to the rail.

'Should we not wait, and take the body ashore for burial?' Diogenes asked. 'I believe members of the sect prefer to be entombed on land...'

The shipmaster shook his head grimly. 'Bad luck to carry a corpse aboard ship,' he said. 'Besides, don't that sort say their god walked on the water? Maybe he can walk across the waves and find himself a burial plot?'

Without another word, the body of the Christian priest Stephanus was pitched over the side and vanished beneath the waves.

'A shame,' Diogenes said to Castus. 'I really thought I was making progress with that man. A keen intellect, for all his erroneous beliefs...'

Pudentianus stood by the deckhouse door, rubbing his grey face. 'It was supposed to be me,' he mumbled as Castus approached. 'I was lying right next to the priest at the beginning of the night... that man came into the deckhouse on some errand – a mistake, I thought... I was suspicious then, but thought nothing more of it. If I had not crossed the cabin to, uh... to comfort the domina Magnilla, it would have been me he knifed! It would be me going over the side right now...!'

'You were *comforting* her?' Castus asked in a low voice.

'Of course!' Pudentianus said, his jaw quivering slightly. 'She was most alarmed by the storm...'

Magnilla herself stood nearby, flanked by her maids, with a scented cloth pressed to her mouth. Her eyes streamed black runnels of kohl down her cheeks, and when Pudentianus made a movement towards her she fled back inside the deckhouse.

The actors from Hippo Regius were extremely apologetic, at least. The killer had been a stranger to them, they claimed; he had joined them at Olbia, after one of their number had suddenly fallen sick. All seemed to believe that the death was a very poor omen for their forthcoming appearance on the Roman stage.

The gathering on deck was breaking up now, some of the passengers slinking away below, while others slumped at the rail to enjoy the fresh air after their night's confinement. Castus made his way to the mast; the water butt had been emptied of its brackish contents and refilled with fresh rainwater. He stooped, drank, and when he straightened up Nigrinus was at his elbow.

'I assume you have your suspicions about the night's events?' the notary said, his lips barely moving as he spoke.

'You do?'

'Of course. I'm starting to realise that you're not entirely as stupid as you appear.'

Castus cleared his throat, then paced to the rail and spat over the side. Leaning back against the rail, he regarded the notary with a hard grimace.

'Well, then?' Nigrinus said, joining him. 'Our killer was no random maniac, we must conclude. Most likely he intended to murder our senatorial friend, and thereby throw our mission into jeopardy. Without Pudentianus, we have no contact with the nobility of Rome, and no base in the city from which to operate. If you had not acted so promptly, he would probably have succeeded. Now – do you think he was one of the same party that attacked us on the beach?'

Castus nodded. He was debating with himself how much he should tell the notary. Not much, he concluded. He would let Nigrinus make the connections himself.

'So we must assume,' Nigrinus went on, 'that the ship you believed was following us from Genua brought these men on our trail. They must have sailed directly to Olbia ahead of us, after their failed attack on the beach. So they knew where we were going. So... we must hope that the remainder of their party have not already moved on to Rome, or our stay in the city could be *uncomfortable*.'

'That's the way I'd guess it, yes.'

'And you have an idea who these people might be? Or rather, who might have sent them after us?'

'I thought that was your province, notary.'

Nigrinus stretched his mouth in a humourless smirk. 'I suppose it should be,' he said quietly. 'But at this stage, I need all the help I can get.'

All through that day they sailed across a rolling sea with a steady breeze from the west. Evening was coming on again when Castus first noticed the glimmering light on the eastern horizon. He climbed up to the sloping bow, leaning from the gilded stempost and peering off into the greyness. The light remained fixed, unmoving as it floated just above the horizon.

'The Pharos of Portus!' Diogenes declared, joining him. 'Bigger even than the famous lighthouse of Alexandria, so they say, which is one of the wonders of the world. We're approaching the port of Rome at last!'

As they drew nearer, Castus could clearly make out the flaming beacon; closer still, and he could see the dark line of the shore, the reaching arms of the massive harbour moles and the tall lighthouse standing on its artificial island at the mouth.

'We'll anchor in the outer harbour before dark,' the ship-master said, 'and go into the dock basin at dawn tomorrow. I suggest that nobody mentions the unfortunate events of last night.'

Nobody seemed eager to do so. As the ship approached the harbour mouth, everyone on deck could see the sleek triple-banked warship pulling out towards them. The light of the beacon fire flashed on the oars as they dipped and rose, picking out the marines assembled on the long narrow deck, the ballistae mounted at bow and stern. Backing her sails, the *Fortuna Redux* slowed and came around as the trireme moved up alongside.

Everyone stay calm, Castus said to himself, praying that the men aboard the warship had not already been alerted to their presence. He could see the boat putting out from the galley, the marine optio standing up at the bow, his helmet plume streaming in the breeze as his men pulled across the choppy waves.

The passengers were assembled on deck with their baggage as the boat hooked onto the ship's side and the marines clambered aboard. Squatting down in the scuppers behind Pudentianus, who had dressed himself in his finest embroidered tunic and patterned cape, Castus tried to look unobtrusive. Casting an appraising eye over the marines, he was not impressed: none wore armour, and their equipment was old and worn. A lazy-looking set of men, bored and aggressive, they spread out across the deck as the ship's owner and the sailing master came forward with the cargo documents for inspection. A couple of them dropped down through the hatches to search below decks, while the rest idled with their spears readied, staring at the assembled passengers with open disdain.

'You there,' the optio said, catching sight of Castus. 'Where'd you get those scars?'

'In the arena at Theveste, dominus,' Castus replied, trying his best to keep the Pannonian inflection from his voice.

'You're a gladiator?'

'Was, dominus.'

'He's my bodyguard,' Pudentianus declared promptly. 'A freedman.' Castus thanked him silently.

'I am Publius Pomponius Bassus Pudentianus,' the young man went on, drawing himself up to his full height. For a moment he managed to look impressively confident, although the optio still towered over him. 'My father is a senator of Rome, and I have already been too long delayed on this voyage.'

'Have you indeed?' the optio said. He turned back to Castus. 'If you ever fancy getting a proper job,' he said, 'consider the navy. We take freedmen in the marines, you know.'

Castus just shrugged lightly. A shout came across the waves: a flag was waving from the trireme. For a moment Castus's pulse jumped, and then he saw a second cargo ship moving slowly towards the harbour mouth.

'We're done here,' the optio called to his men. The marines came clattering up the ladder from the hold and the bilges, and with a last sneer and a spit they clambered back into their boat and set off towards the second incoming vessel.

Pudentianus exhaled hugely and wiped his brow. Already the sailing master was shouting to his crew, and moment later the big mainsail bellied in the wind and the *Fortuna Redux* was under way once more. As the last glow of sunset faded to the west, the ship moved through the narrow channel beneath the burning beacon of the lighthouse, past the massive gilded statue of Neptune standing at the end of the mole, and entered the outer harbour.

'We're here,' Diogenes said with quietly suppressed awe, as the anchors plunged down into the oily-smooth waters. 'I can hardly believe it...'

The land was lost in darkness, but there was a smell on the breeze: dust and smoke. The smell of civilisation, Castus thought as he breathed it in. The smell of Rome.

CHAPTER XIX

Gold and glittering mosaic glass above him; cool marble beneath his feet.

Castus tipped his head back and gazed up at the ceilings of the vast bathing hall. Around him was noise, the voices of thousands of men, the splash and gush of water, laughter and singing, even the words of a poet declaiming his latest work in one of the side chambers, all of it echoing together under the soaring vaulted roof into a single rushing roar. Castus was oblivious to the noise. Although this was not the first time he had been here, he had still not lost his sense of mute wonder.

But as he paced slowly between the milling crowds of naked and semi-naked bathers, he was naggingly aware of a single chattering voice at his elbow, an occasional touch on his arm.

'Yes, dominus, whatever you desire – whatever in the world you require – I, Apelles the Mouse, will provide! Merely name what you want, dominus. You need food? Drink? Lucanian sausage, maybe? Very spicy! Honey cakes...?'

The little rodent-like man had followed him in from the *palaestra*, talking constantly, trying to catch his attention. Castus continued to ignore him.

He looked up and saw painted figures on the ceiling: gods and giants. He saw tall columns of purple and green marble, mosaics in yellow and blue, statues in blinding white and gold.

The hall in which he was walking was larger, he thought, than the imperial basilica in Treveris, but this was only the centrepiece of the baths complex. To either side, through enormous arched portals, were other chambers, thermal rooms, changing rooms and halls for oiling and massage. There were twin *palaestrae* for exercise, and a huge open-air swimming pool. This was the newest and most sumptuous bath in all of Rome, dedicated only six years before in the name of Diocletian; Pudentianus had claimed it was the biggest in the world, and Castus could believe him.

'Perhaps the dominus wishes for company, or for sport? I, Apelles the Mouse, can introduce him to the finest wits, the boldest players in all this district! Yes, indeed, for a small consideration...'

During his years in the army Castus had travelled from one end of the empire to the other. He had seen mighty Antioch, Ctesiphon, the imperial capitals of Nicomedia, Mediolanum and Treveris. He was not, he thought, easily impressed. But these last six days since his arrival in Rome had tested his idea of himself as a man of the world. So much here was far beyond anything he had expected.

Rome was vast. When Diogenes had told him that the city had a million inhabitants, Castus had assumed he was exaggerating. Now he suspected the figure was higher. Half the human race seemed to live here, teeming and swarming in the streets and the fora, covering the hills with houses and apartment blocks as far as the eye could see. On every hilltop were enormous mansions, temples and porticoes; in the valleys between were streets narrower and more squalid than any Castus had known. It seemed absurd, even insane, to imagine that their small party of men could hope to have any influence on a city of such size and energy.

On the first morning, after their journey up from Portus, Castus and the rest of the party had passed through the centre of the city. Crossing the Tiber, Castus had seen the imperial palace rising from the summit of the Palatine Hill, the temples of the Capitol opposite. Pudentianus, riding in an open litter, pointed out each monument as they passed, as if he owned the whole town and was displaying it to his guests. As they entered the ancient forum, Diogenes leaned closer. '*Look up,*' he said, and when Castus raised his eyes he had seen a multitude of statues thronging the pediments and pillars all around him, a legion of figures, painted and gilded, glowing in the autumn sunlight.

He remembered that this was Sabina's home. All those times she had described the place, the houses the size of palaces, the temples of gold and marble, Castus had thought it a mere fantasy. Now he knew the truth, and was not surprised that she missed it so keenly.

'Or is it a girl the dominus desires, hmm, yes? A girl, or a boy? Nothing could be simpler for Apelles the Mouse! Which do you prefer – a young virgin girl, eh? Twelve or thirteen maybe, but so *skilful* in the arts of love...'

Castus turned suddenly on his heel, causing the little man to jump back a step and almost skid on the polished floor.

'I want nothing from you!' he growled. 'Do I look like a wealthy man? Do I have a slave following me with a money pouch?'

'But, dominus,' the man said, the grin sliding over his face again, 'I would surely take your word as bond! You are a soldier, I perceive? A noble soldier, yes, one of the brave legionaries of our invincible emperor Maxentius? Why, certainly I would trust your word!'

'You know nothing about me,' Castus said, leaning closer.

'I told you – get lost, or I'll get angry!'

He raised his fist, flexing the heavy muscles of his arm, and the little man's grin vanished in a twitch of fear. Apelles skipped back a few steps and made a bizarre and obscene gesture.

'Go suck a donkey's cock!' he said, then scuttled quickly away across the marble paving in search of more willing customers.

Castus continued on across the hall, shrugging off his sense of irritation. The people of Rome, he had noticed, were certainly the rudest he had ever encountered. In every street there were people arguing and shouting, waving their arms at each other, exchanging insults. Even buying a loaf of bread was a confrontation. He supposed it was just the effect of so many people from so many different places living crushed together like this. But it was exhausting all the same.

The fact that the little man had so easily marked him as a soldier did not surprise Castus. He had never been convinced by the idea of masquerading as a former gladiator: whatever Nigrinus and his friends might think, professional sports fighters looked quite different from soldiers. Their muscles developed differently, their stance and posture was quite distinct, and anyone who had been in the army could distinguish them with ease.

At the moment, Castus was surrounded by plenty of men who were obviously soldiers. Just as Pudentianus seemed able to instantly identify a rich man at the baths, even naked, so Castus could pick out a soldier. All around him were bodies marked with the welts and bruises of military training, muscles shaped by marching, by humping shields and kit and hefting javelins. Even without the scars, it was easy to spot them. The massive fortified barracks of the Praetorian Guard was only a short distance away from the Baths of Diocletian, and a good quarter of the bathers thronging the halls would be men of the cohorts. Most of them, Castus knew, had been recruited from the detachments of the Danubian army that had marched south with Severus and Galerius years before. Moving through the crowd at the entrance to the thermal chambers, he picked out the familiar accents of the Illyrian provinces, of Pannonia, Dacia and Moesia. These men spoke like him; they looked like him. Strange to think that they were his enemies, and would kill him if they knew his true identity.

Castus and the other members of the expedition were living in Pudentianus's sprawling family mansion, a short distance away from the baths along the ridge of the Quirinal Hill. Nigrinus came and went on his own obscure errands; Castus had ordered Felix to accompany him, partly in case the notary needed protection, but mainly to keep an eye on what he was doing. Felix could report little; Nigrinus was obviously keen that his operations remained shrouded in secrecy. Of them all, only Diogenes seemed to be enjoying himself. He was supposed to be accompanying Castus, but instead he spent most of his time in the libraries and bookshops of the city.

He was welcome to that, Castus thought as he lay on a marble bench in an atmosphere of steam and fresh sweat. A slave scraped oil from his shoulders. Diogenes was as likely to find useful information in the library as he himself was at the baths. He was supposed to meeting somebody here, a contact of Nigrinus, although this was his second visit and for the second time there was no sign of the man.

Next, scanning the crowds, he paced through into the hot baths and then to the cold plunge. Easy to get careless; he reminded himself that this was enemy territory, and he was in danger here. With the bathing ritual completed, and still no sign of Nigrinus's contact, Castus sat on a bench in the circular vestibule of the thermal rooms. Opposite him, a pair of older men stood and observed the younger bathers as they emerged from the steam room, assessing them with a practised eye. A man sauntered in from the main hall, dressed in a silk loincloth and trailed by over a score of slaves carrying towels, scrapers and lotion bottles. Castus watched it all, and his lip curled. This was a fool's errand.

Out through the pillared portals, he moved into the blaze of sunlight filling the vast open-air swimming court. Above him rose the monumental façade of the main hall, ranks of columns, pedestals and statues standing tall over the water. Such splendour, Castus thought as he peered upwards, to impress a lazy and heedless people. Then he took three long strides forward and leaped from the broad marble steps in a long arcing dive into the water.

There were around a hundred other swimmers, and as many again sitting around the edges of the pool, but Castus ignored them for the time being. He was not a graceful swimmer, but his pummelling crawl moved him effortfully from one end of the pool to the other and back a few times with not a thought in his head. Gasping, refreshed, he burst from the water at the far end and strode up onto the steps in the sunlight.

From this angle, he could see the scum of oil on the surface of the water, catching the light in shifting colours. To his left was a group of other men – he marked them at once as soldiers – and as he sat on the steps with the water drying on his skin Castus began to pick out scraps of what they were saying. Their accents were Danubian: one had the flat drawl of a Moesian, another sounded Dacian, and the third was as

Pannonian as Castus himself. He caught the word *Ariminum*, and mention of *the usurper*. It took him a moment to realise that they were talking about his emperor, Constantine.

'Hey, brother,' he said, leaning toward the group of men before his natural reserve could stop him. 'What was that you said?'

The three men stopped talking and shifted around on the steps to look at him. Castus saw the initial hostility in their eyes, then the recognition: he was a soldier just like them, and his words had carried the same accent.

'News from the north,' the Dacian said. 'The enemy's on the Flaminian Way. Mutina's fallen, and they've advanced as far as Ariminum.'

Ariminum was on the Adriatic, Castus knew that. For a moment he felt a spur of fierce pride, and tried not to let it show. *If only I was with them now...*

'I haven't seen you before,' one of the other men, the Pannonian, said. 'You with the Guard?'

Here it was; the moment he had been dreading. Castus knew that he could no longer pretend to be a gladiator. He knew that he had to lie, although the thought of it disgusted him. *I did not ask for this.* He remembered that day on the frozen Danube, edging out onto the ice and feeling it creak and fracture beneath him.

'I'm with the Second Herculia,' he said. It had been true once, at least.

'That's a bad scar on your face there,' the Pannonian went on, with a calculating squint. 'Got that in a fight, I'd say. Recent, too.'

'At Verona,' Castus told him. The less he could tell them, the better. But he knew that every word he spoke took him further into danger.

'You fought at Verona?' the third man said in his flat Moesian drawl. He flicked his head back, impressed. 'That was some fight, so they say. Not too many lived to talk about it.'

'We were in the reserves,' Castus said, gazing back at the water, the splashing swimmers. A knot rose in his throat and he swallowed it down. 'But the enemy broke through. Cavalry cut us up. We were lucky to retreat in formation.'

The three men had shunted over on the steps now, gathering closer to him. Castus was becoming aware that his discomfort fitted neatly with his story: nobody liked to talk of defeat, and he could tell by their moment of silence that they would not press him for the details.

'And now?' the Dacian said. 'You Herculiani are back here in Rome, or what?'

'Spoletium,' Castus said, shrugging heavily. 'Some of us get to come here on leave, though.'

'Sounds like you need it, brother!' said the Moesian, slapping him on the shoulder. 'Where are you from anyway?'

'Taurunum originally.'

They knew Taurunum; the Pannonian was from Cibalae, only a short distance away. In a few moments, all three had introduced themselves, shaking Castus by the hand and the shoulder, glad to draw him into their group.

'I used to be with the Thirteenth Gemina,' the Pannonian said. 'Now a proud soldier of the Eighth Praetorian Cohort! Philocles here used to be in the Fifth Macedonica, and our Dacian friend was in the Eleventh.'

'Castus,' he told them. He had gone as far as he dared into falsehood. *All you had to do*, he thought, *was open your mouth and speak...*

After that it was easy. Only a few moments later, so it seemed, Castus was sitting with the three Praetorians in a shady corner of the palaestra colonnade, where a row of stalls sold snacks and drinks. He was trying not to talk too much, or too quickly – his taciturn act seemed to go down well – but his pulse was racing and he could feel the sweat on his scalp. There were more soldiers gathering around now, and the first three were introducing him all over again to their comrades. Castus sat on a column drum set against the wall of the palaestra, staring out into the sunlight at two fat perspiring men tossing a ball to each other. He tried not to think about the risk he was running.

'We didn't get to hear much about Verona,' the Pannonian was saying, lowering his voice as he passed Castus a cup of wine. 'Although a few men came back from the battle. We were told not to discuss it, in case the civilians got to hear too much.' He glanced around with a suspicious frown. 'Is it true that bastard Pompeianus changed sides at the last moment?'

'Not that I know of,' Castus said. He drank his wine, and tried to keep his hand steady. Now was the moment, he thought.

'What about the army here?' he asked. 'They still got the guts for a fight, do you think?'

The Pannonian snorted. 'Oh, yes,' he said. He swilled his mouth with wine. 'Those bastards from Gaul haven't seen anything yet. No offence, brother... But let them come down here, then they'll see some real bloodshed!'

'The Guard are strong enough,' the Dacian said. 'Between you and me, I wouldn't rate the new levies much, though. The Numidians are good, light cavalry and so on, but these new legions are mostly just half-trained civilians from Africa and Sicily. I wouldn't call them soldiers myself...'

'The only proper soldiers are us in the Guard,' said Philocles the Moesian, waving his cup. 'And the cavalry boys. The Horse

Guards. You can keep the Numidians – they'd quicker run away as fight. The rest are just there to make up numbers, as far as I'm concerned. They're not even billeted in the city – their commanders don't trust them enough to bring them here!'

'Too many Christians among them too,' the Pannonian said darkly. He swirled the wine in his cup. 'They're a plague down there in Africa and the south – the sun makes their brains go soft, I reckon.'

'Do Christians even fight?' Castus asked. 'I thought their god told them not to?'

'They fight when you flog them hard enough!' The others laughed, and Castus grinned along with them, letting the information soak in. The wine was strong, and he kept noticing figures moving in the periphery of his vision, men coming and going, listening in. He fought to remain calm, casual-seeming.

'So, if the enemy got this far south,' he said slowly, 'you think they'll send us out to fight in the field, or try and hold the walls?'

The three soldiers pondered, frowning. There were too many others gathered around them now, Castus thought. He needed to keep a line of escape open.

'Hold the walls, I'd say,' one of them decided. 'Let them camp out there and rot! Winter's on its way, and we've got stores enough to last.'

'I'd prefer to fight an open battle,' the Pannonian said. 'But it's the will of the gods and the emperor...'

'Can you trust the people in the city here, though?' Castus asked them, leaning closer into their circle.

'Trust them? Not at all! But they wouldn't dare try anything against us, if that's what you mean.'

'And whatever happens,' another soldier declared, 'we can be sure the gods will give us victory!' He grabbed the jug and refilled their cups with wine. 'Here's to the emperor, and to the gods!' he said, and slopped a libation onto the paving. Each of them did the same.

'Maxentius!' the Dacian cried, raising his cup. 'May he be victorious always!'

Maxentius, they all said, and drank. Castus swallowed heavily, praying that the wine might wash away his traitorous words.

When he lowered his cup, he noticed a man staring at him from the edge of the group. A face he recognised, pale and raw-boned, with a coarse rust-coloured beard. For a moment he could not place him.

'Centurion!' the Pannonian said, getting to his feet and saluting quickly. The red-bearded man nodded in acknowledgement, but his eyes remained fixed on Castus.

The arena at Verona, Castus remembered. *Gods have mercy...*

'Do I know you?' the centurion said. There was another man with him, a younger soldier with thick lips and a broken nose.

'I don't think so, centurion,' Castus replied, trying to return the man's gaze and not flinch to obviously.

'Centurion Sergianus was at Verona too,' said the Dacian, nudging Castus on the shoulder. 'He escaped from a prison after the battle... only got back here a few days ago...'

Sergianus, that was the name. *Me and my boys won't turn traitor for you, or anybody.* The centurion stared at Castus a moment longer, then blinked and turned away. Castus watched him over the rim of his cup: Sergianus walked a few paces along the colonnade with the younger man at his side, glanced back over his shoulder, then walked on again.

Out, now.

Castus waited, holding his nerve, pretending to drink a little more wine as the three Praetorians talked of some plan to move on to a bar they knew nearer their barracks. He was invited to join them, of course.

'Sure,' he said, feigning a grin. He felt the scar tighten across his jaw. 'Just got to use the pot first.'

Clambering between them, he walked as casually as he could along the colonnade in the opposite direction from Sergianus, then stepped around the corner into the lobby leading to the latrines. Once he was out of sight of the Praetorians he pressed his back against the cool marble wall and drew a long shuddering breath. A heartbeat, then two, and he was moving again.

He had been this way when he had visited the baths before, with Pudentianus. Striding quickly, holding himself back from running, he passed through the long hall of the latrines. A few men glanced at him, but he got through without being challenged. At the far end, through a narrow doorway, he stepped out into the changing rooms. He found his tunic and cloak on the shelf and dressed quickly, fumbling at the straps of his boots; anyone who saw him now would know that he was not a serving soldier, and the penalties for being caught as a deserter were worse than those for a runaway slave.

Cursing under his breath, Castus willed himself to remain calm. He threw the cloak around his shoulders, tossed a copper to the cloakroom slave and strode out into the atrium hall of the baths, heading for the exit doors.

'You!'

One glance over his shoulder, and Castus saw the red-bearded centurion striding from the changing room behind him, fastening his belt. The younger man was right behind him. No doubt now that Sergianus had remembered him. Putting his head down, Castus kept walking, long hard strides towards the exit door and out into the late-afternoon sun.

Do not run, he told himself. *Do not run...* But he could hear the sound of his pursuers now, the grate of their nailed boots on the marble floor of the atrium. He had no weapon – he had carried the shortsword concealed beneath his tunic a few times, but at the baths that would have been impossible. Sergianus and his friend would both have military daggers, perhaps clubs too.

He was halfway along the gravel path through the grove of trees, moving fast towards the gates that led from the baths enclosure, when he heard the shout behind him.

'*Thief!* Stop that thief!'

At once men were closing in from both sides. Like a shout of *fire* in a crowded theatre, calling that word at the baths always got a response.

No chance to hide now. Castus pulled up his cloak and wrapped it over his left arm. Then he started running.

He reached the gates before his pursuers; a man stepped up to bar the way before him and Castus shouldered him aside, then he swung himself around the gatepost. Outside was a broad expanse of gravel in blazing sunlight, milling slaves and litter-bearers waiting for their masters, others touting for business. Castus swerved between them, kicking up dust from the gravel as he ran. The route to Pudentianus's house lay to the left, around the corner of the baths by the old Colline Gate and left along the straight road called the Alta Semita. Castus glanced that way, then turned and ran to the right.

He was out of the crowd around the litters and halfway to the corner of the baths enclosure by the time he heard the noise of pursuit. Sergianus had gathered a crowd behind him, whether fellow soldiers or civilians Castus had no chance to tell. He just kept running, along the wall to the corner, then on across the street and up an alleyway. The noise of his breath, his own footsteps on the cobbles, was loud. The clatter and shout of the pursuit was louder still.

Down the alley he cut right, then left across a muddy courtyard where ragged-looking children sat around a well. He was entering the web of narrower streets now. A group of men in brown workman's tunics turned as he approached and called out, trying to bar the way, but Castus just slammed through them and kept running. A dog erupted, snarling, from a doorway and he heard the snap of its chain as he dodged past.

A stitch was burning in his flank. Sunlight lanced hot between the close-packed houses, and Castus felt the sweat running down his spine beneath his tunic.

He paused for a moment in a wider street, heaving breath as he listened for the sounds of the chase. The glint of light caught his eye: an array of knives, displayed outside an ironmonger's shop, ranks of blades hanging from a rack and spread across a table. He could snatch one and run – better to be armed… Then he saw the eyes watching him from the open doorways on all sides, the suspicious faces. No, he had enough trouble already without another mob at his back.

A cry echoed down the alleyway behind him, and Castus looked back to see Sergianus and three more men coming after him. The others from the bath must have fallen away… He drew a long breath, then shoved himself from the mouth of the alley and bolted across the street into a narrow cleft between the buildings on the far side.

He was moving downhill now, with the sun almost directly ahead of him. Castus tried to get his bearings: he had never been in this part of the city before. The narrow street he was following dropped into a valley packed with small houses, walled yards and blackened old apartment buildings. The road divided: narrower paths on two sides. Castus paused at the corner, looking back again. The younger soldier was there, Sergianus's friend with the thick lips; he spotted Castus, shouted and began to run.

Up the crooked alley, crumbling brick on either side, Castus cut left and then right and found a blank wall ahead of him. He turned, breath caught: he was in a courtyard between apartment buildings, the ground slimy with rotting food scraps and the stink of hot clogged drains filling the air. No exit. A woman with dirty hair peered down at him from a high balcony.

Doubling back, Castus reached the turning of the alley and threw himself against the wall with his cloak bunched around his left fist. At once he heard the approaching footsteps of the soldier chasing him, rapid at first but then slowing. Castus pressed himself against the bricks, not daring to breathe, willing the young man not to glance around as he passed.

At the last moment the man turned, his eyes widening over the bridge of his broken nose as he saw Castus behind him. His mouth opened, but before he had a chance to cry out Castus surged forward and swung his fist into the man's face. The blow crunched against his jaw, but the man did not drop; he had a blade in his right hand, and his left hand whipped out and grabbed Castus by the shoulder. Twisting, Castus trapped the blade in the folds of his bunched cloak, then grappled the man by the neck and tried to break his grip. Just for a moment he was aware of the woman still watching them, impassive, from the high balcony.

The soldier snarled in his ear; Castus heaved against him and swung him back against the bricks. Still he could not break the man's hold, and in a few moments the other pursuers would be upon him... Castus dropped his arm quickly, seized the man's right wrist and twisted it, angling the dagger back towards him. Three tight thudding breaths as they wrestled together, then Castus threw his weight against his opponent; he felt the man's arm buckle, and the blade punch back into his side, just beneath his ribs. The soldier stiffened, gasping through clenched teeth.

For a moment Castus held the soldier in his grip as the life flowed out of him. He could feel the blood spattering the front of his tunic. 'Sorry, brother,' he said.

Then he flung the dying man away from him and ran once more.

Pudentianus's house stood on the slope of the Quirinal, with high porticoes looking out over the valley towards the Forum and Palatine beyond. The main door was up on the Alta Semita, but there was a secondary entrance that led to the kitchens and the private bath suite, at the top of a flight of steps that climbed from the valley. Castus came up that way as the last of the afternoon faded into evening. He was exhausted, and knew he looked harried. His cloak was pulled around his body to hide the bloodstains on his tunic.

'Oh, you are injured!' the cook's wife cried, throwing up her hands as Castus passed the kitchen door. She came after him into the passageway.

'Just a disagreement at the baths,' Castus told her as he stripped off his cloak and flung it aside. 'I'm not hurt.' The woman was already fetching him a cup of watered wine. She was a slave, heavy-bodied and flat-faced, but Castus liked her. He sank down gratefully onto a stool in the kitchen courtyard, took the cup and drank deeply.

'Dominus,' the woman said, leaning closer. 'Please, you must go up... the Young Dominus and the Man from Gaul are arguing! We're worried they'll fall out badly!'

Over her shoulder, the old door porter nodded his agreement. Castus groaned, and tipped his head back against the wall. The 'Man from Gaul' was Nigrinus; to the slaves of the household, everyone from outside Rome was an exotic foreigner. Castus, of course, was 'the Illyrian' to them; he had no idea what they called Felix and Diogenes.

'All right,' he said, hauling himself to his feet again.

A narrow stairway climbed from the kitchen courtyard to the residential area on the upper floor of the house. Castus could hear Pudentianus's raised voice when he was only halfway up the stairs. He jogged up the last flight, crossed the portico of the garden court and joined the knot of slaves at the open doorway of the main reception chamber.

'The senatorial order of Rome,' Pudentianus was saying, his voice high and cracked, 'is not some tradesmen's fraternity that can be summoned upon demand! They are the servants of no man! They are the very custodians of the state, the living embodiment of the majesty of Rome itself, of our oldest and proudest traditions—!'

'Exactly,' Nigrinus broke in. 'Which is why I was sent here to meet with them. Which I cannot do if you continue to prevaricate like this.' He was speaking quietly, in his usual bland singsong tone, but Castus could hear the tense rage simmering in his words.

The two men were facing each other across the chamber, and the contrast was telling. Pudentianus paced angrily, turning on his heel, striking the air with his fingers; Nigrinus was completely still, his face blank beneath the grey-brown bowl of his hair. Beyond them was an open window giving a view over the evening skyline. Diogenes sat beside the window; he raised an eyebrow at Castus.

'I am not *prevaricating*!' Pudentianus fumed. Castus could almost hear the young man's teeth grinding. 'I am engaged in complex and delicate negotiations! Which will be ruined if you insist on blundering into everything I try and do!'

Castus leaned against the doorpost and folded his arms.

'Complex and delicate negotiations?' Nigrinus said, almost whispering. 'What would you know of that, *boy*? I was sent here by the emperor himself to conduct this mission. I have placed myself and those with me in grave danger. I have spent days descending into the slums of this city, seeking out criminals and unsavoury men, even talking to *Christians*. And yet I must bide my time while you dance attendance on your betters, is that it?'

Pudentianus glared back at him, fists clenched at his sides, speechless. Castus had seldom seen the notary so obviously angry, but he gave very little sign of it. The young noble-man's more apparent rage appeared puny and ineffectual by comparison.

'I remind you,' Pudentianus said, 'that you are guests in my family's home!'

Nigrinus wafted a slight bow, but his expression did not alter. 'Get me an audience with the senators,' he said quietly. 'Or I shall arrange one myself. That is all.'

The young nobleman hissed between his teeth, then stormed out of the room. He gave Castus only the briefest glance as he passed, his eyes widening slightly at the sight of his bloodied tunic, then he was gone.

'Oh, there you are,' Nigrinus said, noticing Castus standing in the doorway. His jaw cracked as he yawned. 'Our man at the baths didn't show, I take it?'

Castus shook his head as he crossed to the window, exchanging a quick glance with Diogenes. Behind him he could hear the notary's slippered footsteps leaving the room. Outside, the valley was falling into darkness under a smoky grey sky. The temple porticoes blazed with torches, and all across the city, tiny embers of lamplight were appearing in the shadowed streets and huddled buildings.

The city was a maze. And somewhere, Castus thought, far away across the horizon, the war was drawing closer every day.

CHAPTER XX

'You're certain you understand what is required?' Puden-tianus asked for the third or fourth time. 'You remember everything I told you? Let me do all the talking at first, and only speak if you're addressed directly...'

'I remember, yes,' Castus said, not caring to hide the annoy-ance in his voice. The young man's nervous agitation was wearing at his patience.

They were walking together down a long gravel path. To either side were clipped bushes, occasional glimpses of fish ponds, mossy statues lost in the vegetation. Ahead of them the straight path was enclosed by a box trellis thickly grown with ivy. It was morning, only an hour after dawn, and the air in the Gardens of Sallust had a misty October dampness.

'I suppose I should thank you for agreeing to this as well,' Pudentianus went on. Castus guessed he was talking to stop himself thinking. 'As you know, I was keen to avoid the notary learning of this meeting. In the circumstances, and at this stage, I feel you are a far more suitable emissary...'

Less likely to try and take charge, he means. Castus nod-ded. The young nobleman's desire to cut Nigrinus out of the negotiations with the Senate was understandable, but risky. No doubt Pudentianus believed that Castus himself would be easier to manipulate. *Let him try*, Castus thought, and breathed a soft laugh down his nose.

The damp air deadened the crunch of their footsteps on the gravel. For all the quiet, peaceful atmosphere of this place, Castus wished he had somebody with him. Felix, ideally. But the young nobleman had insisted that they come here alone, and did not give the impression of numbers. Only a single slave followed them: a sour-faced, pockmarked man named Naso, one of the two that had come with Pudentianus from Verona. Castus flexed his shoulders and felt the strap tighten across his chest: the shortsword he was wearing beneath his tunic dug reassuringly into his ribs. After his encounter at the baths, he had resolved never to leave the house without a weapon; he did not want to face an armed opponent with empty hands again.

At the end of the long trellised avenue the path broadened at the bank of an ornamental lake. On a marble pedestal stood a sculpture of a naked barbarian apparently stabbing himself in the chest, while a dying woman dangled from his arm. Castus gave it a quick glance, hoping it was not intended as prophetic.

The men standing around the statue turned as Castus and Pudentianus approached. There were six of them, dressed smartly but plainly. Bodyguards, Castus guessed; judging from the hang of their capes and tunics, he knew several were carrying concealed weapons. There were more figures beyond them, slaves standing with their backs to the group, watching the approaches. Clearly, Castus thought, they were taking no chances on being unexpectedly disturbed.

Pudentianus kept walking, spreading his arms wide. The group of bodyguards parted before him, and Castus saw the man seated on the marble bench at the foot of the statue. He was older, heavily built, with thick iron-grey hair. Beneath his hooded eyes were dark pouches of flesh, and his downturned mouth was framed by weighty jowls. As Pudentianus approached he got to his feet, heaving himself up using a stick, then stood still as the younger man embraced him and kissed him on both cheeks. Castus noticed the rings on the man's fingers and the massive jewelled brooch securing his deep blue cloak. As Pudentianus stepped away, the old senator sank down to sit again, as if the effort of standing up had proved tedious for him.

'Most noble Rufius Volusianus, I greet you!' Pudentianus said. 'May the gods pour blessings upon you!' Compared with the older senator, he seemed barely more than a boy.

'Harrumph,' Volusianus said. Castus recalled what Pudentianus had told him about this man: he was one of the leaders of the Senate, former Consul, former Prefect of the City... Also, it seemed, Pudentianus's uncle.

'We've been hearing a lot about your activities, nephew,' Volusianus said. His voice was so deep it seemed to come from somewhere beneath the ground. Castus noticed that the man's eyes did not move as he spoke; his whole face remained oddly immobile. 'Or the activities of your associates, I suppose,' the senator went on. 'Your friends have been spreading a lot of coin about the city. Hmm. Buying up the collegia and the circus factions. Even the Christians. Glad to see your emperor knows the power of gold. The power of blood too.'

He turned his head, swivelling his leaden gaze to peer at Castus. 'Talking of which,' he said, 'who's this?'

'This, uncle,' Pudentianus said, stepping to one side, 'is the most distinguished Aurelius Castus, a tribune in the army of... of our friend from Gaul.'

'Tribune eh?' the old man said.

Castus felt the scar itching on his jaw. His tongue pressed at the gap between his missing teeth. He was wearing an old

314

brown cloak over a plain tunic; nothing in his appearance marked him as anything but a common ex-soldier.

'Once upon a time,' Volusianus said, in a distant, musing tone, 'our legions were commanded by men of the aristocracy. Our tribunes resembled young gods. Now they look like cookshop bruisers, it seems... Still, that's convenient, I suppose, if one requires some bruising to be done!'

Castus just stared at the man, eyes wide, his back teeth clenching. He could see the bodyguards shifting their stance slightly, smiling to themselves at the old senator's wit. It was so insulting, Castus thought, that he was almost amused himself.

'They're saying in the city,' Volusianus went on, speaking to the air, 'that this *Constantine* is bringing an army of savage barbarians from the forests of Germania to cut all of our throats and burn Rome to the ground. So tell me, Tribune Aurelius Castus,' he said, turning abruptly to address him, 'what does your master want from us?'

For a moment Castus said nothing, holding the man's weighty gaze. He could sense Pudentianus peering back at him, beginning to fidget and fret. The old senator's eyes were like pebbles, trapped in the dull putty of his face.

'The emperor Flavius Constantinus Augustus,' Castus said at last, careful to keep any ingratiating note from his voice, 'desires that the Senate and people of Rome withdraw their active support from the usurper in the coming battle. If Maxentius believes that the city will not stand a siege, he will be forced to march out and fight us in the open field. Then he can be defeated.'

'And if he does not?'

'Then the city will fall to our assault, and many more will die. My emperor does not wish the capital of the world to be dishonoured in this way.' Castus heard the words as he spoke them: he had no real idea of how much he was inventing, and how much was true. Volusianus nodded and turned his dead eyes away.

'The city of Rome has not fallen to a hostile foe in over seven hundred years,' he said. 'Maxentius believes he can maintain himself inside the walls against Constantine, as he did against Flavius Severus and Galerius. Some fortune-teller apparently told him once that if he leaves the city evil will befall him! But it's true that he has become... erratic. Disappointing, in fact. I supported him once, as I'd supported his father Maximian, who came to such an *unfortunate* end in Gaul...'

His voice had sharpened slightly. Did he know that Castus himself had been involved in that death?

'But lately Maxentius has disturbed the harmony of the city too much. He has set his troops on the people, and on the nobility. Many of our conscript fathers have lost their property; many have even lost their lives. But I ask, tribune – could your man do any better, hmm?'

'The emperor Constantine,' Castus said, slow and steady, 'has the greatest respect for the Senate. He wishes to restore Rome to her ancient greatness...'

'And you can give us assurances of this?'

Castus looked quickly at Pudentianus. The young man was glaring at him, almost nodding encouragement.

'No,' he said. 'I cannot, but there is another in our party, a tribune of notaries. He has been authorised to speak in the emperor's name.'

He could almost hear Pudentianus's outraged exhalation. But there was no way that Castus was going to agree to cutting Nigrinus out completely. He had no taste for diplomacy himself, and the notary was the one who had planned all this and had the imperial warrant to negotiate. Besides, Castus feared what the man might do if his schemes were too obviously thwarted.

Volusianus tipped his head back a little and sniffed. 'A very wise man once said, if you want things to stay the same, things must change. So, very well. We will meet with your notary and hear whatever offer he wants to make us. Tomorrow evening, shall we say? The house of Turcius Apronianus on the Esquiline; my nephew can take you there.'

He made a slight stirring gesture in the air with his jewelled fingers, then gazed off towards the lake. Clearly the meeting was at an end.

'Well, that went comparatively well!' Pudentianus said, with a grin, as soon as they were out of earshot. 'You know, I think he even liked you...'

'Is that how he shows it? By insulting people to their faces?' Castus frowned, bemused. The young nobleman's enthusiasm was disconcerting.

'You don't understand,' Pudentianus said, with a condescending air. 'Gaius Ceionius Rufius Volusianus is one of the most powerful individuals in Rome. When a man reaches that level, most of humanity is simply *invisible* to him. That he took any notice of you at all, even addressed you directly, shows that he's already decided to support us!'

Maybe so, Castus thought, pacing along with his hands clasped behind his back. The sun was beginning to shine through the morning mist, and it was becoming humid. 'This is all just a game for you, isn't it?' he said.

Pudentianus smiled back at him. 'Of course!' he said. 'Isn't it like that for you too? Winners and losers – why else would you get involved?'

Honour, Castus thought. *Loyalty. Redemption.* Or was that just part of the game too? He remembered the bloody field after the battle at Verona, the heaped corpses, the dying and the slain.

Darkness was already falling by the time they left the house the following evening. As they descended the street into the valley a damp breeze was guttering the lamps outside the corner bars and cook shops. Still plenty of people about at that hour, and they moved in a tight column, Pudentianus riding at the centre in a covered litter, with slaves from his household ahead and behind. To any onlooker, he was just a wealthy young man on his way to a dinner party. Walking ahead of the litter, Castus kept the hood of his cloak drawn up to hide his face. He was wary, scanning the groups of men that lingered at the street corners. After his encounter at the baths he was all too aware of the dangers of the city; he had slept badly the night before, disturbed by dreams of pursuit and entrapment. The risks they were running were all too obvious now.

Nigrinus trailed at the back of the group, walking on his own. He had said little to anyone since Pudentianus had told him about the meeting that night, only nodded his agreement. Nothing to show whether he was angered by what had been arranged, or content to go along with it. But Castus could sense the notary's hatred for the young nobleman wrapped tightly within him.

They passed through a busy area of narrow streets, then turned to the left and climbed again, around the massive stone walls of a market enclosure. The Porticus of Livia, Castus realised: he was trying to keep his bearings and his sense of direction. Behind him, Felix walked silently, content to blend in with the household slaves. At least, Castus thought, if they got lost in this maze of streets Felix would surely know the way

318

out. Past the market, they climbed steadily up the back of the Esquiline Hill, into a region of high garden walls and shadowed gateways. This was where the wealthy had their mansions; as they walked Castus could smell the fragrance of flowering bushes and greenery. A crescent moon rose before them, and the sound of their footsteps echoed between the blank walls.

They had walked for about a mile when the journey came to an abrupt end. In a narrow cobbled lane that dropped downhill towards a dark expanse of parkland, the litter-bearers set down their load and Pudentianus climbed from the cushioned interior. Castus looked to left and right, but saw only bare mossy walls. He looked up, and saw white stucco pillars and the curve of a dome. Then a narrow door opened in the wall beside them.

'In here,' Pudentianus said, drawing his cloak around him as he stepped through the door.

The smell of woodsmoke and hot ashes met them as they entered the darkened chamber beyond the door. This was the furnace chamber of the bathrooms, Castus realised; they were slipping into the house through the service quarter, just as he had entered Pudentianus's own mansion so many times. Moving in silence, they filed up a darkened stairway and emerged into a wide garden courtyard with pillared walks on all sides. At the far end of the garden, beyond the low clipped bushes and the marble pool, was an arrangement of rocks and statuary. Water poured from a spout near the top to flow down in rivulets, lit by lanterns concealed to either side. A startling effect, Castus thought, especially at night.

'They must be siphoning water from the public aqueducts,' Diogenes whispered in his ear. 'Illegal, but I suppose they make the rules...'

Pudentianus paused at the end of the garden while one of his slaves removed his cloak and another arranged his dining robe and tunic. 'I'll have to go on ahead,' he told Castus. 'The slaves here will attend to you for now, and I'll send word when you are to follow.' There was an assertive tone in his voice: already he was showing off his command of the situation.

'Through here, domini, if you please.' A household slave with a Frankish-looking hairstyle gestured through a wide doorway leading from the courtyard. With Nigrinus scowling behind him, Diogenes and Felix bringing up the rear, Castus followed the slave into a large chamber set with couches and stools, a low circular table in the centre and tall iron lamp-stands in the corners. At once other slaves entered behind them, bearing platters of food and jugs of wine.

'Looks like we won't be dining with the senators,' Diogenes commented as he surveyed the meal spread before them.

'Of course not,' said Nigrinus. 'We'll be brought on once they've finished, to follow the musicians and the jugglers. A fine bit of after-dinner entertainment.' He seated himself on a stool near the door, ignoring the food and drink.

Castus sat on one of the couches, glancing around the room. The chamber would have graced a palace: walls painted with landscape scenes, and a big multicoloured mosaic on the floor showing a mounted huntsman spearing some sort of writhing beast. Even the dishes and jugs were fine worked silver, and the lamps on the tall stands were ornate bronze, shaped like leaping dolphins. He noticed Felix sitting awkwardly opposite him, knees spread. Castus himself had spent enough time in the palace at Treveris to be comfortable with luxury, but he was reminded that Felix had not.

'I believe this is flavoured with silphium,' Diogenes said, sniffing at a dish of roast chicken cutlets in thick pungent sauce. 'Remarkable. Must be worth its weight in gold...' He selected a piece and chewed quizzically. 'Salty,' he said.

There was an open window at the far end of the room, giving a view over the nocturnal city. Castus went to it and leaned on the sill, breathing in the night air gladly. He would not be sorry to leave Rome, magnificent though it was. In the middle distance, he picked out the great ranked arches of the amphitheatre, lit up by torches. A little to the right of the arches, Castus saw an enormous gilded statue, standing almost as high as the amphitheatre beside it and catching the glow from within.

'The Colossus of Helios,' said a voice at his elbow. Castus turned to see Nigrinus beside him. 'Although,' the notary went on, 'Maxentius recently had the face of the sun god recarved to resemble his own son, Romulus. An act of presumptuous impiety, for which the gods will surely punish him!' He smiled, as if amused by the concept.

'You believe that?'

'Of course not!'

For a moment they stood together. Felix and Diogenes were still eating, and neither was close enough to overhear the notary's words.

'When we're taken to the meeting,' Nigrinus said, his lips barely moving, 'you must be very careful what you say. Let me make our case – the young fool will try and involve you, no doubt. He's only attempting to make himself look more important.'

'Isn't this meeting what you wanted?' Castus asked him, growling the words. The notary's sour humour was beginning to wear at his nerves.

'Oh, certainly,' Nigrinus said. 'But I would have preferred to approach the senate on terms of greater equality. As it is, we come to them as supplicants rather than emissaries. Which is the way they want it, of course… Our friend Pudentianus intends to show us off like hunting trophies.'

321

'I didn't see your methods getting us any closer,' Castus said. 'I care nothing for your sense of pride; all I want is to get this meeting done and get clear of this house, and this city, with my men alive and unharmed. Understand? Then we can get back to being soldiers.'

'And that's all that matters to you, hmm?' Nigrinus said, with an arch smile. He shook his head sadly. 'All this effort, and it could so easily be wasted.'

'That's for you to judge, not me. Have you said your piece?'

'Not quite. As I was saying, we must watch what we tell them. The aristocracy of Rome is old and scaly in the ways of power. Treat them as you would a bag of snakes. And remember, they would not hesitate to sacrifice any of us if they could benefit from it.'

'Sounds familiar,' Castus said, with a humourless smile. How long had he known this man? Seven years, he realised, since he had first met him in the praetorium in distant Eboracum. It was longer than Castus had known any of his friends. Yet here they were thrown together again, by chance or fate. They were supposed to be allies, he reminded himself, not adversaries.

'I have a proposal for them,' Nigrinus went on, ignoring his remark. 'I may need you to back me on some of the finer points, but all you need do is agree to what I say. Is that clear?'

'Not really. But don't worry – anything that gets us out of here quicker's fine with me.' Castus went back to the table, leaving Nigrinus stony-faced and apparently consumed in thought.

Sitting at the couch, Castus picked at the rich food, but his appetite was gone. A tight knot of agitation filled his belly. He could feel the pommel of the sword strapped beneath his tunic prodding at his armpit; Felix and Diogenes were also armed.

Nothing in the house suggested threat, but the weaponry was a reassurance all the same.

Castus tried to empty his mind, pretend he was on some long night-sentry duty. His knee was jumping, and he leaned his fist upon it. Then he got up and marched to the door.

'Does the dominus desire anything?' the long-haired slave said, appearing from the shadows. A eunuch, Castus noticed.

'No,' he said. From somewhere deeper in the house he could hear the sound of music: flutes and a lyre. Bronze discs hanging between the pillars of the portico chimed in the faint warm breeze. Standing in the doorway, Castus peered across the garden at the far colonnades. A pair of figures moved over there, slaves passing from one wing of the house to another. For a moment the light from an open door caught them, and Castus blinked and stared. Both of them were wearing sky-blue tunics. Exactly the same as Lepidus's followers; he was sure of it.

He took a step across the threshold, and the eunuch gave him an enquiring glance. Other slaves were positioned along the portico, lingering in the shadows; clearly the household staff had been ordered to keep a close eye on their guests, and not allow them to stray.

But then the sound of a distant gong echoed along the portico.

'Domini,' the eunuch announced to the room behind him. 'Please, follow me.'

CHAPTER XXI

The nine senators reclined on the semi-circular couch of the dining chamber. Above them in warm lamplight rose a broad apse decorated with the signs of the zodiac picked out in gold and bright glass. *The gods in repose*, Castus thought.

He was disturbed to notice that Volusianus, the old senator he had spoken to in the gardens, was not among them. These were rather younger men, although Pudentianus was by far the youngest. The sons of the chief players, he assumed. Doubtless they would pass on whatever was discussed to their seniors.

Two stools stood on the marble tiles before the apse. Castus took one and Nigrinus the other, with Felix and Diogenes standing at their backs. The eunuch who had conducted them from the waiting room faded silently from their presence, and Castus heard the gentle thud of the doors closing behind him.

There were no introductions. Safer, Castus guessed, if they did not know the full names of those who had gathered, treasonably, to hear their offer. But Pudentianus leaned across the circular table, recently cleared of the remains of their sumptuous meal, and muttered to the other men on the couches. Castus heard his own name mentioned, and that of Nigrinus. He was trying not to think about the slaves he had seen outside; it was surely coincidence, he had decided. Or perhaps he had not seen the colour of their tunics too clearly in the lamplight...

'We understand,' one of the senators declared, 'that you have an address from the rival emperor in the north?' He looked eastern, dark-skinned, an Egyptian perhaps, and his voice echoed from beneath the apse.

Nigrinus cleared his throat, a thin scratching sound. 'Conscript fathers,' he said. 'We come to you as ambassadors from the emperor Flavius Valerius Constantinus Augustus, who even now approaches this city with an army of liberation, to free Rome from the hateful rule of the tyrant.'

'Indeed,' said another of the senators, a massively fleshy man with a small beard. 'And yet we have heard this rhetoric before, I think. Just over a century ago, Septimius Severus marched on Rome in a similar fashion. He too gave assurances that the dignity of the Senate would be respected, that no blood would be shed... but within a few years, he had executed scores of our forefathers!'

A ripple of nodding heads and muttered words from around the dining table.

'How are we to know that your emperor will not prove an even greater tyrant than the one we presently enjoy?' the Egyptian added.

'You are right to be apprehensive!' Nigrinus said, and his words carried the slightest touch of a threat. Castus noticed the men on the dining couch stiffen. 'But our emperor Constantine cares only for the harmony of the world, the harmony of gods and men, and for the sublime majesty of Rome... and the Roman Senate.'

Getting to his feet, Nigrinus addressed the assembly beneath the apse, standing like an orator and throwing his thin voice across the room. He must have been preparing this speech for months, Castus realised. 'For the last seven years,' the notary said, 'Constantine has ruled the western provinces with

325

strength, justice and wisdom. None complain of his rule! None have been persecuted, save only those who rose in treasonous rebellion against him—'

'Emperors have a way of deciding what is treason and what is not,' the fat senator broke in. 'All of us have served Maxentius!'

'You have served *Rome*. And my emperor assures you that your service will be recognised. None will be punished for doing their duty. In fact, all the senatorial offices will be preserved in the hands of their current holders. There will be no trials, no informers and no confiscations. Property illegally seized by the tyrant will be restored, and his oppressive edicts revoked. Peace and justice will prevail...'

Castus watched the expressions of the assembled senators. Some remained closed, warily suspicious, while others visibly brightened. In their eyes he saw the flash of greed, the satisfaction of self-interest. As Nigrinus spoke, Castus let his gaze wander around the room. Marble on all sides, statues in niches, dazzling wall paintings. The whole house looked like this: he had seen enough of it during the brief trip from the waiting room to realise that this mansion must be one of the finest in Rome. Or perhaps all the houses of the supreme aristocracy were as grand? Why should men who possessed such wealth, such massively upholstered luxury, care who governed them? Then again, Castus thought, only emperors had the power to take all this away. He felt the stirring of a vague sense of admiration for Maxentius, daring to strike against men so wealthy and arrogant.

Once again he recalled that this was the world that Sabina had known. She would have been comfortable in these surroundings; this was what she had missed for all those years she had spent in Gaul. His mood soured: he could never have given her any of this opulence.

'Tribune?' somebody repeated. Castus sat up sharply. One of the senators had asked him a question.

'My colleague wished to know,' the Egyptian said, 'how you, as a military man, would rate Constantine's chances against our current emperor?'

Castus took a moment to compose his thoughts. He felt the pressure of the room upon him; his unease in addressing civilians was nothing new, but this particular gathering unnerved him. Should he stand up? He decided to remain seated.

'The emperor has an army of thirty thousand men,' he declared. His voice echoed off the high ceiling. 'Most of them are veterans of the Rhine legions. Already we have defeated the tyrant's forces three times. We destroyed his cavalry at Taurinum and his infantry at Verona. If he takes the field against us again, he is sure to be defeated once more.' He heard the fading echo of his words, filled with a certainty he did not possess.

'But Maxentius has fifty thousand, in and around Rome,' the fat senator said.

Castus spoke again before he could think. 'Most of the tyrant's men are newly raised conscripts, poorly trained and poorly equipped. His only disciplined troops are the Praetorians, the city cohorts and the Horse Guards, with the Second Parthica at Albanum, and they muster less than twenty thousand between them all.' He was only repeating what he had heard the soldiers telling him at the baths, but spoken like this his words sounded satisfyingly authoritative. He saw them take effect as the group of senators turned to mutter between themselves once more. The apse they were sitting in had an unusual acoustic property: when the men on the couch spoke together their words were near inaudible, but when they addressed the room the curving space above them amplified their speech.

'Constantine is not the only other player in the game, though,' the Egyptian said. 'There is also Licinius in Illyricum, and Maximinus Daza in the east...'

Nigrinus opened his mouth to speak, but Castus cut him off. 'Licinius is the ally of our emperor,' he said. 'They concluded a pact of marriage last winter.'

'You know this?'

'I carried the messages between them myself.'

Once again a chorus of muttering. Castus caught Nigrinus glancing at him; was he impressed, or annoyed at the lack of diplomatic caution? Impossible to say. Castus found that he did not care. Now he had spoken, he felt the near uncontrollable urge to be out of this room, and out of the oppressive presence of these men.

Nigrinus was speaking again now, pacing in small steps back and forth. 'When the emperor approaches Rome,' he was saying, 'it would greatly aid his cause if the city could be made... uncomfortable for the tyrant. That way he will be less inclined to remain within the walls and chance a siege. I have myself been working with certain of the city factions to inspire demonstrations, or signs of popular disturbance. You might do the same, with your clientele, perhaps, your networks of supporters...'

'You ask that we risk committing sedition, before matters are decided?' another of the senators said.

'Nothing so dramatic, surely! But you might use your influence. The tyrant is a very superstitious man, so they say. Very inclined to prophecy, oracles and suchlike. I believe at least two of you are members of the College of Fifteen. You are responsible for consulting the books of the Sibylline Oracles, yes? If the tyrant desired such a consultation, you might be a position to return a particular reading.'

'A false reading, you mean?' the fat senator said. 'That would be sacrilege!'

'And yet, not wholly unknown,' the Egyptian said, just loud enough for his remark to carry. He probed at his chin, considering. 'What might this particular reading be?'

'Oh, something vague enough to be oracular,' Nigrinus told him. 'And yet sufficient to sway the mind of a man debating the outcome of open battle. Perhaps something like...' He paused, as if thinking. '... *Once battle is joined, the enemy of Rome shall perish!*'

Castus stifled a snort of surprise. Nobody could be in any doubt that the notary had dreamed that one up long ago. Whatever did it mean?

'Certainly it leaves things open,' the Egyptian said. 'And so could not be said to be untrue, either way.'

'But tell me,' said another of the senators, a grave-faced man who had not yet spoken, 'is it true that your emperor favours the Christians unduly?'

Castus exhaled heavily, barely listening to Nigrinus's circling reply – the harmony of men and gods, the security of the state, the importance of unity – and instead issuing a silent prayer that this meeting be allowed to end soon. Surely now, he thought, they had achieved their aim in the city. Could more be done? Surely now they could make preparations to depart, and find their way back to the army. Already Constantine was at Forum Sempronii, they had learned that morning, and his troops were marching southwards daily on the Flaminian Way across the Apennines. *Almighty God, Unconquered Sun, let me be with them soon...*

He found himself staring at one of the younger senators on the couches, reclining beside Pudentianus. The man had not spoken, and seemed to be holding himself back from the debate.

Squinting slightly, Castus observed him from the corner of his eye. He had a lean, handsome face and sharply receding hair; he was familiar somehow, but Castus could not place him. Then the man raised his hand idly and scratched his jaw, and Castus noticed the ring he was wearing: two golden leopards, clasping a pearl. The memory came to him suddenly. Lepidus had worn a very similar ring. And there was a clear resemblance between the two of them.

But now, it appeared, the meeting was concluded; Nigrinus was bowing with stiff courtesy to the men on the couches and pacing towards the doors. Castus stood up, nodded once, and followed him. He expected little result from what he had just witnessed. These men would not, he was sure, stir themselves to any great exertions on Constantine's behalf. Secure in their wealth and privilege, they would continue to sit on their hands and watch from the sidelines as the armies fought and men died. He felt a surge of anger and disgust, and a desire that something should wake these men from their sleep of centuries, disturb their godlike repose.

In the painted vestibule outside the audience chamber the party were directed to wait, while the senators conferred among themselves. There were benches along the walls, but Castus remained standing. How much longer must they remain in this place? Palms in terracotta vases stretched to the panelled ceiling, and against one wall was a huge bronze urn, polished to a mirror shine and set on a fluted pedestal.

'It states here,' Diogenes said, stooping to read the inscription on the pedestal, 'that this was the urn that floated Hercules to the island of Erytheia, which I doubt, although it looks almost large enough...'

Castus noticed that he could see the doorway of the audience chamber behind him reflected in the side of the urn, swimming in the smooth curve of the metal. Within the doorway was the chamber itself, the figures of the senators in their apse like the inhabitants of a miniature golden world. He stepped to one side, and saw in the metal the far side of the vestibule, and a doorway into another room. A flash of sky blue: the two slaves he had seen in the courtyard had passed across the reflection.

Stepping back, he shot a quick glance into the chamber and saw the senator he had noticed earlier, the one wearing the leopard ring, getting up from the couches and walking towards a side door that would connect with the other room. All around the vestibule, household slaves and eunuchs stood sentinel, blocking the exits.

'I need a distraction,' he said to Diogenes, speaking from the side of his mouth.

'What sort of distraction?'

'Use your ingenuity!'

He was already pacing across the vestibule towards the far door. In the next room he could see the senator meeting his pair of slaves and moving away along a corridor.

From behind him came the sudden hollow boom of bronze. A cry, and the slaves at the doorways hurried forward. Diogenes's voice cut through the exclamations. 'So sorry! I just leaned against it a moment – is it dented?'

Castus was already out through the door, slipping into the next room and along the corridor. For once he was glad that his shoes had no hobnails, and he could move quickly and silently. He caught sight of the senator and the two slaves as they turned a corner at the far end of the corridor.

Breaking into a jog, he reached the corner and peered around into a smaller garden court. A fountain trilled at the centre, the water catching the light of the lamps suspended between the pillars. The senator was passing through a low arched doorway at the far side, leaving his two slave attendants to wait in the courtyard. Castus waited, counting his breaths. Then he straightened his tunic and walked casually around the corner of the corridor and across the garden court. The slaves glanced at him, frowning, but did not move to stop him as he followed their master through the arch.

The chamber beyond was semi-circular, and lit dimly with another of the tall dolphin lamps. Monochrome mosaics on the floor, paintings of cavorting nymphs on the ceiling, and around the curve of the far wall a polished marble bench with six holes. Castus suppressed a wry grin: it appeared that the aristocracy of Rome even shat in splendour.

His quarry was already seated at the latrine, frowning as he saw Castus enter the chamber. He opened his mouth to speak, perhaps to call out to his slaves outside, but Castus moved too quickly. The lamplight fluttered wildly as he crossed the floor; then he seized the man by the throat and hauled him up off the bench, pinning him against the wall with a forearm across his neck. The senator's legs were still entangled in his breeches.

'What is this?' the man managed to gasp. 'This is an outrage!'

He raised his hand to try and push Castus away from him, and the gold leopard ring shone in the lamplight.

'Claudianus Lepidus,' Castus said, baring his teeth close to the man's face. 'You know him?' There was a wiping stick tipped with wet sponge beside the latrine; he snatched it up and levelled it at the senator's face. 'Start talking, or you'll get a taste of this!'

A moment of feigned incomprehension; Castus pressed his arm harder, feinting with the dripping sponge-stick. The senator gagged, horrified, then nodded. Sweat was beading on his brow.

'My brother,' he said. 'He's my brother. But… he was exiled many years ago. He was never a member of the Senate. Please – release me and I can explain!'

Castus held the man locked against the wall a moment more, then gave him a last shove and let him drop. He tossed the stick aside. 'I warn you, I'm armed,' he said. 'But I could kill you with my bare hands if I wanted.'

'No need for that, I beg you,' the senator said, clasping his throat. 'I assure you, we are *allies*. In fact, I believe we're related.'

Castus seized the man by the shoulder again, making him flinch.

'My name is Domitius Saturninus Latronianus!' the senator exclaimed, raising his palms in entreaty. 'You're married to my cousin, yes? The domina Valeria Domitia Sabina?'

'Yes,' Castus said, too startled to say more.

'You must understand,' Latronianus went on, still looking queasy with fright, 'my brother is not… an *honourable* man. We have long been opposed in our views and allegiances. He believes that if he serves the tyrant against Constantine, Maxentius will reward him with promotion to the Senate and a share of the property seized from your wife's family.'

'Serves him *how*?' Castus kept his hand on the sword concealed beneath his tunic. There was still no sound from the garden court outside the chamber, but it would not be long before they were disturbed. The senator drew a cloth from his sleeve and dabbed it across his brow.

'My brother has developed a network of informers in the north,' he said. 'Highly placed people who… pass messages and supply information. He has a plan to disrupt the supply lines of Constantine's advance. I know little about it…'

'Tell me.' Already Castus had realised the terrible possibility: could Sabina be one of those highly placed people?

Latronianus gave a loose shrug, glancing around the chamber. 'I believe my brother intends to raise a mutiny among the naval troops at Ravenna, and the garrisons along the roads to the north. Have them restore their old allegiance to Maxentius at the last moment. He's promised their officers gold payments from Rome.'

Castus caught his breath. If Ravenna and the other garrisons declared for Maxentius again, Constantine and his troops would be cut off in the Apennines, with no route of supply. With winter coming on, the tyrant's forces would only have to wait for hunger, cold and desertion to reduce the invading army to nothing.

'Why haven't you acted to stop this?' he said, lowering his voice. He knew well that inaction could be as treacherous as outright treason.

'Lepidus is still my brother!' the senator declared, wide-eyed. He glanced nervously at the sponge-stick lying on the floor. 'It would be impious to turn against my own blood.'

Castus stared at him, disgusted. He saw it all clearly now. Nothing mattered to these men but the fortunes of their own families, their own wealth and prestige. He remembered what Pudentianus had said back in the Gardens of Sallust. *Winners and losers.* It was all just a game.

'But now you've… extracted the information *under duress*,' Latronianus said, with a strained grin, 'you might perhaps act on it. You must understand that we of the Senate could hardly support your man while there is the possibility of something untoward happening! The tyrant has seen off two invading armies already, and those foolish enough to back his opponents openly have paid the price.'

But Castus was already backing towards the door. Clearly it was vital now that he return to the army as soon as possible, and report what he had heard to Constantine's officers. Every further day's delay could give Lepidus the chance to set his plan in motion.

'One more thing,' the senator said, slumping back against the marble seat. He drew a long breath, composing himself. 'Your mission has been compromised, I believe. I don't know how, but the tyrant's spies already know of your presence in the city. You and your friends would be advised to get out of Rome while you still can.'

By the time Castus returned to the vestibule, Nigrinus and Pudentianus were facing each other, only a head's distance between them. The notary had pulled on his travelling cloak, but the young nobleman was still dressed only in his dining robes.

'The meeting is clearly over,' Nigrinus said through thin lips, 'and you are coming with us!'

'You don't give me orders!' Pudentianus hissed back. 'I brought you here, didn't I? Now I say I will remain. It would be discourteous to leave!'

'We must return to your house, as we have things to discuss...'

'Silence,' Castus said abruptly, pushing his way between them. 'The notary's right. We leave as we arrived, together. We go *now*.'

Pudentianus glared at him, and for a moment seemed inclined to protest further. Then he noticed the commanding urgency in Castus's eyes. He snatched his cloak from the slave beside him and marched angrily towards the stairs.

Outside, the night was clear, the moonlight turning the narrow streets into a collage of angled shadows, and the party moved quickly. Slaves went ahead of them with burning torches. Pudentianus had withdrawn into sullen silence, and rode with the curtains of his litter pulled closed and his slave, the pockmarked Naso, marching beside it as if to deter anyone bothering him further.

'You did well back there,' Nigrinus said, sliding into step beside Castus.

'It won't do any good,' Castus grunted in reply. He realised after he had spoken that he had never heard the notary compliment him before. Or compliment anybody, for that matter.

'Oh, I'm not so sure,' Nigrinus said. 'Sometimes people need further encouragement than mere words.'

Castus glanced at him, but the notary was looking more than usually blank, his face in the moonlight a pale expressionless bar. He had been intending to tell Nigrinus what he had learned, but something in his attitude now made Castus uncertain. The brief sense of trust that he had developed for the man was evaporating once more. Shaking his head, he quickened his pace, the words of Latronianus's warning still fresh in his mind. Nearing the front of the group, he joined Felix and Diogenes, just behind the torchbearers. The noise of their footsteps rattled down the narrow cobbled lane, and somewhere close by a dog howled.

Across the back of the Esquiline Hill, their route took them through the twisting alleys behind the Porticus of Livia. There were big apartment buildings looming against the sky now; one of them was half-covered with a ragged lattice of wooden scaffolding, intricate in the light of the moon. Up ahead, the street widened slightly where two branching alleys converged.

Castus felt that warm breath up the back of his neck again, this time a certain presentiment of danger. Something was moving in the shadows of the alleyway. He raised his hand, trying to block the glare of the torch in front of him; he had just enough time to think that he should have positioned himself *ahead* of the torchbearers...

'Halt! In the name of Maxentius Augustus!'

Suddenly the darkness was rushing at them. The two slaves threw down their torches and bolted, and in the spill of flame Castus saw the glint of spears, the shapes of hooded men closing in from all sides.

'Arm yourselves!' he cried, and as his command burst back off the buildings around him he heard the shouts, the crash of the litter dropping to the cobbles, a man's scream. He was fumbling at his tunic, trying to draw his weapon free; a curse, and he grasped the fabric of his collar and ripped it down across his chest. Weapon in hand, he turned to look back, and what he saw drove a grunt of shock from his body.

Nigrinus had stepped away from the litter, his mouth working as he called a command to the men closing in from the alleys. He raised his hand and pointed.

Pudentianus was clambering up from the litter, his voice high and strained. 'What are you doing? This is a mistake! Let us pass!'

His slave, Naso, had snatched up a fallen torch and was brandishing it before him, scattering sparks. One of the surrounding men threw back his cloak, stepped up to him and then smashed the slave across the face with the flat of his sword. Naso dropped, the torch falling from his hand. Castus saw the coarse red beard, the snarl; then Sergianus drew back his arm and struck again, punching his blade through the throat of the young nobleman.

Pudentianus died without a sound, slumping back against the litter. The other slaves bringing up the rear just stood and stared, paralysed by terror.

It had all happened in three heartbeats, and for that brief

time Castus too had been locked rigid with surprise. Beside him, Felix had his short military dagger held in a low grip as he crouched, more like a street-fighter than a soldier. Diogenes too was armed, but clearly confused and disorientated. Then Sergianus dragged his blade from the young man's neck, and the distinct wet suck and hiss of it jerked Castus back into motion.

'Let's go, *now*,' he roared. 'After me!'

Head down, he charged towards the mouth of the nearest alley, scooping one of the smouldering torches from the ground as he ran. He whirled the brand, and the pitch-soaked rags trailed smoke and then burst into flame. No way of telling how many stood against them; six or sixty, the odds were bad. At his heels he could hear Felix and Diogenes, both of them yelling; then he slammed into a pair of figures in the darkness. He knocked aside a jabbing spear with the torch, then plunged the burning ember at a man's face. Lashing with the sword, he drove the other man back; the figure stumbled and tripped, then Felix was leaping over him with a dagger bared in his fist.

Sheer brutal impetus carried them through the first line of the cordon, but there were more men beyond, faces stretched in angry screams, blades wheeling from the darkness. Castus stabbed and swung, barely conscious of what he was doing, the noise of his own voice ringing back at him from the walls on either side. Rage propelled him now; he slammed one man aside with his shoulder, slashed another down with a backhand blow. Somewhere he was cut, bleeding, but the last of the men blocking his way was falling back, terrified, and Castus was through and running.

The batter of hooves on cobbles filled the street. *Gods, they've sent cavalry after us.* The torch was a hacked stump in his hand, and Castus had no idea of where he was or which direction he was running. Shards of moonlight cut the alley, a flung javelin jarred sparks off the wall, then Castus emerged into a courtyard between tall buildings and saw the mounted men ahead of him, sealing the exit to the next street.

'Dominus, here!' Felix was pulling at his arm and pointing upwards. Scaffolding climbed the side of the building: a mass of timbers lashed together, ladders and platforms rising into the moonlight. Felix had already leaped at the lowest spars and was scrambling upwards, with Diogenes just behind.

Ladders, Castus thought. *How I hate ladders.* The horsemen were urging their mounts forward down the alley now, into the courtyard. Armed foot soldiers rushed from the opposite side. Castus drew a long breath, stuck his sword through his belt, then ran at the scaffolding and began hauling himself up after Felix.

Timbers wailed and groaned under his weight, the whole precarious structure shuddering as he climbed. Men were on the ladders below him, but Castus was clambering between the lashed spars and uprights, gaining distance on them. He heard ropes straining, wood splintering and cracking, and now he could feel the night's breeze on his back as he climbed above the trench of the alley.

At the bottom, the scaffolding had been sturdy timbers, but as he reached halfway Castus's hands found only slender poles lashed together. He dragged himself up onto a wooden platform. Felix was just above him, hurling broken bricks down at the Praetorians climbing below. A quick glance down, and Castus felt his stomach dive and his muscles tighten. The narrow alley was flowing with men, alight with torches, and it looked a long way down.

'In here!' Diogenes cried, and Castus rolled onto his side on the platform to see the secretary leaning from an open window. Gripping the slender uprights, he dragged himself around until he could clamber in through the gap. Felix was already ahead of him, disappearing into the darkness of the building, but at the window ledge Castus paused and held himself back. The pursuers were coming up quickly behind them, shouting and clattering on the scaffolding.

Sitting on the sill, Castus turned to face the gulf of the street. He braced his arms against the window opening to either side, jammed his boot heels against the uprights of the scaffolding and pushed. Ropes groaned and popped, wood cracked, and then he felt the upper part of the structure begin to sway from the wall of the building. Men were already screaming below him, some of them jumping from the lower levels. Castus stretched his body from the window, his legs driving out hard against the wooden uprights, muscles burning as he heaved. A grating crash from above, a fountain of collapsing bricks and rubble dust, then the creaking structure of the scaffolding pulled away from the building and crashed down into the dark pit of the alley below.

Hands at his shoulders dragged him back through the embrasure of the window. Felix was there, hard determination in his eyes as he pulled Castus to his feet and led him on into the gloom of the building. They were on the third or fourth floor, puddles of lamplight exposing a narrow corridor, walls of cracked plaster, the rail of a stairway beyond. The air was close and thick, smelling of boiled food and latrines. As Castus edged along the corridor a door opened to his left, and in the brief spill of light he saw a fat woman in a grease-stained *stola*, with two small children peering past her knees. The woman let out a gasp; then the door slammed closed again.

Nearing the stairs, Castus could already hear the noise of the men climbing. Hobnailed boots smashed up the stairwell, and when he glanced over the rail he saw the raised face of

Sergianus three flights below him. The Praetorian snarled, then yelled to the men behind him and charged on upwards.

Felix was at the entrance to the next corridor, crouched and ready to move. No sign of Diogenes. Just beyond Felix, in the darkness of an archway, a small girl in a ragged tunic stood with a knuckle pressed to her mouth, staring at the two men.

'Roof?' Castus asked the girl, and the word was a hoarse bark.

The girl widened her eyes for a moment, then lifted her hand and pointed. In the shadows at the far side of the stairway, a wooden ladder rose towards a faint rectangle of moonlight.

'Where's Diogenes?' Castus said as he pulled himself up the ladder. Felix shook his head. The Praetorians were charging up the last flight of stairs now.

At the top of the ladder, a narrow wooden hatch gave access to the roof of the building. Castus shoved his way through, dragged Felix after him and pulled up the ladder. Diogenes was beyond their help now; he would do better on his own anyway.

Gulping breath, the two men paused and gazed around them. The roof of the apartment block was flat, with a low coping surrounding it. From the open hatchway came the racket of shouting men, women's screams, the thunder of pounding feet.

Castus paced towards the edge of the roof, drawing back involuntarily as he neared the brink. The wind caught him, soft and wet, and when he raised his eyes he saw the roofs of the city spreading around him, a terrain of tiles and flat terraces under the moon. Away to the left were the tall arches and domes of one of the big imperial bathhouses. Beyond them, picked out against the dark mass of the city, Castus could see the summit of the Capitoline Hill and the shape of the great temples at its crest.

But none of the surrounding roofs met the building; none were close enough that a man could leap the gap. They were trapped, and the pursuers would take only moments to find another ladder.

'We could kill them as they come up,' Felix said, squatting down with the dagger in his hand.

'We can't kill the whole Guard,' Castus replied, his breath heaving. He could feel the blood running down his leg, the pain pulsing up from the gash in his thigh, his bruised chest and arms. For all the time they had been running and climbing he had barely thought about what would happen next. The fierce need to escape had driven him on. But now the truth struck him: he had failed. Pudentianus was dead; Diogenes lost; he and Felix were hunted fugitives in a hostile city. And Nigrinus... Nigrinus had been the betrayer. He felt the hope draining out of him, his confusion turning to futile rage.

Felix got up and took three steps to the edge of the roof, peering down. 'There's a way,' he said. 'Down there, climbing.'

Castus felt his heart clench in his chest, and his limbs turned cold. 'No,' he said.

'You can't?'

'I won't.'

'We fight, then.'

Felix snatched up a length of wood and weighed it in his left hand, keeping the dagger in his right. He was still breathing fast, but appeared fearless. Castus's legs were trembling, the energy of the chase dying out of him. He knew there was no way he could climb down the side of the building. He limbs would freeze, his fingers lock and then fail; he would fall, and take the other man with him.

'You go – now!'

Felix stared at him, his brow knotting. 'Dominus?'

342

'Move! That's an order. I shouldn't have to tell you twice, soldier.'

A heartbeat, then Felix nodded. He dropped the club, clasped the knife between his teeth and was over the edge of building almost before Castus saw him move.

Alone now, Castus stood in the sigh of the wind, sword in hand, waiting as the men in the building below him pushed up through the hatchway and onto the roof. There was a time to fight, he thought. A time when it was possible to win. But not now. No chances remained to him.

As they advanced he peered over his shoulder at the city. At least he had seen Rome. When he looked back there was an arc of men around him, all of them with levelled spears. Sergianus walked from between them.

'Hello, boys,' Castus said, and drew one side of his mouth up into a grin as he dropped the sword.

Sergianus kept walking. 'Got you now, bastard,' he said. 'This is for Mikkalus.'

The dead man in the alley, Castus had time to realise. *The one who followed me from the baths.*

Then Sergianus smashed a fist into the side of his head, and the night whirled around him.

PART FOUR

CHAPTER XXII

Ariminum, October AD 312

The waves rolled long and flat onto the dun-coloured beach. Further out, the glow of sunset reflected in pale bands across the sea. Just above the last hissing wash of surf the party of ladies and eunuchs picked their way along the sand, while behind them, on the dunes amid the windblown grasses, stood the line of litters with their hangings streaming in the breeze. Bodyguards lingered discreetly.

'Which sea is that?' Fausta said, flinging out an arm to the east.

'The Adriatic, domina,' one of the eunuchs replied.

'And what's on the far side?'

'The shore of Dalmatia, domina. Part of Illyricum.'

'Ah!' Fausta said. She was still walking. Sabina struggled to keep up with her, but the damp sand was filling the toes of her slippers. She suspected the emperor's wife only brought her household on these pointless excursions to discomfort them.

'And Illyricum is part of the domain of Licinius, yes?' Fausta went on in the same blithe tone. 'Or is it the other one who controls it – Daia or Daza or whatever he's called?'

'Licinius, domina,' the eunuch said, but Fausta was not listening.

'So many emperors these days,' she said, as if to herself.

'Mind you, I expect there'll be one less soon, at least!'

Sabina had grown accustomed to the younger woman's often callous attitudes, but even so she was shocked. Was it her brother's death that Fausta expected, or that of her husband? She seemed to regard either with complete indifference. Even after all these years in her company, Sabina could not decide whether Fausta was genuinely as heartless as she often appeared, or whether it was an act designed to conceal her fear and insecurity.

Night was gathering over the sea now, the light of sunset fading from the shredded clouds, and the wind was picking up. Fausta stood facing the waves, her silk shawl drawn tight over her mouth. Sabina moved closer to her, until they could speak without being overheard.

'Is there any news?'

Fausta shook her head just slightly, the silk fluttering.

'Nothing from Rome?' Sabina asked, her words almost lost in the breeze.

'Nothing.'

Sabina turned to hide her exasperated sigh. Behind her the rest of the party lingered on the sand, the women in tight little huddles, the eunuchs trying to hold their parasols steady. She looked at them, and felt no warmth in her heart. Never had she felt so constrained, so oppressed, by their presence.

Back at Treveris it had not been so hard to endure, with all the delights of the palace and the great city around it. But this journey south in the wake of Constantine's advancing army had been a trial. The last twenty days especially, down the length of the dead-straight Via Aemilia from Mediolanum to the sea, pausing every night in flea-ridden towns and posting stations, sleeping in requisitioned houses little better than barns. At every stop they had been greeted with the same fake glassy-eyed enthusiasm, by citizens who had already greeted a conquering emperor and his army of thirty thousand men eight days before, and now had to extend the same welcome to that emperor's wife. Sabina had hated it.

Soon, she thought, soon she would be in Rome, and could free herself of all this. She would have her property back, her wealth restored, and live as fate and her family had once decreed. But that tantalising idea brought its own stir of sickening anxiety: what would grant her these riches? Constantine's victory, or the wiles of Lepidus?

Fausta, Sabina knew, had found the journey almost as tedious. She too had been separated from her husband for many months, although in her case it was Constantine's choice; he preferred not to be distracted by female company during his campaign. Sabina doubted that many of his officers were as scrupulous.

'I received another letter from my husband earlier today,' Fausta said as she turned from the sea. She raised her voice slightly, so the others would hear and be summoned. 'Although he tells me little of the war, of course.'

She was making her way back up the beach towards the waiting litters, the eunuchs springing forward to lay strips of matting over the fine dry sand. 'Instead he chooses to discuss religious matters,' Fausta went on as she walked. 'Can you imagine? Why he thinks I'd be interested in that I don't know!'

'Religious matters?' Sabina asked. They were walking in single file now, up the rise of the dune.

'Constantine fears that the gods have deserted him,' Fausta announced. She paused a moment, to let the tremor of concerned attention pass along the line following her. 'Apparently he's becoming more interested in the ideas of the

Christians. Their priests follow him everywhere, whispering in his ears... What do you think – is that wise?'

Before Sabina could answer, one of the eunuchs broke in. 'Perhaps it would be wise not to opine on the sacred intelligence of the Augustus, domina?' He was smiling as he spoke, but his words gave Sabina a slight chill.

'Oh, probably,' Fausta went on, unconcerned. She paused at the top of the dune and turned again to peer at the sea. 'What do we make of this *Christianity*, anyway?' she said. 'It seems a simple enough faith. Comforting, I suppose. The idea that there's only one god, and he sees everything and knows everything, even our dreams. And then judges us when we die. But my husband has always been a simple man...'

Mine too, Sabina thought, oblivious to the flurries of stifled outrage from the eunuchs. But Castus had never been at all drawn to the Christians. Quite the opposite, as far as she knew.

'Mind you,' Fausta said, 'I'll never understand all this stuff about god sending his son to earth and then killing him and then bringing him back to life so everyone can live forever. Do you understand that, Sabina?'

'No, domina.'

'I believe these are theological questions, best left for others...' the eunuch insisted.

But now they had reached the litters. Fausta drew aside the drapes of the leading one, beckoning to Sabina.

'Travel with me, sister,' she said. Sabina caught the jealous glances of the other women; she ignored them.

They climbed into the litter together, arranging their gowns as they sat at facing ends and the bearers drew the drapes closed around them. A jolt, a lurch, and they were up and moving, the litter swaying smoothly to the bearers' steps.

Fausta waited until they had turned onto the road and the pace had levelled out before speaking again.

'Have you seen anything of... your cousin?' she asked.

Sabina stiffened, her stomach tightening and a cold flush running down her back. She shook her head quickly. 'He's with the army,' she said. 'I haven't seen him for several days now.'

Six days, to be exact. Domitius Claudianus Lepidus had passed through Ariminum on his way south; his duties as Master of Dispositions, in charge of logistics for the imperial retinue, allowed him much freedom of movement. Sabina had been trying to put her cousin out of her mind, but his shadow seemed always upon her. She had continued to act as a conduit for his messages, though, his reports to Rome on Constantine's movements, the state of his army and the loyalties of his officers; only the promise of what he could give her if he was successful, and the fear of her own punishment if he failed, stopped her confessing everything to the emperor's officials.

'You opened some of his messages, yes?' Fausta said quietly. She had dropped her flippant attitude completely now.

Sabina caught her breath, waiting for the chill to pass. *How does she know?* 'That was how I learned that Castus was being sent to Rome,' she said. 'And that Lepidus was sending men after him.'

'You warned your husband of this?'

'I tried – I sent a note, but I doubt he ever got it... There was another message as well, to Rome, telling Maxentius's people to apprehend the mission when it arrived. I destroyed that.'

'You did?' Fausta said, with a small sharp smile.

Sabina shrugged. 'I cannot bear passivity,' she said. But she was pretending a courage she did not feel. Over and again she had imagined Castus lying dead in some ditch or alleyway, or his body sinking into the depths of the sea. The thought that she could have prevented it, could have saved him if she had acted sooner, horrified her. She had prayed and made sacrifice at every temple on that long road from Mediolanum, and still she woke from nightmares in a panicked sweat.

Fausta was gazing through a gap in the swinging drapes. It was almost fully dark, but the light of the torches carried by the bearers shone through the thin fabric. She was biting anxiously at the carnelian ring on her little finger.

'How disgusting it is,' she said, venom in her voice. 'That vile man, that vile, subtle man... he could bring such harm to all of us.'

And Sabina knew this was true as well. Several times she had passed messages between Lepidus and Fausta, and she knew what they had offered her: if Constantine lost, Fausta would be widowed and bereft, and suspected of involvement in her father's death. But Lepidus could intercede with his contacts in Rome, and effect a reconciliation with her brother, Maxentius. Sabina could hardly blame the younger woman for being caught. Once again, Lepidus had baited his hooks well.

'If only he could suffer some small accident or other,' Fausta said in a musing tone.

'Could it be done?' Sabina asked quickly, sitting forward.

Fausta smiled again, with a slow shake of her head. 'It would be risking too much. He has documents that implicate us, I'm sure. And if it did not succeed...'

Through the gap in the drapes Sabina saw the pitted old walls of the town of Ariminum. The litter slowed as it passed beneath the great arch that marked the beginning of the old Flaminian Way to Rome, then entered the stone-paved main street of the town.

'But you would do well to keep clear of him,' Fausta said as the litter drew to a halt. 'We both would, but it's harder for me. Maybe you could disappear for a while.'

'Disappear?'

Fausta just widened her eyes meaningfully – the expression gave her an appearance of childlike innocence. Then the lids came down again, and her face was perfectly blank as the bearers drew the drapes aside.

Sabina turned the brief conversation over in her mind as she rode the last distance through the cobbled back lanes to her house. Her own litter was much smaller than Fausta's, but she was glad of the temporary privacy. The thought of Lepidus brought her nothing but anger and humiliation, and she loathed the part of herself that was still, inexplicably, drawn to him. At least he had ceased his sexual demands, most of the time. He still claimed that he and Sabina would be wed, once they reached Rome and Castus's death was confirmed, but Sabina wondered if he was growing tired of her. She had realised long ago that he desired only power, and the erotic thrill that power over others gave him.

The litter slowed, then grated down onto the cobbles. Sabina climbed into the spill of torchlight, drawing her shawl over her head. The door of the requisitioned house opened before her, and she walked inside, too lost in her own considerations to notice the agitation of the slaves.

In the gloomy paved court at the heart of the house she threw off her shawl and called for wine. The sea air had left her skin feeling clammy; she would have a bath, she decided, and then go to bed early and hope for sleep. But why were the slaves all staring at her?

It was the barbarian nursemaid who spoke, coming from the bedroom at the rear of the house with a bundle in her arms. 'He was here.'

'Who?' Sabina demanded, affronted for a moment; she had never liked the blonde slave, and found her attitude dangerously close to insolence at times... but then she realised, and a spear of ice passed through her. '*When?*'

'Before one hour,' the nurse said. Elpidia, that was her name, Sabina remembered – or was it Ganna? 'He was angry. Shouting. Angry at you. Domina, we must go!'

For a few heartbeats Sabina was lost in confusion, turning a slow circle between the brick pillars. The barbarian slave was carrying bundled clothes and blankets, she saw now. 'There is a carriage, at the back...'

'Where's the boy?' Sabina said. 'Where's my son?'

'He is safe. This man threatened to take him, but I would not allow it.'

Think, Sabina told herself. She was breathing rapidly, trying to digest what was happening. How had Lepidus discovered what she had done? Now she saw the spreading bruise on the slave's cheek, dark red already rising to blue. He had hit her; he had threatened to steal the boy...

A crash from the front hall, the cry of one of the door slaves, then a man's voice echoing through the gloom. Sabina turned on her heel, retreating. Too late: Lepidus was already striding into the court, unpinning his cloak and flinging it at one of the other slaves. He was grinning, but his eyes were hard.

'Domitia Valeria Sabina, I find you at home, finally!' he announced. 'If you are well, I am well!'

'His excellency Domitius Claudianus Lepidus,' the door steward mumbled weakly, following the man in from the hall.

A child's cry filtered through from the bedrooms at the rear of the house, then a rising wail. Sabina noticed the barbarian nursemaid edging around the margins of the court, her eyes on Lepidus.

'What is this disturbance?' she said. 'You've woken my child!' She hoped her voice would not betray her terror.

'I mean to do more than wake him,' Lepidus said, still pacing closer with that familiar prowling step. Two of his own slaves had followed him in from the street. 'Why did you destroy my letters?' he asked, cocking his head to one side. 'Why did you open and read my correspondence? It was really very disloyal of you!'

Sabina was moving slowly backwards, poised on her toes with every step. Her son was still crying in the back room, a regular pulse of sound. Nobody moved to attend to him.

'Perhaps we could discuss this later... over a meal?' Sabina said. 'Perhaps some wine?' She was stalling, hoping that something would come to her, some plan of action, or just some courage.

'I think not,' Lepidus said. He moved very fast, crossing the court in two quick strides and seizing her by the arm. His fingers dug hard into her flesh. 'I think I want to discuss this now, here.'

The assault shocked her; Lepidus had never been openly violent before. He was dragging her towards one of the bedrooms that opened off the courtyard.

'No, please,' she heard herself saying. 'Not like this, not here – not in front of the slaves...' Still the absurd desire for decorum, for dignity – it was instinctive. But Lepidus paid no attention.

For a moment Sabina struggled against him, but he had

a wiry strength that she could not resist. 'When my husband returns he'll murder you!' she hissed.

'Your husband is dead,' Lepidus declared. He grinned, tightening his grip on her arm as her body slackened, her willpower weakening. 'I'm afraid Aurelius Castus was captured by agents of Maxentius in Rome,' he said. 'He was executed!'

Sabina felt a sudden pain in her chest. Her breath grew short. He was lying – she told herself it was a lie, but she felt sick. Madness was beating in her head.

A flash of green at the margin of her vision, and the slave nurse threw herself forward with a ringing shriek. Her attack caught Lepidus unprepared – he turned his head just as the woman swung a blow at him, and her fist cracked against his cheekbone. He cried out, releasing his grip on Sabina's arm, then reeled back to trip over an urn set between two of the pillars.

Already his two bodyguards had closed in to flank him as he scrambled to his feet. The blonde slave stood in the centre of the courtyard, fists clenched, breathing fast. She made another move towards Lepidus, but he was faster; he sprang forward and shoved her away from him with a stiff-armed blow.

'Secure her!' he yelled to his bodyguards. 'The bitch is out of control!'

Once more he lurched towards Sabina, his glaze of urbane civility gone now, his arms out to seize her again. Breathless, she flinched away from him and raised her hand. Her fingers found the burled head of the long bronze pin that secured her braids, and plucked it free. Lepidus snatched at her, and Sabina swung her hand down with a finger's length of sharp metal jutting from her fist, driving the pin through the muscle of his left forearm. She felt it grate against bone, and twisted. A thin spray of blood spattered her hand.

For a single heartbeat Lepidus stared down at the spike piercing his arm, then he doubled over with an animal bellow of pain.

At once everyone was in motion, everyone shouting. The courtyard echoed with shrieks. Sabina's own slaves, released from their shocked stasis, moved to surround her as Lepidus's men ran to assist their master. Sabina felt the barbarian woman take her by the shoulders, a firm grasp, urging her back towards the far doorway.

'We must go now. Come – there is a carriage ready.'

'My child,' Sabina said, faint with shock at what she had done. 'What have you done with him?'

'He is safe – he comes with us.'

Lepidus had collapsed against a pillar, grey-faced and gasping, clutching his injured arm as one of his slaves tried to extract the pin from the wound. Sabina heard his high scream as Ganna conducted her down the darkened corridor that led to the rear of the house. Then she was outside, in the narrow cobbled lane where a light two-wheeled carriage stood waiting. She was moving in a dream, sickened but strangely exultant as she climbed into the carriage and felt it sway into motion.

The barbarian woman sat beside her, holding the child wrapped in a shawl. Sabinus had stopped crying now, and his face was a white disc staring out from the wool that surrounded his head. Sabina took the boy, clasping him in her lap, and felt the fear and madness pouring out of her. When she went to touch the child's face she noticed that her hand was still wet with blood.

'Will he live?' she said, her voice catching. 'Lepidus?'

'Sadly, I think yes,' Ganna replied.

Sabina glanced from the carriage and saw the black waters of the river as they crossed the long bridge to the north of the city. She was a fugitive, but she was free. For a while at least. Then she remembered what Lepidus had told her. Castus could not be dead – she refused to believe it.

But only the gods could save her husband now. The same gods that their emperor seemed so eager to deny.

CHAPTER XXIII

He had expected chains. He had expected a dank, lightless cell, like the one he had known in the dungeons of Arelate. But as Castus groped up through the levels of pain into consciousness, he realised that he was lying on a bed in a large room, with daylight filtering dimly through an open door. What had happened? His head was pounding, and his jaw felt massively swollen, but when he moved it there was no spear of pain. No broken bones, and the scar had not reopened. His body felt battered, and he guessed he had been dragged down stairs.

Nigrinus, he thought. Nigrinus had done this. Once again the notary had played false; once again men had died for it. He wondered if Felix had managed to escape; there would be people in the city who might aid him, conceal him. Diogenes too, if he had survived. The slaves at Pudentianus's house had always liked him, and would give him shelter if he could get there undetected... As for himself, he was a prisoner. Castus struggled to raise his head, to sit up. Waves of nausea flowed through him.

'Calm yourself,' a voice said. 'There is no fighting here.'

With difficulty, Castus turned his head. The speaker stood a short distance away. He was a small man with a dark, greyish complexion and a soft and pliable look. A eunuch, Castus assumed.

'You are not badly injured,' the eunuch went on in a light and slightly lisping voice. 'No thanks to our Praetorians. Your face is bruised, and you have wounds on your leg and shoulder, which I have had cleaned and dressed. Thank the gods they built you of such strong stuff.'

'Who are you?' Castus managed to say. His skull felt twisted out of shape.

'I am Valerius Merops, *cubicularius*. And you are Aurelius Castus, Ducenarius of Protectores and tribune in the army of the pretender of Gaul.'

Castus could only squint back at him. Of course, he thought, the notary would have told them everything. Merops made a dry fluttering sound between his lips – a laugh of sorts.

'Yes, your friend Julius Nigrinus has been very helpful to us. We knew of your arrival in Rome only a day or two after you entered the city, but we never expected one of your own party to approach us so soon. Your emperor should really not rely on such malleable people!'

Castus grunted, half in anger and half in pain. He made another attempt to sit up, and got his elbow beneath him.

'Calm, I said. You have time to rest before you are needed.'

'Needed?' But the eunuch was already moving toward the door. A moment later, the dim light was gone and Castus heard the grate of a lock. Groaning, he subsided onto the bed again.

Another day passed, and a night, as far as Castus could judge. They had left him water and food, and clean clothes of plain white wool, and when he felt able to lift himself upright he dressed, wincing as he discovered new cuts and bruises. He was still wearing the leather thong around his wrist with the blue stone that Ganna had given him before he'd left Mediolanum. *For protection*, she had told him. He smiled at the bitter irony of that, then pulled his boots on. When the eunuch returned to fetch him he was sitting on the edge of the bed, waiting.

'Do not attempt to flee, or try any violent escapade,' Merops said as he stood by the door. 'Trust me that you are surrounded by guards, and would not leave this place alive.'

Castus had little idea of what place this might be, although he was developing a notion. He followed the eunuch along a vaulted corridor, sunlight dropping in heavy beams from vents overhead. There were no guards in sight, but Castus caught the stir of movement in the shadows and knew that there were men all around him, slaves and soldiers, unseen watchers. They climbed a long stairway that rose into the light.

Merops was moving quickly ahead of him, his slippers tapping at the marble floor. They were in another corridor now, with tall arched windows along one wall covered by ornate grilles that cut the sun into arcs and shards. The opposite wall appeared to be a single expanse of dark marble, polished like glass and reflecting Castus's warped image. The eunuch turned only briefly, gesturing him to follow. At the far end of the corridor they passed through a dim chamber and emerged into a courtyard. Pillared walks surrounded a sunken garden where water streamed into marble basins.

'This way,' Merops said, drawing aside a long yellow drape and motioning for Castus to pass through into the chamber beyond. Pacing through the wide opening, Castus squinted into the blaze of sunlight from the doorway at the far end of the room. Mosaics of marble and glass shimmered across the floor. He could see a portico beyond the doors, tall fluted pillars with the sky beyond, and a single figure seated in a cane chair, silhouetted against the light.

Castus advanced across the chamber and out through the far doors into the portico. As he approached the seated man he saw the face in profile, and caught his breath. He had suspected, but it was a shock to recognise him so easily. A face he had only known from a portrait on a coin. *Preserver of His City.*

Maxentius.

The tyrant of Rome was busy peeling an apple, paring the skin away from the flesh with a small knife. He did not look up from his work as Castus came to a halt a few paces from him. From the doorway, Merops cleared his throat meaningfully. *I will not kneel*, Castus thought. *I kneel only for emperors, not usurpers.*

But Maxentius appeared not to expect it. He finished peeling the apple, sliced it into segments, then laid the knife aside on a circular table beside the seamless twist of skin. With a dish of fruit segments in his hand he reclined in his chair. The cane creaked. 'A fine view, is it not?' the tyrant said.

The portico curved away to left and right, an arcing *exedra* with perfect white columns soaring upwards, and the ground fell away beyond it. Castus stared out between the pillars, and saw below him the full expanse of the Circus Maximus, the brown sand of the racetrack and the tiers of white seats rising all around it, the golden statues gleaming in the low sun. Castus knew where he was now: this was the Palatine Hill, the palace of the emperors.

'Many of my advisors believe you should die,' Maxentius said as he ate a slice of apple. 'They would like to scourge the flesh from your back, and see you crucified in the arena.

To send a message, so they say. What message would that be, I wonder?'

The tyrant appeared younger than Castus had expected; there was a noticeable similarity to his sister Fausta in his olive skin and dark eyes, the softness of his mouth. The dark stubble on his chin did little to make him appear more mature, and there was something in his hair that caught the light. Gold dust, perhaps. Castus stood stiffly, thumbs hooked in his fabric waistband, and said nothing.

'Sit down, why don't you,' Maxentius said, gesturing to a stool. Castus eased himself down onto it, but the rigidity of his spine did not ease. The young tyrant appeared perfectly relaxed, even languid; impossible to imagine Constantine sitting there like that. Castus remembered the emperor in his tent, the night before the battle on the road to Taurinum. That focused intensity, battling with terror. Could this young man ever know such a feeling? Castus remembered that Maxentius had never led men in battle, never had to face the eve of combat.

'So, you come to us from the camp of my brother-in-law,' the tyrant said. 'How is my dear little sister? Have you slept with her yet?'

Castus felt the blood rush to his head. What had Nigrinus told him? His pulse was jumping in the pit of his throat, but he managed to remain silent.

'My spies tell me she's bedded half of Constantine's court.'

'Your spies lie,' Castus said.

'Really? It doesn't surprise me. An emperor of Rome can have whatever he wants, you know. Except the truth.'

In his mind Castus heard Nigrinus's voice, those quiet insidious words he had spoken back at the villa beside the lake. *A debaucher, who has dishonoured many women. Your wife among them, in fact...* Staring at the young man sitting

363

opposite, he felt a surge of fierce rage mounting through his body. How could this gilded youth have led the world to war, pitting Roman armies against each other?

His gaze fell to the table, the paring knife laid beside the coil of apple skin. One lunge, and he could seize it. The blade was no longer than his thumb, but it would be enough to open the tyrant's throat. He could do it, now, easily; there was nobody to stop him. *One man, one blow, and this whole war could end...* His muscles tightened, energy flowing in his limbs. Then the sudden chill of realisation: had Nigrinus intended this along? Had this whole expedition to Rome, the betrayal, the attack, been a carefully constructed ruse to bring him to precisely this point?

No, he could not believe that. Not even Nigrinus could have arranged things so neatly. Besides, he was surely deceived by appearances; the exedra appeared empty of all but sunlight, but there were surely guards positioned in every doorway along its length. He would be watched, and any move he made would be countered instantly. *Emperors are never truly alone.*

Barely two heartbeats had passed since Castus had looked at the knife, but Maxentius appeared to have changed his demeanour. As if he had let one mask drop, and assumed another. Now there was something dark and toxic in his eyes. 'Your notary tells me that you were present when my father died,' he said.

Castus drew a sharp breath. Once again he sensed Nigrinus's long reach, his subtle direction. This was the hook, he realised, that had drawn Maxentius. This was the lure that had saved Castus's life, but might kill him yet.

'Tell me what happened,' the tyrant said. He set aside his dish of sliced fruit and gazed out between the pillars into the sinking sunlight.

Haltingly, Castus related the story of what had taken place three years before, at Massilia and then at Arelate. Maxentius surely knew most of it already, but he needed to hear it all. As Castus spoke, the young man sat motionless. Only a muscle moved in his jaw as Castus told him of his father's last moments, just before he had withdrawn from the chamber to let the old usurper take his own life.

When Castus had finished speaking Maxentius said nothing for a while, then he breathed in and hunched his shoulders. 'It was an undignified end,' he said at last. 'But if what you say is true, the shame of it is not yours. You acted with honour, and I respect that. I thank you for it.'

He raised a hand and rubbed lightly at his lips, then pressed his brow. 'They sent me here as a punishment,' he went on a moment later. 'My father and Diocletian. They sent me to Rome to keep me far away from where the real business of empire happened. From Nicomedia, from Mediolanum. This city meant little to them; it was a backwater, a relic. Just a hollow stage set. Diocletian found the Roman people too rude and riotous for his tastes. But I loved it. I love it still. You see that, yes? You see what I've made of this city? I am restoring it to its ancient greatness. Constantine would never do as much. For him it's just another trophy. But for me, Rome is everything.'

Castus did see it. As he spoke, the young man's face took on a new maturity, a look of sober determination completely at odds with his manner only moments before. Perhaps, he thought, perhaps this man truly could be an emperor? Was his ambition any less reckless than Constantine's? He remembered the dying man of the Herculiani, on the bloody field after the battle outside Verona. Yes, Castus thought. Emperors are all alike. All of them bastards. But all of them had a spark of glory in them.

'And now my brother-in-law is leading an army against Rome,' Maxentius said. 'Will he fight me?'

'He will,' Castus told him.

'And will he beat me, do you think?'

'Only the gods know that.'

'Ah, the gods! If only they were more communicative...' Maxentius had that jesting air again, the slight smirk that flickered across his soft lips. It angered Castus to see it. He was speaking of life and death, and not just his own.

'I'm told Constantine is loved by his troops. Why do they follow him so gladly? Why are they so eager to die in his name?'

Because he treats them as men. 'Constantine is a leader, a fighter. He shows himself on the battlefield, takes the vanguard. The soldiers see him as one of their own.'

'And you are a soldier. Do you see him in that way?'

For a moment Castus said nothing. Too many thoughts were wrestling in his mind, too many memories. The man he had just described had thrown himself into the thick of the fighting at Verona, endangering his own troops, heedless of those that died for him. But he remembered the night outside the praetorium in Eboracum years before, the figure raised upon a shield and wrapped in a purple cloak as the rain fell and the massed soldiers bellowed his name. Castus had been there with them, shouting along with them. They loved Constantine because they had made him.

'Constantine Augustus is my emperor,' he said. 'I acknowledge no other. And if you mean to kill me, give the order. I will tell you nothing more.'

Maxentius just shrugged lightly, nodding. 'I think you will live a little longer,' he said. 'Tomorrow is the day of the Augustan Games. You will join my retinue, as a guest. Perhaps, if you are lucky, you will witness something of the majesty of Rome. Then I intend to send you back to your emperor, so you can tell him the truth about what you have seen.'

The noise reached him as he moved along the wide tunnel, the cavernous roaring drowning out even the crack of the guard's hobnailed boots on the marble floor. Ahead of him, Castus saw the light increasing in intensity. Then he stepped out into the open air, and for a few moments he could only stand blinking, his senses overwhelmed.

The great stadium of the Circus Maximus, which he had seen the day before from the exedra of the palace on the hillside above, was a crucible, alive with molten humanity. A quarter of a million people it could hold, so Merops had told him, and from where Castus was standing there appeared not an empty seat. The stands heaved, bright with the colours of the racing factions, with the flash of gold and gaudy clothing, and the noise of the crowd filled the air like thick vapour. A blinding glare came off the sand of the racetrack; sweepers moved across it like pond-skaters alone in a vast emptiness.

'Come,' said Merops, taking Castus by the arm. The tunnel from the palace had disgorged them directly onto the wide podium beside the imperial gallery; now the eunuch led Castus to one side and down a short flight of steps, the two guards stamping along behind him. Above them on the podium rose the imperial gallery itself, a pillared eminence with a pediment like a temple, where the inner circle of Maxentius's officials and advisors were seated.

Castus found himself positioned to the right of the gallery, beneath an awning. The men around him appeared to be functionaries of the court and senior military commanders.

He sat down on the marble bench, and the two guards placed themselves to either side of him. Both were Praetorians, and neither wore weapons openly, but Castus knew they were armed. The gallery above him was ringed by a cordon of Protectores, all of them carrying spears and gilded shields. There would no opportunities to strike against the usurper here.

He had still not fully digested what Maxentius had told him the day before. Would he really be allowed to go free, after all that had happened? It seemed too much to hope. But Castus had clung to that thought all through a sleepless night, and he clung to it now. *You can tell him the truth about what you have seen.* If the gods willed it.

Now a redoubled roar went up from the stalls, and Castus jerked his gaze around to the left. Between the pillars at the front of the imperial gallery, Maxentius had appeared. Gone was the lounging young man Castus had seen on the exedra: the figure standing above him in the sunlight wore armour of gilded metal, flashing as he moved. On his head was a jewelled diadem, and cradled in his arm was a golden sceptre capped with a translucent blue-green orb. Rose petals showered down around him in the sunlight.

'*Emperor Marcus Aurelius Valerius Maxentius Augustus,*' the herald cried, '*Everlasting! Pious son of the deified Maximian Augustus! May he be praised always and happily throughout the entire world for his victories!*'

Raising his right hand, two fingers extended, the tyrant of Rome acknowledged the massive acclaim of his people.

Trumpets rang out from the far gates of the stadium, and the first ranks of men paraded out into the light. But these were not athletes or gladiators, not racing chariots and teams of horses. These were troops, armed and armoured for battle with their standards before them. '*Maxentius Augustus!*' the crowd chanted. '*Maxentius Augustus!*'

The majesty of Rome, Castus thought. This is what he had been meant to see: not the vast multitude of the city's people assembled for the games, but this display of military might. The column of marching men was thousands strong, and moved with fierce discipline. The Praetorian Guard took the lead, then came squadrons of Numidian light cavalry on their prancing horses. After the Numidians were the Horse Guards, men and mounts clad in glittering scale armour, every lance with a streaming pennant. Another two cohorts of the Guard, and then came the legions. Castus watched them as they passed along the far side of the track. The herald on the platform below the podium was crying out the names of the units. *The First Legion Valeria Romuliana. The Second Legion Valeria Martia.* Not names Castus recognised. These would be the newly raised troops, he realised, the men from Africa and southern Italy. Sure enough, many of them had no body armour, and their march lacked the regularity of the Praetorians. But they appeared spirited enough. They looked like soldiers.

On and on the column extended. There must be twenty thousand men at least, Castus estimated, and they would only be a fraction of the tyrant's full army. The head of the column had reached the curve at the far end of the track, and Castus stood to watch them as the lead units marched back up the length of the stadium and drew to a halt before the imperial gallery. Now his eye began to detect the gaps in the formation, the ragged step and the fraying lines. They had been well drilled for this display. But how well they would stand up in battle might be another story.

For a moment he thought the volley of screams from his left, beyond the podium, were some new surge of popular fervour. Then Castus smelled the smoke, and saw the black smudge rising against the sky. All around him men were leaping to their feet, craning over the seats to try and see what was happening. Up in the gallery, the Protectores had moved forward at once to screen the emperor with their shields. Below them in the stalls the crowd rippled and flowed as panic drove through them.

'The stands are on fire!' said the guard to Castus's right. He jumped forward, clambering down over the seats in front of him. At once Castus sensed another man sliding into his place.

'So it begins,' a voice said in his ear. Castus locked his body, forbidding himself to turn. He would recognise that dry hiss anywhere.

'You did this?' he whispered from the side of his mouth.

'Friends of mine,' Nigrinus whispered back. Down on the sand, the assembly of troops was milling in confusion, some of the new recruits breaking ranks. The Praetorians were still standing firm, Castus noticed.

'Listen to me,' Nigrinus hissed in his ear. 'Our mission was betrayed. I did what I had to do, to limit the damage.'

'Pudentianus?'

'More use to us dead than alive.'

Castus was holding his breath, not daring to move but wanting more than anything to turn and seize the notary by the throat. Now he felt something pressing into his back, sliding down into the sash that bound his waist.

'See that this reaches Constantine,' the notary breathed. 'If it's discovered, we are both dead men. Understand?'

Slowly Castus lowered himself back into his seat. The object that Nigrinus had given him was digging into the base of his spine, not a slim tablet or a scroll but something hard and knotted. Smoke was billowing out across the racetrack, threading between the ranks of the soldiers assembled on the sand. He said nothing, and a moment later the notary was gone.

CHAPTER XXIV

In the grey of dawn the Flaminian Gate loomed huge and dark over the road, the single arch closed and barred, lamps flickering in the two tiers of slot windows overhead. The sky was already bright, outlining the crenellations of the ramparts, and when Castus glanced up he saw the spearpoints and helmets of the sentries on the wall walks. He turned in the saddle and glanced back at the six men who had escorted him down the long straight street from the centre of the city to the walls: mounted troopers of the Horse Guards, wrapped in their cloaks against the morning's chill. His own mount was a pony, a bristly and intractable beast; compared to the fine mounts of the escorts, he felt as though he was riding a mule. But he knew he was lucky to be alive at all.

'If it were up to me,' Merops said, leaning from his carriage, 'you would not be permitted to leave like this. If it were up to me you would not be permitted to *live*. But the Augustus has spoken. So – return to your Gallic pretender and his army. Inform them of the clemency of the emperor Maxentius, of his mercy, the invincible strength of his army, the impregnable defences of his city. I trust we will not meet again!'

'Likewise,' Castus said. But the word was gall in his mouth, his whole body creased and bitter with defeat. How could survival and liberation feel so much like failure?

The gates swung open, iron hinges wailing, and the barred portcullis grunted upwards. Castus dug in his heels, and the little pony trotted forward into the mouth of the arch. For a moment the sound of the hoofbeats echoed under the stone vault, then Castus was out again and the sun was in his eyes, the road stretching long and straight ahead of him across the flat land towards the belt of trees on the far horizon. He heard the creak and boom of the closing gates, the heavy rattle and clash of the portcullis, and Rome was behind him.

For several hundred jogging paces he dared not look back, expecting at any moment the snap of a ballista and a bolt whining over his head to hurry him on his way. None came, and when he did at last turn and stare back at the walls and gate he saw nobody watching him, nobody following. The early sun slanted across the tops of the ramparts, illuminating the massive brickwork of the walls and the twin drum towers that flanked the gates on the northern side. There was a damp autumnal feel in the air.

Riding onwards, he followed the straight road between clusters of old tombs half-obscured by undergrowth, ruined walls of old buildings, copses of trees. He could feel the object that Nigrinus had given him pressed tight against his side – he had concealed it inside his tunic, in case he was searched before leaving the city. In his saddlebag, along with the hardtack and cheese he had been given for his journey, was a more ordinary message, a safe conduct issued in the name of Maxentius Augustus, giving him leave to pass through the guarded strongpoints on the road. This was the Flaminian Way, the route to the north, and Castus knew that all he had to do was follow it and he would meet Constantine's advancing army. Either that, or come upon the scene of their defeat, somewhere in the distant hills that smoked across the horizon.

This would be the third time, Castus thought grimly, that he had returned alone from a mission. The first had been in Britain, when the Picts had wiped out his century and only he had staggered back from captivity. Again, last winter, he alone had returned of the despatch party sent to the court of Licinius. Did the gods love him, or did they just want to humiliate him? Bleakly, Castus wondered what his reception might be, if he managed to reach Constantine's army. He had Nigrinus's 'report', peculiar object though it was, but he had lost both the men he had taken with him. Pudentianus was dead and he himself had been captured by the enemy and displayed like a trophy at the games. It would not be an honourable return. But then he thought of Lepidus, the man who had sent killers after them, and who had surely betrayed their mission. The man who had seduced his wife. At least the thought of finding Lepidus and making him pay fired Castus's blood – but he had no more than his own word as evidence against the man.

The straight stretch of road ended at the river, the yellow Tiber curving between meadows and thickets of willow. A stone bridge spanned the river, and a detachment of guards was posted upon it. The optio in command scanned Castus's safe conduct without great interest – he gave the impression that he could not read, but recognised the imperial seal – before waving him on. As he rode across the bridge Castus glanced to his right and saw the river rushing from the arches beneath him. On the far side the ground rose, big bluffs of red rock jutting up, and the road turned sharply to follow the riverbank. A bottleneck, Castus thought, gazing over his shoulder with an instinctive tactical appraisal. He could see the soldiers on the bridge watching him.

Beyond the bluffs the road curved again, before heading straight across an open expanse of meadowland enclosed by a wide bend in the river. There were still a few tombs along the verges, massive old things encrusted with vegetation, one of them almost the size of a fortress tower. To the left, away from the river, the high ground dropped in a steep escarpment that edged the plain. Castus slowed, glancing around at the land in the low sun and the lingering vapour of early river mist. The place was a natural killing field. *If I was going to trap an army marching on Rome*, he thought, *I'd do it here.* He felt a slight shiver up his back, a breath of presentiment. Then he kicked at the pony and rode on.

All morning he continued northwards along the Flaminian Way. The road ran into hilly country, with the river coiling in its green valley away to the right. On the rolling summits pines stood proud against the sky, lifting fleecy dark heads on slender trunks. The only traffic on the road was heading south: heavy bullock carts laden with animal feed, tanned hides, vegetables and grain. Once Castus passed a line of soldiers tramping back towards the city, ragged exhausted-looking spearmen who marched by with barely a glance at him. He rode on, counting the milestones as he passed.

At the thirteenth stone he paused, dismounting to eat and swig water from his flask. His thighs and buttocks ached from the saddle, and he left the pony cropping grass while he paced up and down, flexing his legs. The road here had climbed to a hilltop, and he had a long view in all directions, the countryside hazy in the sunlight. To the north an isolated ridge rose steep and massive, crested with bare rocky peaks and fringed with dense woodland. The river lay on the far side, and beyond it Castus could see the blueish line of the mountains, the Apennines that ran down the spine of Italy.

Then he turned to look southwards, and saw the group of riders far away on the distant road, coming in his direction.

Eight of them, their horses moving at a rapid trot. They were still a mile or two distant, but as Castus shaded his eyes and peered into the sun he could make out the spears and javelins the riders carried. He had no weapon, not even an eating knife, and the riders were moving with a sense of purpose.

Back in the saddle, he hauled the pony away from the grassy verge and set it cantering over the brow of the hill and down the far slope. Open country on either side of the road here, fields and scattered copses of small trees, not even a farmhouse that might give him some cover or concealment. For another couple of miles he kept up the pace, on across the valley and up the far slope as the road climbed again. His legs were burning, and a tide of sweat was running down his spine. At any moment he expected the first shout behind him, or the thunder of hooves on the road. All he could hear was the pony's maddeningly slow thud, the clink of the bridle as the animal tossed its head and the water slopping in the flask tied to the saddle horn.

From the top of the next hill Castus could see the wooded broken country off to the right, stretching away towards the flanks of the big rocky ridge. A glance back, and he saw the eight riders closing the distance fast. Setting his teeth, he urged the pony on into a gallop, down the slope on the far side of the hill. The animal was labouring under his weight, blowing hard, and he was bouncing in the saddle as he rode. Up ahead of him, Castus could see a solitary rider on a mule; the man paused and turned to stare back at him.

As the ground levelled Castus hauled on the reins, and the pony jolted and plunged to the right, off the road and across the dry ditch into the scrub on the far side. *Come on*, he hissed through his teeth, kicking with his heels. *Come on, move...* His breath was hot in the back of his throat. When he looked up he could see the trees ahead, but he had misjudged the distance:

he would never reach them before the riders crested the hill behind him. Cursing, he bent low over the saddle horns and slapped at the animal's flanks with the reins, willing it to speed. He had a good idea now who was pursuing him so intently.

Halfway to the trees Castus let out a cry of triumph: the gully of a stream bed crossed the open ground ahead of him, thick green foliage rising from its banks. If he could reach it before he was spotted from the road he could hide it there... But as he risked a glance back he saw the eight riders silhouetted on the hilltop. He heard one of them shout, and then all eight dropped into a gallop down the slope after him, their cloaks billowing out behind them.

Into the stream bed, leaves and spiny branches whipping around him, Castus turned the pony and galloped through the shallow water and up the bank. No chance to hide now; the stream would slow his pursuers, but not for long. As he came out of the bushes on the far side he could see them fanning out along the brink of the gully, urging their horses down after him.

A last sweating gallop and he was into the trees, crouching low over the pony's mane. Undergrowth crashed around the animal's legs, but the ground was uneven here, rutted and steep. The trees were not as dense as they had appeared from the road either: it was a network of copses and thorny hedges, separated by patches of scrubby open ground. But Castus could see the ground rising ahead of him, the trees stacked more thickly. If he could get up between them, he might stand a chance of escape.

Then the trees fell away on either side and he was on the lip of a grassy dell. The pony shied, snorting, and plunged down the dip. Castus was thrown forward in the saddle, and he had only just regained his seat when the animal gave a sudden jolt. Twisting, Castus had time to see the shaft of a javelin jutting from its haunch before the pony staggered and threw him from the saddle as it went down. For a heartbeat he felt himself flung, helpless, in the air; then he hit the ground with his shoulder and slammed down onto his back with a punch that burst the air from his body.

For a moment he lay still, a wave of tranquillity washing over him. It was a relief not be jolting around in the saddle, a relief to lie on a bed of soft decaying leaves, staring up at the trees. Then the pain ripped through him and he cried out, baring his teeth. Somehow he had cut his forehead, and there was blood in his eye. He worried that his shoulder was broken. *Move*, he told himself, *get up and run*... He screwed his eyes shut, sucked in a breath, and tried to roll onto his side.

A studded boot came down on his chest, pressing him to the ground; then he felt the sharp iron point of a spear against his neck. He opened his eyes and saw the figure standing over him, the rusty red beard and the shining skull.

'Looks like we've run you to ground, bastard,' Sergianus said.

Two of them grabbed his arms, hauling him up and dragging him, a dead weight between them. Castus struggled to focus his mind, to fight against them, but he was still stunned. At least, he thought, none of his bones were broken. He kicked at the ground, and one of the men let out a high, whinnying laugh.

At the far side of the dell was a fallen tree, crusty with moss, and they hurled him down against it. All eight of the men, Castus now saw, were wearing military belts and tunics under their cloaks. Praetorians, although he had guessed that already. One of them, a big man almost as brawny as Castus himself, had drawn his long, broad-bladed spatha and was swinging it in the air, the metal singing. Another was gathering sticks; a fire-pot smoked on the ground beside the heaped kindling.

'Your emperor let me go free,' Castus managed to say. He

knew it would do no good. The whinnying man laughed again. 'I have a safe conduct...'

'The emperor Maxentius is a merciful man,' Sergianus said. 'But we are not. You killed our brother Mikkalus, knifed him in a dirty alley, and we reckon you haven't paid the price for that yet.'

Castus bit down on his words; there was no point trying to speak now. He flexed his arms, but the two men on either side were gripping him tightly. He felt their calloused hands, smelled their sweat and their stale breath.

'However,' Sergianus went on, 'as you say, the emperor promised to let you live, and return to your army. We are loyal soldiers of the emperor, and so cannot disobey him... But first we want to make sure that you can't bear arms against us again...'

One of the soldiers had Castus in a grappling headlock, holding his left arm and torso pinned against the fallen tree. The other man, the one with the whinnying laugh, seized his right arm and dragged it out straight. The swordsman moved closer, his blade flashing in the sunlight.

'No!' Castus cried. Horror lanced through him. He realised now what they were going to do. Blood was beating fast in his neck.

Sergianus was grinning, his teeth glinting through his beard. 'Don't struggle,' he said. 'My friend here might miss and give you a cut on the head! You'd look even uglier without an ear. Oh, don't worry, you'll be going back to your army all right, just as the emperor promised. But without your hands! Let's see you saluting your beloved Constantine with a pair of stumps...'

The swordsman lifted his blade, and the whinnying soldier gripped Castus's forearm tightly, holding the hand stretched out. Castus closed his fingers into a fist, heaving against the man gripping his neck. His legs were kicking, heels beating against the turf, and the soldier was laughing breathily in his ear. On his exposed wrist, Castus noticed the leather thong with the bright blue bead that Ganna had given him shining in the sunlight. If he ever needed protection, it was now; but already it was too late.

He closed his eyes, raging despair filling his body as he waited for the whip of the descending blade and the shock of blinding pain. To be caught like this, after so many escapes. So many glances at death. It was absurd, hilarious – he felt nervous laughter heaving in his chest, punching at the back of his throat.

A sharp crack, and Castus opened his eyes to see the big swordsman sway and reel, his eyes rolling upwards and blood bursting from his nose. Then his legs folded beneath him and he toppled forward. The sword fell from his grip and jabbed into the turf, stuck upright.

The soldier holding Castus by the wrist had flinched, his grip slackening; Castus wrenched his arm free and swung his fist, cracking it into the face of the man pinning him down. He felt the man's nose break, and wrestled him aside. Then he flung out his arm again and seized the hilt of the sword. Twisting, he stabbed backwards and drove the blade between the ribs of the soldier with the whinnying laugh. Blood spattered across him as he pushed himself to his feet.

Five men standing; the soldier next to him still on the ground, clasping his broken nose. Another slingstone arced from the trees and struck the man beside Sergianus on the leg; he yelped and dropped to one knee. Castus got the sword in a two-handed grip and stabbed downwards, killing the soldier on the ground. Then he vaulted the fallen log and started running for the trees. A javelin flew past his shoulder.

He could hear the confused fury of the men behind him. One of them screamed as another slingstone found its mark. Powered by the wild energy of escape, Castus scaled the slope and threw himself forward between the trees. They were coming after him now, and they had spears and javelins, but he had a good lead on them and he was charging, leaping through the thorn thickets, slamming the undergrowth aside as the forest closed around him and the sounds of pursuit died away.

Castus ran until he could run no more, then he hurled his back against a tree and stood with the sword in his hand, breathing like an ox, waiting. Thorns had scratched his face and hands, and his shoulder and ribs ached from his fall from the horse, but he was alive, the blood racing in his body. Slowly he shortened his breath, listening to the sounds of the forest around him. He had no idea how far he had run, and it was dark here, the dense leaves obscuring the sky.

A man stepped from the bushes ahead of him, and Castus tensed. He crouched against the tree, sword levelled, as the man moved closer. Then he grinned.

'You lost your mule.'

He saw Felix shrug, his face creasing into a rueful smile. 'It was borrowed anyway.'

'So did the notary play us false, or did he not?' Felix said. 'I don't understand.'

'Both, I think,' Castus told him. They were sitting beside a tiny flickering fire, in a clearing high on the steep side of the rocky ridge Castus had seen from the road. Beyond the reach of the fire's fitful glow the night was solid black, the forest silent. Felix was skinning and gutting a hare he had killed with his sling a few hours earlier. Castus watched the man's big corded hands working with the knife and the blood streaking his fingers.

'He knew the enemy were closing in on us, I think,' he went on. 'So he pretended to go over to them, to buy himself time to speak to the senators.'

'What about the young lad, Pudentianus?'

'A sacrifice. Nigrinus hated him anyway, but his death would have shown the senators what they're up against, I suppose. In case they needed reminding. Anyway, the notary's got in with the tyrant's people now, working his usual devious tricks.'

'Bastard,' Felix said. There was no apparent anger in his voice, but Castus could tell the word was deeply felt. 'If I see the whore again, I'll kill him.'

Castus just grunted, nodding. Felix had already told him, haltingly and in no great detail, about his own flight from the ambush. He had concealed himself in the city, returning to the places he had known as a youth – the slums and the brothels of the Subura district – then slipped out from the southern gate with a party of travelling musicians bound for Capua. One of the musicians would be missing his mule. But Felix had seen nothing of Diogenes during his time in the city's more infamous quarters.

Castus remembered the strange object Nigrinus had given him; he had not wanted to examine it while he was held in the palace, and had not had a chance since. Shrugging the neck of tunic forward, he reached down inside it until his fingers closed around the small bundle he had carried safely stowed just above his waist belt. He drew it out, and held it up in the light of the fire.

'He gave me this,' he told Felix. 'No idea what it is.'

The object resembled a small ball of twine, wrapped tightly around a lump of bone. 'Maybe there's a message on the inside,'

Castus said, pulling at the knot that secured the end of the twine in place.

'Hssht!' Felix hissed, raising a bloodied hand. Castus frowned at him across the fire.

'*Astragal*,' Felix said. 'I've seen one of them before. There are holes drilled through the sheep-bone, see, and each stands for a letter. The twine goes through the holes to spell out the words, if you know the code. Unwrap it and it's useless.'

'Eternal gods!' Castus placed the wrapped bone carefully on the ground beside him. He was unwilling to touch it now, in case it started unravelling.

'What was it you did, exactly,' he said, 'before you joined the army?'

'Bit of everything,' Felix told him, and his crooked teeth shone in the light of the fire.

Advancing armies left devastation in their wake; they also, Castus soon discovered, created emptiness ahead of them, a zone of deserted villages and abandoned fields, like the bow wave of a ship moving through water. For three days he and Felix trekked northwards, and everywhere there was desolation; the population had vanished in fear of the scouts and foragers of one army or the other. Castus carried only a sword, Felix his sling and knife, and they had lost their mounts and the safe conduct that would take them through the Maxentian checkpoints. They camped at night, took food and water from the empty villages by day, and tried to keep in sight of the road.

On the first day they swam the Tiber; by the second they were hiking into the steep green valleys of the Apennines. The ides of October had come and gone, the date when they had originally planned to intercept Constantine's advancing army at Spoletium. Castus considered finding a secure place and waiting until the vanguard of the army appeared. But they could have been waiting for days, and the army might never come. They moved on.

Several times, from high vantage points, they gazed down at the road and saw troops moving, squadrons of Numidian light cavalry or detachments of marching soldiers. They avoided the towns and the larger villages, the few huts that still showed the smoke of hearth fires.

And just after dawn on the fourth day, as they scrambled along the banks of a rushing mountain stream, they were captured.

CHAPTER XXV

'Where in the smoky black arse of Hades did you spring from?'

The drillmaster stood with his fists planted on his hips, his seamed red face pulled into a disbelieving grimace. Castus was sitting on a folding stool outside the command tent of Legion II Britannica, packing his mouth with good army bread and washing it down with sour vinegar wine.

'Rome,' Castus said, chewing heavily. He swallowed, then gazed into his cup. 'You'll like it there. The wine's decent.'

Only a few hours had passed since Castus and Felix had been caught by the party of exploratores in the valley three miles to the south of Spoletium. The exarch commanding the scouts had not believed Castus's story, of course. Two men dressed in ragged civilian clothes, scrub-bearded, one with a plundered sword: they were either brigands, deserters or enemy spies, and the exarch had ordered them bound and escorted back to camp under guard. Castus had been grinning all the way.

'Are you back to lead us, then, tribune?' Macer said. He was staring at Castus as if he had just appeared from a crack in the earth.

'Isn't Vitalis still in command of the Second?'

Macer's lips tightened and he glanced away. 'Your friend

Vitalis was wounded at Mutina,' he said. 'Javelin in the thigh. We left him behind at Ariminum, and I've been at the front ever since, more or less.'

The drillmaster looked old, Castus thought, more so than his years. Beneath his ruddy tan there was a greyness in his face, his single eye bleary and reddened. The campaign was taking it out of him. From what Castus had seen of the legion, it had taken it out of them all.

'We've been losing men ever since Verona,' Macer said. 'A score went down with campaign fever and never recovered, then some more fell at Mutina before the place surrendered. There's been skirmishing all the way through the mountains. Barely half the men that marched with us from Divodurum are still with the standards.'

'What about the officers?' Castus asked him.

Macer scrubbed at his white hair. 'They've been hit worst,' he said. 'Half the centuries are led by optios now. Brocchus is still carrying the eagle, but most of the other standard-bearers are new men.' He paused, clearing his throat quietly. 'Attalus died,' he said. 'Cut up by enemy scouts on the road just short of Cales. And Gaetulicus, the last of your rapists from Mediolanum, he lost his guts to the sickness before we left Verona. Judgement of the gods, I reckon.' He angled his head and spat.

Castus nodded, then sucked down a mouthful of wine. He was not sorry about Attalus, or Gaetulicus, but the loss of so many others was bitter news.

'Tribune,' Macer said, squatting down on the turf beside him. 'I know we had our differences. Our disagreements, you could say.' He sniffed, uncomfortable, and rubbed his head again. 'But we need a commanding officer. I can't do this on my own; I wasn't made for it. I've seen you on the field – you're a decent leader, and the men need somebody they recognise, somebody who knows them.'

'I'm not your commander,' Castus said. He was still just a tribunus vacans. An officer without a unit. And the judgement of the gods awaited him too.

When the scouts brought him to the camp he had been taken to the command tent and made to wait under guard. Not until Leontius arrived was he recognised and released from his bonds. It was to Leontius, and then to Evander, that Castus had made his report. While a secretary had scratched at a wax tablet, taking it all down in shorthand, Castus had narrated the essentials of the failed mission to Rome. He tried to connect the events in the right order, to remember everything. He told them the names of the senators they had spoken to, and the names of the legions in Maxentius's army. He repeated what the Praetorians had told him at the baths: the strengths and weaknesses of the tyrant's troops, the poor training of the recruits, the large number of Christians in their ranks. He told them of the betrayal of the mission, the death of Pudentianus, Nigrinus's double dealings, and what had happened at the palace. He repeated what Sabina's cousin had told him about Lepidus.

'This is Claudianus Lepidus?' Evander said, breaking in. 'The Master of Dispositions?'

Castus nodded. He saw the two senior officers exchange a glance. The secretary had filled four tablets with notes, and Castus had a dry mouth and an aching head. He doubted he had ever spoken at such length in his life.

'Do you have any further evidence against him?' Evander asked.

'No, dominus,' Castus said. 'But the notary Julius Nigrinus told me to deliver this to the emperor.' He placed the twine-wrapped sheep-bone on the table beside the secretary's tablets.

Evander leaned closer, peering at the object, then picked it up carefully between finger and thumb. 'Very well, tribune,' he said. 'You're dismissed. For now. Get something to eat, you look like a starved dog.'

Now, sitting outside the command tent in the legion lines, Castus looked to his left. The walled town of Spoletium climbed the slope from the valley where the army was camped towards the wooded summit of the hill. Somewhere within the town the emperor Constantine had established himself and his retinue; Evander was there now, with the tablets of notes and the mysterious coded message. Soon enough, Castus thought, he would discover what verdict had been passed upon him.

Breathing in deeply, he tipped his head back into the sunlight. All around him spread the regular rows of army tents, the camp ovens still smoking after baking the morning bread. He closed his eyes, and listened to the rough gnarled voices of the soldiers, the curses and the laughter. This was home, he thought. The relief of getting safely back here was enough for him. Let the gods decide what they would.

'Tribune!' a familiar voice cried. Castus opened his eyes and stood up quickly.

'Centurion Modestus,' he said, and almost laughed. He had the briefest memory of Modestus as he had once been, a drunkard and a shirker, back in the old legion fortress at Eboracum. Now he was a tanned veteran, a centurion's staff in his hand and a vigorous spring in his step. Marching up to Castus, he seized him by the shoulders and pulled him into a firm embrace.

'Thought you'd buggered off and died,' Modestus said, and kissed him loudly on the cheek. Then he turned and whistled.

Two slaves were following Modestus, carrying a brass-bound chest between them. Eumolpius trailed along behind them. The slaves set the chest down, and the orderly unlocked it and threw back the lid.

'It's all here, dominus,' Eumolpius said. 'I kept it safe, just as you ordered.'

'Reckoned we'd lug it along with us,' Modestus added. 'Else some sneaky bastard'd make off with it, no doubt.'

Castus knelt beside the open chest. Metal gleamed within. He reached down and took the gold torque, flexing the loop of it around his neck. His ring was in a leather pouch, and he slipped it back onto his finger. Then he saw the sword.

'I had the armourer replace the blade,' Eumolpius said. 'It's perhaps not as fine as the old one, and I haven't sharpened it.'

'You did well,' Castus told him. He closed his hand around the gilded eagle hilt, then drew the long spatha from the scabbard, holding it up in the sunlight with a flush of true pleasure.

The chest also contained his armour, the muscled cuirass, manica and gilded helmet, and his folded clothes and military belts. Standing, Castus stripped off his ragged tunic and flung it aside. He pulled off the worn old boots he had been wearing, and the breeches too. Finally he shed his loincloth, and stood naked while Eumolpius and two slaves flung buckets of water over him, watched by a dozen grinning legionaries.

He rubbed himself down with a coarse towel, and was dressing in the musty clothes from the chest when Eumolpius handed him something else.

'I almost forgot!' the orderly said. 'It came for you just after you left Verona. I kept it in case you... well, in case you ever came back.'

* * *

Castus looked at the narrow tablet, his own name inked across it. Breaking the seal with his thumbnail, he unfolded the leaves of it and stared at the flowing letters. In the bright sun they were almost illegible, and he retreated to the cool shade just inside the open flap of the tent. Frowning heavily, he stared again at the tablet, the chicken-scratched letters. Mouthing the words to himself, he began to read. And his pulse quickened.

Husband. Shame has made me flee from you, and now I struggle to write these words. If you cannot forgive me, then please try to judge me fairly, for the sake of our son if not for me. There is no excuse for what I have done but I regret it. Truly I regret it. I have betrayed not only you but our emperor. I would take an honourable way out but I am weak, I find. My cousin, Claudianus Lepidus, means to destroy you and those who travel with you. I cannot indict him without indicting myself, and others more exalted than me. Be on your guard, and trust no man. I have been blind but please know that you have my love. Remember that what we call duty is often only pride. May the gods protect you and guide you safely. SABINA.

Castus closed the tablet, then pressed it to his forehead for a moment. He was breathing very deeply, very slowly. He was still sitting there in the shadowed tent, unmoving, staring ahead of him into nothing, when the two Protectores arrived with the summons. He slipped the tablet beneath his belt, then stood up without a word and followed them.

The paved road climbed steeply up the hillside towards the arched gate of Spoletium. The Protectores led Castus at a rapid pace; Felix followed behind him, dressed in a clean tunic but still unshaven and wolfish. Castus too was bearded, his hair grown out, his face bruised and scratched, but he was dressed as a Roman officer, the torque gleaming at his neck and a sword belted at his side. He marched fast, and felt ready for whatever was coming.

In through the gates, they climbed the last slope and passed beneath an old arch, the reliefs and inscriptions worn to indistinction. Spoletium stood on a hillside, and the regular grid of streets appeared warped by the inclined ground, turning to steps in places. The Protectores did not pause, stamping along with their nailed boots clattering on the worn paving. They crossed the broad open space of the forum, then halted before the tall inlaid doors of a large townhouse. The doors swung open, and they gestured for Castus to enter.

A sentry took his sword, and silently motioned for Felix to remain in the vestibule while Castus moved on into the building. The sun was high, but cool shadow still suffused the central courtyard, a fountain trickling at the heart of the enclosed garden. At the far side, another set of doors opened, a purple drape shifted aside, and Castus entered the sacred presence of the emperor.

'*The most distinguished Aurelius Castus, tribunus vacans*,' a eunuch solemnly declaimed. Castus took four long paces, then sank to kneel on the tiled floor. The air carried the faint aroma of incense.

'You may stand,' Evander said. He was sitting at a table to one side of the chamber, and Castus could see the sheep-bone before him, the twine that had bound it unravelled now. At the far end of the chamber, wrapped in a plain military cloak, the emperor stood with his back turned, apparently lost in thought.

Castus assumed a parade stance. The two Protectores had followed him into the room, and there were several eunuchs and a secretary around him too. He recognised the other officer with Evander as well: Agrippinus, the chief of the agentes in rebus. The emperor did not move.

'I have informed the Augustus of everything you told me in your report,' Evander said. 'We have also deciphered the message you brought from Julius Nigrinus, Tribune of Notaries.'

He turned to Agrippinus, who picked up the sheep-bone and turned it lightly between his fingers. 'The message was only two words,' Agrippinus said. 'The first was a password, proving that the message was genuine. The second was a name.'

'*Lepidus*,' Evander said. 'It appears that the notary wishes to confirm the accuracy of what you have told us.'

Castus blinked, his mind blank for a moment. Had Nigrinus known all along? Speechless, he merely nodded.

'It seems the notary has done well,' Evander went on, 'although we can only guess at his methods. It's a shame that Flavius Ummidius, the chief of his department, could not be with us to congratulate him.'

Castus remembered the old man with the papery smile who had presided over the meeting at the villa beside the lake. 'Flavius Ummidius is not here?' he asked.

'Flavius Ummidius is dead,' Agrippinus said. 'He died, it seems, of fright. Only a day or two after your departure, he discovered something in his bedchamber, a figurine of some sort, marked with his name and stuck with nails. It was too much for his heart, sadly... Of course, we suspect the dark designs of the tyrant.'

Castus frowned, nodding. It seemed a very unlikely thing for Maxentius to have ordered, or Lepidus. He barely noticed that Constantine had turned to face him.

'Tribune Aurelius Castus,' the emperor declared in a cold and ringing voice. 'We are satisfied that you have conducted yourself with honour and determination. The information you have gathered in the camp of the enemy is of great worth. Therefore, I order that you be reinstated as commander of the Second Legion Britannica.'

Throwing his cloak back from his shoulder, Constantine paced slowly across the floor. Castus recalled that the last time he had seen this man had been on the moon-drenched battlefield outside Verona, in the mesh of the fighting. The memory of what he had said and done that night brought the blood rushing to his face.

'I misjudged your loyalty,' the emperor said stiffly. 'I make apology for that.' Before Castus could reply, he stepped forward and gripped him in an embrace. 'It's good to see you back with us again, brother,' Constantine said.

Then he turned on his heel and paced back to the far end of the room.

'There is one thing you must do before taking up your command,' Evander said. 'His excellency Domitius Claudianus Lepidus, Master of Dispositions, is currently residing in a house just outside the northern gate. You are to take a party of men, go to the house, and summon him.'

'Summon him, dominus?'

'Of course. Summon him here so he can be questioned. He must answer to a charge of treason.'

'Yes, dominus!' Castus said, straightening up and saluting. The emperor remained in his attitude of deep thought, his back turned once more.

'Make sure no harm comes to the man, won't you?' Agrippinus added.

* * *

Dropping quickly down the sloping streets and stepped alleys from the centre of town, Castus marched out through the northern gate of Spoletium with Felix at his side and six dismounted troopers of the Schola Scutariorum at his back. The troopers had been part of the sentry detachment at the emperor's residence, and all wore helmets and carried spears and shields. They crossed a bridge over the shallow river beyond the walls, then climbed the dusty tree-lined track on the far side to the gates of the house.

In through the gateway, shoving aside a pair of startled slaves, Castus marched up to the main doors while a pair of troopers moved around either side of the house to seal off any rear exits. Raising his fist, Castus hammered on the wood panels of the door. Silence followed. He could hear a bird singing in the trees back along the road. The door looked solid enough; he hoped he would not have to find a ram and break it down.

A bolt rattled, hinges squealed and the door edged open slightly. A flat-faced man peered through the gap.

'We want to talk to your master,' Castus said.

The man peered at him, his jaw working. Castus could see the calculation in his features, the spark of fear in his eyes. Then the door swung closed again.

Before the slave could slip the bolt into place Castus hurled himself against the door, flinging it open. He felt the heavy wood crash against the man's body, then he was over the threshold and striding in through the vestibule, with Felix and the two troopers crowding behind him.

There were two more slaves at the far end of the vestibule, bodyguards in sky-blue tunics, but they carried only staves. One glance at the armed men advancing on them and they threw down their weapons and backed away. Castus pushed past them.

'Where is he?' he demanded, seeing a man in a patterned robe emerging from a side chamber of the courtyard. Lepidus's procurator, or one of his clerks, he guessed.

'The master is dining!' the man exclaimed. 'If you would care to wait a moment...?'

'We would not.'

The dining chamber was easy to find. Castus could smell the aroma of spiced food even from the courtyard. His stomach roiled. He still could not admit to himself what he was about to do.

'Give me your dagger,' he said quietly to Felix. The small man slipped the weapon from the sheath on his belt and passed it, underhand, to Castus. The two troopers had taken up positions flanking the doorway. 'Wait here,' Castus told them.

Throwing open the doors, he marched into the chamber. A quick glance took in the panelled wall paintings, the mosaic floor, and a young slave boy in a very short tunic attending his master. Lepidus was dining alone, reclining on a single couch. There was a stack of tablets and rolled documents on the low table beside him; the man was working while he ate. Lepidus wiped his mouth with a napkin as Castus approached, and dropped the tablet he had been reading, but did not rise.

'If you've come looking for your wife,' he said, 'she's not here. I got tired of her moods and left her at Ariminum.'

Castus stood in the centre of the room, one hand on the hilt of his sword. 'You,' he told the boy. 'Get out. Close the door behind you.'

The boy obeyed promptly.

'Stand up,' Castus told the man on the couch. Lepidus was screwing the napkin between his fingers, a nervous smile twitching across his mouth. Castus noticed that his left forearm was bandaged, a thick wad of dressing tied against it.

'You know there was never a chance that Sabina would be faithful to you,' Lepidus said. 'Why should she? A dumb brute, she called you. You know that? She laughed at you, she—'

'Stand up,' Castus repeated. His hand itched on the hilt of his sword, but he knew the man was goading him.

'Now you want to take me before the emperor,' Lepidus said, the nervous smile still on his face. 'They'll torture me, I suppose. But the things I could tell them... Your own dear wife would be next. And the emperor's wife too. Fausta – I know you're fond of her. Sabina told me all about it. Maybe you too, then, eh?'

Exactly, Castus thought. He had known at once why the emperor's men had sent him after Lepidus. They could have chosen anyone, any of the Protectores or the other tribunes, somebody unconcerned. They had chosen Castus because they knew that for him it was personal. And if Lepidus died, the plot died with him.

'I have plenty of money here in the house,' Lepidus was saying. He touched his face, and his hand was shaking. 'It's yours – all you have to do is call your men off and look in the other direction...'

Castus drew the dagger from his belt and tossed it to the floor, the iron ringing as it struck the tiles.

'You sent slaves to kill me and the rest of my party,' he said. 'They failed. Instead they killed a sailor called Fish-hook and a Christian priest called Stephanus. Now I'm giving you the chance to do the job yourself.'

Lepidus stared at the dagger on the floor. He tried to speak, but his jaw was trembling too much. He wiped his fingers through his hair, then rubbed at his bandaged arm.

Castus raised his hands, keeping them clear of his own weapon. 'Pick it up,' he said. 'Either that or you're coming with me.'

The man on the couch swallowed thickly. He let out a brief laugh. Then he threw himself at the dagger. His reaching fingers missed the hilt and knocked it away from him, and Castus stepped back. Scrabbling, Lepidus managed to grab the dagger and straighten up. A look of wild ferocity lit his face, and he lunged with the blade.

Castus took another step back, dodging the man's clumsy stroke, then with one swift motion he seized the grip of his sword and slid it from the scabbard. He drew his arm back, then stabbed Lepidus through the body.

Lepidus lurched against him, clawing at his neck and shoulders.

'I guessed you'd be no good at this,' Castus said, and gave the sword a wrenching twist. Then he shoved the man away from him, dragging the blade free as he fell.

He was wiping his sword on the dead man's tunic as Felix and the two troopers pushed in through the doors.

'His excellency attempted to attack me,' Castus said, and shrugged as he kicked the dagger away across the floor. He gestured to the pile of documents on the table. 'Burn all these,' he said, and pretended not to notice the quick glance the soldiers exchanged. 'Burn any other letters or lists you can find as well.'

Lepidus's treason, his negotiations with the commander at Ravenna and the others, with Sabina and with Fausta: all of it would go up in the flames. If the emperor's men wanted him to do their dirty work, he would do it properly, in his own way. Let them accept the consequences. The guilty would be tortured only by their own consciences.

A brief swell of nausea as he stared down at the body, a fluttering sense of shame in his chest. *What we call duty is often only pride.*

A pool of blood was spreading across the mosaic floor, rich crimson against the bright tiles.

CHAPTER XXVI

They smelled the river before they could see it. The scent of wet sedge, mud and water carried on the misty night air, and the six riders moved slowly, each man wrapped in a dark cloak. For the last mile the Tiber had been on their left, but it had swung away in a wide bend and now it was ahead of them. Castus felt his senses growing steadily sharper in the darkness.

'He crossed over there somewhere, dominus,' the exarch said quietly, pointing into the murk. 'One of my men found him, more or less where we are now.'

Castus peered towards the river, then nudged the flanks of his horse and the big grey mare moved forward again, slow and steady over the uneven ground. He was glad to have his familiar mount back again; compared with the unfortunate pony he had ridden north from Rome, Dapple's calm strength and solidity were doubly welcome.

'And you're sure there are no enemy troops on this side of the river?' he asked. The exarch and his men, with several other units of exploratores, had been scouting the area north of the Tiber since midday.

'Not as far as we know, dominus,' the exarch said. 'In this darkness, they could have small patrols out, perhaps. But their main force is far south from here, inside in the city.'

Or so you believe, Castus thought.

Constantine's army was camped at Saxa Rubra, two miles back up the river, at the ninth milestone on the Flaminian Way. It had taken them six days to march down from Spoletium over the last passes of the Apennines, in a column nearly twelve miles long, moving at the pace of the wagons and the siege train and the few remaining camels. The only enemy resistance had been at Ocriculum, where an advance party of the Divitenses had fought a running battle with a squadron of Numidian cavalry. Now less than half a day's march would take them to the gates of Rome. The scouts had reported that the stone bridge over the Tiber had been broken, two of its three arches demolished, and the enemy had withdrawn towards the city. Clearly, Maxentius had opted to keep his army inside the walls and stand a siege. Back at Saxa Rubra the troops were relaxing after their long march; the next day, the engineers would have to repair the bridge for the army to cross, and there would be no fighting any time soon.

But something was not right; Castus could feel it. He remembered this open ground he was crossing now, the escarpment that rose somewhere to his right in the darkness, the bottleneck between hills and looping river at either edge of the plain. He had passed this way on the day he left Rome, and he remembered the strange intuition, something close to a certainty, that the battle would be fought here. Almost, he thought, like a message from the gods.

Intuition alone he could have discounted, gods-sent or not. It was not intuition that had brought him down here two miles from the camp in the midnight mist.

Earlier that evening, a pair of exploratores had found him in his tent in the legion lines. Castus had just finished eating, and was cleaning his kit. The scouts had taken a captive, they explained, who claimed to be a soldier of the Second Legion.

'We thought he was an enemy spy, dominus.'

'Not the first time you made that mistake,' Castus muttered to himself.

But when they brought the ragged figure into the tent he could see why they refused to believe he was a soldier. The thin man before him was soaking wet and smelled terrible, his hollow cheeks were covered by a patchy beard, and for a few long moments Castus did not recognise him.

'Apologies, dominus. I had to swim the river.'

'Diogenes!' Castus cried, leaping up from his stool and clasping the man by the shoulders, shaking him with fierce joy. Runnels of brown water dripped onto the tent's matting floor. Then he was calling for Eumolpius to bring towels, warm wine and clean dry clothing, pushing Diogenes down onto a stool while the man gulped out his story.

He had spent nearly twenty days hiding out in Rome, he told Castus. Pudentianus's old door porter had concealed him in a neighbour's kitchen for most of the time, but Diogenes had heard enough of the outside world to know that the atmosphere in the city had changed. News of the approach of Constantine's army had thrown the people of Rome into a state of barely suppressed panic, everyone convinced that they were about to be sacked by ferocious barbarians from Germania and Britain.

'Only today I heard,' Diogenes said, sitting with a blanket wrapped around his skinny shoulders and cup of warm wine in his hand, 'that the crowd in the circus were chanting the name of Constantine! Some faction or other was leading them, it seems. The Praetorians stormed the stands to try and shut them up, but everyone heard it. "Constantine shall never be defeated," they were chanting...'

Nigrinus, Castus thought as Diogenes filled in the last few details of his story: he had been smuggled out of the city earlier that evening, but had had to cover the last distance on foot and swim across the river, then had got lost in the mist on the far side.

'But before I crossed over,' Diogenes said, with more urgency, 'I saw something happening on the southern bank. It was about half a mile downstream, I think, close to the broken bridge, and hard to make out in the mist, but it seemed like a large number of men were building something down there.'

'Building what?'

'I couldn't tell, dominus. But I saw boats in the river, moored along the near bank. They looked like barges to me.'

'Barges,' Castus said. He pondered a moment, then nodded and stood up quickly, calling for Eumolpius to saddle his horse. He had an idea, but he would need to see things for himself before he could be sure.

The mist parted and the river was before them, the black water flowing smooth and fast. Half a mile downstream, Diogenes had said, but in these conditions it was impossible to see anything like that far. They would need to move closer.

'Fan your men out to the right,' Castus told the exarch. 'We don't want to get trapped against the river if there's anybody out there.'

He tugged at the reins, and the grey mare turned and moved along the bank, skirting the stands of willow and thickets of brush that loomed from the swirling darkness ahead. For a long time, Castus saw nothing, heard nothing but the slow thud of the horse's hooves on the damp turf and the steady whisper of the river. The air was cold, and the wetness was soaking through his cloak.

Then he heard it: the voices of men from the far bank, the muffled clatter of wooden boards. He gave a low whistle, summoning the exarch to him, then slid down from the saddle. Passing the reins to the scout, he picked his way forward on foot, scrambling down the crumbling earth of the bank into the mud at the water's edge. Sound travelled much more clearly here, and as he probed his way forward Castus began to make out the shapes on the opposite bank.

A waterbird burst from cover, startling him, and he threw up his hands but managed to silence his cry. He held his breath, waiting, but there was no response from the darkness across the water. A few more steps, then a few more; the mist swirled aside and Castus saw what he was looking for. He drew a long breath. Then he scrambled up the bank and ran back to the horses.

The return to camp seemed to take an age, but less than half an hour had passed before Castus rode in past the sentries at a gallop, calling out the watchword, and cantered between the tent lines to the imperial enclosure. He dropped from the saddle, Dapple still blowing and stamping, and threw the reins to a sentry. Then he was striding fast, ordering men out of his way, a note of urgent command in his voice. He could see the sentry braziers burning outside the great pavilion that housed the emperor's own quarters, and the lamplight from within.

The two Protectores on duty halted him at the door of the pavilion. Castus knew one of them, but the other was a stranger.

'Sorry, brother,' the Protector said in a hushed voice. 'Nobody goes in there. The Augustus is conferring with his Christian priest and can't be disturbed.'

'The priest? Why?'

The man shrugged, and Castus caught the swift apprehensive glance that passed between him and his fellow guard.

'Then where's Aurelius Evander?' he said.

'Here,' a voice said. The flap at the door of the pavilion lifted aside and Evander emerged, a pair of eunuchs trailing

403

behind him. The Commander of the Field Army of Gaul looked unusually harried, his face drawn and unshaven in the glow of the braziers. Castus noticed that he was wearing his sleeping tunic beneath his cloak.

'Dominus!' he cried, saluting quickly. Then, more quietly, he asked what was happening in the pavilion.

'The Augustus has had a dream,' one of the eunuchs announced. It was Festus, the Superintendent of the Sacred Bedchamber. 'A dream of great portent, it seems. He believes that the Bishop of Corduba to be the only man who can explain to him its meaning!' The irritation in the eunuch's voice was obvious.

Castus frowned heavily. In his experience, dreams seldom meant anything good. They were best forgotten as soon as possible.

'You arrived with some velocity, tribune,' Evander said, stifling a yawn. 'What brings you here at this hour?'

'Dominus, I believe the enemy are about to cross the river in force.'

Evander's expression changed instantly, tightening to a look of stern attention. He gripped Castus by the shoulder, steering him a few steps away from the pavilion. 'How can you know this?' he demanded. 'The Milvian Bridge is broken, the scouts said...'

Quickly Castus outlined his reconnaissance along the riverbank. 'The enemy have constructed a bridge of boats,' he told the commander. 'They must have built it in sections and moved it up under cover of darkness. There's a mass of men on the far bank, and as soon as the bridge is in place they'll cross over and take up a position on the plain before dawn, with their cavalry occupying the high ground on the right of the road.'

Evander was blinking, struggling to take it in. 'You're certain of this?' he said. 'I mean, you couldn't have been mistaken, a trick of the mist perhaps, cattle on the far bank – such things can be deceptive...'

Castus felt the scar on his jaw beginning to itch. He knew, as Evander surely knew, that certainty was impossible in these situations. But his intuition had surely been proved right: either Maxentius had changed his mind about remaining in the city, or his withdrawal to the shelter of the walls had been a ruse all along.

'Dominus,' he said. 'If we prepare to march now we can take up an opposing position before they've had time to properly deploy and prepare the ground. Perhaps we can even seize the heights before their cavalry get there...'

Evander shook his head promptly. 'Don't presume too far, tribune,' he said. 'It would take hours to assemble the men and break camp, and we'd need a strong cavalry force if we wanted to hold ground.'

Castus clenched his back teeth in frustration. But he could see that Evander was thinking, his mind running through options. 'I must speak to the Augustus,' the commander said. 'Only he can order an immediate advance. Remain here.'

He turned back towards the pavilion, and only then did Castus notice the large number of other men that had gathered around them, tribunes and other officers, Protectores and civilian officials, drawn by the currents of rumour. Castus imagined those same currents running through the whole camp around him, all thirty thousand fighting men and the great mass of slaves and civilians that had marched with them. But it would take more than rumours to stir such an army into motion.

As Evander approached the pavilion, the two Protectores stepping smartly aside, the doors flapped open again and another figure emerged into the braziers' glow. Castus recognised the dark features and white hair of the Christian priest, Hosius, the Bishop of Corduba. The man was dressed in a plain unbelted tunic, and his feet were bare.

'Bishop,' Evander said, drawing himself up stiffly. 'Is the Augustus still awake?'

'Our blessed emperor is resting,' the priest declared. He spoke as if to address the whole gathering of men around the pavilion. 'But his mind is at peace.'

'I must speak to him. The enemy is preparing for battle.'

'He knows!' Hosius said, and smiled. 'Almighty God has sent him a powerful vision. A promise of victory!'

Still smiling, the priest walked away towards his own tent with his head held high, the gathering of officers parting nervously before him.

'Ten years ago we were feeding the likes of him to the beasts,' the guard muttered from the side of his mouth. 'Now look at him.'

There was no more sleep that night. In the darkness the centurions roused their men and had them prepare their weapons and armour. A party of scouts went out along the river, and returned an hour later with the confirmation of Castus's report: the full enemy force was in the process of crossing the river and taking up a position to block the road.

It was still dark when the tribunes and senior officers assembled in the large tent beside the imperial pavilion. Lamps burned, casting weary faces into harsh shadow, but there was a tense aggressive energy in the air, every man charged with the certainty of coming battle. Castus knew many of them: Leontius of VIII Augusta, the tribunes of the Divitenses, the Minervia and Primigenia legions, and Hierocles, the commander of the Protectores. Hrodomarus of the Bucinobantes stood proudly in scarlet and gold, a younger and much slimmer version of his father King Hrocus. But many were new men, and many were missing: Vitalis of course, also Florius Baudio, who had been killed on the advance through the Apennines just short of Spoletium, and several more. The campaign had already reaped a harvest of the commanders, and the fiercest battle was yet to come.

Together they listened as Evander explained the situation, and gave the orders for the march and deployment. The troops would leave camp in battle array, leaving all the wagons and the siege train behind them. Only a thin screen of cavalry would cover the advance; the men must be ready to fight at any moment. Evander told them the order of battle, and the watchwords they would use to identify themselves in the darkness. He reminded them to check that all their troops wore the feathered helmet crests: there could be no mistakes, no confusion once the action commenced.

Every man nodded, many of them scratching notes on tablets. Standing to one side of the group, Castus committed everything he had heard to memory. It was simple enough: no clever tactics, no complex manoeuvres. Evander's plan was to hit the enemy with one massive frontal assault, and it was a plan that suited Castus perfectly.

A breath of night air entered the packed tent as the flap opened, and then the gathered officers were looking back, shifting aside to form a lane. Castus craned his neck to look over the other men's heads, and saw the emperor marching between them, two Protectores and a group of civilian officials and eunuchs at his heels.

Constantine stepped up beside Evander and turned to address

the gathering. As one, the officers threw up their hands and cried out the salute.

'Fellow soldiers,' the emperor said, his voice hoarse but strong. 'One final battle lies between us and victory. Tomorrow we lift the yoke of tyranny from the city of Rome, and restore the ancient splendour and liberty of the city of our ancestors.'

Something in the emperor's manner seemed changed, Castus thought. He remembered speaking to Constantine before the battle at Verona, and noticing his fear. He was not afraid now, but seemed possessed of a strange, glazed calm, the sort of invulnerable aura that drunkards could assume, but totally sober, totally cold and clear.

'I have received a message, a sign,' Constantine went on, sweeping the assembly with a fervent gaze. 'A sign from the Greatest God. Many of you here were with me in Gaul, three years ago, and witnessed with me the celestial vision of light.'

Castus found himself nodding, holding his breath. He remembered the moment well, although he had not seen any-thing very clearly at the time: it had been a vision of the sun god, so men had said. The mighty Sol Invictus, in his guise of Apollo.

'Brothers,' the emperor said. 'The truth of that vision has been revealed to me in a dream.' His brow was creased, and he dabbed at his face with his fingers for a moment, as if stunned. 'Before we enter battle, our front-rank troops must mark upon their shields the saving sign of the Greatest God. With this sign, the divinity will deliver us certain victory.'

A rustle of breath, of muttered words, passed between the gathered men. One of the imperial slaves had stepped up beside the emperor with a board, and on the board was painted in broad strokes of black ink a symbol. Castus stared at it, perplexed. From the sounds they were making, most of the other men were perplexed too.

The greatest god, he knew, was the Unconquered Sun. His own legion carried Sol's symbol upon their shields already: the red solar wheel. The same symbol appeared throughout the army, from standards to belt buckles, helmet crests to tunic embroidery. It was on many of the coins issued in Constantine's name. All recognised it. But the symbol inked on the board the slave was holding was something different. Two crossed lines, with a third drawn through the middle and a curl at the top. Castus knew it from somewhere, but could not place it.

Was it some variant on the solar wheel, perhaps? Such things could be revealed in dreams, Castus supposed. As the emperor made his departure and the gathering broke up, he noticed Aurelius Evander glancing in his direction. His expression was troubled.

'It's a Greek symbol,' he heard somebody saying. 'It stands for good luck.'

'I'm not so sure, brother,' somebody else said.

But as Castus left the tent and walked out into the damp pre-dawn chill, heading for the lines of his legion, the suspicion in his heart was gathering. With a sense of dark unease, he realised that he knew what that symbol meant. He had first seen it many years before, scratched into the doorpost of a house in the north of Britain. It was nothing to do with luck. Constantine's army would be going into battle marked with the sign of the Christians.

CHAPTER XXVII

'Cavalry on the heights,' Leontius said, peering into the hazy grey dawn. 'All of them, looks like.'

Castus nodded. It was as he had expected. Above the line of reddish bluffs that edged the plain, the enemy horsemen had already occupied the high ground. He could just make out their streaming draco banners and unit standards between the trees that edged the escarpment. Maxentius would have his Horse Guards up there, Castus knew: two thousand scale-armoured lancers, with mounted archers and the Numidian light cavalry in support. Their intention was obvious. They would charge down from the heights in a swinging left-hook punch, aiming to crush the flank of Constantine's army and leave his infantry trapped with their backs to the river.

'Still a lot of motion up there, though,' Leontius went on, squinting. 'They haven't managed to get into formation yet.'

The two officers were on horseback, a hundred paces in advance of the Constantinian battle line. Hrodomarus of the Bucinobantes was with them; together they would be in charge of the left centre of the battle line. Behind them their troops were already assembled in vast silent blocks, waiting for the signal to advance.

If the enemy cavalrymen on the heights were still in an unready state, Maxentius's infantry was even less prepared.

From where he was sitting, mounted high on his grey mare, Castus could see the enemy front line stretching across the plain between the bluffs and the river. They would be formed deep, sixteen ranks most likely, the best array for poorly trained troops. A second line of the same numbers behind, perhaps a third in support. Together they formed a massive phalanx, but after their river crossing the lines were in chaos: even from this distance Castus could clearly hear the scream of the trumpets and horns, the shouts of the commanders as they tried to muster their men. Only in the centre was the line strong, where the ten thousand men of the Praetorian Guard stood in formed ranks beneath their proud standards.

'Have you seen the Augustus?' Leontius asked Castus, lowering his voice. Castus shook his head. In all the milling confusion of breaking camp and marching to the field, he had seen nothing of Constantine.

'I got a glimpse of him just after first light, over on our right with the cavalry,' Leontius went on. 'He looked… *possessed*. He's either mad or inspired by the gods, brother. I pity those poor bastards over there when he tears into them.'

Inspired by the gods. Castus wished it were so. But if some divine spirit fired their emperor, it did not seem to be that of the ancestral gods of Rome. Raising his eyes, Castus searched for the gleam of light. But the heavens were closed: a skin of mottled grey cloud hid the sky, and only a faint radiance in the east showed where the sun had risen above the misty horizon. The distant land beyond the curve of the river was blurred, indistinct, and the air was stirred only by a slight damp breeze.

'What are they doing here?' Hrodomarus demanded, leaning from beneath the massive fur cape he wore over his mail. Over to their right, ahead of the centre of the battle

411

line, three figures in loose tunics were standing in the open ground, raising their empty hands to the clouded sky.

'Christians,' Leontius spat. Castus could see that the central figure was the white-haired Spanish bishop, Hosius. 'They're praying to their god, I suppose. The Augustus must have given them leave to do it.'

'This is not good,' Hrodomarus said, with a contemptuous sniff. 'Too much already the signs on the shields!' He gave a last dark look at the praying Christians, then turned his horse and rode back to the ranks of his warriors.

Castus waited only a little longer. He gave a brief salute to Leontius, who returned it. There was nothing more to be said now. All knew what the next hours would bring. Tugging on the reins, he turned Dapple and walked her back towards his waiting soldiers.

The array of Constantine's army almost mirrored that of the enemy. The emperor himself with his main cavalry force was on the right wing, the infantry drawn up across the plain. But instead of the solid shield wall of the Maxentian troops, Constantine's men were assembled in attack columns, each blunt-headed wedge a fortress of locked shields, auxilia and light troops positioned in the gaps between. The Second Britannica formed four of the columns. As he glanced along the lines Castus saw that every man wore the crest of feathers on his helmet, and every front-rank shield was clearly marked with the symbol that Constantine had decreed, scratched in chalk or charcoal over the brightly painted blazons. The sight, he had to admit, was impressive. He could only guess what effect it might be having on the enemy.

He reached the left-hand edge of his legion's formation, and as he approached Macer took several strides forward and saluted.

'All ready, tribune,' the drillmaster cried. Macer would be leading one of the attack columns, and his face was glowing with fierce pride.

Castus returned the salute, then rode on along the formation. The men in the front ranks were all veterans. They had marched with the legion all the way from Divodurum, and most had fought on the Rhine and in Britain before that. They knew Castus, and many called out to him as he passed, or raised their spears in silent salute. Castus saw Felix, freshly shaved now but still with his look of rangy strength. Then there was Modestus, and Diogenes, recovered from the night's exertions, standing firm and steady in the second rank. He saw the other men, recognising them, nodding a greeting here and there. No fear in their eyes, no tremors in their stance. They had marched a thousand miles, fighting all the way, and now they were poised on the brink of one final clash. Rome, the eternal city, heart of the empire and citadel of the tyrant, lay only two miles away on the far side of the Tiber. Their morale, their discipline, was iron-hard now.

Reaching the right of the formation, Castus slipped down from the saddle and took his shield from Eumolpius. The orderly took the reins and led Dapple back through the lines. Castus flexed his right arm, warming his muscles, and the segmented bands of the manica slid together with a slight rasp.

No time for speeches, for bold addresses. The men had all the courage they would need. Castus could feel the formation at his back almost humming with tension, every man straining for the note of the horn that would set their columns into motion. Opposite, across the misty plain, the enemy line was still milling and shifting as the Maxentian commanders struggled to get their massive, unwieldy formation into order.

Already Castus could hear the yells, the reverberating rattle of spearshafts on shield rims. But there was no cohesion to it, no sense of collective intent. By comparison, the disciplined silence of Constantine's men was all the more imposing.

Distant trumpets wailed from away to the right. The cavalry were moving up the slope, the emperor himself leading his horsemen towards the enemy flank. *Wait*, Castus told himself. *Wait...*

Now he heard the signal for the centre to advance, and almost at once the vast clatter of armoured men moving forward in unison rolled across the plain. All along the left wing men were edging forward, every rank shuffling up behind the one in front. At this moment, Castus knew, the only desire in a man's heart was to close the distance before them, to bring on the moment of confrontation. To stand and wait in close formation, sweating even in the damp chill of the breeze, was a test of endurance. He felt the desire himself, and knew it well.

Then, close and sudden, the brass yell of the trumpet. Behind him, Brocchus raised the eagle of the legion and the centurions cried out the order, and as one the men of the Second Britannia began to move. The sound of their advance was an iron pulse, gathering momentum.

Castus drew his sword as he marched. The head of each column, the blunt fist of every advancing wedge, was formed by locked shields; the ranks that followed held spears to strike over the backs of their comrades.

The distance between the two armies was closing now. Castus felt the dew-damp grass swishing against his bronze greaves. He smelled the river away to his left. For the first time, or so it felt, he saw the ranks of the opposing army leap into focus: they were no longer an undifferentiated mass of men but individuals. He saw their shield blazons bright in the dull haze of morning, their helmets and the snarling faces beneath. The watery gleam of their spears. *Gods*, there were a lot of them... Before, when he had ridden out with Leontius, and even when he had rejoined his legion, he had felt detached from what was happening, strangely heavy in his limbs, his blood slow and thick. He had felt the pressure of a sleepless night upon him, emptying his mind. Now he felt the familiar prickling rush of fear, the sudden sensitivity in his fingers, in his face. All of his senses were acute, the world around him growing bright and vivid even through the day's murk.

It was madness to be advancing like this, against such a massive host. Madness to try and drive a narrow wedge into the heart of that swollen enemy phalanx, and split it as a mason split a block of stone. Castus allowed himself the thought. He allowed himself, just for a moment, to dread the enemy blades, the wall of muscle and steel that faced him. His knees were weak, and he feared he would stumble. He thought of his son, of Sabina, of everything the world held that he would miss if death took him. The thought steadied him. He would not die, not this day. Surely the gods would not allow that?

Then he felt the energy of battle bloom inside him, like the intoxicating rush of strong wine, driving away the fright. His blood was singing in his veins; he felt the strength of his arm, the breath in his lungs, and he knew that he was grinning, the scar on his jaw pulled tight.

One hundred paces. The trumpets sounded and the advancing columns drew to a halt. Men shuffled and jostled, tightening the formation and dressing the lines, barely needing the barks of the centurions to direct them. There were missiles dropping among them now, the enemy archers and slingers

moving up to the front to pelt the head of each advancing
column. Castus kept his shield up, his eyes on the wall of
men ahead of him as the stones and arrows fell. The troops
opposite were not the raw and frightened recruits he had
seen earlier: he saw the blazons on their shields, recognised
the devices and knew this would be no easy fight. Legion II
Parthica was one of the crack formations of the old Roman
army. Every other heartbeat Castus heard the sharp *thock* as
an arrow punched into a shield board close to where he was
standing. A few anguished cries too, as missiles found their
mark deeper in the formation.

Light troops were moving up into the gaps between each
attack column. To his right, Castus saw a loose horde of
Mauretanian archers swarming forward, lean and muscular
dark-skinned men in short sleeveless tunics. Their thick hair
was elaborately bunched and coiffed, and many of them carried
spare arrows stuck through it, giving them a bizarre and
savage appearance; they advanced at a run, shooting in rapid
flurries, dashing forward and dancing back as they rained
arrows into the enemy formation.

'Glad they're on our side,' said Brocchus, standing at
Castus's shoulder with the eagle grounded before him.

Cheering from the right, and a rolling thunder of hooves;
Castus glanced in that direction and saw the cavalry powering
up the slopes onto the high ground, Constantine's purple and
gold draco standard streaming at the fore. Only a moment
later the first cries of battle drifted across on the damp air, but
so distant that Castus could barely distinguish them over the
noise of arrows falling around him. Had the emperor's cavalry
managed to strike the enemy horse before they had formed
to oppose them? So much of the battle could be decided over
there on the flank.

Warmth flooded across the side of his face, and Castus turned his head to see that the sun had burst through the low clouds to the east, spilling a sheet of silver light across the field. Castus glanced down and saw the wink of colour below the cuff of his armoured bronze sleeve: the blue bead amulet Ganna had given him, still tied to his wrist. He raised his sword hand, lightly kissing the bead. For luck, he thought. Then he lifted the sword high above his head, the new blade flashing in the sun.

'*Victory and Rome!*' he cried.

At once the cry was echoed back at him from the mass of men behind him, a thousand-strong yell bursting forth in unison. Over to his right Castus could hear the horns signalling the centre legions to begin their charge, and even as the brass notes were fading a vast yell went up from the heart of the line, and the men began to surge forward. Gazing from behind the rim of his shield, Castus watched the attack columns of the Minervia and Primigenia legions advancing, a fast march at first, quickening into a jog and then into a run. He saw the ranks of the Praetorian Guard tighten to oppose them, but the rushing wedges of armoured men closed the distance with breathtaking speed. The columns held together, shields tight, and they looked like machines, like mighty rolling engines of war. Two more heartbeats, and they crashed into the front ranks of the Praetorians. Shields boomed together, and the noise was like grinding iron and bone, cut through with screams. At the moment of impact, Castus almost thought he could see a mist of blood spraying up, bright in the morning sun.

'We'll be next,' Brocchus said grimly. 'Gods be with us now...'

He had barely spoken before the trumpets sounded behind them. The Second Britannica gave a massed collective shudder and began to move. Castus kept his head down behind the rim of his shield. The men pressed close on his left flank and pushing up behind him felt like extensions of his own body. When he raised his eyes he saw the enemy, very close and distinct now, their mouths open in shouts of rage and defiance. He saw a centurion, his face blanched white, yelling at his own men to close their ranks tighter. Several of the enemy were already hurling darts and javelins: too soon; the missiles fell short.

The men at the front of the column broke into a jog, their armour and equipment clattering around them. Now the javelins were arcing out from the men at the centre, raining cruel shanked steel into the opposing line. Castus watched the missiles fall, judging the moments that remained. His life had contracted to a simple choice: break through the mass of the enemy formation or to die in the attempt.

Twenty paces. Castus felt his heart like a fist in his chest, the pulse beating in his neck. He threw his head back. 'BRITANNICA!' he yelled.

'*Britannica! Britannica! Britannica!*' the men behind him shouted.

Then he bellowed out the order to charge, and broke into a run.

For a few heartbeats he was conscious only of the rushing momentum, the impetus of the charge. Thoughts sparked through his mind. *Don't slip now, don't stumble.* Vital to keep the formation together, even at the run, to hit the enemy line in one solid mass like a battering ram. And then there was nothing but the fury of his blood and noise of his own heaving breath.

One quick glance, the enemy line rearing up before him, sickeningly close, then Castus dropped his head and threw his shoulder into the hollow of his shield. The collision almost punched him back off his feet. Then other men were piling in behind him, crushed against his back, all of them yelling, and the noise was an explosion of thunder that drowned all thought, all feeling.

He was forcing his way into a thicket of spears, a wall of shields and armoured bodies. Iron all around him, and he could see no more than an arm's reach to either side. A blade struck his helmet, grating across the gilded bronze with a shriek that made his teeth ring. Pushed from behind, shoved from in front, he struggled to stay upright, to keep forcing his way forward. His boots skidded and stamped at the wet grass underfoot. There was a noise in his ears, a frenzied bellowing like an agonised bull; Castus realised it was coming from his own throat.

His sword arm was trapped against his body, and he wrestled it free and angled his blade around the rim of his shield. He stabbed wildly, underarm, grunting with each blow. Each fifth stab found flesh: unprotected thighs, hands, faces. Heaving at his shield, Castus sensed the wall ahead of him beginning to flex and weaken. He dragged the shield to his right, hooking the rim around the edge of an opponent's shield and twisting, levering open a gap and then slamming his sword into it. The man fell suddenly and Castus stumbled forward, clambering over the dying body as others pressed in behind him. He heard the shouts from the rear of the enemy: 'PARTHICA! PARTHICA!'

Into the second rank now, Castus got his sword up and slashed over his shield. He saw the white-faced centurion in front of him and struck at once, jabbing his blade between the man's cheek guards. He could sense the enemy giving ground, their lines beginning to fray as the blunt head of the wedge pressed between them. Moving forward was like trying to breast a powerful current, a rushing tide. Castus felt his legs trapped among fallen men; he lifted his boots, stamped, kicked. He realised that he had his eyes closed; when he opened them, men's faces were only feet away from him. He saw their widened rolling eyes, the tongues straining in their mouths. For a moment he was shoved hard against one man and he felt teeth gnash close to his cheek. A sword whipped past his face so close he could smell the bloodied steel.

Behind him he could hear a man screaming: *'Help me. O gods, help me!'*

Another voice, Brocchus, screaming back: *'Get on your feet! Get up and push!'*

Castus felt a bright haze surrounding him. He knew he had been hit, probably more than once. The palm clenched around his sword hilt was hot and sticky. Still he forced himself forward, lashing out with a wheeling blade.

He had carved his way deep inside the enemy formation now, the men of his legion bunched close around him. But he could sense the opposing mass gaining strength and solidity, starting to press tighter on every side. Castus felt a flash of panicked intuition. The enemy had brought up their second line, he realised. His column was trying to hack their way through a massed phalanx thirty-two men deep. They were in a vice, and they were being slowly crushed, and the enemy would not give ground.

The momentum of the advance had stalled and died, and Castus heard men falling behind him, dying in the seething crush. He backed a step and found himself pressed up against Brocchus: the eagle was raised above his head in both hands and he was striking down with the spiked butt. Parthica shields on all sides, a dense pack of men, but they were keeping their distance. Castus realised that he was standing on the bodies of the slain, his boots sliding in blood and filth.

He tried to shout, but his throat was locked and he could only gasp for breath.

Forward; the only way was forward. If he died here, he would die on his feet and not trampled in the mess of the slain. Castus raised his sword, then swung it down and the knot of men behind him jolted into motion. Shields raised, they pressed forward in a last ragged charge, hurling themselves at the ranks of the enemy.

It was like slamming into a solid wall. For a few moments, a few heartbeats, shields banged and ground together, iron clashed and whined. Castus kept his head down, striking blindly, pushing forward with all his weight and strength.

Then, sudden as a sunburst, he felt the mass of enemy troops ahead of him shiver and begin to break. Castus lifted his head, and could not believe what he was seeing. The enemy formation was thinning rapidly, their lines unravelling and disintegrating. Blinking, dazed, Castus saw the rear-rank men stumbling backwards out of the fight with confusion on their faces.

He looked to his left and saw the yellow and red shields pushing forward, each marked with the smudged black charcoal symbol of Constantine's dream-vision. Realisation came to him – these men at the rear of the enemy phalanx were the conscripts, the men from southern Italy and Africa. *They were Christians...* and the sight of their own symbol etched on the shields of the enemy was collapsing their morale. They were breaking from the rear, men spilling away in terror as the cohesion of the array collapsed. Now, for the first time, Castus saw open ground around him, the churned turf thick with fallen bodies.

Wheeling his sword above his head, he let out a savage roar of triumph. '*Haaaaaah!*'

Brocchus was yelling too, brandishing the eagle as the second column came smashing obliquely through the ranks of the enemy. At the head was Modestus, his face and torso sprayed red; the two columns meshed at once, driving the attack back into the disordered enemy phalanx. Castus felt too battered to speak, but his men needed no order. With the enemy breaking all around them they pressed forward, their hacking advance turning into a rolling tide of destruction, the melee turning to outright murder.

Here and there knots of the enemy tried to make a stand, but the men of the Britannica surged over them, bearing them down and trampling them underfoot. At their head, Castus kept himself staggering forward, his shield a lead weight in his left hand. Men appeared before him and he struck them down without thinking, without feeling.

Then the ground ahead of him was clear, only a litter of discarded weapons and shields on the turf to show where the enemy lines had crumbled. Castus realised that the sun was high to his left, the sky blue and the morning getting hot. Steam was rising from the damp grass.

Looking to his right, Castus saw a struggling mass of soldiers still locked in combat. To his left the Maxentian recruits were streaming back towards the river and the bridge of boats, with Hrodomarus's warriors in pursuit. But there were cavalry out on the plain as well, their own or the enemy's he could not tell. And now his own men were breaking formation, cheering as they spilled forward across the field.

An arrow thwacked into Castus's shield.

'Hold!' he yelled, the word rasping in his throat. 'Form a line! Modestus – pull your men back and form them!'

Modestus was shouting too, but in bursting through the enemy phalanx the columns had lost all order. If the enemy rallied, or if even a small force of cavalry opposed them, they could be cut to pieces. Castus saw Macer striding ahead of his men and bellowed at him. The drillmaster had lost his helmet, and his hair was stiff with sweat and dried blood. He was grinning, and appeared demented.

'Macer! Hold them – *hold them*!'

Castus was breathing hard, confusion beating in his head. What was happening? Was the battle won? There were only a few hundred paces to the bridge of boats, but the ground was filled with milling enemy troops.

Then he dropped his gaze, and his breath caught.

Right in the centre of the field, the Praetorians were retreating. But they were not falling back in confusion, as their comrades in the other legions had done. They were still moving in formation, in a close-order block of shields with their standards at the centre, every man taking two steps back and halting, then two steps back and halting, oblivious to the rain of darts and arrows falling on them. Castus could only stare in wonder. It was the most impressive feat of discipline he had ever seen on a battlefield.

A batter of hooves, and Eumolpius was beside him, sliding down from Dapple's saddle with a waterskin over his shoulder.

'How did you get here?' Castus gasped, then seized the skin and drank deeply. He coughed, choked, then leaned forward and spat bile onto the grass. Then he drank again. His men had formed a line once more, but many had sunk down to their knees, too exhausted to stand. He would let them rest – they needed it.

'The emperor's cavalry's broken the tyrant's Horse Guards!' the orderly was saying, stumbling over the words in his excitement. 'The enemy are fleeing on the right, down off the high ground towards the broken stone bridge, and the emperor's pursuing them!'

'Is he?' Castus said, wincing as he began to feel the pain of his cut hand, his lacerated thigh, his bruised shoulders for the first time.

'Tribune!' Modestus called. 'Signal!' He pointed to the rear. Castus turned and saw the red banner waving, heard the trumpet's cry. *General advance on the left.*

'That's it,' he said, passing the waterskin back to Eumolpius. 'Now get back there.' He jerked his thumb back over his shoulder, and Eumolpius leaped up into the saddle again.

'Advance!' Castus shouted, raising his sword, but the men had seen the signal and were only waiting for his order. Falling into step, in a close formation eight men deep, they began to move forward across the steaming grass towards the disordered ranks of the enemy.

The riverbank was a slaughtering ground.

As his advancing troops crested the slope that dropped to the water, Castus saw the warriors of the Bucinobantes butchering the fugitives in the shallows. Everywhere enemy soldiers were throwing off their helmets and mail and splashing into the water, trying desperately to swim clear of the savage barbarian spears. A band of Mauri archers had pushed forward through the advancing legionaries and were lining the bank, pelting the swimmers with arrows. Already the Tiber was flowing red.

Further downstream, around the curve of the river, Castus could see the floating pontoon bridge packed with retreating troops. The bridgehead was a furious chaos of men and horses scrambling to get onto the bridge and escape to the far bank. Beyond it, the broken stone arches of the Milvian Bridge still stood above the flood; even there, men were crowding the approaches, trying in vain to clamber across.

Castus stared at the river, and felt only a mounting sense of horror. The banks were heaped with the slain, wounded men groaning and screaming. And on the pontoon bridge, thousands of men of Maxentius's broken army struggling in panicked flight, so tightly packed that they could barely move forward. He saw men falling from the bridge, shoved off into the water to struggle and thrash before sinking under the weight of their armour. The river upstream was already churning with mud and blood, bodies and staggering men. Cavalrymen of the Equites Dalmatae were riding along the bank, herding the fugitives into the water.

'Tribune!' Brocchus said, grabbing his arm and pointing. Away to the right, the crowd around the bridgehead had opened, men falling aside as a party of horsemen came galloping through them. Castus saw the purple draco standard; but this was not Constantine. The lead rider wore armour of burnished gold, tall purple plumes on his helmet, the same gleaming panoply that Castus had last seen when he had sat in the Circus Maximus, watching the tyrant's army in review.

Maxentius forced his way out onto the bridge, his horse kicking aside the fleeing men of his own army, the remaining troopers of his cavalry guard following behind him. On the riverbanks, the archers continued to rain arrows into the seething water, killing men before they could drown. Castus could only gaze at the slaughter, open-mouthed. He remembered sitting in the exedra of the palace as Maxentius had told him of his plans to restore Rome to greatness. Where was that greatness now?

The tyrant and his guards had reached the central span of the bridge, their panicked flight almost halted in the press of men struggling around them. Then Castus heard a massed wailing cry go up. One of the boats carrying the central span had broken free, and the roadway above it was sagging under the weight of the crowd. For a few heartbeats Castus saw the crush of bodies as the men on the bridge scrambled to get clear, the tyrant's horse backing and kicking; then there was a loud groan of timbers, a crack, and the bridge gave way.

Screaming, the horde on the bridge surged and slid, bodies cascading into the foaming water as the timbers of the roadway collapsed beneath them. Maxentius was still up on the bridge, his armour gleaming golden in the sun. Then his horse shuddered and reared. Slowly, almost gracefully, it toppled backwards, bearing the rider beneath it. Together they crashed down into the churning water, and the Tiber closed over them.

The tyrant was gone, but the battle was not yet done. As he tore his gaze from the bridge Castus saw a staff officer cantering up from the rear – he looked immaculate on his white gelding, but when he spoke his voice was a high cracked yell.

'The Praetorians are still holding on the riverbank! Form your legion, tribune, and swing them around against their flank!' Castus gave him a brief nod, and he rode on.

There was a hornblower beside him, and Castus ordered him to give the signal to form column of attack. The man blew a dull farting sound, coughed and spat, then blew again and the notes rang out loud and true. As the men formed up Castus turned and looked back at them: only half his legion were still with him, the rest scattered across the field in disarray.

Those that remained were stumbling, their eyes empty and their faced glazed from the slaughter, but Castus knew that they still had the strength to fight. Raising his sword, he felt the tremors of fatigue running up his right arm. Then he swung the blade down, and the column behind him lurched forward into a jog, their shields clattering against their sides.

The crowd around the bridgehead parted before them, most of the demoralised enemy troops already throwing down their weapons. Castus led his men straight through them; other columns were converging around him, all as battered and bloodied as his own men but moving with a regular disciplined step. Ahead of them they could see the block of Praetorian survivors, backed up against the riverbank with the water foaming red at their heels. Only a few thousand remained, huddled within their ring of shields, and all around them were archers and light troops with javelins, showering missiles upon them.

'Surrender!' an officer was yelling. 'Your emperor is dead! Throw down your arms!'

But the Praetorians were holding fast, determined to fight to the end. Castus remembered the men he had met at the baths, those soldiers from the legions of the Danube. Men like himself. Had they fallen already, somewhere in the mesh of combat, or in that slow disciplined retreat across the field? Or were they standing still, in that grim bulwark of shields upon the riverbank?

Leontius was calling to Castus from the head of his own Eighth Augusta column. 'Wedge attack!' he cried. 'Drive in their flanks!'

The horns screamed, and Castus felt the men at his back already beginning to surge forward. Raising his shield, he threw himself into a charge. He could barely feel his legs as he ran, only the breath dragging at his throat and the ache in his arm as he tightened his grip on his sword. Then the battle cry rose around him, the wall of shields broke as the Praetorians surged forward into a counter-charge, and Castus slammed himself between the bodies of the enemy.

There was no order to this fight. No formations remained, only the fury of combat. The Britannica wedge had smashed aside the charging Praetorians and thrust deep into their flank, but now men fought as individuals or in small knots, hacking and striking. Castus forced his way onwards, punching with his shield. There were three men at his back, and he could hear their screams as they fought. All around him the enemy mass was breaking up. Somebody aimed a spear at him from below, and he slashed down and killed the man without even looking at him.

Then the struggling bodies ahead of him parted, and Castus saw the riverbank, a last group of Praetorians still holding together, ringed by the slain. At their centre, pouring blood from a dozen wounds, was Sergianus.

The red-bearded Praetorian took two steps back down the bank until his feet were in the water. But he had seen Castus advancing on him now. He raised his sword, grinning. 'Bastard!' he yelled. 'Come and die!'

One last charge, and Castus was down the bank and into the river, water bursting around him in a reddened froth as he waded between the corpses piled in the shallows. The knot of men around Sergianus had scattered, and the Praetorian stood alone, shield raised, sword levelled. Castus closed with him in two thrashing strides.

Sergianus swung at him, and Castus caught the blow on his shield and turned it aside. Water dragged at his legs, and he almost staggered. He drew his arm back, pressing forward with his shield, and then slashed a low wheeling cut. Sergianus stumbled, throwing his arms wide, and Castus's blade sheared into his thigh and chopped his leg from beneath him. The Praetorian gave a shuddering gasp, falling to one knee in the water. For a moment Castus hung back, breathing hard, staring at his stricken opponent. Then he took one more step forward, planted his boot firmly in the wet mud of the riverbed, and drove his sword down into Sergianus's neck.

The body sagged as he dragged his blade free, then subsided into the bloody water.

Back up on the bank the legionaries were already raising hoarse cheers of victory. Men seized Castus by the shoulders, by the arms. Hands pounded at his back, but he could feel nothing. Away to his left he saw a group of Second Legion men gathered around one of their fallen comrades. They parted as he approached, and there was Macer, lying on his back with blood streaming down his face. Castus knelt beside him; the drillmaster was still clinging to life, his thin lips drawn back in a snarl. He was lying against a mound of bodies, and the ground all around him was dark and marshy with blood.

'Best way to die, lad,' Macer said. 'Couldn't see me as a farmer anyway...' He raised his hand, clasping Castus's forearm. His grip was still strong, but weakened almost at once. Then the old man stiffened, breath hissing between his teeth, and his hand fell slack.

Castus climbed to his feet. He had dropped his shield back at the river, but the sword was still in his hand. His entire right arm was red to the shoulder, the bronze links of the manica oiled with blood.

When he gazed back towards the river he saw the banks heaped with the dying and the dead. His own men, those of other legions, Praetorians all sprawled together in a tangle of hacked limbs and bleeding bodies. Beyond them, the Tiber flowed placidly in the sunlight, rolling its freight of corpses down towards Rome.

CHAPTER XXVIII

It would not be a formal triumph. It would be considered unseemly, Nigrinus knew, to celebrate a victory over another Roman army, the deaths of fellow citizens, even the death of a man now universally reviled as a tyrant, his statues smashed, his name chiselled from the monuments. Instead, Constantine's entry to the city of Rome would be an adventus, a ceremony of imperial arrival and greeting.

No, Nigrinus thought, it would not be triumph, but it would certainly resemble one well enough. The streets of the capital were decked with garlands, crowds gathered all along the route, people climbing onto the rooftops and thronging the public porticoes to acclaim the conqueror from Gaul. Constantine would ride through the city in an open carriage, seated upon an ivory throne, and all around him his troops would march in procession with their spears garlanded with laurel.

Already Nigrinus could hear the cheering drifting across from the north, where the imperial cavalcade would be proceeding down the long straight street from the Flaminian Gate. Over to his right, on the broad steps that fronted the Porticus of Octavia, Nigrinus could see the senior members of the Senate waiting in dignified ranks, every man dressed in the heavily starched and densely folded white toga of his office. The Consuls were there, and the Prefect of the City, and behind him Rufius Volusianus. All of them waiting to greet their liberator, Constantine, and escort his entourage across the *pomerium*, the sacred boundary of old Rome.

Nigrinus stood alone and unobtrusive in the crowd. He wore an expression of bland indifference, and only occasionally did the dry shadow of a smile cross his lips. But inside he was exultant. The victory of Constantine's army the day before on the meadows beyond the Milvian Bridge was an answer to many of Nigrinus's godless prayers. It was the culmination of his efforts, and it would guarantee his path to promotion and high status. And then, he thought, and then... He could look down on all those who had slighted or disparaged him throughout his life, who had ignored him or underestimated them. Yes, he thought, and he could *piss on all their heads*. This may not be Constantine's triumph, officially speaking, but in Nigrinus's closed and secretive heart it was his own.

Was it not he, Nigrinus, who had induced the tyrant to forsake the security of the walls of Rome and chance his fate in open battle? He had lavished much gold on the city factions, and promises of more gold to come. The seditions they had instigated, the unrest among the Christians, the rumours that had flown about the city of Constantine's unstoppable advance: all had been Nigrinus's work. But more importantly, the suggestion he had planted in the mind of the tyrant himself, that he should consult the Sibylline Oracles, had tipped the balance. He had no idea whether the senators of the College of Fifteen had returned the ambiguous message he had given to them, the message that the sorcerer Astrampsychus had plucked from his smoke nine months before in the cellars of Treveris. But whatever they had told him, it had worked. Maxentius had marched, and met his doom, almost as if, Nigrinus thought, he had led the man with a halter. It gave him a cold thrill of power.

Now the noise of the procession was getting closer, the pulse of chanting coming from the streets to the north-east. In front of the Porticus of Octavia was a wide paved area where the emperor's carriage would pause, and Constantine acknowledge the greetings of the Senate. The crowd was getting thicker too; Nigrinus had to crane his neck to see, or risk getting jostled.

'Julius Nigrinus, is it not?' a voice said. Nigrinus flinched, startled – he did not enjoy being recognised in crowds. The man who had addressed him was a senator, balding but smooth-faced, with an urbane handsome look. Nigrinus nodded a greeting to him, then replied with a tight-lipped smile.

'A great and happy day for us all, no?' Latronianus said. He was wearing his white ceremonial toga, and eight slaves in sky-blue tunics flanked him and kept the crowd away. 'For you more than most, I would say?'

Nigrinus merely shrugged.

'They tell me,' the senator went on, 'that the body of the tyrant was fished from the Tiber early this morning. Still wearing that golden armour, indeed. Apparently his head was struck off and mounted on a spear, to be carried at the front of the procession! Rather barbaric, I think, but it certainly sends a clear message.'

That would be Constantine's doing, Nigrinus thought. He had observed, over the years, a strong taint of vindictive cruelty in the Invincible Augustus. Why was it that emperors, the rulers of the world, were so unable to govern their own emotions?

'But why are you standing down here?' Latronianus cried, raising his eyebrows. 'You'll see nothing! Several of my colleagues have positioned themselves up there on the upper storey of the theatre. It's reserved for dignitaries. I was about to join them – much better vantage point. Perhaps you would care to be my guest?'

Nigrinus glanced up at the high stone arches of the Theatre of Marcellus. One side of the curving outer gallery looked down onto the open area before the porticus steps. There were already people packing the arches, but he could see the figures in the white togas standing in immaculate solitude. Yes, he thought, he might do better up there. He had no slaves to shield him from the gathering crowd, and Latronianus's eight men would serve him well.

'We've heard some quite extraordinary stories about you,' Latronianus said as they walked together across the paving to the lower arches of the theatre. 'Some, I confess, had reason to doubt your intentions. I'm sure you don't blame them. But you must be due a great reward for your labours, I expect?'

Nigrinus pursed his lips, about to demur, then stopped himself. He did expect a great reward, yes. But he did not care to discuss it with this man.

They reached the arches, Latronianus's slaves moving ahead of them to open a path through the crowd. The stonework of the theatre was scratched and scrawled with graffiti. Men moved through the crowd selling hot greasy snacks and punnets of roasted chestnuts, and the people gathered inside the arches had the heedless levity of a crowd at the circus or the amphitheatre. Nigrinus decided that he would be glad to leave Rome. The city had been great once, centre of a mighty empire, but now it was no more than a festering pit, a sink of decadent luxury and vile poverty grotesquely intermingled. Diocletian had been right to despise the place.

As he passed through the arch, shepherded by Latronianus's slaves, Nigrinus glanced back at the senators waiting on the porticus steps. He noticed Rufius Volusianus peering in his direction, and as the old man caught his eye he raised his hand slightly and gave a brief wave. Baffled, Nigrinus waved back.

Broad stone stairways led up from the lower to the upper gallery; the nearest ones were already crowded with people, beggars and trinket-vendors, but Latronianus led Nigrinus around the curving arcade to another stairway, far from the throng. As they began to climb, a slave stepped up beside the senator and whispered quickly in his ear. Latronianus frowned, then made a tutting noise.

'A trifling matter I must attend to,' he told Nigrinus. 'Go on up – my colleagues will be waiting. I'll join you in a moment.'

Nigrinus paused, staring back at him, then turned and began to climb. It was cool in the heavy shadowed darkness of the theatre's interior, almost cold, and strangely quiet after the noise in the street outside. But even here Nigrinus could make out the sound of chanting. Getting louder now – the procession must almost be in sight. How annoying, he thought, to be an emperor. To have people chanting your name at you everywhere you went...

He turned at the landing and quickly scaled the next flight. At the top was a corridor, a glare of sunlight at the far end. Nigrinus was pacing towards the light when two figures appeared, silhouetted. And now he heard another man coming up the stairs after him, quick leaping footsteps. He paused, squinting. The two men ahead were barring the corridor, and one of them was holding a knife.

'What is this?' he managed to say. His knees were weak; he feared he would have to support himself against the wall. The silhouetted figures in the corridor advanced slowly, while the third man waited on the stairs.

'Sadly,' one of the figures said, 'the noble men of the Senate will not be able to meet you. But they send their regards. And their farewell.'

With an icy shock, Nigrinus recognised the soft boneless

figure. He recognised the voice too, that slight lisp. It was Valerius Merops, Maxentius's eunuch. Had he too been playing a double game all this time? Nigrinus cursed himself for not knowing. He cursed that he would never know.

Reaching behind him with trembling fingers, he found the small knife he wore concealed in his girdle. He always carried it with him, intending to open his veins if he were ever captured. He could not abide the thought of torture. He drew the knife, but his chest was quaking, his bowels were loose and he felt the urge to vomit.

Merops and his assistant were pacing closer. From outside, Nigrinus could hear the cheering gathering in volume. He swallowed heavily, sucked in a long breath through tight lips, then turned and hurled himself back down the stairs.

He caught the man on the lower step unawares, colliding with him and pushing him back against the wall. With his eyes closed, Nigrinus let out a clenched cry and drove the knife up under the man's jaw. He felt the blade bite, the spurt of blood hot against his fingers. The man did not even gasp.

Heaving the body across the steps behind him, Nigrinus leaped down to the landing. His shoes slipped on the worn stone floor, but he caught himself and ran on down the lower flight, the noise of his footfalls booming. He had flung the bloody knife away from him. All his life he had been afraid of blood, anxious that he should not weaken at the sight of it. He had caused the deaths of so many, but had never before raised his hand against another man. He was laughing as he ran. He had never known it was so easy to kill.

At the bottom of the stairs he doubled the corner into one of the ground-floor passages. He must flee, get away from here and conceal himself somewhere. Down the passage, he saw light filtering from his left and turned again. He was following the curve of the arcade now, and every few steps he saw the flash of sun between the arches.

Rounding the curve, he saw the crowd gathered at the end of the arcade, many of them already raising their voices in acclamation of the approaching procession. Nigrinus was panting, his sides aching. He would lose himself in the crowd.

A man stepped from a shadowed opening to his left, and with one straight arm shoved Nigrinus back against the wall.

'Know me, do you?' the man rasped. Nigrinus saw his pockmarked face, the angry scar across his brow. Pudentianus's slave, he remembered. Naso.

Then the slave punched him hard in the belly, driving the air from his lungs. Nigrinus barely felt the blade go in.

He sagged, his knees folding beneath him, and slid down the wall. Naso had vanished. Now he could feel the pain pulsing up from his wound, and when he looked at his hand it was daubed in bright red. *Got to move...* Scraping at the wall with his free hand, Nigrinus dragged himself upright. Hunched, he staggered a few steps towards the light, then a few more.

The noise burst around him, the screams and cries of the multitude. Forcing his legs a few steps further, Nigrinus slumped against one of the outer arches. He could see the procession coming around the corner and moving into the open paved area before the Porticus of Octavia. Marching at the front was a single soldier, carrying the severed head of Maxentius, tyrant of Rome, impaled on the end of his lance. They were not cheers of acclaim Nigrinus was hearing, but screams of hatred and abuse, as the mob pelted the grisly remains of what had once been their emperor with ordure and broken roof tiles.

Nigrinus dug his fingers into the stone, trying to hold himself upright. If he could see, if he could at least glimpse Constantine... His body felt numb, but his limbs were burning, agonised. He could feel the blood soaking down his legs, pouring onto the cobbles beneath him. Then his legs gave way beneath him and he dragged his fingers scratching down the side of the arch as he fell.

His last exhaling breath was lost in the jeering of the mob.

CHAPTER XXIX

The imperial city of Rome had rarely looked so impressive. The rains of early November had washed the dust and smoke from the air, and in the low autumn sunlight the city appeared to gleam. Against a leaden sky the temples on the Capitoline Hill rose clear and distinct.

Aurelius Castus stood on the balcony of a house on the slope of the Aventine, taking in the view. Across the valley he could see the pillared exedra of the palace, where he had met with Maxentius the month before. Below it stretched the vast stadium of the Circus Maximus. The stands down there were still packed; Constantine had decreed ten days of games to celebrate his entry into the city, and the Roman people had responded with their usual enthusiasm. Castus might have expected them to be glutted by such things, after the constant lavish spectacles laid on by their previous ruler, but apparently they had an inexhaustible appetite for entertainment.

He would not be joining them himself. Since the glorious adventus, he had kept himself apart from the jubilation. He had seen too much of emperors and the business of empire. In his soul he no longer cared what Constantine said or did, or what was said or done in his name.

And what would he do, in fact, the latest emperor of Rome? He had already forgiven all those supporters of Maxentius who remained in the city. Only the Praetorians had been punished: the entire ancient corps had been disbanded, and the survivors exiled to the frontier armies. The barracks of the Horse Guards had been seized, and then given to the Christians to turn into a grand new basilica. They at least were jubilant, and praised their new ruler.

Constantine himself would remain in the city until the spring, and then march north to Mediolanum, to meet with his brother emperor Licinius and decide how to divide the Roman world between them. Maximinus Daza still ruled in the east; would they join with him and split the empire three ways, or would there be further war? When he considered these things, Castus saw only the heaped corpses along the banks of the Tiber, the river running with blood. Too many men had died to bring Constantine to victory. Too many Roman soldiers had been killed by men they could have called brothers.

Castus clasped his hands behind his back. He breathed in slowly, stilling his mind, then turned and paced into the reception chamber of the house. This had been one of Sabina's father's properties once, seized by the tyrant after the old man's execution. Maxentius had given it to a tribune of the Praetorians, but that man had died at the Milvian Bridge, and now Castus had commandeered it as his own lodgings. He would have the deeds made over to his wife in time. It would be easy enough to do: in Rome, officers of Constantine's victorious army could have anything they wanted.

But there was only one thing that Castus wanted.

Standing in the reception chamber, he listened to the voices filtering through from the vestibule, then from the inner court-yard. Eumolpius appeared in the doorway, dressed in a freshly pressed white tunic.

'The domina Valeria Domitia Sabina,' he gravely intoned, eyes to the ceiling.

For ten days Castus had rehearsed this meeting in his mind, tormenting himself with possibilities, rejecting them all. In his heart he had forgiven his wife, or at least tried to, but still he felt all too keenly, too painfully, the distance between them. Now he stood, straight-backed and silent, and watched her as she entered the room.

Sabina still wore her travelling clothes, the hem of her long tunic spattered with the mud of the Flaminian Way. She looked drawn and tired. Castus had expected her to be remote and aloof, or to fling herself at his feet in some feigned display of repentance. But he was surprised to see the tears in her eyes.

'This house,' she said, gazing around at the walls as she wiped her cheek with the back of her hand. 'I always loved this house. It was my favourite. I never expected to see it again. How did you know?'

Castus said nothing. He had not known. But had his wife really thought she would never return to Rome? A woman like her, raised in this city, could never have truly believed that a Gallic usurper and a half-barbarian army might be victorious. That, he thought, was how Lepidus had snared her. Castus could imagine it, and in a way he could not blame her. And with Lepidus dead, and Julius Nigrinus rumoured to be dead too, there was no one who could speak of what she had done. Except perhaps Fausta, and she had reasons of her own for remaining silent.

Now Sabina crossed the room and stood before him. She laid her hands upon his shoulders, then lightly touched a palm to his cheek.

'Husband,' she said. 'I've missed you.'

She leaned forward, and kissed him on the lips.

'They told me you were dead.'

Castus did not move, did not speak. The scar on his jaw burned with a cold fire. For so long he had been angry, but he felt nothing of that inside him now. Sabina's eyes held a clear sad honesty, and she smiled as she looked at him.

'A truce?' she said.

'A truce,' he replied. Then he embraced her. Both of them knew that much time must pass before they could ask for more.

Sabina left the room with her maids, but Ganna remained waiting by the door, the boy cradled in her arms.

'How is he?' Castus asked as she approached.

'Growing heavier every day,' Ganna said. 'Soon he will be as big as you, I think.'

The child stirred as Castus took him from her. Wide-eyed, he gazed at his father, then cried out a stream of incomprehensible words: *'Babamah! Mumbada! Walala!'*

'He speaks your language now?' Castus asked, and Ganna smiled.

The weight of the boy in his arms was strangely comforting. Castus stared down at him, frowning, moved. Then the boy reached up with his small hands, clouted Castus on the chin, and chuckled.

'He has the right idea,' Ganna said.

Supporting the boy in the crook of one arm, Castus pressed his hand to the woman's cheek. The blue amulet she had given him caught the light. She closed her eyes, then turned her head, kissing his wrist.

Sabina was standing in the doorway, and Castus noticed the quick play of conflicting emotion across her face. Pained realisation, a brief swell of anger, and then resignation. Her expression cleared and she glanced away, then crossed to the far doorway that led to the balcony. Castus handed the child back to Ganna and went to join his wife. The distant roar of the circus crowd was drifting up on the breeze.

'They love him now. Constantine,' Sabina said. 'The hero of the Roman people. I heard an orator saying that he's ascended to the summit of the world. His deeds and his fame will live for evermore. And so on. It must be strange, don't you think, to become a godlike being?'

Castus just grunted. The thought of eternal fame held no attractions for him. All his life he had wanted only to do his duty, support his emperor and his brother soldiers. He wondered if he could ever want anything so simple again.

'And what of us?' Sabina asked. 'We must live in our less exalted realm, with all our failings, I suppose.' She took his hand, a slight subtle pressure. Castus could hear the wry smile in her voice. 'Once we are gone all our great deeds will be forgotten.'

Far away across the city, a flight of birds circled over the temples of the Capitoline Hill, their wings catching the sunlight. Castus watched them for a moment. He felt a slow surge of exultation rising within him.

'Then thank the gods we are mortal!'

AUTHOR'S NOTE

The battle of Milvian Bridge, fought on 28 October AD 312, was one of the most significant clashes in Roman history. Constantine's victory over Maxentius gave him control of the western empire, and of the city of Rome itself. And yet the battle is more famous for something that probably did not happen. The so-called 'Vision of Constantine', a heavenly apparition sent to the emperor by the Christian God on the eve of battle, supposedly convinced him to convert to the new religion and laid a path for the spiritual transformation of the empire over the following century. But this vision is not mentioned in the earliest accounts of the battle at all. Two imperial panegyrics given shortly after the event make no reference to celestial manifestations, the pagan historian Zosimus ignored the story, and the Christian writer Lactantius claimed instead that the emperor was visited by God in a dream, and instructed to mark the shields of his troops with 'the heavenly sign'.

It was the churchman Eusebius who first supplied the story of the emperor's vision. Constantine, he claimed, had witnessed 'with his own eyes the trophy of a cross of light in the heavens, above the sun, and bearing the inscription *Conquer by This*'. It is not entirely cynical, I think, to relate this anecdote to the solar apparition that Constantine reportedly saw in Gaul two or three years earlier. This vision (mentioned at the end of my previous book, *Swords Around the Throne*) was described at the time as a sign from the sun god. It does not seem unlikely that the Christian emperor of later years chose to reinterpret this older vision, and install Christ in the place of Apollo.

To what extent Constantine was or was not a committed Christian at the time of his Italian campaign has long been a matter of academic speculation. He may have come to see the unity of the Christian religion as a way of drawing together the various faiths and sects of the multicultural later empire under one all-powerful divine order. He may simply have believed it was true; only two years later he was declaring to a synod of bishops that 'I myself must be judged by Christ'.

But the Roman world of the early fourth century was still resolutely traditional in its religious inclinations. The Christian population of the empire in AD 300 is estimated at between 5 and 10 per cent, concentrated in large urban centres like Carthage, Alexandria and Rome itself. This is around the same percentage as the Muslim population of Europe today. Whatever else might have motivated Constantine's religious beliefs, they were clearly not a mere bid for popularity.

As always, in putting together a plausible description of these events I have tried to draw on as many of the more reliable ancient sources as possible. Panegyrics XII and IV, of AD 313 and 321 respectively, offer detailed, if often highly florid, blow-by-blow accounts of the action; Lactantius and Eusebius, and the later writers Zosimus and Aurelius Victor, add further – albeit often contradictory – material. Beyond this, I have tried to find expeditious solutions to the cloudier aspects of strategy and tactics: the defeat of the Maxentian *clibanarii* at the battle near Turin, for example, could have happened in a number of ways. I have chosen what appears to me the most likely, and happily the most dramatic too.

In the autumn of 2014 I was able to visit many of the locations of Constantine's advance, from Susa in the Italian Alps through Turin, Milan and Verona to Rimini (ancient Ariminum) and then southwards. In the quiet little city museum of Spoleto I found the tombstone of Florius Baudio, a Protector who may well have fallen in battle while commanding Legion II Italica Divitensis; other tombstones of this same legion mark out the trail of Constantine's advance on Rome.

The Milvian Bridge (Ponte Milvio) still crosses the Tiber to the north of the city. The probable site of the battle itself, on the plain north-east of the bridge, is bisected by highways and largely covered by military training facilities, while modern apartment blocks loom from the red stone bluffs to the west. I visited the site on the anniversary of the battle, but between the hurtling traffic streams on the Via Flaminia Nuova and Tangenziale Est I was unable to discern any echoes of that distant clash of arms. Imagination, as usual, made up the deficit.

The visitor to Rome today can admire the massive walls, repaired by Maxentius in preparation for siege, and the hulking ruins of the great Baths of Diocletian, which now house a church and a museum. Finds exhibited in the Museo Nazionale Romano, the Musei Capitolini and the Vatican attest to the opulence of aristocratic life in the fourth century. The 'imperial regalia' of Maxentius, presumably concealed in a cellar beneath the Palatine Hill following his defeat and only recently discovered, is now displayed in the Palazzo Massimo alle Terme.

The Arch of Constantine was erected at the heart of the city by a grateful Senate in AD 315; the vigorous frieze that runs around the main structure tells the story of the emperor's advance, the final battle and his triumphant entry to Rome. Prominent in one of the scenes of marching troops is a baggage camel; those who doubt such animals were used by the Roman army are referred to finds of camel bones from military contexts dating to the third and fourth centuries. One even comes from the foothills of the Julian Alps.

Much of the comprehensive literature on Constantine's campaign and defeat of Maxentius tends to dwell on the religious implications of his victory. Alongside the works mentioned in my previous books, Iain Ferris's *The Arch of Constantine* provides a concise survey of the famous monument, while Raymond Van Dam's *Remembering Constantine at the Milvian Bridge* is an engagingly oblique study of the various interpretations of the conflict. Neil Christie's *From Constantine to Charlemagne: An Archaeology of Italy AD 300–800* gives a detailed picture of the ancient landscape and its cities, with some invaluable maps and plans.

Maxentius has long had a bad press. His reputation was blackened by his opponents, and Christian historiography casts him as a satanic figure and a persecutor of the faithful (which he almost certainly was not). A brief, but more balanced, appraisal is offered by Mats Cullhed in *Conservator Urbis Suae: Studies in the Politics and Propaganda of the Emperor Maxentius*. John Curran's *Pagan City and Christian Capital: Rome in the Fourth Century*, meanwhile, covers the social world of the eternal city in the later age.

There are always certain books that, found by chance, prove unexpectedly useful. This time it was Garrett G. Fagan's *Bathing in Public in the Roman World*, which contains a wealth of vivid detail about the society of the great imperial bathhouses. Kyle Harper's *Slavery in the Late Roman World, AD 275–425* is an engrossing study of that most notorious, and ubiquitous, of ancient institutions.

My thanks go to Ross Cowan, for an enlightening discussion

on the events of Constantine's Italian campaign and the battles of Turin and Milvian Bridge. Once again, I offer my sincere gratitude to Rosie de Courcy for her insightful editorial support, to my agent Will Francis, and to Head of Zeus for their continued enthusiasm for my work.